Praise for Reavis

The Broken Truth
The Second Tucker Snow Thriller

"*The Broken Truth* starts with a bang and never lets up. A wild, unpredictable ride."

—Johnny D. Boggs, nine-time Spur Award winner

Hard Country
The First Tucker Snow Thriller

"*Hard Country* crackles with authenticity as Tucker Snow shows us what it takes to be a lawman, and a good man, in a sprawling state like Texas. I'll read anything Reavis Z. Wortham writes!"

—Marc Cameron, *New York Times* bestselling author

"An action fan's dream. Nonstop excitement. Wonderful characters. A terrific locale. And a startling bulletin about how your car is watching you."

—David Morrell, *New York Times*
bestselling author of *First Blood*

"A stunning success! *Hard Country* checks all the boxes: a nonstop thriller plot, characters who are so real we're sure we've crossed paths in real life, and a breathtaking portrait—both searing and sympathetic—of a small town, from an author whose compelling voice and keenly observant eye transport us there. Wortham is known for his protagonists, and Tucker Snow is one of his all-time best: sharp, uncompromising, wry, thoroughly human, and the one thing we don't see enough of nowadays: a dyed-in-the-wool hero. I was going to set aside a weekend to read the book. My problem? What to do with the rest of Saturday afternoon and Sunday—yes, *Hard Country* is the definition of a one-sitting read. Bravo!"

—Jeffery Deaver, *New York Times* bestselling author of *The Bone Collector* and *Hunting Time*

"*Hard Country* is easy to love, a beautifully crafted and fully realized thriller of rare depth and pathos. The debut entry in Reavis Wortham's new series is structured along classic lines reminiscent of the best from Ace Atkins, Don Winslow, and even James Lee Burke. This is thriller writing of the highest order that grabs hold from the very first line and doesn't let go until the last. As timely as it is terrific!"

—Jon Land, *USA Today* bestselling author of the Caitlin Strong series

"*Hard Country* is the best thriller I have read in a long time. The story sizzles with action as Tucker Snow brings justice to where it belongs—and in the manner in which it deserves to be brought. What really sets *Hard Country* apart from most books in the genre is the emotion and heart that Wortham brings to the page. Bravo!"

—John Gilstrap, author of *Harm's Way* and the Jonathan Grave thriller series

The Texas Job

The Ninth Texas Red River Mystery

"Reviewers taking on a Wortham novel will make heavy use of

cowboy-movie images. [As the story unfolds,] the unkillable Ranger goes from hero to superhero, 'a man made of hard bone and corded wire.' None of this will put off Wortham's admirers, who can't get enough of 'the sweet natural cologne of leather.'"

—*Booklist*

"Readers who've already seen Tom grow old in earlier installments of Wortham's Texas Red River series will be rubbing their hands in eager anticipation of what happens next. A...powerful tale of a solitary hero confronting a web of conspirators against hopeless odds."

—*Kirkus Reviews*

"Set in 1931, this well-crafted crime novel features Texas Ranger Tom Bell, a supporting character in *The Right Side of Wrong*. Authentic settings and richly drawn characters complement Wortham's striking depiction of the Texas oil boom and the unavoidable corruption, greed, and anarchy that accompany it. Hopefully, Bell will be back in a sequel."

—*Publishers Weekly*

Laying Bones
The Eighth Texas Red River Mystery

"Wortham adroitly balances richly nuanced human drama with two-fisted action and displays a knack for the striking phrase. ("R.B. was the best drunk driver in the county, and I don't believe he run off in here on his own.") This entry is sure to win the author new fans."

—*Publishers Weekly*

Gold Dust
The Seventh Red River Mystery

"Center Springs must deal with everything from cattle rustlers to a biological agent that the CIA said was safe, but were wrong, and a real fight between the government and those who actually know what the term 'gunslinger' means. Murder is everywhere, and readers will never forget this Poisoned Gift once they see it in action. Wortham has created yet another Red River Mystery that hits home in a big way, making it all the more terrifying."

—*Suspense Magazine*

"Richly enjoyable…reads like a stranger-than-strange collaboration between Lee Child, handling the assault on the CIA with baleful directness, and Steven F. Havill, genially reporting on the regulars back home."

—*Kirkus Reviews*

"It's a pleasure to watch [Constable Ned Parker and Texas Ranger Tom Bell] deal with orneriness as well as just plain evil. Readers nostalgic for this period will find plenty to like."

—*Publishers Weekly*

"Reading the seventh Red River Mystery is like coming home after a vacation: we're reuniting with old friends and returning to a comfortable place. Wortham's writing style is easygoing, relying on natural-sounding dialogue and vivid descriptions to give us the feeling that this story could well have taken place. Another fine entry in a mystery series that deserves more attention."

—*Booklist*

Unraveled
The Sixth Red River Mystery

"The more I read of Reavis Wortham's books, the more impressed I am by his abilities as a writer... His understanding of family feuds, how they start and how they hang on long past their expiration date, is vital to the storyline. Wortham's skill as a plotter is demonstrated as well. He's very good at what he does, and his books are well worth reading."

—*Reviewing the Evidence*

"This superbly drawn sixth entry in the series features captivating characters and an authentic Texas twang."

—*Library Journal*

"Not only does Wortham write exceptionally well, but he somehow manages to infuse *Unraveled* with a Southern Gothic feel that would make even William Faulkner proud... A hidden gem of a book that reads like Craig Johnson's Longmire mysteries on steroids."

—*Providence Journal*

Dark Places
The Fifth Red River Mystery

"Readers will cheer for and ache with the good folks, and secondary characters hold their own... The novel's short chapters fit both the fast pace and the deftly spare actions and details... The rhythm of Wortham's writing, transporting us back in time, soon takes hold and is well worth the reader's efforts."

—*Historical Novel Society*

Vengeance Is Mine
The Fourth Red River Mystery

"Wortham is a masterful and entertaining storyteller. Set in East Texas in 1967, *Vengeance Is Mine* is equal parts Joe R. Lansdale and Harper Lee, with a touch of Elmore Leonard."

—*Ellery Queen's Mystery Magazine*

* "Very entertaining… Those who have read the author's earlier books, including *The Right Side of Wrong* (2013), will be familiar with Center Springs and its rather unusual denizens, but knowledge of those earlier volumes is not required. This is a fully self-contained story, and it's a real corker."

—*Booklist*, Starred Review

The Right Side of Wrong
The Third Red River Mystery

"A sleeper that deserves wider attention."

—*New York Times*

* "Wortham's third entry in his addictive Texas procedural set in the 1960s is a deceptively meandering tale of family and country life bookended by a dramatic opening and conclusion. C. J. Box fans would like this title."

—*Library Journal*, Starred Review

Burrows
The Second Red River Mystery

* "Wortham's outstanding sequel to *The Rock Hole* (2011)... combines the gonzo sensibility of Joe R. Lansdale and the elegiac mood of *To Kill a Mockingbird* to strike just the right balance between childhood innocence and adult horror."

—*Publishers Weekly*, Starred Review

"The cinematic characters have substance and a pulse. They walk off the page and talk Texas."

—*Dallas Morning News*

The Rock Hole
The First Red River Mystery

"One of the 12 best novels of 2011. An accomplished first novel about life and murder in a small Texas town... Wortham tells a story of grace under pressure, of what happens when a deranged and vicious predator decides that they're his promised prey...a fast and furious climax, written to the hilt, harrowing in its unpredictability. Not just scary but funny too, as Wortham nails time and place in a sure-handed, captivating way. There's a lot of good stuff in this unpretentious gem. Don't miss it."

—*Kirkus Reviews*

"Throughout, scenes of hunting, farming, and family life sizzle with detail and immediacy. The dialogue is spicy with country humor and color, and Wortham knows how to keep his story moving. *The Rock Hole* is an unnerving but fascinating read."

—*Historical Novel Review*

Also by Reavis Z. Wortham

The Tucker Snow Thrillers
Hard Country

The Texas Red River Mysteries
The Rock Hole
Burrows
The Right Side of Wrong
Vengeance Is Mine
Dark Places
Unraveled
Gold Dust
Laying Bones
The Texas Job

The Sonny Hawke Mysteries
Hawke's Prey
Hawke's War
Hawke's Target
Hawke's Fury

THE BROKEN TRUTH

THE BROKEN TRUTH

A TUCKER SNOW THRILLER

REAVIS Z. WORTHAM

This one is for my little brother, Rocky Lane Wortham, who wholeheartedly accepted his name and, with that, has always followed his own road.

Cover design by *the*BookDesigners
Cover images © xiaolin zhang/Shutterstock, Sunti/Shutterstock, Rejdan/Shutterstock, Bob Pool/Shutterstock, EcoPrint/Shutterstock

Published by Poisoned Pen Press, an imprint of Sourcebooks
P.O. Box 4410, Naperville, Illinois 60567–4410
(630) 961-3900
sourcebooks.com

Cataloging-in-Publication Data is on file with the Library of Congress.

Printed and bound in the United States of America.
SB 10 9 8 7 6 5 4 3 2 1

"I am the hawk and there's blood on my feathers, but time is still turning, they soon will be dry."

—JOHN DENVER AND MICHAEL TAYLOR

Chapter 1

The white Ford dually pickup ahead of me pulled a cattle trailer at speeds way too fast for a gravel road, chasing its headlights through the hot Northeast Texas night. I knew better than to follow closely behind the thick cloud of dust boiling up under its tires and sparkling in the red and blue flashing lights on my state-issued Dodge truck.

The wash of bright, twinkling stars in the night sky looked as if someone scattered a handful of glitter across a black ceiling. The most recognizable constellations, the Big and Little Dippers and Orion's Belt, were as distinctive as a planetarium. The Milky Way's sweep of stars, dust, and gas reminded me of smog.

George Strait sang about making Amarillo by morning on my radio, tuned so low it was barely noticeable. It was kind of a joke, because at that hour I was over six hours away from the panhandle.

In today's modern times, I was chasing cattle rustlers.

I'm Tucker Snow, a special ranger for the Texas & Southwestern Cattle Raisers Association, the oldest livestock alliance in Texas. TSCRA special rangers are officially commissioned by the Texas Department of Public Safety or the Oklahoma State Bureau of Investigation and have the authority to investigate and arrest in both the Lone Star State and Oklahoma. Some folks also call us special agents or cattle cops.

For the past week, I'd been cruising the back roads in that part of Northeast Texas just south of the Red River, investigating a rash of cattle thefts involving farm and ranch owners in the area.

More than a few victims I'd tracked down over the phone didn't know if they were missing stock at all. It might take weeks, or months, for those weekend ranchers who lived in cities hours away to notice if any cattle were missing, or even if fences were cut or down. I spent way too much time educating those *amenity* landowners about what the old-time ranchers knew from hard day-to-day work and experience.

After gathering all the info I could, I spent several nights sitting up on just such a ranch owned by a Dallas gentleman who visited his property only a few times a year. He left the acreage under the oversight of a foreman who rolled in once a week to put out hay, check their water supply, and make a lazy head count.

What was I looking for? Likely places where someone might back a trailer up through a fence to a catch pen or a corral to load up a few head. The sitting and waiting was almost like deer hunting, requiring just as much patience.

I was about to give up and go home for some sleep and to see my teenage daughter, Chloe, before she left for school. It was just me and her, and I made every effort possible to be there when she was home.

Dealing with the deaths of her mother and little sister was hard enough, but only months earlier she'd been kidnapped along with another young girl and taken to Oklahoma. My brother, Harley, and I went and got them, leaving a pile of bodies behind, but Chloe was wrestling with an emotional roller coaster that often plunged her into dark days.

That was always in the back of my mind, and I was rolling it over when my phone buzzed with a call from a night-owl woman who'd seen a loaded cattle trailer go by in the early morning hours a couple of days earlier. When she saw the same truck and trailer pass by again at close to three in the morning, she found my card.

Luck was on my side. Instead of being two counties over, I was close by, and for once technology worked in my favor. My GPS led me to the lady's house and behind the rig only minutes later.

Metal fence posts and lines of bob wire on both sides of the dirt road flashed past, and gravel rattled against my truck's undercarriage as I tried to pull the truck over.

A cottontail bounced left to right over the bar ditch, disappearing into the shadows created by tall Johnson grass, brush, and cedars growing in the fence. Whiteface cattle standing inside the wire watched us pass with casual indifference, while a herd of whitetail deer in the next pasture tensed, heads upright, eyes glowing in our high beams.

Please don't jump the fence please don't jump the fence...

Deer are bad about doing exactly the wrong thing at the wrong time. They're almost as bad as squirrels, who possess the worst critical thinking skills of any animal in the world. Though the brush guard on the front of my pickup would absorb most of the blow from a deer, I didn't want to hit any of the animals who were minding their own business until a cattle thief raced by.

Easy, Tuck. If one of those mamas makes a run for it, keep an eye on the fawns.

Though Sara Beth had been gone for several months, I still heard my wife's voice from time to time, especially if there was danger nearby. Some folks might say I was a brick short of a load, hearing voices in my head, but I always countered that authors experience the same thing and people call *them* creative.

Sara Beth was my best friend and therapist, and she stayed in the back of my mind, sometimes offering up bits of advice and caution. Long ago I learned to ask myself what she'd recommend in any given situation, and it worked nearly every time.

Her voice in my head even woke me one night when there was an intruder in the house with me and Chloe, right after we'd moved into the new place. Nonbelievers might say I heard something in my sleep and my late wife's voice was my subconscious warning me of that danger, but it was her. I'm convinced of it.

Red brake lights flickered for a moment as the driver took a hard right turn a little fast on the road zigzagging between farms and pastures. It fishtailed a couple of times, and I took pressure off the accelerator to slow my pickup, expecting the trailer ahead to snap back the other way and yank the other truck off into the ditch.

Instead, the driver compensated for the shifting weight of the cattle loaded behind him and drove even faster, earning my respect for his skills behind the steering wheel. I've seen trailers with less of a load flip over on a dry concrete road in a heartbeat.

Half a second later, the entire rig went dark and the fleeing vehicle rushed through the night using nothing but the light of the setting moon.

I wasn't expecting a kill switch. I'd seen it more than once as a special agent investigating cattle thefts. This was a pro outfit from the get-go.

I dropped back a little more. The kill switch wouldn't give me time to react if the guy hit his brakes.

The dust cloud thrown up by the trailer was so thick I had to hit my dimmer, as if driving in fog. He wasn't gonna get away, though, even if he gained some distance. Gravel popped beneath my tires, and the truck took a notion to feel greasy and slide sideways for a moment. I let off the gas to regain control and then punched it again.

Keeping one eye on the road, I ignored the radio mounted under the dash because it'd been on the fritz for two weeks. Instead of picking up the microphone handset, I thumbed my phone awake and cursed under my breath at the single bar.

Technology again. I waited to get a better signal.

Chapter 2

Five foot two and a hundred pounds soaking wet and full of bananas, Toby James pulled a strand of brown hair behind one ear and adjusted her hat. She saw the fast-approaching emergency lights in her side mirrors and hit the kill switch to go dark as she picked up an old-school walkie-talkie riding in a cup holder and pushed the transmit button with her slim forefinger.

"You copy?"

Bill Sloan's voice filled the cab. "Hey, gal. Wassup?"

"Y'all get that tire changed?"

"Sure did, and in record time."

"Good." With one hand white-knuckled on the steering wheel, she didn't take her eyes off the road. "We have trouble. The laws just lit me up."

Sloan was the ringleader of a small theft ring who identified the ranches and farms to steal their cattle. He was running buddies with Fred Belk, a lean cowboy and former Army staff sergeant recently back from being called up for National Guard service. They all grew up in the area and knew many of the families and their branches in Ganther Bluff.

Sloan was the best at what they did, rustling and driving. He and Fred watched that pasture full of cattle for two weeks, monitoring one rancher's schedule to check the stock and feed before choosing the right night.

They loaded the stock without issues and took off, but Sloan blew a tire. He and Fred changed it with ease, but it put them behind Toby and her trailer full of steers. Now they were back on the job to block any law enforcement officer who stumbled upon the truck and trailer.

Sloan's job was simple. Break some minor law to get their attention and pull him over, and while they were writing him up, or chasing him down the next country road to draw them away, Toby'd roll on with a trailer full of money on the hoof.

"Dammit."

In her mind, Toby saw his face flush at their bad luck. They'd been together for nearly two years, and in that time she'd seen that reaction to anger and frustration more than once.

"How far ahead are you?"

His breathing was heavy on the open channel, and his voice was full of concern. "Just a little bit. Keep straight to the next crossroad and turn left. That'll bring you around, and I'll cut in between y'all in a couple of minutes."

"Hurry."

"You bet."

Chapter 3

The truck and trailer ahead of me seemed to be making random turns each time the driver reached a crossroads in an alternating checkerboard of crops, pastures, farms, and ranches.

I tried twice to call Chief Deputy Frank Gibson, who was the acting sheriff in our county following the recent death of Sheriff Jackson. I needed to tell him where I was, but each time I tried, I got a No Service signal. I figured I'd wait until the rig neared the highway and the closest tower, then I'd tell Gibson where to cut them off, and we could make the arrest.

Off to the right at about two o'clock, I caught a brief glimpse of headlights flickering through the trees and coming my way.

The big rig slowed for the upcoming intersection, but I still hung back out of the dust cloud. The headlights racing in were going to intersect the road we were on. He'd get there at the same time as us, but I hoped he'd give way when he saw my emergency lights.

The rig in front didn't hesitate, but hooked a left as if the driver didn't see the oncoming car that slowed and stopped in the middle of the intersection after the truck and trailer were straightened up and running again.

The sedan sat there idling and blocking my way. I stood on the brake, slid for a minute, and ended up forty yards away to study on the new situation. "What are you doing, fool?"

Talking to myself was a habit I was trying to break.

Chapter 4

They'd already decided that getting pulled over by the local constabulary was no big deal for Sloan, if that happened. He knew them all and had worked for ranchers around the area for so long, he was on a first-name basis with most of the deputies and the local constables who prowled the county precincts and farm roads.

Fred Belk pointed with one finger when they pulled up behind Toby's departing truck and trailer.

"Girl's using her head, running dark." One foot on the brake and in the way of a lawman's truck, Sloan watched her grow smaller.

Knowing something was coming, Fred braced himself in the seat. "Now, what're you gonna do?"

"Stop that guy from following her." Sloan glanced to the left at the pickup's lights. "Get aholt of something."

Bracing himself, Fred snatched up the walkie. "We have it, gal. Get gone."

In the distance, the rig's lights immediately came on as Toby put the hammer down on the straightaway, growing smaller.

"You gonna block him?"

Sloan shook his head. "Nope. I can't afford jail time, and things have changed. It isn't just getting in the way now. Interfering with an officer is gonna sting, and I think we can get away."

"Wait, what!!!???"

The next minute was wild-ass driving when Sloan whipped his Charger in tight donuts, throwing dust and gravel into the air and blocking the road with his insane driving.

Beside him, Fred Belk grabbed the dash with both hands and gasped. "Damn! Hold my beer is *right*!"

Laughing like a loon and driving like a drunk cowboy, Sloan spun the tires and threw dirt by the buckets.

A veteran of rodeo buck-outs, Fred threw back his head and howled like a wolf.

Chapter 5

The Charger's driver shocked me by turning the car into a spin in the middle of the crossroads, doing donuts and throwing gravel in a huge circle.

"What the hell is this guy doing?"

Didn't he see my flashing lights?

Before the dust got too thick, my headlights lit the interior occupied by two males, both in billed caps with outlaw scarves tied over the lower halves of their faces.

I laid on the horn as they threw up a plume thick enough to rival a volcanic eruption. The disappearing cattle trailer was just a shadow in the dust that drifted between us. Now I understood. The rig's running lights were dim behind the intentional screen thrown up to cover the escaping rig.

The wheelman stopped spinning the sedan, shifted gears, and backed toward me like a rocket.

I hadn't been expecting *that.* Still unfamiliar with my relatively new pickup, I reached up for the shift lever, only to recall the shifter was now a dial on the dash.

The Charger slid to a stop only a few yards ahead, and

thinking he was going to back into me, I twisted the dial to Reverse. The guy shifted again and stood on the accelerator and brakes at the same time, throwing a blizzard of rocks up behind his tires. They exploded against my grill and windshield like buckshot pellets. Stars frosted the safety glass.

I instinctively ducked at the noise and impacts, and stayed down as the assault continued for a shocking length of time, thinking that the passenger might take that opportunity to step out with a gun.

Not one to run, though, I finally got mad and partially raised up. The Dodge's rear end fishtailed back and forth, throwing up an even stronger barrage of road gravel before he finally took off.

I sat up and floored it to follow him, only to shoot backward and into the bar ditch. Slamming on the brake and cussing the engineers who took away my shift lever, I snapped the dial to the right and hit the gas.

Off-balance, my right back tire was in soft sand and the other on grass. The tire bearing the least amount of weight spun and whined. Cursing a blue streak, I hit the brakes and fumbled with the dash to find the right button to shift into four-wheel-drive. Blood pounding in my ears, I took a deep breath to calm myself and again accelerated, this time slower.

The gears meshed, and I pulled back onto the road. The Charger was nothing more than taillights by the time I got straightened out and took in after it.

Pickups aren't speed machines, and the muscle car could have outrun me by that time. Still, I stayed on the pedal and managed to keep him in sight until his brake lights flickered and he turned right at the next country road after using his turn indicator.

Something's up. Remember when?

Sara Beth was right.

When I was a kid, my dad and I saw a dove flutter from a thick yaupon holly and drop to the ground in a flurry of gray wings. I hurried forward to catch it, but the bird stayed just out of reach. Fifty yards away from Dad, it seemed to recover and flew away.

He was still standing beside the bush when I returned, grinning. "Couldn't catch it, huh?"

"No, but she was hurt bad."

"Look in here."

I was small enough that he picked me up to see three little balls of fuzz in a nest. She wasn't hurt. She led me away, but I knew better now.

The Dodge wasn't trying to get away that overcast night; it wanted me to follow, leading me away from the cattle trailer. He was running block, and I had no intention of following him.

"Nope."

Ignoring the way they went, I took in after the trailer again, and luck was with me. I shot through the darkness, following the curve of the road and still drifting dust until all of a stinking sudden I came up on the cattle trailer on a curve that wasn't going as fast as I expected.

Sara Beth's calm voice came again.

Watch it.

The only thing that kept me from ramming into the back of the trailer was the quick flicker of my lights in his reflector that gave me enough time to brake.

Chapter 6

When they saw the state truck hadn't taken the bait to follow them away from Toby, Sloan whipped around at the next gate turnout and put the pedal to the metal.

Fear rose in his throat as the stakes increased. He didn't want Toby's arrest on his conscience. He picked up the walkie. "Toby, he didn't follow us. I have another idea. Where are you?"

She paused for a moment, and he knew she was keeping one eye on the road and looking at the navigation screen on her truck's dash. She told him where she'd be in a minute.

"Good. I'm circling the Reynolds ranch. That'll bring me up on your right when you go past Cottonwood Creek Road. We're going to Plan B. Slow way down and let him catch up at the crossroads, but don't stop."

Her tense voice came back. "He's already caught me."

"Okay, roll your windows down, and when you hear the pops, get gone."

"What pops?"

"The ones that'll tell you to put the hammer down."

Rocks and pebbles hammered the Challenger's undercarriage,

and it didn't take long to reach the place he was looking for. It was the exact mirror of the terrain they'd used to block the chase only minutes before, but this time there would be a different ending.

Fred Belk rubbed both palms against the tops of his jeaned thighs. "What's plan B, and I don't think I'm gonna like it."

"I don't imagine you will. There's his lights."

—

After rushing down the gravel road toward still another T-intersection, Toby saw headlights heading in her direction and took her foot off the accelerator. When there were no emergency lights, she assumed it was a local.

She moved to the right, almost into the ditch as a dark-colored Suburban without front tags moved over to give her room. The brights on her Ford lit the interior full of men who stared ahead as if ignoring the excitement on the rural road.

The vehicle passed and slowed even more at the sight of the Dodge's rotating lights behind the cattle trailer. Brake lights went on as it moved over to give the truck enough room, then continued on its way as if all the action was common for the area.

Toby's stomach tightened as the SUV drove away, but she was where she needed to be. There was nothing but pasture on the four corners, as if he wanted the open country around them. She stopped at the intersection, giving herself three escape options. Behind her, the Dodge's rotating lights lit up the open pastures on either side of Toby and her trailer.

—

From their incoming vantage point, Sloan and Fred saw Toby at the crossroads in front of them with the official vehicle several yards behind. If she turned left, she'd be gone down another zigzagging farm road. Straight, she'd run north until she hit the highway six miles away.

If she turned right, she'd pass them, but at that moment she sat there idling, waiting to see what Sloan and Fred had in mind. Sloan held his breath as a dark SUV drew close to Toby. That was a lot of action for a rural intersection at three in the morning, but it continued straight to disappear to their left.

With a sigh of relief, Sloan dismissed the SUV that proved not to be a part of the pursuit. "I don't like this one damned bit, but I'm not gonna let Toby or us go to jail."

He frowned at the flashing lights and slowed. They crept up to within a hundred yards of the idling dually and trailer and the lawman some yards behind.

Fred leaned forward in his seat. "He's just sitting there. What now?"

Sloan rubbed a hand across his dry mouth. "Your turn. Pop his tires!"

"You're kidding! Just take the ticket."

"No way. I done told you this is more than just getting in the way." Sloan shook his head. The original idea of simply cutting a patrol car off until Toby could escape went out the window.

What they'd done back there in front of the lawman's pickup went way beyond a simple misdemeanor. When they finally drove off, it'd be a felony.

"Whoever's in that Dodge'll take me to jail, and I'll miss my next doctor's appointment. I can't afford that." Sloan paused. "And I can't let Toby go to jail, neither."

Lit by the dash lights, Sloan saw the look in Fred's eyes and knew he was asking more than his old friend wanted to give, but they'd been together all their young lives and were closer than brothers.

Calm as if they were in church, Fred drew a deep breath. "Don't ask me to shoot at lawmen anymore after this. I won't do it no more. It ain't right."

"I won't."

Sloan slapped Fred on the arm in thanks as his old running buddy opened his door and pushed out of the off side. Looking back over his shoulder, Sloan caught a glimpse of Fred sprinting fifty yards down the gravel road with his rifle to get away from the Charger.

As Fred stopped beside a head-high cedar growing up through a bob wire fence and threw his tricked-out AR to his shoulder, Sloan mouthed, "Bye bye, tires!"

Chapter 7

I backed up and stopped some distance away. I reached for the phone to call the Chief Deputy at the same time my right front tire blew with a pop and hiss of air. Before I could react to the unexpected blowout, a shot echoed off the dark trees around me, and I recognized what it was at the same time a second pop flattened the other tire on that same side.

I was taking fire.

This time I saw the flash at about two o'clock on my right and over a hundred yards away as the truck and trailer turned left at the crossroads and sped away.

Dropping the phone onto the console, I snapped the dial into reverse for the second time that night and backed away as fast as the truck would allow on two soft tires. High-speed reverse in the dark isn't easy at best, and I was all over the road, praying I wouldn't take to the ditch before getting out of range.

Another round punched through the right rear fender with a thud, telling me the shooter still had the angle. He was shooting across the corner of a wide pasture and had a clear target for another few seconds. I missed a third and possibly fourth flash, because my attention was on the road behind.

A grove of trees finally interfered with the shooter's sight line, and I was in the clear. Turning the pickup sideways across the road, I reached for the phone, but it slid off the console and was gone.

The gunfire stopped, but with the truck between us, I rolled out and yanked the back door open to grab my rifle. Blood pounding in my head and ready to fight, I flicked off the safety and hurried to cover behind the engine block.

The gunman obviously had a night vision scope on his rifle, but that wasn't unusual for our part of the country. Lots of hunters used them for predator- or hog-hunting, and more than one poacher went to jail for taking deer out of season and at night with the new technology.

This guy I was hunting was something.

The next thing I knew, someone behind the vehicle opened up with what sounded like the same kind of rifle, emptying an entire magazine with a steady strobe of semiautomatic muzzle flashes aimed my way.

I ducked behind the protection of my wounded truck as rounds whizzed by high overhead with a dry, nasty, insectile tone. When the shooting stopped, I raised up to fire back, but all I saw was the vehicle disappearing into the darkness.

For several minutes I was torn about what to do. That was unusual for me. Before Sara Beth's death, I made decisions in an instant, but now I sometimes overthought things.

I needed to call the chief deputy and tell him what was going on, but I was afraid to move right then. The car itself might be gone, and I could tell it was a sedan of some kind, but for all I knew, the first shooter might have stayed behind and was looking for me through that nightscope of his.

These guys had already proved they were full of tricks.

I didn't want to give him any more chances at me. My inclination was to charge the source of trouble, but night vision scopes changed the game. So I waited as long as my patience would allow, even though I have a barely contained rage that often tries to rip its way out.

Experience taught me to control it back when my brother, Harley, and I were working undercover narcotics for the Texas Department of Public Safety. Deep breaths and consciously calming down helped put the monster back in its cage.

When no more shots came my way, I scanned the area using my peripheral vision to defeat night blindness. Staring directly at something in the dark won't work, but Harley and I learned years ago that looking to the side of our objective often revealed details in the night.

Night sounds returned, and as far as I could tell, it was over.

Hands shaking from shock and subsiding fury, I leaned into the cab to find my phone. It wasn't on the floorboard, nor the back floor. Designers of trucks apparently didn't consider dropped items of immediate importance, and the seats were in the way.

Periodically popping back up like a prairie dog to check my surroundings, I dug around with a small flashlight until I located the slender phone in that narrow gap between the console and the passenger seat. My heart finally settled in those five minutes enough for me to see I had a weak signal.

Relieved, I punched up Chief Deputy Gibson, who answered in a bright voice. "I was beginning to worry about you."

"Probably for good reason."

"You sound like you've been running."

"Just took fire out on County Road 3838."

The electrical system flickered and hissed, and the cab went dark. The call dropped because it had routed through the truck's media system, and I wanted to shoot the pickup myself. Trees met overhead, and I suspected they blocked the direct signal from the phone.

Rifle in one hand and the infernal device in the other, I crept down the road, walking in the ditch to present less of a target, and squatted beside a cedar to break up my shape.

I punched the screen again and it was so light I almost dropped the phone before I could find the control button to dim it down. The shooter was obviously gone because there was no way he could have missed that light.

Gibson answered on the first ring. His siren muffled his voice. "You hurt?"

"No, but my pickup's electrical system squirreled out and I lost you. I guess one of those holes he shot in the truck hit a chip or something. The whole thing's dead, so I had to get in the open to call again." I told him exactly where I was. "Shooters are probably with the cattle thieves I was chasing, and they're gone by now."

"You sure you're not hurt? I've heard of people being hit and not knowing it for a few minutes."

"No. I'm good and nothing's leaking. He shot out enough tires so I couldn't move, though, even if the truck worked. He put one round into the fender just for grins, too, I guess. I don't have any holes in my hide, though. I believe the second shooter covered the first one until he could get in the car. They're gone now."

"We're on the way."

"I can hear that, but I'd rather you get after him. The shooter's probably following that trailer."

"It's just me right now. You have any idea which way he was headed?"

"I think both vehicles were going west, if I'm not turned around." For the first time since I was an adult, I wished I knew the stars.

"I'll send out a BOLO and get over to you as soon as I can."

"I'm not going anywhere." Some distance away, I saw lights on in a farmhouse, likely awakened by the gunfire. A few shots in the night are common, but when somebody empties a couple of magazines in a steady string of shots, folks in the country are gonna get up with a gun in their hands.

Through the trees on a fence line, a single pole light lit a house and barn. Rural East Texas is seldom completely dark. There are always lights in the distance, from more pole lights, houses, trailers, and even barns.

Now that the adrenaline was wearing off, my spirit wilted. I've always thought that pole lights are one of the most depressing sights in Texas, and couldn't tell you why to save my life.

The night was filled with the calls of night birds and crickets as I walked back to the truck and settled behind the wheel with the rifle across my lap, trying to puzzle out what had just happened.

Chapter 8

Back in the Charger, Fred Belk thumbed fresh rounds into his AR's empty mag while Sloan took skinny seldom-used back roads to get out of the area.

Hands shaking from adrenaline, Fred dropped a round and felt in the darkness by his feet until he found it. "Damn. I didn't like that one bit. Us old boys ought not be shooting at one another when we're all on the same side."

"What side is that?"

"Well, right for one, and country folks. I think that coulda been the new cattle agent we've heard about. The one who went to Oklahoma and shot up Jess Atchley and those meth dealers who took his daughter." He slapped the magazine into the well and repeated the process with Sloan's empty rifle. "I heard Atchley took his own daughter, too. Intended to sell her...put her to work. That stock agent got her back, too."

"Don't believe everything you hear, but you're right. I think that's Tucker Snow we just lit up." Sloan's eyes flicked to his rearview mirror to make sure they weren't being followed.

"I don't like shooting at guys like us."

A shiver went down his spine. "We're not law."

"What I meant was that neither one of us ought to be shooting at a man who's just doing his job and went to protect his daughter." Fred took a long swallow of beer, as if he was dry as the desert. "We'd do the same thing for our family."

"I was shooting so high those rounds came down a mile behind him."

Sloan checked his speed when the car drifted to the right on the loose surface under his tires. They were free, with no chance of being chased, so he let off the accelerator and took the next right when the lane intersected with an oil road.

"You know as well as I do that he didn't know that. Especially after I put all those holes in his truck."

Enough time had passed that Sloan figured Toby was close to pulling into Mitch Ramsey's back pasture, where the rancher's health issues prevented him from checking his stock for weeks. He relaxed and leaned back in the seat. They'd be there in a few minutes and unload the stock in Crawford's back pasture to be free and clear at dawn.

"I didn't want you to be the only one shooting toward him." Sloan didn't want anyone to be in any deeper than he was, because most of the money they made on these thefts was for his own medical expenses. If anyone went down for the rustling or shooting, it would be him for trying to stay alive.

Making money was easy when you used your head, only he needed more of it. They reached the highway and he maintained a steady pace to the Crawford ranch. Relief flowed through Sloan, and he turned up the volume on his radio.

The Red Hot Chili Peppers filled the sedan as Fred slid lower in the seat to a more comfortable position. It was the first time Sloan felt completely healthy in a week, and he was taking advantage of it.

Two minutes later his phone buzzed, and Toby was on the line. "This is better than that dumb walkie-talkie. I'm at the pasture. Be careful."

"Good job, babe." Sloan whacked Fred's arm in celebration. "Hey."

"Hey, what?"

Sloan became serious. "I love you."

"Me too," Toby answered. "You boys hurry up and get here."

Chapter 9

Days later, after I got my new truck to replace the one that was shot up by cattle thieves, the temperature was well into triple digits. I cruised down the two-lane hardtop wishing it would cloud up and rain. I wasn't the only one, because anyone who made a living by dryland farming or relying on grass and water for livestock, was in the same dry-docked boat.

Heat waves shimmered above the two-lane highway, and water mirages vanished as I drew near. I understood how the thirsty old-time pioneers out in the desert felt as they approached a cool, blue lake only to find sand, rocks, and biting reptiles.

Crisp, brown grass, weeds, and drying brush lined both sides of the road. In the pastures beyond, pools shrank so fast you could almost watch the water level go down. Man-made watering holes for livestock are called pools in Northeast Texas, ponds in deep East Texas, and out west they're known as tanks.

It wasn't uncommon to see damp mudholes full of rotting fish carcasses lying high and dry after the water evaporated from the pools. I knew several old boys who spent uncounted hours pulling cattle from the soft mud after they sank belly-deep in search of water.

Trees lining dry creeks seemed to say to hell with it and dropped their leaves to sleep through the rest of the summer. Cows and horses stood in what shade they could find, staring at passing vehicles as if hoping they'd bring fresh cool water.

Mitch Ramsey was waiting beside his farmhouse when I turned my pickup off the blacktop county road and drove across the cattle guard to follow a packed gravel drive leading past a barn and new sheet metal shop. An Angus mama cow and her calf watched me from inside a corral made of welded drill stem pipe. A second matching corral contained two slick, fat steers.

Mitch must've gotten a deal on the used pipe, because in addition to the corral, he'd used the material for fences, posts, and even grape and climbing vine arbors on the front and side of his white frame farmhouse. I liked the look that made the structure and other parts of the farm appear to be part of the land itself, and not something stuck out in a pasture with no thought to how it blended in with the countryside.

Sara Beth and I used to laugh at houses some folks built in rural areas. With no apparent forethought, they bought a couple of acres, usually pasture, scraped it clean, and then poured a concrete slab right beside the road. In my opinion, country houses should always be on a pier and beam foundation, sitting off from the road and surrounded by trees to help it look established. They look better sitting high above the land, instead of at ground level.

Most of the time those brick monstrosities, often with glaring white columns holding up second-floor balconies and porticos, should have been constructed in a suburban neighborhood or, in the case of one gothic outrage not far from where we lived before Sara Beth left our world, on a hill surrounded by bare-limb trees.

When I punched the Off button on my truck, wishing for the old days when keys unlocked doors and fired up starters, the calf bawled loud enough to be heard in the next county. In response, its mama bellered right back.

Stepping out of the cool cab, I set my hat, adjusted the big key fob in the front pocket of my Wranglers, closed the truck's door, and threw the mama cow a look.

Taking off a pair of worn leather gloves, Mitch ambled in my direction with a peculiar gait that came from a fairly new artificial leg.

We shook, and his hands felt tough enough to go without gloves. I studied the cow. "These the ones you called me about?"

"They are." He chuckled when the mama lowered her head and pawed the ground. "She don't like *you* much, neither."

"I don't believe I owe her money."

"She don't want money, nor nuggets neither. She wants to stomp you into strawberry jelly. That old gal's already taken a run at me twice this morning when I came out to feed these steers. She hit that fence hard enough to shift the posts."

The steers watched as Mitch propped himself on his artificial leg and rested his good knee on one of the feed pen's crossrails. His jeans formed to the back of his new titanium leg. Throwing an elbow over the next rail a little under shoulder height, he leaned there as comfortable as if he was in bed.

He used a thumb to wipe sweat off one eyebrow and jerked it toward the other pen. "They came up yesterday and that old gal's mean as my first wife." He stuffed the gloves into the back pocket of his jeans as he talked. I knew he did that so he wouldn't lay them down and forget where he put them. I've formed the same habit myself.

He waved an index finger at her. "I've been around mama cows who don't like you messing around with their calves, but that one takes the cake. She was wandering around the barn there for a while last night and stayed between me and her calf. Every time I'd move, she'd paw and snort, so I put feed in the trough and filled the other one with fresh water before I went in the house to eat supper.

"I didn't know if they were looking for water or feed, but she was in here eating when I came out. She didn't like that very much when I shut the gate on her."

"No brand?"

Mitch paused and rubbed the day-old whiskers on his jaw. He flicked a finger. "Nope, nor the calf. No tags or paint, neither."

I glanced past the house toward a line of trees in the bottoms some distance behind the house. "She might've come up from the river. She may be wild."

"Not unheard of." Tilting his sweat-stained straw hat back on a white forehead with his thumb again, he coughed softly before sliding a pack of cigarettes from his shirt pocket and lipping one out. "Some folks don't believe there can be wild cattle in this part of the state, but these Red River bottoms are sometimes wide open, and I've heard of 'em making their way here from time to time."

"Most of the time that's out west."

"It is." Cupping his hands against the hot breeze, he lit the smoke with an old-school Zippo etched with a military insignia still visible on its worn and scratched side. A coughing jag caught up with him, and when it was over, he drew deep on the cigarette. "That's better."

We both grinned at the old joke. Back in college, I had an old shop teacher who chain-smoked. He'd get on one of those coughing spells, and when he finished, he'd fire up another one and grin at us students. "It's a bad habit, but it sure tastes good."

Mitch let a stream of smoke out of his nose. "She could get water pretty easy down there on the river, but the grass is going fast. I 'magine she smells the hay or nuggets I shake out. Maybe the corn I'm feeding those steers, too."

Mitch slipped the lighter back into his jeans pocket. He blew a long stream of smoke through his nose that flowed across his thick mustache like an ocean wave. "I heard of y'all arresting some folks out near the New Mexico line here while back for rounding up strays and not reporting them."

I shrugged, not wanting to get into the details of a case still working its way through the courts. "Y'all" was relative, since special rangers for the TSCRA have specific districts assigned to us through the Texas Department of Public Safety .

Out of thirty special rangers, I'm one of those stationed along the Northeast Texas and Oklahoma border and commissioned to investigate crimes in both states.

A former smoker myself, I breathed in the sweet smoke from his cigarette floating in the clean country air. "People wouldn't believe what all we run into with this job."

"How long you been working for the cattlemen's association?"

"Quite a while."

"Long enough to see something like this?"

"Her?" I jerked my chin toward the mama cow, who watched us like a hawk.

"Yep."

"Not so much here in Northeast Texas. You put those two up to feed 'em out?"

The Angus steers I was talking about cleaned up the last grains of corn in a trough. Finished, one walked over to a galvanized forty-gallon water tank to drink. The other raised his head to blink at the still irritated cow in the adjacent pen.

"Yep. I intended to load 'em up and take 'em to the processor next month, but these days folks are buying their own steers for slaughter, and it's hard to get a kill slot."

"Small processor?"

"Yeah, he's about thirty miles away."

"Have you thought of having one of those mobile units come out?"

Mitch nodded. "I did, and it was the same problem. They're all booked up."

We watched the mama cow go over to the fence separating the two pens and paw at a pair of steers. I grinned. "I've never seen anything like that ol' gal in my life."

"What do you want to do with her?" The cigarette between Mitch's lips bobbed as he spoke.

"Well, since I don't have any reports on a missing cow and calf, I shouldn't take them with me."

"I don't want that crazy thing." Mitch drew on his cigarette. Smoke came out when he spoke. "I'd let 'em go, but I don't need her hanging around here. She's dangerous. If you don't do something, I might have to shoot her."

I watched her, studying on our problem for a few minutes. "Well, I can take her out to my place, I guess, and get her off your hands for a while."

After the death of my wife and youngest daughter in a car wreck caused by a meth-head, I sold my old house, bought a ranch, and moved to Ganther Bluff with Chloe, my oldest daughter.

The place didn't have one head of stock on it, and I'd kept it that way on purpose.

I threw a glance at my pickup. "I didn't bring my trailer."

Mitch grinned. "Let's load her up in mine, and I'll take her out there for you."

"That'll cost you in gas."

"This is costing me in antacids."

"Fine, then."

I watched his gait. We'd known each other for quite a while, and I'd heard about the cancer that started in his shin and threatened to spread throughout the rest of his body. The doctors took the leg off above the knee and declared him cancer-free.

It was his lungs I wondered about because he fired up another toonie. I called to his back. "You want some help hitching up a trailer?"

"Already have one on the hitch." He chuckled and disappeared around the corner of the barn.

The growl of a diesel dually rose in volume as he drove around and pulled a little four-wheel bumper-pull stock trailer to the gate.

Mitch backed it up with little effort, and when he was close to the gate, I opened it for him. He stopped when the trailer blocked the opening, and I swung the doors wide.

"Don't turn your back on her."

"She's behaving."

"Look at them eyes. She's crazy as a Bessie bug."

I can't tell you how many cattle I've loaded in the past, and Mitch's experience was invaluable, so I figured between us we had it handled. All we needed to do was walk the perimeter of the pen and herd her toward the open trailer door.

It worked halfway.

The calf took one look at us and squeezed up against her mama. The cow acted like she wanted to go in the trailer, but halfway across the small pen, she changed her mind and charged. I went up the fence like a monkey and she just missed me with that big old head that banged hard into a support post.

She backed up and saw Mitch waving his arms at the calf. It headed for the open trailer doors.

"Look out!"

Mama charged again, and despite his artificial leg, Mitch went up and over the fence in a flash. Mama cow whirled back toward me, and I felt like I was back in the rodeo arena as a young man trying to ride bulls. At that moment, I figured mad rodeo bulls were safer.

Way to go, cowboy!

This was exactly the situation where Sara Beth would have thrown her head back with a wonderful laugh that came from deep down. She was always full of life and, more often than not, saw joy and humor in nearly everything.

Safely out of the pen, Mitch plucked his phone out of his back pocket. "Hang on."

He punched at the screen and spoke for a minute while I sat on the top rail and watched the cow. "I hope you're calling for somebody to bring you a rifle."

"I just saw Bill Sloan and Fred Belk drive by. They're turning around to come help."

"It'd be nice if they have a horse trailer on the back of their truck."

"If they did, it'd belong to their boss, Jim Crawford, but they're young and dumb."

We laughed as a half-ton Ford pickup pulled across the cattle guard and parked beside my Dodge. Slender and bent-shouldered,

Sloan took his time getting out of the truck. Fred was faster and looked like a wrestler.

Mitch met them, and they shook hands. He laid a hand on Sloan's shoulder. "How're you feeling?"

"Better than I look. I can still work, and that's all that counts."

"He's still ugly," Fred said, pulling on a pair of gloves.

"Meet the boys." Mitch introduced us and we shook. He gave Sloan a soft pat on one arm. "They helped out quite a bit while I was in the hospital here while back. Kept an eye on the stock and made sure nobody ran off with my tractors."

"It wasn't nothing." Fred nodded toward Old Sorehead. "Need some help with this contrary old gal?"

"We do. She has a mind of her own." Mitch turned and led the way. He spoke quietly to me. "Sloan's kidneys are giving up on him. He's on dialysis now."

Sloan went back to the truck for a couple of lariat ropes. Despite being drawn down by his disease, he looked as if his entire life was spent working cattle or plowing fields.

Now there were four of us. Mitch pitched me a pair of leather gloves, and I pulled them on as their little blue heeler, Maggie, looped the corral half a dozen times, either to burn off energy or because she liked to run. She saw the pair in the pen and sat down to watch, ears pricked forward.

Fred Belk climbed over the fence. "Maggie, put her in the trailer."

Born to herd cattle, the little heeler slipped through the fence and loped around behind the cow. I thought she'd seen the end of her bad ways because of the dog. Tame as an old milk cow, she started across the corral with the dog walking behind.

Sloan bent and stepped through the rails. "Let's get a couple of ropes on her; then we can just pull her in."

That mama cow charged him fast as lightning, and he went up the fence in a flash.

Embarrassed, Sloan quietly rolled his rope as Mitch grinned. "Dang, that was pretty."

Fred built a quick loop and threw a glance toward the barn. He flipped it over the calf's head. "Y'all help me drag her into the trailer and be ready."

I saw his plan, and the three of us quickly had the little one inside and tied to the front end by the lariat ropes stuck through the slats. We'd left the trailer door open, and Mama charged inside like the whole thing was her idea from the start.

Fred slammed the door, and she lost her mind. It was as if we'd locked King Kong in there.

"She's gonna kick that trailer to pieces." Sloan kept his distance.

Mitch waved at the boys. "Thanks, y'all! Tuck, let's get her on the road, and she might settle down."

I jogged to my truck and hoped all the fences back at the ranch were in good shape.

If not, the .45 on my hip might be the only way to keep Red River County safe.

Chapter 10

Several weeks later, it was still hot and getting hotter. La Niña had a firm grip on Texas and the South. The dry and warm winter helped set the stage for the hot summer that was sucking all the moisture from the land.

The old-timers always said that winters like the one we'd just experienced resulted in dry ground which heats up fast in the summer and continues to dry out. The whole thing is a vicious cycle that only fresh cold fronts in the fall could turn around, unless one of those rare early-season Pacific hurricanes blew over Mexico and brought us rain.

The dirt parking lot at the Bethany sale barn outside of town was packed with rigs of every size, throwing up a continuous haze of dust that filled the nostrils and settled on the vehicles parked nearby. Pickups, trucks, trailers, and even more than a few sedans lined up in long, wavering rows that stretched across the lot and even down the sides of the two-lane leading out of town. It was bumper to bumper on the highway, with pickups and cattle trailers waiting their turn to pull into the lot.

More than a few parked their empty trailers to form a ragged line in front of the sale barn, planning to have them filled with stock by the time they left. *Drought* was the word of the day, and stockmen were unloading their cattle as hay and feed prices rose so fast you could almost see vapor trails in the air.

The air was thick with blowing dust, bellering cattle, and the smell of cow shit. The old-timers always said cow flop smelled like money and usually followed that comment with a laugh. With prices so bad, I doubted very many people would be cheerful enough to joke about it.

The sixty-seven-thousand-foot sale barn was huge, though it paled in comparison to some I've been in. I parked near the front door and joined the flow of cattlemen coming in and out. Cool, dry air was a relief as I stepped into what some called the lobby. Many knew me, and so making my way inside was a slow process of howdys, handshakes, and a few snatched moments to talk about concerns, life, and in some instances, families.

Sara Beth's death was still fresh enough that more than a few old boys cut their eyes at me with nothing more than a nod and a look of sadness. Everyone knew what had happened back in the fall, too, when my baby brother, Harley, and I tangled with a family of meth dealers who had the misfortune of dealing from their house across the road from our little ranch.

They crossed us in exactly the wrong way, and now those who had survived the encounter were twiddling their thumbs down in Huntsville prison.

Two years younger than me, Harley had worked with me before I joined the TSCRA and he retired after being seriously injured on the job. He's the exact opposite of my own personality.

We were an unusual pair, twenty years earlier. Country boys who wound up in big city law enforcement. Under an unheard-of special dispensation from the governor, we worked together as undercover narcotics officers for the Texas Department of Public Safety. Arrests, fights, gunfights, car chases, and living two distinct lives apart from our families, we cut a swath through the dealers and their drug pipelines until both of us figured we'd used up most of our luck on the day he was shot.

The kid he never grew out of still lived in him, and it showed through in almost every way with wisecracks and eternal optimism. His eyes always smiled, even when someone irritated him, and his whole demeanor was lighter than mine. However, once he got a mad on, you better hunt a hole. He's the kind of person who'll shoot a bad guy, piss on him, go have breakfast, and not lose a minute of sleep that night.

Directly across from the door was a wide sales counter. Hallie Arney looked up from a mountain of paperwork in front of her. Her short dishwater-blond hair had so much hairspray on it, I couldn't help but think it looked as if she was wearing a helmet.

She threw me a grin past the line of farmers and stockmen either filling out forms or cashing in tickets for the sale of their cattle. "Well, a brand inspector. Where you been?"

A steady stream of cross traffic wove between those sunbaked men, either going into the attached Beef House restaurant on my right, or the arena on the opposite side.

"Out doing my job, Miss Ma'am." I picked up a sale catalog and stuck it into my back pocket.

She waved me off as if I was a fly and went back to talking with a farmer who'd run out of money for razor blades.

The lowing and mooing of agitated cattle from the outside was a low hum in the background, punctuated by bellers and shouts of the cowboys in the arena as they pushed stock into the sale pen, then back out, to the continuous rattle of the auctioneer.

Hallie flashed me a grin and pointed with her chin at the low swinging bat doors leading to the sales area behind her. "Busy day."

"No kidding." I nodded at the grizzled farmer whose face was a roadmap of deep lines etched by the sun and three packs of cigarettes a day. "How're you doing, Bert?"

"I'd be better if these prices would go up."

Instead of standing there commiserating over something neither of us had any control over, I gave him a little slap on the shoulder and pushed through the waist-high swinging doors in the counter and through to the back. Buster Blakely, the sale barn's owner, and another man in a starched shirt and high-dollar straw hat were deep in a conversation reaching back a hundred years ago.

Buster held up two fingers as if counting and pushed his cap a little higher on his forehead. "I'll run both of 'em through the arena, Ed, but I can't sell 'em for mules, because they ain't."

The man wore a pristine hat that was decidedly out of place among a sea of sweaty, broken, brimmed hats and dusty caps with a variety of farm- and ranch-related logos. He wanted to be angry, but held himself in check. "I bought those two mules only last year to pull the wagon."

I had the feeling that Ed was a city boy dabbling in some form of farming or ranching. His clothes were new, pressed, and the look he was going for was a long way off. "Drugstore cowboy" came to mind.

Buster took a deep breath, trying to get Ed to understand what he was saying. "I understand, but like I said, they're hinnies."

"You're making that up."

Buster swallowed his frustration. "Look, a mule is the offspring of a mare and a jack. That's a male donkey."

I leaned into Hallie. "Who's he talking to?"

"Some feller out of Dallas. Bought a little place south of town and wants to be a cowboy. He was in Fort Worth a couple of years ago and saw a chuckwagon competition. He got the bug and decided to go all in. Bought him a wagon and a recipe book and went to town on the whole idea, but somebody sold him a team of hinnies for mules, and a guy at a competition made fun of him, so he's here to sell the team and start over."

"I know the difference." Ed frowned. "Now."

"Buster," I stepped closer. "I've been eavesdropping." I stuck out my hand to the weekend cowboy. "Name's Tucker Snow. I'm a special agent with the TSCRA."

The man looked confused.

Buster jerked a thumb in my direction. "He's a livestock agent. Some folks call them brand inspectors."

"Cow cop," I added.

The guy shrugged as if he didn't care one way or another who he was talking to. "So you're sure." He turned toward the door leading into the arena, as if a pair of mules would walk up to him to make things right.

"I'm sure." Buster dug a tin of Skoal from the back pocket of his jeans and slapped the edge against the palm of his hand to pack it. Twisting off the metal lid, he pinched out a dip and stuck it into his bottom lip.

The dude sighed and stuck his fingers in the front pockets of his jeans. "I never thought about country folks taking me."

"There's bad in all places." Buster crossed his arms and tightened his bottom lip around the fresh dip. "Who'd you buy the team from?"

"Young couple. Found them online when I typed in mule team for sale in the search engine."

Now I was really interested. "They from around here?"

"Said they were. I met 'em out at Herschel's truck stop with the money. They met me out around where the big rigs fill up. I bought 'em legal. I have a bill out in the truck."

"Don't need it."

The guy shrugged and from his body language, I believed him. "Like I said, found them advertised online and met a young couple at the truck stop."

"Let me guess. Not only were they parked out back with the big rigs, it was all cash."

"Yep. They tried to sell me the trailer, too, but I didn't need it."

"They give you a name?"

"Loren and Tracey Smythe." Instead of saying *Smith*, he pronounced it with a formal *Y* sound, as if they were Brits.

"You realize they were saying Smith."

He looked embarrassed. "I know, now."

"Would you be able to identify either of them if you saw 'em again?"

He shrugged. "Maybe."

"Look, I'll have to do some more investigating to find out if your animals were stolen in the first place. You may have a case of fraud here, but I'll need to dig around for a while. Give me your name and number, and I'll see what I can do."

I wrote down his information and gave him a pat on the shoulder. "Hang in there."

"Can I sell my team?"

I paused. "That's between you and Buster."

He looked crestfallen as I went back to work and Buster headed into the Beef House for dinner. Hallie picked up a sheaf of papers and handed them to me. "I have these for you."

She knew most everyone who came through the sale barn,

but when strangers appeared, there was always a bunch of tickets she kept off to the side so I could give them a look to check the brand and ownership of the stock.

Cattle theft is still a thing in Texas and Oklahoma, and anywhere else in North America where folks raise stock. I took the stack of papers and glanced up at the busy lobby full of cattlemen going back and forth between the offices, the sale arena, and the Beef House restaurant on the far side. Each time someone opened the door, the smell of sizzling steaks, hot grease, frying onions, and coffee wafted out to compete with all the odors coming from the arena.

Because I knew so many of the ranchers, farmers, and stockmen through my job as a special ranger, I only glanced at some of the tickets. I wasn't looking for lists of hundreds of cattle. Thieves usually concentrated on small scores, a few head here and there that might not be noticed for days, or even weeks.

I settled into a creaky wooden chair at a desk not far behind Hallie and flipped through the papers. I separated them into two stacks, those names I recognized and those I didn't. Plucking a small notebook from my shirt pocket, I went through my list of reported thefts that weren't isolated to just cattle.

There's a lot of money sitting around ranches and farms, and much of it's equipment. There are always people who'll steal anything not nailed down, from saddles to tractors. A steady list of hot items filled the pages in my book.

Hallie stamped a paper and handed it over to a rancher in a sweat-stained straw hat. He nodded and turned away.

Hallie said, "Hey, Tuck. I've had two people today ask me if I'd heard anything about stolen log splitters."

I raised an eyebrow, waiting for her to continue.

She tapped a pen on the desk in front of her. "Both of 'em

said somebody just drove up, hitched the splitters on, and drove off. Is there some hot market I don't know anything about?"

I flipped to a fresh page in my notebook. "Not that I've heard. Who was it?"

She gave me the names.

"Well, I'll keep an ear open." More for show than anything else, I opened my phone to the Facebook Marketplace page and typed in log splitters. A whole list came up and I scanned them, looking for locations in or close to Ganther Bluff. I didn't figure to see they'd already been posted for sale, but as Harley and I always said, thieves aren't usually former valedictorians of their class.

Chapter 11

Finished with the paperwork at the sale desk, I went into the arena, which smelled of cow manure and pee, old dirt, and fresh coffee. I found a seat high up in the semicircular arena stands with a view of the dirt-floor pen. Bright stadium lights overhead made it easy to see the stock as they were pushed through one gate in the sale area, held there for a quick examination by the buyers, then released back into the maze of cattle pens and aisles.

The auctioneer behind a table positioned above the action kept up a steady drone of information as a couple of cowboys herded in everything from one single beefalo calf to steers sold in lots, stockers, or cow/calf pairs.

The auctioneer rattled off the owner's name, weaning dates, vaccination and deworming programs, and how they were fed. Two ring men scanned the sea of cowboy hats and billed caps, watching for signs from bidders and, when someone made an offer, calling to the auctioneer for a loud, "Yup," sending the asking price ever upward.

The experienced buyers didn't shout or raise their hands. They kept their bids quiet by catching a ring man's attention by either the flick of a finger, a nod, or even one instance I learned to notice, a single raised eyebrow.

A buyer to my left whose name I couldn't recall made a disgusted sound when the gate below opened and the pen filled with black Angus steers. It was odd to see half a dozen red hides mixed in the bunch, and the man tipped his hat back as if that was a signal to talk.

"You know, I'd take the whole lot, but I can't."

"How come?"

"Them red 'uns. My boss won't let me bid on a mixed herd, even though that steer's Angus, too. We market *black* Angus, and if anyone saw me buy red cattle, he'd have a fit."

I knew what he was talking about. Folks think that good beef comes only from black Angus cattle, but that's all marketing. As far as beef was concerned, red and black Angus are the same, but manipulated consumers believe what they see and hear in advertisements. "Cut out the red ones. Those are slick-looking steers."

By the time those words were out of my mouth, the auctioneer pronounced them sold and they were already moving them out of the ring to bring in the next lot.

"I could have, but my head would be hanging from the boss' wall if he found out. That's our business now, just like everything else in this world, all smoke and mirrors."

I was about to answer him when a man under a truck stop cowboy hat took an empty seat beside me. He smelled as if he'd dumped a bottle of cologne down his shirt. In addition to the cheap stamped hat, he also wore an oxford shirt, some kind of jeans that were likely popular in urban dance clubs, and a pair of boots that would have been at home on a motorcycle's foot pegs instead of a sale barn.

The antique theater-style seat creaked under his weight when he sat down, and he held a sales ticket in one hand. He used it to partially cover the lower half of his face, as if there was any likelihood that competing bidders would see his mouth move. His eyes were hidden behind a pair of dark shades. "You're Tucker Snow."

Out of courtesy, the cattle buyer beside me quit talking, gave the newcomer a glance, and studied the herd of steers below.

I noticed the man's fingers were pale and smooth, the nails trimmed. My internal radar screamed "danger close," but there was nothing in evidence that made me think it was true. It wasn't unusual for strangers to stop me to talk about everything from a special ranger's resemblance to Texas Rangers, to my badge, gun, and in the case of those in the know, my work.

"I am."

Maybe he was one of those weekend ranchers. That would explain the clothes, but he had a smirk on his face that I already wanted to knock off onto the floor. It immediately reminded me of a guy I went to high school with and couldn't stand back then. The last time I saw Mark Lovitt, I felt the same way, especially after he made it clear that he was still interested in my wife, though we were long out of school and she and I had two girls.

The guy spoke softly behind the paper. "You were talking to Mitch Ramsey, right?"

Slumped down in the seat with one leg crossed over the other, I cut my eyes at him without answering.

"And you also talked to," he studied the paper in his hand, "Luke Strawn not long afterward."

I'd visited Strawn's little ranch not long after I was over at Mitch Ramsey's place, but I'd be damned if I admitted to a private conversation with anyone to a stranger. I turned so he could see the badge above the left-hand pocket on my shirt. "How can I help you?"

"Well, sir, I represent the interests of Mr. Ramsey and Mr. Strawn in a legal issue that needs to remain only between them and the company that employs me."

"Well, then keep it amongst yourselves."

He frowned. I don't think my side of the conversation was going the way he expected. He tried again. "This also involves you in a situation that you should keep confidential, but it's important to my company that we get your full cooperation in this matter."

"You just said a lot of words and nothing else." I considered his statement for half a second. Mitch and I only talked about that old mama cow and her calf. What in that exchange could interest this guy? "You a cattle buyer?"

He snorted. That sound, attitude, and the grin on his face set my teeth on edge. It was one of those feigned, maddening looks that said he was smarter than most other people and considered himself above everyone else. It said he knew a secret, and there was no chance he'd let you in on the details.

That smirk reappeared, and I had the fleeting thought that my old grandmother would have slapped it off his face with one big floury hand. "Frankly, what you were discussing with them is none of your business."

My face flushed with anger, and I hate when people have conversations about something I don't know, thinking I have all the information. "I work for the state and do my job."

"I can make it worth your while to work with us, and help you understand our business is extremely important and you'd be doing our country a favor, as well as yourself."

"Buddy, you're circling the drain here in more ways than one, and I'm about done with you. I don't know what you're talking about, but either ask me a question or get to the point. It sounds like you're trying to bribe me, or at the very least you're interfering with the lawful duties of an officer. That's a Class B misdemeanor and it could put you in jail for about six months...to start with."

"The subject you were discussing with Mr. Ramsey is being handled by my company. If you would, I guess, simply forget you ever talked to him and Mr. Strawn, it would be beneficial to all of us."

"If you're wanting me to look the other way about that cow and calf Mitch called me about, it's a tiny matter that you're blowing out of proportion. If you're threatening me in any way, or trying to bribe me, you're making a sad mistake."

A brief frown flickered across his forehead.

He seemed to not care that others were around, and that was a dangerous signal. People who aren't concerned if they're seen or overheard while doing something possibly illegal or embarrassing can be capable of anything. The sea of men filling the stands around us seemed to be paying us no attention, their eyes either on the stock moving through the sale pen, or their own conversations. I knew better.

"I just need for you to curb a couple of your investigations." The guy gave a shrug and feigned interest in the heifers in the arena. "Stick with cows and equipment."

"You're contradicting yourself and barking up the wrong tree, pal."

I turned to look right at him and the guy seemed to be considering his approach. "Your discussion with Mr. Ramsey, for example, could create problems for those gentlemen and yourself. If that happened, I'd hate for your daughter to find herself in certain uncomfortable situations."

I don't get mad often. Most of the time it's merely aggravation, but when I do lose my temper, it can be bad. It's moments when I see red, and that's unfortunate for everyone concerned. The next thing I knew, I was standing over him, trembling with fury. "Outside, buddy."

I didn't recognize my own voice. Those sitting around us tensed, finally watching the exchange as the auctioneer sold the lot of calves in the pen and waited for the hands to bring in the next animals. Many were older cattlemen or buyers who'd seen similar exchanges between competing stockmen in the past for a variety of reasons, while a number of younger men watched, not sure whether to stare at or ignore the entire situation.

This wasn't a visible cell phone crowd, or not as much as in some places. If this exchange had been on the street in a town or city, you can bet half a dozen people would be recording our exchange. However, most of those around us were simply watching, and maybe hoping for a fight.

The slim man unwound from the creaky seat and rose like a snake, the brim of his new straw hat only inches from my own. His voice was low and condescending. "Easy there, fella. I have everything under control, so I expect you to do the same. Come on out and let me give you the full message from my boss. Lead the way."

"Not hardly."

He gave an exaggerated shrug and headed for the door. Blood pounding in my ears, I held out two hands to indicate that I didn't want anyone following us outside. Eyes old and rheumy, dull and bright watched us make our way down the narrow steps.

The infuriating man led the way without turning around, and I felt like a high school kid going outside to fight. Once he was several feet away, I used the same steep, narrow aisle down to the concrete walk around the semicircular pen.

That took me only inches from two dozen heifers trotting in the soft sand on the other side of the steel arena, and my eyes locked in on the auctioneer's. He raised an eyebrow, and I shook my head as I traversed the arena and out into the lobby. His rhythmic chant of repeated numbers and filler words followed us as the doors closed behind.

I was wound tighter than a watch's mainspring. This smug stranger had brought my daughter into whatever it was that he was involved in, and that was the wrong thing for anyone to do.

Sara Beth spoke from behind the veil. *Easy, hoss. Just chill and maintain.*

It was an old expression we'd shared in college. When anything threatened to anger us, we calmed the other with just that one word, *maintain*.

We pushed through the doors into the heat of our Texas furnace. Sunshine felt heavy on my shoulders, and once away from the doors, I could already feel sweat in my armpits.

A few feet from the door, he turned as slow as Christmas, holding both hands up between us. "Easy. That was the only way I could get you out here where we could really talk."

I closed the distance, so close I could smell the cinnamon gum in his mouth. "You better start making sense, buddy."

"Chill out. I'm here to let you know it would behoove you to let my company handle those little issues I was talking about. That's all. Just step away."

Frustrated to no end, I wanted to grab his shirt and shake the guy until his hat flew off. "You're not making any sense."

An older rancher and young man who could have been his son passed on their way to the door, knowing something was up, but too country to get involved. The older guy nodded, and they went inside.

"I'm supposed to tell you that you're doing a fine job, but my boss feels you're investigating issues involving Mr. Ramsey and Mr. Strawn that don't fall under your purview. He suggests that you leave them alone and stay away and never talk with them again."

"Buddy, you have about two seconds to make sense."

He seemed to look over my shoulder at someone, but I've been around way too long to fall for that old dodge. Maintaining eye contact, I waited for him to answer my question.

"Well, here's the deal. I can offer you a significant amount of surplus cash for any charity you wish. It'll be our gift."

"What's your name? I'll need it when I arrest you."

"Uncle Tuck!" That young voice was as familiar as my own, and it was followed by his brother's. "We're here!"

Without turning, I knew it was Harley and his seven- and eight-year-old boys, Danny and Matt. Keeping an eye on Mr. No Name, I stepped to the side and held out a warning hand, still without turning around. The boys looked like little versions of the adults doing business in the sale barn.

Probably due to my body language, Harley's voice told me he understood. "Boys!"

The footsteps hurrying up on the gravel stopped, and Harley stepped into view. "You kids go over there right now."

He moved up close and from the corner of my eye I saw him take up a position to see more of the parking lot. Little Brother and I'd worked undercover for so long back in our younger days that we thought alike. He recognized the situation and reverted back to the old ways. Tough as nails, Harley would fight a buzz saw, our daddy said, and he was right.

"What's up, Tuck?"

"This guy and I were having a talk, but I'm finished." I knew the boys were watching, and right then all I had from this guy was a few words that still didn't mean anything to me. I couldn't arrest him, for he hadn't made any specific threats or offered an outright bribe. "The best I could tell, we were talking about nothing."

As much as I wanted to, you can't arrest someone for being an asshat.

No Name gave Harley that smirk. "Mind your own business, buddy." He likely took Harley for just another farmer or rancher, since he was dressed like the rest of them.

The results were immediate and would have been catastrophic had the boys not been watching. My little brother has always been more explosive than me, and during our years working undercover, I saw his eyes harden more than once. When they did, people usually got hurt, or shot.

Right then I was the one who wanted to hurt someone and didn't want Harley to be the instigator. He was retired from law enforcement and it was me wearing the badge. "Harley. This guy and I were just talking."

Expressionless, Harley tilted his head. "I don't know who you are, but if my brother here will let you go, I suggest you find somewhere else to flash that stupid look around."

The man's slitted eyes slid off me and again made me wonder who I was dealing with. "You're Harley Snow, owner and CEO of Lone Star Tactical. I should come down and take your course on surviving urban chaos, though truthfully, I love chaos and I doubt you have much to teach that I don't already know."

"We can start right now." Harley took a step forward at the same time someone in the parking lot tapped their horn. It was only two short blasts, but it was as if No Name received a message in Morse code.

Holding his hands at waist level, he took a step back. “Gentlemen, this has been an enjoyable conversation, but I’m afraid I’ll have to leave. It *shore* has been nice to visit with you all.” He emphasized the words *shore* and *you all* to mimic country dialect.

I fully expected him to say, “Yeehaw,” which would have sent me over the edge, but instead, he spun on one foot and walked around a truck. Harley thew me a look that said he wasn’t finished and started after him, but stopped when two black Suburbans passed us, weaving through the dirty trucks and trailers.

As if choreographed, a new black Ford half-ton pickup driven by Asshat slipped in between them, and the three vehicles pulled onto the highway, disappearing in a short caravan.

“What’n hell was that all about?” Harley watched them drive away as the boys joined us. Sensing the tension in the air, the kids went against their natural instincts and remained quiet. “And who was that guy, and how does he know me?”

“I don’t have any idea,” I said. “But I intend to find out.”

“How?”

“I’m going to talk with Mitch Ramsey.”

Chapter 12

In violation of Texas state law, two black Suburbans without license tags on their front bumpers were parked side by side in the sale barn's full lot, facing the main doors. The first SUV, which initially led the way into the crowded lot half an hour earlier, idled quietly, hiding four air-conditioned men inside behind dark-tinted glass.

The second contained four more men, also hidden by tinted windows that reflected the surroundings like mirrors. The only man of color, a well-dressed man with gray at his temples, sat in the back behind the passenger seat and studied the locals going in and out of the sprawling sale barn.

The phone in his coat pocket vibrated. He plucked it out, glanced at the screen and replaced the device without answering. Two cowboys walked past, studying the clean, shiny vehicles as if they were alien spaceships. Knowing they couldn't see inside the SUVs that stuck out like sore thumbs among all the trucks, the man flicked his fingers as if dismissing the two strangers.

Shaking his head, he addressed the broad-shouldered man sitting beside him. "I told them I'd handle this. They insist on calling every hour for a progress report. If my supervisor wanted to do it himself, he should have gotten his ass out from behind that desk and joined me."

"He'll never expose himself in that way, sir. You know how the higher-ups there at ChemShale operate."

"That's the difference between a hands-on guy like me and a paper pusher."

Wendel Cross closed a file and laid it on the seat between him and the big man with scarred knuckles. He shifted his position to get a clear look at his undercover employee talking intently with the stock agent beside a muddy pickup. "Pierson doesn't look anything like these people, Strap."

The giant laced his fingers in his lap. Brown hair cut high and tight, his demeanor screamed ex-military, while his accent was pure Texas. "It's *his* version of a local boy."

"Look at those guys around us. Worn-out jeans stuck in the tops of their boots, and that guy's shirt so faded you can almost see through it. Some of these people are barely getting by."

Dirty straw cowboy hats, sweat-stained baseball-style caps with farm and manufacturer logos, jeans, and worn-out boots were the standard uniform for the men who mostly climbed out of pickups and even a few dusty sedans.

"Sir, I think some of these old boys you're talking about have more money'n God. They just prefer to spend it in other ways, usually on equipment and cattle."

"Well, no matter. Pierson looked like a drugstore cowboy going in there. No one who lives around here is going to take him for a local."

"That's because he dressed himself." Strap laced his fingers and rested them in his lap. "I doubt he'll make any headway with that stock agent anyway."

Cross's phone vibrated again. He checked the screen, punched it off, and returned it to his pocket. "If this thing rings one more time, I'll let you answer it."

"That probably wouldn't be a good idea, sir."

It rang again, and instead of fulfilling his threat, Cross answered. "Are they finished with that farm?"

He listened for a moment, nodding. "It won't come back to us, will it?"

Strap kept an eye on the front door. It opened, and he pointed. "Mr. Cross, they're coming out."

Completely self-assured, Tucker Snow exhibited the confidence of an experienced lawman, but he also looked pissed.

"Fine. I want every piece gone. Is the cleanup crew finished?" Cross listened. "All the dirt is gone? Good." He punched off without saying goodbye and addressed Strap.

"Ramsey went nuts when the guys offered to pay him and his wife for their troubles."

"In what way?"

"When he heard about the material, and that we had to remove it, he was going to call the media. They said he threatened us with the EPA."

"Shouldn't have done that."

"So do I need to go out there?"

"No. They did what was necessary, and we're beyond that."

"It might come back on us."

"There's always that danger, but we'll get it all handled." Cross drummed his fingers on the door's armrest. "Speaking of that, I should have let you handle this part, but people tend to notice you more than guys like Pierson."

"I doubt very many people would have paid any attention to me here today. I could have put on my jeans and blended in."

"Not the way you're built. I'd prefer to keep you out of sight until you and the boys need to do your thing." He watched the stock agent and Pierson as they talked. "This isn't going to work. Pierson's pretentious. I can almost feel how pompous he is from here."

"I don't know what those words mean, sir. I was raised in the country."

"Don't give me that. You graduated at the top of your class."

Neither man looked at the other, focusing their attention on the small drama only thirty feet away.

"There were thirty-two of us." Strap shifted his weight in the seat. "That wasn't such a tough chore."

"And college? Top ten in your class at A&M, if I recall what I read in your jacket." Cross chuckled. "And I'm not going to stroke your ego by talking about how successful you were in the military, so you can talk like a country bumpkin if you want, I know different."

Strap answered with a grin, watching Pierson's body language and that of the brand inspector. His eyes narrowed. "Another player's coming into the picture."

Mr. Cross adjusted himself into a more comfortable position on the leather seat and watched a man and his two boys cross the lot toward the pair. The youngest kid, who looked like a little cowboy, tilted an oversized hat back on his head, pointed, and said something to his dad. "How do you feel when you're talking to that fool?"

"Pierson?" Strap kept his eyes on the evolving situation. "I don't feel anything. He's been a good hand and does the right things at the right time, but he's the kind of guy I never liked. He thinks he knows it all, and in my line of work, that'll get you killed."

"You're absolutely right." There was silence for a beat as Cross absorbed the discussion. Still not comfortable, he tugged at his suit vest and adjusted the Windsor knot in his black tie. Apparently satisfied, he leaned back, fingers absently playing with a heavy ring on his right hand. "Things look like they might be getting complicated."

The kids followed a rangy man in jeans, Western shirt, and billed cap. They broke into a run and made a beeline for the brand inspector and Pierson. The special agent held out a hand, and the boys slid to a stop as if trained.

Strap nodded in appreciation when the man they assumed was the boy's dad read the scene in a flash. He angled away from his initial line of travel, called something to the boys who immediately responded by backing away and slightly behind the man. He checked his surroundings, and stepped forward, completing a wide triangle.

Triangulation.

There was an exchange between the three of them, and Strap nodded again. "Professional."

"That's Harley Snow. The special agent's brother." Cross tapped the file. "Damn the luck at him showing up right now. He's as dangerous as a rattlesnake, but I think he's no match for you."

"I don't like snakes. I'd rather not find out, sir."

"Nor would I, and because of Pierson's faults, and those two men who look ready to start a gunfight, we're going to Plan B."

"What is that, sir?" Strap watched the exchange, intent on the men's body language.

"Diplomacy doesn't seem to be working. So let's get to the reason I keep you gentlemen on the payroll."

Strap put his hand on the door handle when things seemed to ramp up between the Snow brothers and Pierson.

"Cliff," Cross spoke to the driver, who met his eyes in the rearview mirror, "tap us out of here."

The driver tapped his horn two quick times, and Strap sat back. Seconds later they watched Pierson turn from the brothers and head for his truck.

Strap took a deep breath, thinking. "The same way we handled that situation down in Laredo?"

"It's different down there. More of the Wild West."

"So what do you want us to do?"

"Take the team and make this guy go away. I don't know how much he got from Ramsey, but he's the kind to dig around and then keep digging until he uncovers something that I haven't anticipated."

The military veteran looked uncomfortable. "Sir, this is a lawman, and his brother is a former officer; neither of them are anything like we're used to. Can I make a request?"

"Sure. Request away."

"Let's try and reason with Snow before things get Western. We really don't know what he talked to Ramsey about. Their discussion might not have moved past that old cow and her calf."

"So?"

"We go out to his house, I'll talk to him and explain that he needs to back off, and make it worth his while. I know what I look like, but maybe if I talk to him as one old country boy to another and make the offer, he'll take us up on it."

"You mean give him money." Cross frowned, thinking. "That won't work with Snow, but it might make a difference with Strawn, now that Ramsey is gone."

"That's a good place to start." Strap nodded. "He can't be making much. A little money in the right place, he sells his farm, and we send men in to clean things up like at Ramsey's."

"He won't live long enough to enjoy it. Did you read this file?"

"No sir. I did not."

"Strawn has the same medical issues that won't go away. Like Mitch Ramsey. And that was the Ramsey issue on the phone just now. It's handled."

"None of this should have happened, sir."

"You're right. And the reason came down to money, the exact same thing you want to give Mr. Snow. I wish we'd caught up to that load sooner. Two years is way too long for this kind of material to have been out there."

"Every action or thought on this earth now comes down to money." Strap tapped his shirt pocket, looking for the pack of cigarettes that wasn't there. He'd quit smoking long ago, but old habits die hard. "We should have located that load and paid the owner for what he had before it got to this county."

"There are a lot of should-haves in this conversation."

"I just don't like putting pressure on an officer. We're all in the same business, in a way."

"You're talking about your old profession."

"Yessir. I served my country and so did they. I have a lot of respect for people like that."

Cross picked up the file, weighed it in his hands. He watched farms and pastures pass outside his window, and wished he was back in his office in Houston. "What are you now, my conscience?"

Strap spoke with care. "I just say we go to Snow's house and make him think we work for the government. I know how good you can talk, and you can make the case for him to let us handle things ourselves. Convince him it's in the name of national security and public health. I think that would be best for all." He paused, seeming to consider his words. "Sir."

"That's never worked in the history of this organization." Cross felt his irritation rise.

"If it doesn't, *then* you can let me and the boys do our thing."

"Why are you so hands-off with this guy? What's he to you?"

Strap looked uncomfortable as steel fenceposts flashed by. "Sir, I was raised on a farm ninety miles from here. I know how these country people think, and if you put pressure on them, they'll dig in their heels and won't budge for hell or high water."

Cross dropped the file and watched a fully loaded trailer pass, throwing up dust that coated the polished clear-coat hood of their SUV. "I hate this country bumpkin shit."

"These people aren't bumpkins. They have a value system that's old, stretching back to the pioneers. They're gracious, but they'll fight like junkyard dogs if they're wronged."

"Their Bibles and their guns."

"Damned right, sir. Look around us. This is the largest unofficial army in the world, and most of these old boys can shoot. They're salt of the earth, and we need to remember that in the future."

"So you think that's all it'll take to make this go away? Talk?"

Cross considered the man beside him, wondering if Strap was being genuine, or maybe after his job. "No, but it's worth a try."

Chapter 13

Later that hot summer day, Harley dropped Matt and Danny off at his house. Chloe was already there to hang out with his wife, Tammy, as was Jimma, the stepdaughter of a drug dealer who lived across the road from my new house.

Tammy filled in a lot of holes in Chloe's life since Sara Beth and her little sister died. I tried not to put too much adult pressure on Chloe, allowing her to be a typical high school kid, but the trauma of losing her mother followed by what happened with the meth dealers weighed on her young shoulders.

That was especially true after the dealer, Jess Atchley, kidnapped her and Jimma from her biological mom, and took them to Oklahoma. It would have sent any other kid straight to a therapist, but Jimma, who was abused by Atchley, was tough as whang leather. After Atchley went to prison, and her mother died from one of the most dangerous drugs I'd ever encountered, Harley and Tammy began the paperwork process of adopting Jimma.

Since that drugstore cowboy had brought him up, I needed to go by and check on Mitch Ramsey. Harley rode with me out to Ramsey's place that afternoon. I'd been thinking about going by anyway to tell him I still had that crazy old cow out at my place. She'd settled down after I put her out, and seemed almost docile, but I'd seen that before. Out in the pasture, contact with me or any other human was almost nil.

Cows in pens, corrals, or loading chutes can go crazy for reasons no one can understand, and I guess cow whisperers could say they feel as if they're in danger and are fighting back in the only way they know how. No matter, I wanted to give her a little more time to raise that calf before we loaded her up for the sale barn.

Bigger calves bring more money, and there was no cost to take care of them. Our ranch had almost fifteen hundred acres of grass, and over twenty pools for water.

Harley rode shotgun in the truck's cab, and that usually meant he fidgeted like a toddler wanting to get out of a car seat. Before long he had the blowers on high and the temperature as low as it would go. Satisfied with his adjustments and as was his habit, he checked the Ram's glove box, then the little storage compartment before lifting the armrest to see what was inside.

"You looking for anything in particular?"

He raised an eyebrow. "Nope. Just seeing what you have in there."

"Some folks might call that snooping."

"Your brother would call it being aware. I see two boxes of .45 ammo, one box of 9 mm and I assume that's for me, four boxes of .223 for that rifle back there under the seat, one box of .380..."

"That's for my backup pistol."

As we talked, he poked at the media center on the dash, going through the sound and navigation system's files. "I know that. Four knives, three pairs of wire cutters, two pairs of binoculars, and I think one of 'em's mine." He raised the armrest to reveal a deep storage compartment filled with curled and stained papers, receipts, and sales programs. "There's about a gazillion little notebooks in here that look like they're all full..."

"And you leave those and all that paper where they are. It's my filing system."

"Right. I remember that from when we were kids. You had your stacks all over our room, and if memory serves, you threatened to kick my butt if I moved any of them."

"I knew where everything was."

"I'll give you that." He sighed. "You could find whatever you wanted in those raggedy-ass stacks of paper." He moved a drift of pages around on the dash. "Looky here what you have baking in the sun, a first aid kit that's not much more than Band-Aids, and a buttload of hand sanitizers."

"The big trauma kit's in the back floorboard storage bin. What's your point?"

"No point. I guess I'm just nosy, but I think you need more ammo."

"I'm not in the business of shooting people. I'm more of an investigator."

As we followed the two-lane northeast of town, he studied on my comment and went through the stations, and finally leaned back with a sigh, adjusting the seat belt across his chest.

We passed pastures, fields, woods, farms, and larger ranches while he grunted and grumbled to himself. He finally said what I'd been thinking. "I swear. Radio is a wasteland these days. Country music is dead, and the only thing out there is this bubble-gum pop rap crap from guys who don't understand country."

I grinned. "Don't get your panties in a wad. They play some George Jones every now and then."

"Yeah, but I have to listen to that other stuff way too long." He sang, "Oh baby, let's go out through the pole beans and build a big fire in someone's pasture, baby, and drink some beer, gonna get you, dance all night on the tailgate of my pickup, baby, and tailgates and whiskey and rain and I don't know real country so I'll say, 'If the creek don't rise,' and"—he went into a falsetto that was downright creepy—"and I'm gonna say, baby, some more because that's all us new fake country beer singers looking for a party know to say, baby, that and beer..."

"Good lord." I shook my head and turned the radio back on. A political talk show was better than his singing, though his take on what passes for country music wasn't far off.

He wasn't finished. "Country used to be about heartache, the land, and life in general. Now it's about brand names and parties all set to a rap cadence. That's the kind of crap that guy you were talking to back at the sale barn would have on his radio."

Harley was quiet for a minute; then, he was back on that guy again and I finally knew why he was so amped up and twitchy. "I wish I'd gotten there a little sooner to talk with that snarky bastard."

I grinned. "The way he was acting, there would have been very little talking."

"That boy pissed me off the minute I saw him. You wanna bet he ain't married."

"No way."

We passed an enormous metal barn sitting alone in a pasture. "Well, if it makes you feel any better, I thought of any way I could cuff him, but I couldn't come up with a reason that would stick."

"He threatened Chloe's safety, and in my opinion, yours."

"My word against his, and it was so veiled that even the worst defense attorney in the country would have him back on the street before I finished the paperwork."

"That's the problem with courts today. Back when we were working, the charges stuck."

"That's what you want to remember, but there were plenty of them on the streets in only a day or two. You know as well as I do some of those guys we hauled in had arrest records that were pages long."

"That wasn't *our* fault."

"Never said it was. We did our job; it's the system that's failing the public. Especially the district attorneys. Law enforcement can work perfectly, but if there's no prosecution, crime'll spin out of control."

"It's when the DAs accept plea deals and won't hold offenders accountable. Long rap sheets are the result of a lack of prosecution."

"That's right! They hide behind prosecutable discretion, but you realize you're preaching to the choir."

Law enforcement does its job, but plea deals result in offenders being slapped on the wrist, or released on a variety of legal issues, allowing them to reoffend over and over again. The DAs cry their caseloads are too heavy, so they have to prioritize their efforts to the most serious offenders, allowing others to prowl the streets, preying on innocent civilians.

He had a captive audience and continued talking as if I were a new acquaintance. "No cash bonds. That's the biggest debacle I've ever seen. We arrest an asshole, book them into the jail where they're printed and told they will be contacted and given a court date. Good God! Remember that guy who had over a hundred arrests for theft, and was released every time?"

I spun him up, just for fun. "It's like those so-called illegal aliens crossing the border and being detained, and then released into the country with the promise of being called in for a hearing."

"Right! In my opinion, we need to bring back chain gangs, especially for violent offenders…"

It was nothing new. We'd been over that ground a thousand times, but it always helped pass the time when we were on the road.

Chapter 14

Cowboy Pierson's fingers raced over the keyboard in his lap as the old and dented air conditioner below the cheap motel room's window hummed and vibrated. The damp air coming from the vents smelled of mildew and old dust.

He would have used the desk provided by the midcentury motel, but it was filled with liquor and beer bottles. They'd been in the Red River Lodge for far too long, and the place needed a good cleaning and airing from the four men who only went by last names they'd chosen after joining the company. Barnes roomed with Pierson, while Sanz and Truitt denned up in the other room that shared a connecting door.

Mr. Cross was at the opposite end of the U-shaped vintage motel, but had a room to himself. His driver and Marco slept in the unit on one side, while Strap's unit bookended Cross's room. He'd chosen the Red River in Clarksville, Texas, because of a distinct lack of security. No cameras meant they didn't worry as much about being recorded, though the new shiny SUVs looked out of place parked amid faded pickups and old sedans that smoked and rattled each time their owners turned their ignitions.

Instead of sitting on one of the two unmade beds, Mr. Cross stood just inside the door beside the faded curtains that weren't completely closed. The little sliver of light was enough for them to see, but not wide enough for pedestrians to look inside.

"They're on the road to Mitch Ramsey's place." Pierson was in regular work clothes, which were 5.11 brand pants and shirts. Their tactical gear was as familiar as the military fatigues they'd all worn in the past, but it was commonplace enough not to draw too much attention.

When anyone did notice, they assumed the men were first responders and therefore not interesting enough to record in their memory banks.

Mr. Cross turned to look out the gap and into the quiet parking lot shaded by tall pine trees and spoke to those who'd gathered in the room. "We're finished there, right?"

"Yessir." Seated on the bed with his back against the scarred headboard, Strap laced his fingers.

"This cow cop is getting too nosy."

"He's doing his job, sir."

"His job is interfering with ours."

Strap nodded and focused his attention on the blurry tube TV resting on a table that looked as if it came from a garage sale.

"Did you get a bug inside the truck?"

Pierson didn't meet Mr. Cross's eyes as his fingers moved across the laptop's mouse pad. He was the tech guy who wanted more than anything to become a member of the team that Cross referred to as Hard Hitters.

"It was easy to stick one under the truck, but getting inside would have taken too long."

"I'd like to hear what he's saying to that brother of his." Mr. Cross turned back into the room. A third man sat at the round table only a couple of feet away, intent on his cell phone. The other mimicked Strap's position, feet on the bed and propped up by two pillows. "What do we have on the location of Snow's daughter?"

Strap side-eyed his boss, then pretended to be interested in the toes of his shoes.

Pierson answered. "She's with the brother's wife and his family."

"Do we have a locator on her car?"

"We do."

"Keep me apprised of her whereabouts at all times."

Strap barely turned his head to see the man on the other bed. Barnes met his gaze for a moment, then went back to the phone in his hand.

"We may have to take more drastic measures soon." Mr. Cross put his hand on the doorknob. "I want to know everything they're doing if they really are going to the Ramsey place. Get a drone in the air."

"Will do." Pierson typed a quick text.

"Text me as soon as they get there." Cross opened the door to a flood of hot air that immediately elevated the inside temperature. "I'll be in my room."

Chapter 15

The entrance to Mitch Ramsey's tree-shaded ranch was almost directly across the highway from another property that was close to the same size. I'm sure it had a house somewhere at the end of a long, winding gravel drive, but we couldn't see it.

We passed an overgrazed pasture and a grove of drooping trees that looked like a city park and came to Mitch's place. The twin sixteen-foot pipe gates were standing open, and I slowed and turned left onto the drive leading to the house. Harley was riding easy on his side of the truck and didn't notice what I saw.

He perked up when I stopped just beyond the entrance. "What?"

"There's something wrong."

"What?"

Any other time you would have thought we were back on our Abbott and Costello routine that helped bleed off tension before we stepped into dangerous situations or when making an arrest in the old days. We did that a lot back when we were working undercover.

"This place is empty."

"You mean no one's home." Harley looked around.

"No." I took in the ragged grass growing beside the gravel drive that was already going to seed.

Farms and ranches are always littered with everything from tractors to flatbeds, riding mowers, and a hundred other pieces of equipment. This place was empty as a house and land listed on the market after the owner dies.

It took a minute for me to realize another change. "His catch pens are gone. His trailers, too."

Harley lowered the shades over his eyes. "Steel cattle panels?"

He had the idea I was talking about metal panels of varying lengths and heights that ranchers use for temporary corrals and catch pens. They were similar but much smaller than familiar freestanding crowd control barriers that cities and municipalities use to keep parade viewers on sidewalks or in specific areas, or traffic safety fences that are easily moved. Cattle panels have surged in popularity since we were raised on our dad's farm.

"No." I shook my head. "They were permanent, set in the ground and welded."

We pulled up close to the barn where I'd parked weeks earlier. The imprints of the pens were distinct in the areas stomped into nothing but bare earth by hundreds of hooves. The scent of stale urine and old cow flop was still strong, but it was all dry and starting to crumble in the hot air.

I killed the engine, and we stepped out into the heat. There wasn't anyone around to throw guns on us, but Harley stayed beside his door, as if expecting trouble. It was ingrained in both of us through years of experience to remain near the vehicle, to use the doors for protection if someone started shooting.

A crow called from a line of trees leading down to the bottoms, and a couple of buzzards circled in the slightly cooler air high above. The entire place was silent. I walked over to where the pens once stood, kicking at a clump of struggling grass sprouting in the middle of where steers headed for their kill slots were fattened on corn.

I couldn't make sense of what I was seeing. "Who would pull out fence posts?"

"Salvage thieves?"

I considered his idea, looking around at the silent house and barn. "Could be, but now that the price has dropped per ton, I'm not sure it'd be worth the time and trouble to pull these up." I waved toward the pipe and cable fences running alongside the highway. They were much older than the corrals and in need of painting. "And those old fences haven't been touched."

"Might have been someone wanting something simple as pens at their place." He scanned the buildings and pastures around us. "We've always said people will steal anything not nailed down. Or maybe Ramsey might have sold them."

"Mitch didn't say anything about selling out the last time we were here. He'd been through so much trouble to keep this place and make it work, even after he lost his leg. I can't imagine him putting the place up for sale."

"Maybe he needed the money to pay off medical bills. From what you told me, they've been snakebit for a while." Harley turned to look back at the gate. "There isn't a for sale sign out yet."

"Somebody might've bought the place before it ever went on the market. Might have sold the corrals to help pay for it after they closed."

"Could be, but I'd expect to see some kind of activity from the new owners." Harley walked to the metal barn, opened the door, and peered inside. "Empty as your head in here. I know a guy who bought a place that a welder owned for years. There was scrap metal everywhere, and they made quite a bit of money from selling it. Didn't help much in the long run after they paid for the property, though. Bought some equipment with it, as I recall."

Studying the grounds, I went to the house. Even the furniture on the front porch was gone, but you could see the light outline of a lounge set on the faded boards where the sun couldn't reach. Discolored spots showed where the legs had stood. I stepped up and peered into the window. The living room was empty. Even the curtains were gone.

Inside was a repeat of the porch. Phantom pictures on the walls showed where frames had hung for years, and ghost outlines of a couch and chairs on worn hardwood floors were evidence of a long life in the old house.

I stepped to the edge of the porch and looked down the length of the house. Mud wrens were already building a nest under one eave. I watched the little birds fly around the house, concerned by my presence.

Fresh clumps of dirt at the edge of the flower beds indicated someone had been digging. Thumbs stuck in the pockets of my jeans, I studied the flower beds that were black with fresh compost, wondering what plants were gone, and why someone had taken even the flowers.

It was possible. People who move to new places often take heirloom plants with them, bulbs from their grandparents, great-grandparents' homesteads, or even an old aunt's flowers that might have been moved from place to place as families relocated.

Sara Beth did the same when we first got married; she'd dug up daffodil bulbs from her mother's garden to plant in front of our new house. The thought flashed through my mind that I should have done the same when I sold that house after she died. I made a mental note to go back and ask the new owners if I could dig a few of those bulbs and some peonies she'd planted, and move them to the ranch house. They came from her daddy's place after he passed.

It would be great to see them bloom. A piece of Sara Beth and baby Peyton at the new place.

Maybe it would seem more like home.

"Barn's empty." Harley's voice snapped me back into the present. "Already a couple of yellow-jacket nests starting up in there, though."

"So's the house." I jerked a thumb over my shoulder as he walked around.

I looked over the flower bed and missing arbors. The dry and dying grass was beaten down around the flower beds, and now that I looked at it, around the pens. It wasn't just digging. Something was missing. In my mind, the fresh material I'd noticed confirmed what'd happened.

"That's what's missing." I scanned the area. "Somebody took the arbors that were here."

"Wonder why."

"They were metal, too. I'm thinking that salvage idea might make more sense, but it would be more likely if it was copper."

People steal new copper pipe from houses under construction and make a killing off the sale.

"But all this was made from old drill stems that aren't nearly as valuable."

The silent farm seemed to be dying around us. There was no longer any life in the buildings, pastures, or on the grounds. It reminded me of one day when I was a young man and my dog passed away from old age. I loaded him in the back of my truck and drove him up to my grandparents' place to bury him beside other old dogs who'd gone on ahead through the years.

Their truck was gone when I pulled up the red gravel drive that cold, gray winter day so many years ago, and the little frame house was closed up and silent. I'd been looking forward to seeing my granddad that day, both for emotional support and for his solid presence, but it was just me.

It was something I had to do myself.

I dug the hole under a bodark tree not far from the house, taking care to get far enough away from the other gravesites of dogs my family'd owned through the years, and laid my old friend down. I covered him with the fresh dirt, and went back up to the house. I sat on the front porch and listened to the silence, until a *V* of complaining geese passed by overhead. Hearing their plaintive honking gave me a sad feeling on a lonesome day.

That's how Mitch Ramsey's abandoned farm felt that evening, and I was glad Harley was there to help chase away the blues with Sara Beth and Peyton's names on them that threatened to gather around me.

It's easy for me to get melancholy these days, and I couldn't help but think the house behind me was already dying. Empty houses without life in them seem to fall apart in a matter of months, if not weeks.

A truck went by on the highway. The driver tapped his horn in greeting and kept going. Both Harley and I threw up a wave. That's what country folks do.

I stepped down and joined him as a pair of dove flew overhead, peeping with the effort of flying hard and fast. "Selling out so fast doesn't make any sense. I'm gonna have to ask somebody why."

"It sure is suspicious, coming on the heels of that guy back at the sale barn."

"That coincidence itches in the back of my mind, for sure."

Harley jerked a thumb toward the barn. "Those dents where the tires of his equipment sat are already growing over. How long ago did you say it was when you were by here?"

"A few weeks."

"Plenty of time if he sold out, right after you were here."

"I'd believe that, but he didn't mention it at all. We talked about livestock, and he called a couple of old boys to come help load up that mama cow and her calf I have over at the house."

"He ever call you about them?"

"Haven't heard a word. Most of my time since then's been other places." I slipped my cell phone from the back pocket of my jeans and flipped through a long list of calls. "Here it is."

I told Harley the date, and he leaned over the back of our truck, in the time-honored position of country folks. "I don't see any cattle down in that pasture. I guess he sold 'em all before he left."

"He didn't go through the sale barn here, or I'd have heard about it."

I mirrored Harley's position over the truck bed and glanced back toward the front gate at a Dodge Charger that passed, slowed, and then shifted into reverse.

Harley squinted at the car. "Know who that is?"

"Nope, but it sure reminds me of that Charger that ran block for that cattle thief before I came over here to Ramsey's place."

We watched the sedan come down the drive and recognition dawned. "Wait. Never mind, those are the two boys who helped us load that crazy cow." I had to think. "Bill Sloan and Fred something. Only met them the one time here."

The engine rumbled as they pulled up close to my truck. Bill killed it and they climbed out. Fred had a beer in his hand, and I tried not to grin.

"Ranger Snow." Sloan looked pleased to see us. "It's Saturday night! Y'all want a beer?"

We shook, and I introduced them to Harley. "Naw, I'm still on duty, and it's Agent Snow."

"Sloan ain't supposed to be drinking." Fred took a long swallow. "Doctor's orders, but he didn't say I had to stop."

"Fred, I can't remember your last name."

"Belk. Good to see you again, sir. Beer, Harley?"

"I'm not driving, or on duty."

"Neither were we." Fred laughed at his own joke and went to the car and opened the trunk. He returned with a small cooler that sloshed with ice and water. Sitting it over into the bed of my truck with no effort at all, he flipped off the lid. "Harley, grab what you want."

There must have been more than one brand, but Harley went with our old standby, original Coors Banquet. He nodded thanks and cracked open a can. "Good to see y'all know good beer." He put a finger on his own straw hat. "You don't see many cowboys driving cars."

"It's easier for this dumbass to get in and out when he goes to the doctor." Fred paused, as if a secret had slipped out.

Sloan let him off the hook. "Doing dialysis, and it takes a lot out of me. It won't be long, though. I'm on the transplant list, and it could be any day."

"Something's gonna kill me." Sloan finished his beer and I realized it was alcohol free. Near beer, as I'd heard growing up. He pitched the empty on top of the ice after squeezing it flat, and fished out a fresh can. "Somebody call you over trouble out here?"

"No." I shifted toward my truck's tailgate as the two young men took their paces around the bed. "Just came by to see Mitch about that crazy cow and calf y'all helped load."

Sloan laughed. "We shoulda shot her. What'd she bring at the auction?"

"Haven't sold her yet. Nobody claimed her, and I'm waiting for the calf to put on a little more weight so she'll bring more, then I'll donate the money to a good charity."

"Too bad about Mitch," Fred said, tilting his hat back.

"I haven't heard anything. What happened?"

"Well, his cancer came back with a vengeance. I heard he was dead three days after you were here, and it wasn't a couple of days before his wife sold out lock, stock, and barrel."

The hair tickled on the back of my neck. "How can that happen without me knowing it?"

Selling a ranch was a big deal, and everyone in the county should have been talking about it, but a man had died and his wife sold out without a word? Country people are close, oftentimes related to each other, and someone should have known what was going on.

The rural grapevine was even better than the internet, and through phone calls and ever-evolving social media, the residents were nosy and interested in what was going on with other families. At the very least, folks living in the area would have taken some of the equipment off his hands, and if it was sold at auction, I should have been there.

It was eerie.

Fred looked around, as if there might be eavesdroppers or an unseen listening device. "Here's the truth. The whole thing's weird. We went by one afternoon and there were dozens of trucks out here, big eighteen-wheelers along with rigs with augers and box trucks. When we went past to feed twenty-four hours later, the place looked like it does now."

"Anyone talk to Anita?" Her name popped into my mind,

though I had only met her once. I remembered her because she was one of those old country gals that was tough as leather and could cook *and* cut calves when he needed her.

Sloan shook his head. "I grew up around here and our family knows just about everybody. My mama called out here, but she wouldn't answer. She left a message and when Miss Anita didn't call back, she had me bring her over. Most everything was already gone, and a big guy with shoulders as wide as a barn door met us right here where we're standing.

"Big bastard didn't run us off, but that's how it felt. Said Miss Anita was already gone. Moved to Idaho, or Montana. I disremember, but it was up in there somewhere. I asked him who he was and he said he was with a company that helped big outfits sell out when their owners got too old or were unable to work the place and the family wasn't interested in ranching anymore."

The phone buzzed in my back pocket and I slid it out to see the word BLOCKED on the screen. Spam calls from unknown numbers were regular occurrences, but I seldom saw that word.

"Special Agent Snow."

"I need to tell you we always know where you are."

Chapter 16

Still reclined on the sagging bed in his shabby motel room barely cooled by the wheezing window unit, Strap listened as Mr. Cross called Special Agent Snow. He looked peaceful, awaiting orders, but inside, Strap was twisted in a knot that reminded him of those days when he and the others were in the military, preparing to step into hostile territory.

He'd worked for ChemShale for over a decade, and this was the first assignment that made him uneasy. In the past, Mr. Cross handled issues with breathtaking speed, and his team usually had to only look menacing whenever necessary for their "targets" to get the message. They sometimes had to rely on their training, and once down on the Rio Grande, things went Western when an assignment brought them up against a Mexican cartel.

When the smoke cleared, two of Strap's men were in shallow graves, and the corpses of more than two dozen gangsters swelled in the South Texas heat. It was an operation that shouldn't have gone sideways, but their experience with ChemShale and previous jobs brought them out on top.

This was different. These were like the people he grew up

with and took an oath to his country to protect. Oh, hell, it was all about money, and he knew that from the start. ChemShale made it clear that everything they did was in the best interests of the country, and sometimes those interests were contrary to how he felt, but there was always a hope they were working on the right side. Still, he had a constant niggling doubt that maybe what they were doing wasn't completely right.

But the money was good at first, and better after he returned from military service, and again, that's what mattered. Another couple of years and he could retire and disappear to Bora Bora where the people there welcomed everyone with open arms. After that, there would be no more lies swirling around like gnats, and he could fulfill a boyhood dream of living on an island in the tropics and never again hearing anyone talk about oil, drilling, or national security linked to some vague notion of what was best for those who didn't know any better.

Mr. Cross liked to call them the uninformed.

Chapter 17

As the strange voice came through the phone's tiny speaker, the hair once again prickled on my neck, and I couldn't help but look around. "Who is this?"

The caller's voice was precise, almost clipped. It came from someone who sounded accustomed to being an authority figure. "I called to offer my condolences on the death of Mitch Ramsey. It was a terrible blow to the family that hired my company to handle his last wishes and to liquidate his assets."

"What…?"

"I can't tell you much more…"

I put the phone on speaker for Harley, not caring if the young men heard. In fact, I kinda liked the idea of them being there as witnesses.

"…except that everything was done according to the law, of course. Mrs. Ramsey is well, and living with her sister. She's now extremely well off and will never worry about money again."

"You have a name?"

"Why, you sound cross, sir. And that name appears to be appropriate, so call me Cross."

"Fine. This smells fishy. Why are you calling me with all this info, and especially right now? What's it to me, and how the hell do you know where I am or what I'm doing?"

"Well, I've been told you're performing your duties, and so I felt it was necessary to help you. Being a good citizen, you might say."

Harley leaned forward. "How the hell has this happened without anyone around here knowing about it?"

"Oh, on the contrary, many people knew, but there was money involved, and as you know, Harley, everything in this world is about money, and it can do wonders to seal people's allegiances."

Harley's eyebrows went up and he mouthed, "How does he know me?"

My answer was a raised eyebrow, and I shook my head as the voice continued.

"Mr. Ramsey's wishes were followed to the letter, and his will stipulated that everything be sold immediately after his death. You had no need to know, or to be involved, therefore you heard nothing, like most of the people in this county."

"He seemed healthy the last time I talked with him."

"Cancer is a bitch. Mr. Ramsey didn't want people worrying or talking about him, therefore it was all kept quiet. Why do you think he wanted that troublesome cow off his hands? He simply didn't feel well enough to deal with it."

Did you get that, Tuck? Sara Beth caught it, too. *He knows about that cow and calf. Creepy.*

Hearing her inside my head was almost funny because that's the way she always talked.

I said, "So, if I believe all this, and I'm not saying I do, why is everything down to the corrals gone?"

Cross chuckled. "People are peculiar, aren't they? You never know what dying people are thinking."

I tried another tack. "Mr. Cross, I'd like to meet with you for a few minutes to talk about this. You're not coming through very clear out here in the country."

He chuckled again, and it was beginning to get annoying. "That is simply untrue. Our signal is strong, but you can take me off speaker if that'll help. If I want to talk with you in person, it will be my idea and under my terms."

Harley leaned away from the truck and scanned the area around us while I studied the phone in my hand. Just to be stubborn, I left it on so the others could hear.

"About meeting face-to-face?"

"I'm afraid that won't be possible. I'm several states away at the moment, and doubt I'll be back to your region any time soon."

By region, I wondered if he meant Northeast Texas, or my assigned region through TSCRA. That region included about a dozen counties in Texas and Oklahoma. If that's what he meant, he was better informed than I expected. But then again, you can find anything on the internet these days.

"Your insurance company must have a lot of power behind it."

There was that laugh again, and I found it almost as annoying as that individual we'd talked to at the sale barn. "I never said we were with an insurance company, but I suppose insurance is what I do. I alleviate issues and take the weight off our clients' minds. How about that explanation? Is that clear enough?"

That's when I knew the guy at the sale barn that morning and the man named Cross were working together. From the corner of my eye, I saw Harley walking alongside the barn, looking up at the eaves. He sure wasn't trying to find wasp or dirt dauber nests.

"Look, your employee this morning made some comment about my family, and specifically my daughter. He crossed a line, and it's one I think you've crossed before. I don't like this at all, and you can bet I'm going to find out who you are, and what happened to Mitch Ramsey."

"Well, he was cremated. I can tell you that much."

"Are you talking about that asshat at the sale barn, or Ramsey?"

"You know what I mean."

"I hoped it was your drugstore cowboy."

"I had the same thoughts, sir. You have my assurances that your family is safe, Agent Snow, and that includes your brother's family."

Despite his words, the man's comment came through as a threat, and I took it as such. It was a good thing Harley didn't hear that part. Had he been within listening distance, he might have managed to reach through the phone and pull part of that guy through the little speaker, and it would have been a part near and dear to the man.

Harley came back to where I was standing. He shook his head, curled his fingers as if around an empty tube and peered through a hole while making a cranking motion with the other. He mouthed, "No cameras," and that's when I realized he was looking for security cameras, which Cross might have been using to watch us.

Cross chuckled. "Archaic, Harley, but effective. No there are no cameras there, but as you're starting to realize, we have eyes everywhere."

My little brother froze and his eyes went glassy. I've seen that look many times, and more than once, people on the receiving end went to the hospital. In more cases than I'd like to admit, some went into the ground.

For a long beat, none of us moved, and then Fred tilted his hat back and looked up at the sky. Barely moving one finger, he pointed upward and we all got his message.

Slow as molasses in the wintertime, Harley walked to the barn and disappeared inside.

I nodded and returned to the infuriating conversation. "Cross, I'll be talking with anyone who knew Mitch, and then I'm going to have a visit with Strawn and figure out what's going on here. I have a feeling you and I are going to meet face-to-face soon, so you need to be ready."

"That sounds awfully close to a threat, Agent Snow, and a man wearing a badge shouldn't be suggesting violence."

"It wasn't a suggestion, but take it any way you want. I'm looking forward to talking with you in person."

He chuckled, and I felt the hair prickle on the back of my neck. "It won't be long, and when you least expect it."

Chapter 18

ChemShale's primary agent in the field, known as Mr. Cross, almost threw the phone against the wall when the brand inspector said Strawn's name through the receiver against his ear. A red rage washed over the man who prided himself on maintaining his composure in all weather.

Cross looked out the window at the hot, humid parking lot outside of the Red River Lodge. While the interior was tolerable from the air conditioner running full blast, the world outside was everything people despised about Texas in the summertime.

He turned back inside with a blank expression. Some might think he was considering the harvest gold carpet, the peeling paint walls, the useless 1960s room divider between the bedroom and the sink, and a simple clothes rod visible from the room. The art on the walls was far from interesting. Old muddy-colored prints of cowboys and cattle mixed with two hunting scenes featuring pheasant and bobwhite quail hung above the dusty TV.

He didn't see anything except the end of Tucker Snow's future. "This will be the last time we speak, Mr. Snow. I'd hoped this information would answer whatever questions you might have about Mr. Ramsey. I'd like to continue our conversation, but I have another, very important call coming in on the other line. Good day to you, sir."

He punched the call off and turned to Strap, who swung his legs over the side of the bed and tilted his head to emphasize that he was listening. Cross's lips were tight and he struggled to maintain a calm disposition. "That idiot Pierson revealed Strawn's name." He turned back to Strap. "Get your people over there and sanitize Strawn's property right now."

"We did, sir. Two days ago when you were in Houston."

Cross relaxed. "Well done. I should have known I could count on you."

"There's one problem that we're dealing with on the bodies, though."

"And they are?"

"Both men had titanium joints and rods, as well as extensive dental work. All that material has ID numbers, so our contacts reached out to let me know about that and asked what to do with them. Those parts are a lead right back to Mr. Ramsey and Mr. Strawn, if anyone starts looking."

"And I was more worried about that metal absorbing radiation that could be measured."

"It's a conundrum, all right."

Cross cut his eyes around the room. "That damned agent is going to dig around. I can feel it." He awakened his phone and punched up an app. Seconds later he brought up a blinking blue dot, signifying Special Agent Snow's phone and location. It was still at the Ramsey site.

Using the room's old-fashioned push-button phone on the nightstand, he punched three numbers for Pierson's room and he answered. "Pierson. What do you see from that drone?"

"They're still standing beside Ramsey's barn. Another truck is there, along with two others."

"Law enforcement?"

"From what I can tell, it's civilians."

Heat waves shimmered above the scorching parking lot as Cross studied a point across the room. "I've had it with this project. It's time to wrap this up and get back to Houston. This man has vexed me to no end, and now he is my enemy. You know what to do."

He hung up. "That means you, too, Strap."

Strap nodded and seemed to turn in on himself. "Sir, I will address the problem with Special Agent Snow..."

"And his brother."

"Yes, sir. His brother, too." He took a deep breath and let it out slowly. "But you know how I feel about women and kids."

"That's the reason I like you, Strap. You have standards and morals. It's an Achilles' heel that can be exploited."

"Understood, sir. And the items with serial numbers on the medical devices?"

"Have the medical replacements delivered to the fields. Drop them down Site 3223 before they cap it. They'll be gone forever. In fact, I'd like you to be the one to put them in the well, so I'll know it was done properly."

Cross's eyes flicked to a leather briefcase at his feet. He never went anywhere without it, and hell would freeze over if he left it unattended in his room. The leather case was filled with files concerning individuals he dealt with, and the root of all their problems, Well Site 3223, which was the first drilling location using a new technique that involved DrySoil, a chemical developed in the ChemShale labs.

It was the site that caused all the trouble they were cleaning up.

"Achilles' Heel is what the guys have started calling that well."

"Fitting." Cross picked up the briefcase as if leaving, and then put it back down. "If we can't contain this situation, it will become ChemShale's Achilles' heel."

"We all have one, people, businesses, and governments." Strap sat on the edge of the bed, his feet planted on the linoleum floor. "It'll be a day out there to get back out to Martin County and most of another to return here."

"I'm fully aware of how big this state is."

They both dealt with individuals who misunderstood the size of the second-largest state in the union. A little over eight hundred and fifty miles from El Paso to the Louisiana border equated to twelve and a half hours on the road, and that was all interstate driving with no lights and averaging between seventy-five to eighty miles per hour. Like most Texans, Strap grew up referring to distance across the state not in miles, but in hours, and when he was younger, they were often measured in six-packs.

At that time, no one knew how vast the world's oil domes could be, and in fact, those repositories were discovered only twenty years earlier, when a handshake agreement between Richard T. Crane of Crane Plumbing Supplies and the king of Saudi Arabia opened discussions on economic cooperation between the West.

After they met, King Abdulaziz Al Saud sent pure Arabian horses to the U.S. as a gesture of friendship, thus establishing those fine horses in America, and arranged for a geologist to visit his country and explore for oil.

After World War II, an oil scramble and a consortium of drillers had the idea to drill worldwide until oil began to run out, then return to the U.S. and an already-established supply.

Wendel Cross's grandfather worked as a wildcatter for Earlene Oil. Their busy little company drilled hundreds of wells, struck oil, then capped them and marked their locations. It was a U.S. insurance policy developed ten years earlier with the intent to remain a worldwide force.

Now in the new century, drilling techniques changed and oil extraction became more scientific. Once-productive oil fields began to dry up, and the complicated process of drilling in shale brought them back to life, but only temporarily. Then came ChemShale with a new drilling process that utilized old sites drilled and capped off in the '40s.

It didn't occur to Cross that he was proposing the exact same process that started the entire devil's loop of dangerous repercussions that his predecessors initiated way back in 1954. Some idiot thought it was a good idea to store radioactive material in an old oil well, waste from the first, almost disastrous attempts to manufacture hydrogen bombs. It was a catastrophic mistake, thinking that the best idea was to stuff the deadly materials deep in the ground and forget about them.

And forget they did. Those involved with depositing the material likely passed away through the years, or honored their contracts and orders to forever remain silent. That erased what institutional memory there might have been and which would have proven invaluable when ChemShale reopened the well to extract more oil with the DrySoil process.

Other countries started to run dry, and when the price per barrel of oil became ridiculously expensive, the market required the United States to unseal those marked wells and utilize alternate methods of extraction.

The company reopened those sites using a highly sophisticated process of extraction referred to as RAE, Romancing and

Extraction. The technology involved injecting a fluid they'd developed called DrySoil, which acted as a sponge. It was extracted, processed, and the oil separated. Once done, the now unusable DrySoil was disposed of, right back in the well, where it eventually hardened to the consistency of concrete, ensuring underground stability and lessening the possibility of future geological shifts and the resulting earthquakes.

However, who would have thought DrySoil would absorb all that naturally occurring radiation along with the crude through the drill rods that were a hundred times hotter than the natural contamination that was the result of drilling in the West Texas oilfields?

When those same rods drilled through leaking nuclear waste that had been dumped in abandoned wells, the result born in Hell carried the guarantee of poisoning and death from Satan himself.

Who could have known? For sure not the ones who developed the drilling process without BLM or the Texas Railroad Commission's approval, and had kept it a secret for the past ten years. Strap knew better than to dig too deeply into what Cross called the politics of crude. As a hands-on employee of ChemShale, his job was cut-and-dried simple.

He was to do the bidding of those above him, the ones who paid him more money in one year than his daddy earned in his lifetime.

Cross drew a deep breath. "You don't have to make that drop in Martin County within the next day or two. Deal with this issue here before you go, and do it right now."

"As in this minute."

"That's what I said."

"Sir, these contaminated rods are lethal, and they're killing people as we speak. Shouldn't I find them all before they get into other people's hands, or continue to dose people with enough radiation to kill a horse?"

Cross wasn't a fan of Strap's soft handling of some situations. "You worry about women and children and welders and people who handle this stuff without protective gear, yet you've done unspeakable things on my orders."

"Which brings us to that unknown couple who bought those rods to start with."

"What about them?"

"Well, with all due respect, we still don't know who the Smythes are, or how they redirected that load."

"Money. It all comes down to money."

"Yessir, but with all you have at your disposal, we can't find Loren and Tracey Smythe."

"I have Patel working on that. He'll get back to me when he knows."

"It's been over a year."

"What's your point?"

"I do my job, sir. Our people should be doing theirs, and faster."

"Do yours now, then, and in the order I told you. I have my plan and methods."

Strap stood. "Fine then."

Chapter 19

Harley came out of the barn as I ended the call. Dust puffed under his footsteps. He wiggled his phone back and forth. "I just called one of my buddies to hire an Uber to go pick up Tammy and the kids and get 'em away from the house."

I didn't get his statement. "Why an Uber?"

"Because that son of a bitch is watching us somehow. I don't want to let anyone know where they're going, and if my truck or yours is bugged, they can follow us everywhere. Fred, you look like you were in the military."

"I was." Fred finished his beer, bent the can, and pitched it into the back of my truck. "And I still serve in the National Guard."

"You think there's a drone up there?"

He didn't look up, but instead made eye contact with Bill Sloan who tilted his head in a "go ahead" gesture. "That's the only way that guy could be watching us, unless he's somehow tapped into the cameras on this truck."

Such an idea had never occurred to me. "Can they do that?"

"If there's a computer involved, you bet they can."

Harley put on hand on the side of the truck. "That's what Don Wells told us when you took your other truck to Fort Worth here while back. The computers in these cars are siphoning off information every time we get in. I guess it's possible they can use your backup camera, or listen to us through your sound system."

I hate technology, and was beginning to despise it even more. I wished for an old-school truck with gearshift levers, hand-rolled windows, and no technology other than a standard radio. That's why I bought an old '85 pickup recently and planned to use it more and more. Being tracked by any entity raised the hair on the back of my neck.

The sky above us was blue, with nothing but a buzzard circling over something half a mile away. I found myself suspicious of even that, and squinted at the big bird, wondering if it was really alive, or a drone designed to look like one.

Sloan's face was tight with concern as he tilted his head up to look at the sky from under the brim of his hat. "Fred, how high can one of those drones fly and still see us?"

"Well, they can fly up to thirty thousand feet, but they need to drop down to fifteen hundred to two thousand feet for the cameras to make out detail, or at least that's what I've heard."

Harley scanned the horizon that we could see. "They aren't camouflaged as buzzards, are they?"

He and Sloan chuckled. "Nossir, but they might look like UFOs."

I thought for a moment and looked at Harley. "So you think they may be listening somehow, too. Tapped into our phones?"

"I'm not taking anything for granted."

That's when I saw he'd taken his phone apart and held the battery and chip in one hand, and the body in the other. I laid my own device on the bed of the truck and motioned for him to follow me. We walked a hundred yards into the pasture. I hoped that was far enough.

"You had your friend call an Uber."

"Yep. We've worked together a long time and understand each other. We talked in code and I had him take the girls to stay with Tammy's friend from college, Shelly. She's divorced and lives over in Gainesville. They should be safe there and we can contact them later."

"You're expecting trouble."

"I'm always expecting trouble, but I know how you think. We're going over to Strawn's place to look around, right?"

"Yep."

"Those guys are going to be watching. I say we stay here and have those boys over there go to my house. Sloan hasn't said, but I think he's ex-military, too." He watched them over by the truck for a minute. "Let's go by the house and pick up my war bag. It still has everything in it that we used up in Oklahoma when we got Chloe back. Then we'll be on an even playing level with whoever's watching us."

"What do you expect?"

"War, and we'll take it to 'em."

Chapter 20

Chloe and Jimma were in the living room when Tammy blew in like a hurricane. Her brown ponytail stuck through the adjustment hole of one of Harley's ball caps featuring the Lone Star Tactical logo on the front.

One weekend after Harley retired from the police department, he agreed to teach a mixed group of male and female citizen students to survive what he called "urban chaos." It quickly became a must-take course for hundreds of people in North Texas, and he soon launched the company that trained civilians to deal with dangerous situations and included self-defense from physical assaults, survival in mass shooting situations, church and home safety, and firearm training.

"Girls, pack some clothes quick and be ready to go in five minutes. I'm getting the boys together and we're leaving."

The wild look in Tammy's eye sent a cold chill down Chloe's neck. She'd been through a lot over the past couple of years, and every time an adult came in with that expression and issuing orders, something was wrong.

It's against human nature to immediately respond to such a

direct order without asking questions, and two high school girls have a lot of questions. Jimma rose and glanced down at her cell phone as if it would have an answer to Tammy's urgency.

"Why? What's going on?"

"I'll tell you when I can. We don't have much time."

"We're in danger." Chloe delivered the statement with a low tone of dread.

"Yes." Tammy hurried across the room and threw the deadbolt on the front door. She reached up to the top shelf of a bookcase between the door and window and pulled down an old-school fanny pack. The girls knew it contained a Lady Smith .38 revolver. She looped the strap over her head and one shoulder, settling it against the side of her chest.

There were guns in strategic locations throughout the house, and they were all loaded. Harley was a firm believer in having weapons ready. Both of his boys were already familiar with them and knew that under no circumstances were they to touch the firearms. That went for Jimma also, when she came to live with them.

Growing up as the daughter of a lawman, Chloe was as familiar with guns as any kid her age, and could shoot with the best of them. She took the back of Jimma's arm. "This is serious. Come on."

The Labrador retriever, Kevin, joined them in the living room. The big dog paced from one person to another, sensing Tammy's fear. His tail hung low, as well as his head.

The girls headed upstairs where the boys were watching cartoons, Kevin close on their heels. On the way past the back patio door, Chloe saw Aunt Tammy had the upper and lower deadbolts thrown. Chloe yanked on the drawcord, closing the curtains as she passed.

Tammy took the stairs two at a time. Though calm, her voice was higher than usual from fear. "Boys! Fire drill!"

"What?" Danny rose from the playroom couch. "Fire drill? We're not in school."

"Your dad wants us to practice." Heart racing, Chloe split off into Jimma's room and threw a few things into backpacks, as the boys complained. By the time they were back down the stairs, Tammy had Matt's and Danny's packs by the door.

Nerves jangling, Chloe hurried to the front window and peeked through the plantation blinds. The street looked normal, but as a kid who'd lost her mother and little sister to a car wreck, then herself had been kidnapped only months ago, she took nothing for granted. Tears rolled down one cheek, and she almost slapped them away.

Tammy ushered the boys to the couch. "Sit right there until I tell you to move."

The rambunctious boys obeyed and for once sat still, eyes wide and waiting. Kevin woofed, concerned.

Chin quivering, Jimma perched on the edge of the couch, as if ready to leap up and run. She smoothed her dishwater-blond hair as if it was sticking up, a nervous habit. "What's going on?"

"Harley called." Unable to sit down, Tammy moved to the blinds and scanned the street. "He said Tuck and another guy had a run-in, and the guy threatened us."

"How?"

"Didn't say, but Tuck took it seriously. We're going to Shelly's house for a little while."

"What about school?" Danny was always looking for an excuse to miss class. He was one of the few kids who looked forward to visiting the dentist's office or anything else that kept him away from school.

"We'll see."

He fell back against the couch. "That always means you don't know."

"That means that..." Tammy sighed. "You're right. I don't know right now, but you guys be ready to go when I say."

"I thought this was a fire drill." Matt always analyzed any situation.

"It is, in a way." Chloe moved over and sat beside him. "You stick close to me if we have to go outside. Lots of people get in trouble during fire drills when they wander away. Remember, in school you always stay close to your teacher and class so they know where you are."

Jimma pulled her backpack close, as if it contained items more valuable than extra clothes. "Why don't we just drive there ourselves?"

"Harley said he was sending an Uber, so that means he doesn't want us to."

The boys leaped to their feet. "Yay! We get an Uber ride!"

"Some people can track the Suburban." Chloe recalled a conversation after she and her dad returned home from the Oklahoma kidnapping. "People can track new cars and trucks." She thought for a moment. "And they can track our phones if they know how. We'd better turn them off."

Jimma instinctively thumbed her phone awake, and Tammy plucked hers from a back pocket. "That's a good idea. Girls, turn them off and take out the SIM card."

"How?" Jimma turned her phone over and examined the back.

Chloe rose and went into the kitchen. She came back with a paper clip. "Like this."

She bent the clip and inserted one end into the tiny hole on the side of her iPhone. The SIM card tray popped out, and she removed it. "Like that. Hand me yours."

Jimma held the phone against her chest for a moment, then passed it over. Chloe popped that one out too and handed both back to her. She tucked the paper clip into her shirt pocket at the same time Tammy turned back from the window.

"The car's here." She opened the door, and the boys shot out like rockets, followed by the big Lab. Tammy picked up the heavy daypack Harley called his bugout pack.

The rest of them followed, and Tammy locked the door behind them.

Chapter 21

"We're playing with fire here." Fred Belk dug a can of Skoal from his back pocket, twisting around and fighting the seat belt. "Every time we're around that stock agent I feel like he can see inside my head."

"He's not that good." Bill Sloan chuckled.

"Apparently not, since we pulled up there in the Charger. I don't see how he didn't put it all together right then and there."

"I told you. His mind is on more than a car he chased through the dark one night several months ago."

"Maybe, but I'm like those guys. I don't want anybody tracking everything I do, and I especially don't like it that people can make threats from a long way off here in *my* country. It ain't American."

Fred crushed the empty can and dropped it down by his feet. He opened another he'd stuck in the door and took a long swallow. It was rodeo cool, but more than once he'd consumed warm, and even hot, beer in the military. "By the way, you know you're not supposed to drink, and that includes that fake beer of yours."

Sloan snorted. "And I'm not supposed to do too much, or eat hot dogs or chili, or take in too much salt, and not use bad language, neither, but I'm gonna enjoy what I can before that new kidney comes in."

Fred tilted his hat back. "I still think you got it over in Afghanistan. Burn barrels or..."

"Those damned shots they kept giving us. Sometimes the same ones over and over. You'd think the military could at least put together a database that kept up with what chemicals they shot in our veins and when. Some of the vets I know call it the cost of doing business, but things happen. Murphy's Law, if you ask me." Sloan absently rubbed a burn scar on his hand that was the result of welding Mr. Ramsey's drill-rod corral. They did a good job on both projects, and he was proud of the work he'd put into the ranch.

And now it was gone.

"Well, we better steer clear of that agent." Belk watched fence posts flash past for a minute. "Tucker and his brother crossed somebody dangerous. They have troubles we don't need to be around."

"Hell, I *like* trouble. That's what I miss about being in the army. There was always something going on. Excitement. I wouldn't mind joining up with them and finding somebody to shoot."

"I think that's why you're enjoying this rustling business. You like the high."

"You're half-right about that. I like the money the most, though. But this thing they got tangled up with is fun, too. I'm wondering who these guys are that're messing with Snow."

"Well, whoever they are, it's better them than me when they get that Harley guy mad. He reminds me of some of those rangers we saw in the sandbox. Did you see his eyes? I 'spect he don't mind pulling the trigger on somebody when he thinks they need it."

Sloan's phone rang and he checked the screen. "Mr. Crawford. Probably wondering where we are."

"He knows it takes a while to make a run to town. He sure does keep close tabs on us."

"I know, but he's a good guy. He's always worried about me falling out and nobody being around. He's the best I ever worked for, and he leaves us alone most of the time."

"At least he don't bother us at night."

"Speaking of that, are we picking up another load anytime soon? You feel like it?"

Sloan slowed and turned on the farm road leading to the Crawford ranch in Red River County. "Sure are! Toby's been keeping an eye on a place down near Mt. Pleasant. It's a good-size ranch running stockers. It's owned by a big-shot out of Houston. He's never there, just a ranch manager and his hired hand who don't do much more than throw out some hay from time to time."

"You can't manage cows like that. You know good and well they check 'em from time to time, and how about when they're vaccinating?"

"You know what I mean. It's a big place, and two men can't be everywhere all the time."

"When are we doing this?"

"Day after tomorrow."

"After your dialysis appointment?"

"Yep." Sloan took a long breath. "I'll be glad when I'm off that damned machine."

"Where are you on the donor list?"

"A long way down." Sloan mentally calculated how much he'd need to cover the cost of dialysis until a donor kidney was available, not to mention his part of the surgery when it happened. His insurance was barely enough to cover head cold medicine. If it wasn't for his penchant for rustling, he'd be so far in the hole they'd have to ship in sunshine.

"At least we still have the money for those last cows squirrelled away."

"Nothing I like more than selling stock directly to buyers."

"Cash money."

They high-fived. "Cash money."

Chapter 22

A whippoorwill called from the creek bottom down behind the house as the sun settled toward the treetops. Unlike cities made of metal, concrete, and bricks that hold in summer heat after sundown, the country cools quickly after shadows overtake the landscape.

I needed to sit outside and think, but my usual thinking spot beside the firepit was on the west side of the house, far away from the nearest shade provided by the wide red oak in the pasture two hundred yards from the house.

I was worried about Chloe, Tammy, Jimma, and the boys. They were safe for the moment, but I couldn't shake the bad feeling that stuck as tight as a tick.

It was just the two of us, Chloe and me, and I was woefully inadequate in the mothering department. Teenage girls are nuts in the first place, swimming in estrogen, and I did the best I could, but there were certain things Sara Beth had handled in her own easygoing way.

She was the one who understood teen angst and emotions. I simply wasn't geared toward those types of issues, or young hormonal girls. Most of my adult time was spent dealing with human vermin, not youngsters with a bright future.

I leaned on Harley's wife, Tammy, to take up the slack for me. After they started the process of adopting Jimma, there were occasional weekend nights when Tammy, Chloe, and Jimma scheduled girl time.

With that whole crew plus the boys at his house, Harley often called to say he was on the way over to sit with me for a while. We did that a lot, sometimes not talking but sharing each other's presence.

I relaxed on the east-facing front porch overlooking Long Creek Road and took a sip of cold Coors. The gravel byway once stayed hot from cars driving between a meth house not two hundred yards from my place, back to Ganther Bluff.

Before Harley showed up, two black Suburbans rolled down the road to the T-intersection a quarter of a mile to the north. They slowed, turned left toward my house, and sped up, leaving twin rooster tails of dust that blended into one. The SUV in back followed too closely, and I doubted the driver could see past the cloud the other car threw up.

City people. The same ones who were at the sale barn last week.

Sara Beth in my mind was right.

Country folks know better than to follow that close. I could imagine the air filter in the second car was fast clogging up. The lead SUV let off the gas when they neared my pipe gate and turned up the short drive.

A slug of adrenaline dumped into my system when they slowed. Those guys had something to do with the smarmy wannabe cowboy at the sale barn. I'd already convinced myself the guy calling himself Cross was in one of the Suburbans at the sale, and here they were.

Seeing me in the rocker, the SUV stopped twenty yards up the drive, instead of continuing farther to park behind my new truck. The second vehicle hit the brakes a little harder than necessary and slid for a couple of feet.

From my angle, I noted the lack of license plates on the front bumpers, leading me to think they might be government-issue. In Texas, plates are required by law on both the front and back of vehicles. I filed that piece of information away for further consideration.

A tickle in the back of my mind rose, and I remembered passing a dark SUV without front plates the night of the firefight. It cruised past at three in the morning as I tried to pull over the trailer full of cattle. Was it full of these guys?

Seven doors opened at the same time. Precision timing.

Military backgrounds? Was this tied in with some armed service branch, or guys who'd trained together for so long they thought alike?

Questions swirled around my head like in cartoons.

Despite the heat, seven men wearing identical dark suits and shades stepped out. One caught my attention as he emerged from behind the driver in the second car. From his size and bearing, I figured he was ex-military, and that could even equate to ex-police, since veterans often gravitate to police work. SWAT came to mind.

The smallest of the group, a slim, gray-haired light-skinned African American man came around from the far side where he'd ridden behind the second car's passenger seat. A position of power.

He scanned the yard, the barn, and the grounds around the house. I couldn't help but think how overdressed he was in a three-piece suit only yards from a barn and long-unused feed pen. There was a silent exchange between him and the others as he rubbed a chin sharp enough to double as an axe.

My spidey senses tingled throughout my body. I set the bottle on the porch railing.

A couple of his cronies spread out to watch the house and barn, but the others remained beside the dust-covered black SUVs and waited. Their actions were professional. I was right. The result of either many years working together, or training.

I bet on the latter.

"Mr. Snow." Gray Hair walked across the short grass and stopped at the edge of the porch, putting one polished shoe on the bottom step.

The man immediately rubbed me the wrong way. I didn't like the way they drove up, he was too loud, and to top it all off, instead of waiting for an invitation to join me, he stepped up onto the porch.

"You're Cross."

He stopped, feet planted wide apart. Every man I've ever known who stood like that was full of himself. "I'd like to talk with you for a couple of minutes. We spoke on the phone earlier."

I was glad I hadn't taken off the pistol in the holster on my right hip and still wore the TSCRA badge on my shirt. I 'magine I looked more like a rancher than a lawman. Tilting the squatty bottle of beer, I took a swallow of the yellow-belly to buy some time.

A flicker of annoyance crossed his eyes. "You've been rubbing up too close to matters of national security. I'm here to ask you in person to stop and let my people handle it."

"I still have my short- and long-term memory. We don't have to retrace those steps. You said you'd be by on your terms, so let me give you mine. Rural crime is my job, and I'm investigating a number of things both here and in Oklahoma. They're under my jurisdiction, and by asking me to step away, you're interfering with lawful investigations."

"I understand. You're a...special agent for the cattlemen's association, Snow."

Most folks get our jobs wrong, and usually mess up the title. "I'm a special agent for Texas and Southwestern Cattle Raisers Association. Not the cattlemen's association. Folks sometimes call me a brand inspector or *Agent* Snow. Now, I'm already tired of dancing with you. What do you want?"

A red tinge formed at the edges of my vision. I fought hard to stay in control for years, but with Sara Beth's loss, I was fast losing the ability to keep the rage under control.

He missed the emphasis. "Yes. As I said, we were talking about the late Mr. Ramsey and the recent sale of his property."

I'd had enough. "Why are we starting this conversation from *scratch*?" Then it dawned on me. "You or your handlers bought the Ramsey place and you have it, and me, under surveillance. Insurance of some kind?"

He slipped both hands into his pants pockets. "As I told you on the phone, we work for a company representing his best interest."

"Nope. He's dead, according to you, and you just said it was a matter of national security. Try again."

"We're an environmental group, in the middle of our own investigation."

"Environmental group, but you can just as easily say you're a doctor, you're a lawyer, or an Indian chief."

"Is this some kind of comedy routine?"

I switched tactics. "So you're with the EPA?"

"In a manner of speaking."

"So you're not representing Anita Ramsey, then, like you said."

One of his men near the lead car's front fender stepped out of sight around the corner of the house. I didn't like that one bit.

"I'd suggest you whistle your dog back around here where I can see him, buddy."

Another plume of dust came down the road leading to Long Creek. From the color and make of the pickup, I knew it was Harley. As usual, his timing was perfect and my rising anger subsided, for the moment.

Cross saw I was looking over his shoulder. He didn't turn around. "That would be your brother, Harley."

"I'm tired of this." I stood. There was no way he should have known that. Temples pounding, I slowly raised my left hand and pointed back the way they'd come. The other was free and wanting to grip the butt of my .45.

"Mister, you have about five seconds to tell me what this is all about, because when my brother coming down the road there opens his door, there's gonna be trouble."

Something flickered past Cross's eyes and he held up his hands. "No trouble. None intended."

"You're tracking us, and there's no reason for that."

A brief smile flickered across his lips. "We track a lot of people. It's the way of today's world. Data miners do it all the time, and people tolerate it because they don't know. I'm here to make you an offer. I'd like to buy this ranch, and the company I represent has authorized me to double the price you paid for it.

"If you don't want to do that, we can put you on our payroll as a consultant. You can retire from your current position, won't have to get up in the mornings, or wear a badge and gun. We'll call when we need you, and I would bet that would be only once every two or three years.

"With that much money, you can move anywhere and not have to work, and in fact, from what I've seen of your dedication to the job, and Harley's exceptional company, we'll buy him out as well. That comes with the guarantee that if you two will agree to work for us as, let's call you extension agents instead of consultants, we can provide an excellent salary until you turn fifty-five, at which time you can retire a wealthy man with full benefits that will exceed anything you can draw from the state."

Harley pulled into the drive and took a hard left into the yard when he saw the men fanned out in front of me. He positioned his truck so that when he got out, it was between him and the others that sat idling quietly. I recognized the maneuver. He knew Sun Tzu's book, *The Art of War,* front to back, and took the old Chinese warrior's advisement, leaving the two vehicles a way out in the event of trouble.

Blocking them in with no hope for escape would change the situation in a flash if everything went south.

He remained in his truck for a moment, and I knew he was absorbing the scene behind a pair of dark Oakley shades. At the same time I knew he was making sure the Beretta M9 under his shirt was free. Knowing my brother, he also had an M4 rifle within arm's reach.

Back when we were younger, it would have been in a rack in the back glass, but such common-sense devices had fallen from favor as more and more city dwellers considered guns evil. In my mind, they could be close to proving their worth.

He opened his door, stepped out, and paused beside the left front tire, leaning on the hood and keeping the engine block between him and the SUVs. It was when three of the men in suits spread out between him and Cross that I noticed a change in his body language.

"Cross, that yard dog over there named Harley doesn't like what he sees. You'd better call your boys back."

Instead of doing as I suggested, he kept his back to Harley and the situation developing between us. He smiled, showing teeth as white as a Labrador pup's. They had to have been veneered because no one his age could have teeth so bright.

"My men are fine."

My face flushed, and I knew Harley was tight as a watch spring. "Your men are poking a bear."

"Let's get back to our conversation."

"We never started one. The answer is no to your offer, and don't bother to bring it up again." I was still seated, but I shifted to free up the Colt 1911 on my hip. Cross was a pro; his eyes narrowed as he registered the adjustment and understood its meaning. So did the big guy, who tightened up and adjusted his angle in response.

"Now, you have one man I can't see on the far side of my house." I spoke directly to Big Guy. "Call him back around here, and get those three away from my brother."

Instead of the big guy answering, Cross answered for him. "I wish you'd relax."

I watched Harley absorb the situation in front of him. His attention shifted, and the next thing I knew, his hand was on the butt of the Beretta he carried under a loose-fitting shirt. His voice snapped flat as a slap across the newly mowed grass.

"You, beside the house! Hands where I can see 'em!"

Cross's eyes flicked to the opposite side of the house toward where his man had disappeared. Had that individual continued, he'd have come up slightly behind me, and I cursed myself for letting something like that happen.

I stood and grabbed the butt of my .45, while pointing at

Cross with my other hand to catch his attention. "Cross! Call your men off, now!"

The air filled with commands from several directions as his people shouted orders at us. Each one reached under their suit coats, and I assumed their hands rested on the butts of pistols on their belts. All we needed was one spark to set off the dance.

We ignored their commands to release our weapons, and Harley angled himself to draw, still protected by the truck. "I said hands, now!" It was a trained command I'd heard for decades, but the tone was what counted, and he was about half a second from drawing.

Another stranger in my yard sounded frightened. "Sir, do not draw that weapon!"

Others in the yard assumed combat positions, shouting commands with increasing volume at Harley, but I thanked the Lord that no one had yet drawn a weapon.

Big Guy's voice was deep, and it rolled across the yard like thunder. "You, behind the truck, Harley! Stand down!"

"Don't move!" I stepped forward, crowding Cross. His eyes widened, and I believe he realized just how close to gunfire the situation had reached. "Cross!"

His eyes locked on mine.

"Call them off now! If shooting starts, I'll kill you first."

A beat.

I was almost there, the butt of that Colt felt wonderful, and in only another heartbeat I could pour out all the rage I carried from Sara Beth and baby Peyton's death and I could be with them again for all eternity.

It almost happened, and then Cross spread his arms, palms turned upward. "Boys, relax!" His tone softened. "We're just talking. That's all."

"A conversation never happened."

I wanted to shoot the well-dressed man who stood cool and calm in the heat, to beat him with both fists until I couldn't raise them anymore, and at the very least, slap cuffs on him.

Like an alcoholic, I needed it so bad I could taste it, but there was still no solid reason to arrest him or any of his people, though at the very least Harley would want to charge them with being assholes.

"Get back in your cars and get gone." Then it all drained away and I didn't care what happened next, but there's no way I'd let them know it. "I don't want to ever see you again."

Cross built a slight smile and ran his hand the length of his tie. "You won't."

I'm not sure what his signal might have been, but as one, his men relaxed. Those facing Harley spread their hands and backed away, still watching him. From my right, the man who'd been around back appeared with his arms well away from his body. He crossed between us, not looking left or right.

Like filings to a magnet, they converged on the SUVs.

Cross turned his back to me and stepped off the porch. He gave Harley a little wave, then strolled across the grass and around behind the second Suburban. Doors slammed and the lead car made a wide turn, rolling off the gravel and leaving deep ruts in the dry grass.

The other followed, making the same maneuver, and they pulled through the gate and sped away.

Harley watched them leave and walked over from his truck. The skin around his eyes and mouth was tight. "That war is almost here."

It was all I could do not to melt into a puddle, but then wasn't the time. "I'm afraid you're right."

Chapter 23

Cross stared straight ahead as they drove away from the agent's house. He was furious at the way that cow cop spoke to him, and blamed himself for letting Strap put him in such a position.

"Strap, your soft sell idea didn't work. We now do it my way. Call Houston and get some more men up here."

The big man nodded. "Yessir. How many?"

"As many as it'll take to alleviate this problem."

"How do you want to do it?"

"That man offered to shoot me."

"He would have, sir. You were on his property, and to be more specific, on his porch. You don't know these people like I do."

"You expected that?"

"I did."

"There's one more house up here that wound up with those drill stems and some of that pipe. They've also refused an extremely generous offer. Husband and wife. No kids. Name's Crawford. They have to go as well. Use them as bait for that damned special agent."

"But the material will still be there."

"Contain the couple, then bring in the team you used at the Ramsey house. Same as there. Have them come in as a construction crew and remove all the material. Put up a new fence, as if the Crawfords decided to upgrade. They didn't get as much of the drill rods, because from what I understand, Ramsey gave them just enough to build a fence across the front. Some is stacked behind the barn."

"Sir, I don't want to seem argumentative, but the Crawfords have no knowledge of where those drill pipes came from or who Ramsey bought them from. They haven't shown any radiation symptoms, either, so there's nothing to spark anyone's interest."

"You're wrong." He tapped a file on the seat between them. "Jim Crawford has been diagnosed with stage two lymphoma. He and Ramsey welded that Strawn man's fence together, along with some local I haven't identified yet. His wife recently went into the hospital and has lung cancer."

"How could one load of contaminated material cause so many problems?"

Cross continued as if Strap hadn't spoken. "Your construction crew will provide a complete update out front. New fence and gate. Then call Snow and report some...rural issue in their name."

"Of course they won't be there."

"Of course."

"Sir, maybe there's another way to deal with these folks."

"There is, and you know who to bring in. Do what I say." Cross barely reacted to his employee's refusal to carry out his exact orders. "Make it authentic enough that there's no question. Snow will show up, and that will be the end of this problem. Maybe he drives up on a crime in progress. No matter what, I want him gone."

"Sir, you saw Snow's brother, and we've both read his file."

Cross sighed and rubbed his forehead. "Why is it never easy?"

"Because it isn't, in my experience. Sir, there might be collateral damage beyond anything we've ever seen." Strap watched the countryside pass in a blur of speed. "People will put two and two together. The agent and his brother dying at the same time will raise questions."

"It won't matter. We'll be long gone." Cross paused, thinking. "Damn that idiot with Harrison Brothers."

Strap knew he was talking about the trucking company who brought the trouble to Northeast Texas. "It's always about the same thing, money."

"How much did he make off of that pirated truckload?"

Strap told him, and Cross shook his head. "And look what it cost us. One greedy driver who couldn't bother with delivering the hot stems to Ormand's sells it directly to an East Texas redneck, and look where it got us. Dead people and all this trouble."

"That driver couldn't have known about how radioactive those pipes were. I imagine he'd done it a dozen times in the past."

"But this contaminated load came from 3223, where those damned fools tried to bury radioactive waste to save *money*, and *that* caused me all this trouble."

"Bad luck all around, sir."

Cross checked his phone for the hundredth time that day. "All right. Let's get this done."

Chapter 24

"Damn that was fun!"

While we sat on the back porch, watching the sun go down under a radiant orange sky, Harley took a sip of Coors and punched at his phone. Coyotes tuned up along the creek, and the mama cow and her calf paused in their grazing to look that way.

"Nothing's fun about nearly getting shot." I shook my head at baby brother, who loves that kind of stuff.

"It was for me! Takes me back to when we were working undercover. Remember those two guys in the pickup when I stuck a gun in the driver's face and told him he was under arrest? He thought about pulling a pistol, and for a second there, I thought he would. That's what it was like today. Makes me want to go back to those days."

"Not me." I'd rather just investigate and go home with the same number of holes in this body I started with.

We faced two different directions, sitting perpendicular to the setting sun, so each of us had a different sight line. I didn't expect trouble right then, but a person can never be too careful. From my position, I'd already seen one of Frank Gibson's deputies drive past, making sure it was quiet at our house on Long Creek.

I'd called Frank as soon as Harley and I decided the threat to our families was real. He listened as I explained the situation, and said his department would be on standby as long as we needed them and would respond the moment I called.

There wasn't much to do beyond that. People threaten each other all the time, and our only legal recourse was to file a no trespass or a restraining order against Cross, but there was no physical reason to do even that. The truth that abused spouses had learned the hard way is that someone served by such papers could walk straight through that invisible legal line and do whatever harm they wanted.

That's where Harley and I differed from most of the populace. Neither of us had ever played by the official rules. We often bent them to fit the situation, and always came out on top.

Few cars and trucks had passed out front. Before we eliminated the meth house that had been operating only a few hundred yards away, the gravel road was an interstate full of addicts driving by at all hours of the day and night. That's how I came to understand what was going on over there. Now the only traffic was locals going to work in the mornings, hauling cattle and hay during the day, and everyone returning to their homes in the evenings.

Night traffic was usually, in my opinion, young folks doing what they've done for decades, going to visit friends, dating, or simply getting away from the old folks. I was glad Chloe wasn't showing any of those symptoms, not right then anyway.

But it was coming.

Ignoring the ongoing acts of life and death among the local wildlife down in the creek bottoms that had repeated millions of times in the past, Harley frowned at the cell phone in his hands. He cut his eyes at me and his good mood vanished. "Bad news."

"What's that?"

"I'm trying to check the cameras and they're down. The guy that came around the house did something to the security system. Either that, or some genius with a laptop got into the Wi-Fi, maybe? I don't know."

"How'd he do that?"

"Don't know. I'm not a technician, but he somehow got into the system and deleted everything. The cameras're deader'n hell. How long was he back there out of your sight?"

"Not five minutes."

"Well, he's a pro. In fact, they're all pros, and I saw that the minute they spread out on me."

"There was nothing I could do. I'd hoped we could review the surveillance and use the pictures to find out who they are."

"My idea too, but they wiped it all." He punched at the screen, his face changing by the minute. "These guys are good. He did something I don't understand. He deleted the entire account, not just the cameras, and I'll bet a thousand dollars he wiped everything on the cloud."

"This is a secure system. We made sure of that."

Harley paused and stared across the pasture. "It wasn't him."

"What's that?"

"It wasn't that guy beside the house. He didn't have anything in his hands. I don't think you can do this with a cell phone. I was kinda busy, and there were a lot of guys and moving parts. How many were there?"

"Eight." I paused and thought about it. "No. Seven. There was one door in the first car that didn't open."

"Someone stayed inside." Harley shook his head. "That's who did it."

Months earlier, he and I worked closely with a security company to put in a system to keep an eye on the meth house, and the road that passed in front. When the situation between the dealers and me all fell apart, I needed it for protection.

And in five minutes, the guy who stayed in the car while the others kept our attention must have opened up a laptop, accessed the account, and took it all down with the click of a few keys.

He lowered the phone and took another sip. "Do you have online banking?"

"Most everyone does."

"Go get your laptop and check your account."

My heart sank when I realized what he was saying. I went inside and emerged with my computer. It only took a couple of seconds to log in and my heart stopped. "There's only one dollar in my account."

"Savings?"

I looked. "One dollar."

"How much did you have in there?"

I told him, and Harley's face fell. "He cleaned you out."

"Not completely. They were what I call operating accounts and that few hundred dollars won't be missed that much. I have another account under an LLC that's never gone online. That's where I keep most of our cash."

I didn't say *my* cash, because it was part of Sara Beth's estate and belonged to the both of us. I know. It's a weird way to think of it, but that's how my mind works. Chloe didn't know about it, though it was written in my will that she inherited everything someday in the future. That day had come pretty close earlier that afternoon.

"Well, that's your operating capital right now."

"I'll contact the banks in the morning."

"Cancel your credit cards right now. Taking all your money is supposed to make you reconsider his offer. They're squeezing you better than anything either of us could have thought of."

While he sat there and finished his beer, I contacted my credit card companies and went through the laborious process of getting new cards. Finished with that, I dialed up Secure Lock, a personal protection company that monitors for identity theft and personal information. I hoped they had connections with other entities that dealt with cash and property. I was suddenly afraid that Cross's man might have accessed websites somewhere and put their name on our home and property.

It was dark when I finished. Sick at my stomach, I closed the laptop and we sat together, watching the last glow of the setting sun, which soon gave way to darkness. The stars emerged, and a meteorite flashed past, but I couldn't enjoy the sight.

My phone rang and I answered.

"Is this Agent Snow?" It was a man's voice that quavered with age.

"It is. Who is this and how can I help you?"

"I'm Arthur Hope, and I bought some heifers online that were supposed to be delivered today."

"And they aren't there."

He paused. "How'd you know?"

"I don't know for sure, Mr. Hope, but online theft is getting pretty popular right now."

"Well, I don't know what to do."

"How about I come by late tomorrow afternoon and take your statement and give your computer a look. That work for you?"

I sighed to myself. The job never ends, and this man needed me as much as anybody. "Sure 'nuff. What time?"

"I can't say. I have to be in Oklahoma in the morning, so I'll give you a holler when I'm on the way."

"Fine with me. See you then."

I punched the phone off and heard my crazy mama cow's warning for the coyotes to stay away. "Little brother, I think we're dinosaurs. This whole thing's spinning out of control, and things aren't like they were when we were younger. It's all electronics and technology, and I'm afraid you and I can't do things the old-fashioned way."

"You're just coming down off the rush. You'll feel better tomorrow. We'll handle things the way we always did, and everthing'll turn out just fine."

"I doubt it. You know, I like the old days better before computers. Cattle theft was hands-on, and when you caught 'em, a tall limb and a short rope stopped that kind of nonsense pretty quick."

Harley finished his beer and we sat there in silence for a good long time. I didn't think he was going to answer, but he did.

"It still works just as well."

Chapter 25

Wendel Cross's driver took him to DFW Airport, north of Dallas, after he told Strap to handle the situation with "complete autonomy." Strap waited for an hour watching fuzzy, off-color tube-style television at the Red River Lodge before coming to a career-changing decision.

He tucked a Sig Sauer behind his belt, letting his shirttail cover the weapon. "Guys, I have to do some prelim. Stay here and off your phones until I get back."

Pierson looked up from his ever-present computer. "We go tonight?"

"We go when it's time." Strap went to the window to check the parking lot. "And I mean it about the phones."

Propped against pillows on the bed farthest from the door, Julian Truitt waved a hand toward the phone on the nightstand. "These are drop phones."

"Doesn't matter. They ping off towers just like your regular phones." Strap paused. "You guys did leave those behind, right?"

Pierson and Truitt nodded at the same time. Pierson tapped his shirt pocket. "These are the only ones we have."

"Good." Strap settled a John Deere cap on his head and unconsciously used both hands to make sure the rolled bill still retained its shape. The vented cap allowed cool air to reach his head, but did little to protect his ears from the blazing sun. "Y'all relax here until I get back, and tell the boys over there in the other room to do the same."

"Exactly where are you going?" Pierson rolled his head back in that insolent way everyone hated.

"To do my job."

Stepping outside and again checking the parking lot, Strap slipped behind the wheel of his assigned SUV and drove out of town, paying particular attention to the speed limit and traffic laws. He wasn't worried about the onboard computers tracking him. The company removed all the programs new cars come with, so there was no problem taking the vehicle wherever he wished.

They could leave no trace behind.

Turning his phone off, he flicked on the radio and dialed in a classic country station. Following protocol, he'd memorized his destination. The information came from one of Cross's many files, and was the location of Tammy Snow, who was at her college friend's house, along with her kids and the agent's daughter, Chloe.

Gainesville, Texas, was almost exactly two hours from the Red River Lodge, and a straight shot down Highway 82, past farms, ranches, fields, and miles of wide-open country. It'd been years since Strap was on that particular road, and he was disappointed to see the highway was now mostly two lanes each way, separated by a wide median.

Businesses fleeing the ever-increasing sprawl of the metroplex found land thousands of dollars per acre cheaper than anything within an hour of Dallas. Huge metal buildings for trucking companies, trailer manufacturing, and a variety of big equipment dealers grew like weeds where pastures and fields once produced cattle and crops.

Before long, it would be rows and rows of houses marching across the land. He sighed, thinking about how determined the world was to cover every square foot with concrete. The little mom and pop farms were fading fast, and by the time he reached retirement age, they'd all be absorbed by mega producers.

The speed limit varied from sixty miles an hour in some places, to seventy-five in the less traveled areas. He kept the needle exactly on the proper number, leaned back, and marveled at what he was doing.

Strap had never failed to follow orders, either in the Marine Corps or after getting out and going to work for ChemShale, at the request of Mr. Cross, who'd said more than once that Strap was exactly what he was looking for. Strap operated under a certain moral code that he kept to himself. He did everything Mr. Cross requested...up to a point.

Only on two occasions did he violate those instructions, and they involved women and children. He had no problem eliminating either one in defense or support of his country, he'd killed both when it was necessary while wearing a uniform. However, this was his country, his home state, and particularly a rural area much like he'd grown up in, and those people reminded him of kinfolk.

That's why he was on the road, alone.

He checked the clock located just above the speedometer. Four hours total to drive out there and back fell into his self-imposed window of time, with half an hour to do what was necessary, before the boys back at the motel began to wonder what was going on.

It was a sure bet none of them would mention his absence to Cross, because they never questioned a word he said. Obedience was essential to staying healthy with the man from ChemShale. Their boss made it clear when they went to work for him that money would flow into pockets and their jobs were secure, but their families were collateral and, once in the fold, no one would risk raising Cross's ire.

However, Strap had no family to worry about. He'd vanished without a trace at the age of eighteen, crossing the border into Mexico and finding a talented young man named Celino Serrano who forged a birth certificate, passport, and driver's license that changed the young man's name from Robert Goines to Strap Harrison.

With those documents and enough other information to give him a solid background, he went into the military only to disappear within the system still again when certain people higher up than he knew saw value in his skills that served until he was released to ChemShale.

Two hours and three minutes later, he pulled up to a street in an older Gainesville neighborhood. Driving past the address, he continued down the length of the block, looking for cars parked along the curb that could contain one of ChemShale's surveillance teams.

Using cameras, and traditional bugs planted by one of their technicians, they also utilized new technology by listening in through smart TVs and those Alexa and Echo devices.

Finding the street clear, he parked at the curb and, without hesitation, stepped out of the truck into the furnace-like heat. He rang the doorbell. One of the two boys he'd seen at the Ganther Bluff sale barn answered, backed by his brother, who was obviously irritated. "Matt, Dad said never to answer the door."

Strap gave them a grin. "He's right. I'm a stranger to y'all, but you must be Danny."

They looked surprised he knew that name. "I'm one of your long-lost cousins, Arthur. I'm from Paris."

Danny dug a finger into one ear, thinking. "He means Paris, Texas, not Paris, France."

Cool air flowed past the boys and onto the porch. "I know."

"Guys, is Tammy home?" The lies and use of her name also lent a sense of familiarity to keep the boys relaxed and not inclined to shut the door.

"She's in the kitchen with Chloe and Jimma." Matt, the youngest, was always the helpful one.

Knowing better than to go inside, even if invited, Strap peeked past them and into a living room kept dark from pulled shades and drawn curtains. Before they could continue the conversation, Tammy came around the corner, wiping her hands on a cup towel.

Seeing the man in the doorway, she hesitated for a moment, her eyes flicking to the right at a barrister bookcase. The top shelf full of books was the only one with the horizontal glass door open. Strap was confident there was a pistol resting in there.

He grinned and shuffled his feet, as if wiping dirt off the soles of his shoes. "Tammy. You don't know me, and what I'm about to tell you will scare the bejeezus out of you, so pick up that pistol right there by you and listen to what I have to say. It's important."

Shock wiped all expression from her face. The wife of a former undercover narcotics officer, trained by her husband, took immediate action. "Boys! Kitchen now!"

The tone of her voice caused them to spin and sprint past her to the kitchen. She snatched a Glock 43 from the shelf, and turned her head. "Intruder! Kevin!"

The family had trained for just such an event, and he should have expected it based on Harley's business. A yellow Labrador appeared beside the woman, head lowered and growling.

Everything Strap planned to do and say went out the window, and he waited for Kevin to come around a corner, waving a gun. "No! Wait! Tell the girls to stand down and not make any calls! Point that weapon at my chest, but call them off please until I tell you why I'm here."

Drawn tight as a watch spring, Tammy centered the pistol on Strap's chest and took two steps back to presumably see into the kitchen. "Hold it, girls."

"Aunt Tammy, what's happening?" The teenage voice was high and reedy with fear.

One of the boys chimed in. "Mom! Are you all right?"

Strap couldn't see the kids, but he hoped they weren't responding to their training. Damn, this family was good! He remained at the door with both hands in sight. He lowered his voice. "Can you call off the dog?"

"He hasn't done anything."

"Except make me nervous." The sight of those bared white teeth had Strap on edge. "I'm here to help you."

She waited a beat. "Kevin, down."

The big dog dropped to his stomach, keeping his eyes on the man at the door.

"The dog's name is Kevin?" Relief washed over him.

"What do you want?"

"Tammy, you're in danger. That's why I've showed up at your friend's door here. Your phone is monitored, and so is hers. Some bad people your husband has run into could be here at any time."

"How did *you* know we were here?"

"The whole world is watching, if they know how. I work for a massive company with tentacles everywhere and unlimited resources. One person traced your husband's friend's credit card when he hired the Uber to pick you up. It's terrifying, I know, but my company knows everything about you, and that's why I'm here."

He lowered his voice even more. "I don't want to come in. I'll stand right here in the door and talk, so please listen to what I have to say, but have the girls turn off their phones, unplug the TVs and smart speakers."

"Unplug what?"

"Echo Dots, or Alexa."

She thought for a moment, and still holding the Glock steady on Strap's chest, she turned her head. "Girls. I have this under control. Turn off your phones, and this sounds strange, but unplug the TV in the living room." She spoke to Strap. "We don't have an Alexa."

Relaxing now that she'd engaged, Strap took a deep breath and, remaining in the doorway, told her everything he could to get the six of them out of the house and away from the danger that was planned to come from his team.

With that information out there, it would soon be time to retire and reinvent himself once again.

Chapter 26

"I swear, that man don't never get in a hurry." Mrs. Crawford used her toes to tilt the rocking chair on her back porch overlooking a pasture full of cattle. A couple of chickens scratched in the sand, completely oblivious to a large hawk circling overhead.

"But he's steady." Toby laughed. The elderly couple had adopted her as one of their own after she and Bill Sloan started dating. "I never saw a man his age work so hard and long and never complain."

"Oh, he complains all right, but that's at night after supper, when he's watching the news, and I'm the only one here to listen to him."

Toby's phone rang as she was sitting with Mrs. Crawford on the old lady's porch. She dug it from her back pocket and recognized the number that belonged to the unnamed man who sold her the stolen drill rods.

She gave the gray-haired woman beside her an apologetic smile. "I'm sorry, but I need to answer this."

Mrs. Crawford rose and stood for a moment to allow her joints to adjust to the load. She put one hand on the slender shoulder of the slight young woman. The scent of onions on her hands reminded Toby of her own mother, who seemed to live in front of the kitchen sink.

"You go right ahead, honey." Mrs. Crawford gave her a pat. "I need to go inside and get that old man ready to go to town anyway."

She limped away, and Toby answered. "Hello?"

"You're the woman who bought those rods from me a year and a half ago. Tracey Smythe?"

She smiled at the alias she and Sloan had used more than once. She crossed one leg over the other and noted the dust on her boot. "I bought drill metal from someone who had this number."

"Fine then. You'd recognize me if you saw me. Anyways, I need to tell you that I made a mistake and shouldn't have sold them. Do you still have those rods, and can I get them back?"

"I didn't buy them to stack 'em up somewhere. I know where a few are, but we sold the rest and they've all been used."

"Can you tell me who you sold them to?"

"No."

The one-word answer seemed to surprise the man on the other end. "Look, I have some people who want those back and will pay anything for them."

"I can't sell what I don't have."

"These people will do whatever it takes to get them back."

A chill ran up Toby's back. "Is that a threat of some kind?"

"It's a threat they used on me."

Toby peeped over her shoulder at the closed door leading into the farmhouse kitchen. Maggie the blue-heeler lay in the shade against the wall, eyes closed and waiting to go back to work herding cows.

Toby rose and walked out into the hot sunshine that felt like weight on her shoulders. Glad for the protection of her hat, she stopped in the shade of a pecan tree. Seeing that she was close, the hens trotted away.

"Look, we sold it all and spent the money." She glanced at the barn fifty yards from the house where the rods were stacked out of sight. "There's some left on a ranch and they're planning to use them for a fence, but that's all I can tell you." She turned toward the county road where Mrs. Crawford wanted the fence.

"Look." The man's voice revealed his rising desperation. "I need your help."

"I'll do what I can." In that moment Toby realized she had a way to make some serious money that would go a long way in paying for Sloan's upcoming transplant. She did some quick math, factoring in how much to give the Crawfords for the material, and still come out ahead on their personal finances. "But I'm gonna need six times what you paid for each rod."

"Damn. That's a lot."

"You said they didn't care about the cost."

"Done. Where are they?"

"The Crawford ra…Crawley, that's the Crawley ranch. They're stacked behind the barn, but I'll need cash."

"We need to do this fast."

"That's fine for me."

"What's the address?"

She knew better than that. Of a certain age, the Crawfords were about to leave for a weekly doctor's appointment. "It'll have to be tomorrow, but I'll meet you out at the Love's just outside of town. You pay me half, and then I'll lead you out to the ranch."

"I know that one. Why wait 'til tomorrow?"

"There are a lot of moving parts here and I'm not in charge of any of them."

"And can you help me with the rest?"

"Like I said, they've been sold and used. The rest of that's up to you."

She hung up when Mr. Crawford came out in his Sunday clothes for their trip to town. In Wrangler jeans, starched blue shirt, he stopped on the porch and set his ever-present straw hat just right on his head, covering the fringe of silver hair that was all he had left up topside. Seeing Toby standing in the pecan tree's shade, he paused to give Toby a wink.

Knowing the missus wouldn't be far behind, Toby retraced her steps, met him on the porch, and saw he had something in his hand. Mr. Crawford smiled when she walked up. "I been meaning to give you something."

She climbed onto the steps to join him out of the sun. "A surprise for me?"

"Yes, ma'am." He held out a shiny black object.

Toby took the surprisingly heavy metal critter, which she realized was an owl the size of her palm. "Where'd you get this?"

"Well, I made it for you, with Bill's help."

She examined the little art project.

"I was a pretty good welder back in the day, but it was always on fences or tractors and broke shredders and such. Bill told me he could do this kind of work, and I asked him to show me how. This one wasn't my first. They were a rabbit and a figure sitting on a toilet, but they were pretty ugly. I thought this turned out kinda cute."

She cupped the little big-eyed owl in both hands and stood on her toes to kiss his cheek. "This is awful sweet, but you could have made it for Mrs. Crawford."

"I did." He rubbed his recently shaven cheek she'd just kissed. "Hers is a flower. It was supposed to be a peony, but I think it looks more like a rose. Anyway, we never had a daughter, and I kinda figured you'd like it, and all…"

"What'd you make it out of?"

"Some old drill rods we got from Mitch Ramsey. He had 'em in the back of his truck one day up at the store, so I talked him out of a couple."

A sharp pain of guilt burned through Toby's stomach at the thought of how they were using the old couple, and once again she was awash in guilt over it.

Chapter 27

It sometimes seemed that I lived out of my state-issued truck. I hadn't been in it for very long, but the dash was already filled with papers, notebooks, and sales programs. Papers drifted into the back seat and on the floorboards, along with other necessary ranch and farm tools.

Still numb from the attack on my bank and worried about my family, I had to clean up that mess with the people who'd come to my house and get to work that couldn't wait. I handled a lot of it as I drove because I'd become good friends with the bank president. Sherri Turner was one of those tough old country gals who'd worked her way up from a teller when she was fresh out of high school.

I explained what had happened and she listened without interrupting, tsk-tsking in sympathy. "Don't you worry, hon. I'll take it all from here, and I sure am sorry for your troubles."

Still worried, I agreed to let her handle it. Harley had contacted the security company, and they were on their way out to reset the system and get the cameras up once again.

No matter what was going on with me, I still had a job to

do and that took me up to McAlester, Oklahoma, to talk with a farmer who'd lost nearly two dozen steers and suspected they had been stolen. He'd piqued my interest when he told me about the unfamiliar truck and trailer that he suspected hauled off his cows, and the Dodge Charger that was seen in the area at the same time.

Harley rode shotgun and listened in on the conversation. That morning we'd picked up four disposable phones and delivered two of them to Tammy at her friend's house. She and Chloe agreed to use them only when we were sure no one could eavesdrop either in person or through any electronic system, and the girls had orders not to call unless they were in danger.

He and I kept two of them to call the girls.

Harley canceled several of his urban chaos classes, but I didn't think it bothered him. He was in a sense working again, and the opportunity to help me arrest—or for him to shoot—a bad guy had him buzzing with delight. He thrived on the excitement and adrenaline when we were working together, while I was more like an old packhorse that plodded along and dealt with the details of our jobs.

The two black warbags on the seat behind us spoke volumes. Better armed than some entire countries, we were ready for whatever was coming.

Now convinced that we were on a dangerous train with no conductor, I called my supervisor, Jimmy Meeks, to let him know what I was doing.

As usual, he answered on the fifth ring. I could never figure out why five was the magic number for him. "What's up, Tuck?"

"Headed up to Oklahoma to check on some missing cattle. I'm calling because I think they were taken by the same people who were running a fraud operation around here a few weeks ago. Male and female team going by the name of Loren and Tracey Smythe, but those are aliases for sure."

"I remember them."

"Well, the report I got says there was a Charger running block and two men in it. The landowner in Oklahoma says someone saw a cattle trailer pulled by a Ford where those cows were took. It sounds like the same team I tangled with."

"The ones that shot up our truck?"

I felt like he was grinning on the other end, but there was no way to be sure. "Yessir."

"You think they're back in business?"

"That's my guess. I've gathered enough information to tie them into other thefts down here, which will bring more charges, up to maybe first-degree felonies."

"How many head did they steal that night you were after 'em?"

"Thirty, but that was only in that load. The full count was eighty-three. I figure they've switched states and started the business all over again. That's where I'm going, to McCurtain County."

With ranchers and farmers selling so much stock, the sale barns in Oklahoma were overwhelmed with the volume of cattle coming through their pens. The *Smythes* and those like them knew how to play the game and disappear into the crowds. If only such people put as much energy into doing what was right, instead of breaking the law, they'd be living comfortably and not faced with jail time.

"The rustlers here in Oklahoma hit a ranch owned by Richard and Pauline Anderson. They disabled a security light and rounded up some calves in a pen with a loading chute. Took twenty head and were gone."

I watched Harley punch at the radio on the dash with a forefinger. "I figure it was a ranch hand that knows the area, but I could be wrong."

"Let me know what you find."

"I will, and then I'm coming back this afternoon to check on a report from a Mister Arthur Hope, who called me last night about missing stock he'd bought online and haven't been delivered." I glanced over at Harley and slapped at his hand. Just like when we were kids, he went right back to fooling with the radio. "I'm going to call you on a different phone in a few minutes to tell you about something else. Harley's here with me so he might weigh in."

A long sigh came through the truck's sound system. Meeks knew that if I was going to use another phone, something big was up. "It's trouble if Harley's in there with you. But I'm glad he is."

"It is, and he is."

Harley frowned. "Hey, I'm right here, and I can hear everything you two are saying."

"I hope you know what I'm thinking, too." Meeks's voice came through sharp, but we both knew he was kidding.

"I don't know why y'all are always ganging up on me."

"I'll call you in a few minutes." I punched off.

When we reached the little town of Valliant, we stopped on a tall Oklahoma hill and walked a distance from the truck. After learning what the computers in trucks can do a few months earlier, I didn't want to be anywhere near it when we talked.

I doubt those with a sound technical knowledge can listen through a vehicle's sound system, but I wouldn't put it past anyone who knew how. Right that moment, computers in the truck had already tracked us to that hill, and were digging through my cell phone for data to use later without my permission.

For all I knew, that bunch from ChemShale had a tracking device somewhere on it, and maybe even bugged the inside.

The dash and seats were so cluttered, they could have put one anywhere and I'd never know it.

We called Meeks on the drop phone to bring him up to speed, and the least I can say is that he wasn't happy with what was going on.

"How do you get into so much trouble?" He sounded exasperated. "I have twenty-nine other agents and none of them ever have these kinds of issues."

"I don't go *looking* for it. That meth deal wasn't my fault, and now I have guys in dark suits and shades coming to the house and threatening me. What else could I do but call Harley?"

"I'd tell you to reach out to the local sheriff, but the last time you did that, it didn't go so well."

"That's because crooked lawmen were a family business in Ganther Bluff, but that's all in the past. I'm not interested in taking that chance, though. I still don't want to spread these troubles around, and don't know who else to involve but you. One call to a TV station or paper, and it'd be out in no time."

"Well, I have a couple of people who need to know. I'll talk to them and we'll keep everything quiet on our side. This is more to cover our asses than anything else."

"I understand."

"Harley."

He leaned toward the phone in my hand. "Yessir."

"Don't shoot nobody. That retirement badge can go just so far."

"I promise I won't shoot at anybody who don't shoot at me first."

Meeks sighed and hung up.

We were on the way back to Texas when my phone rang again through the sound system, interrupting the radio. It always startles me, and I still can't get used to that sudden ring that seems louder than the music we were listening to—this time it was George Jones singing about little yellow sticky notes all over his empty house.

The little two-lane we followed wandered and twisted through the countryside, so I slowed and glanced at the screen to see a phone number without a name pop up. That wasn't unusual. Phone scammers had become a way of life for everyone who owned a cell phone, and even for those who still had landlines. Most of my calls were from people I've never met, so out of necessity, I answered them all.

It was a 903 exchange, one that reaches from Sherman to the west, to Texarkana on the east, and down south below Tyler. Hoping it wasn't spam, I punched the icon. "Hello."

"This is Jim Crawford. I'm looking for Special Agent Tucker Snow."

Looking for a place to pull off so I could talk, I slowed. Up ahead was a little wooded pull-out rest stop that looked as if it had been constructed by the WPA. I rolled to a stop off the highway and glanced over to see a hand-mortared rock wall with a small spring at the base. Water dribbled from a pipe jutting out to the side. Unusual for our part of Texas, it looked like it belonged up in Arkansas.

"This is Snow. How can I help you?"

"I'm a member of the TSCRA and need some help."

People usually want to be polite and visit for a second, but I always preferred that they get to business. "Be glad to." Opening the console under my right elbow, I took out a pad and pen. Harley got out to fill an empty bottle with spring water. "What's up?"

"Well, I have some hay for sale and a guy I never met from Texarkana bought it."

He didn't have to go any farther, because I've run into that old scam a dozen times through the years. I felt sorry for the guy, because I'd heard it a hundred times. "Let me guess. He bought a lot of hay, most of what you had and sent you a cashier's check for it, but he asked you to pay to have it shipped through a third party."

"You got it. He had a company to ship it to him, and asked..."

"That you cash the check that was for much more than the price of the hay, and he asked that you wire the extra money to that guy to pay for transportation and delivery."

There was a moment of silence on the other end. "I got taken."

"Probably. The check was counterfeit."

"It looked legitimate."

"They're good at what they do. He knew you'd move fast, because you needed the sale. It looked good just long enough to go through."

"Can you come out here?"

"Where do you live?"

He told me, and it was right on the way. I was anxious to get back to the house and into an old 1985 Dodge truck I'd bought not long after getting the one I was in. I needed a truck without all that fancy tracking technology, and we intended to use it to go to Gainesville and check on everyone there.

Neither Harley or I could come up with a plan for the girls. They couldn't stay at Tammy's friend's forever, but we were on high center for a little while longer.

"I'll be there in a couple of hours."

"That's perfect." Mr. Crawford gave me the address and I punched the number into my GPS. No matter what kind of troubles I had, there were still criminals out there who needed to be cuffed.

Chapter 28

Pierson grinned at the guys he'd come to think of as *his* team. Barnes and Sanz sat on the ends of the two sagging beds in the Red River Lodge. Truitt and Warren slouched in chairs pulled in from the other room. All four remained quiet, intent on the conversation Pierson had initiated with a call to Special Agent Snow. Learning that he'd initiated the call, they drifted in close to see what was up.

With the phone to his ear, Pierson nodded as if the special agent on the other end could see him. "Perfect."

With that one word ending the conversation with Tucker Snow, he leaned back and surveyed the men as if they answered to him. "Well, now that's the way you do it."

He dialed another number and leaned back with his insolent look. When Tracey Smythe answered, he went through another storyline and arranged to meet her at the Love's truck stop.

When he hung up, Pierson was so full of himself he could bust. "Damn, I'm good." He turned off the phone he'd taken off the body of its owner. "That was easy."

Norman Barnes snubbed out a cigarette in a red plastic ashtray on the bedside table. "We don't have the materials yet."

"I will by the end of the day. That's the last of the rods, and we're getting close to wrapping things up around here. We meet her at the truck stop and I can follow y'all back to the ranch. At least this'll go right."

Barnes and Gabriel Sanz looked concerned. Barnes leaned forward with one elbow on the knee of his tactical pants. "Pierson, Strap's gonna shoot you when he gets back."

"Hey, I don't remember hearing that I work directly for that big bastard, and besides, he's been gone way too long." That superior, narcissistic look returned to his face. "Mr. Cross wanted this job done now, and done right. I have the seniority here, and the experience."

He switched into his "cowboy" accent. "This ain't my first rodeo, so I say we take that nosy agent and his know-it-all brother out and finish up."

Running one hand over his short haircut, Sanz spoke to the floor. "Strap called in another team to help us. He did that because these two Snows are badasses."

"Nobody's more badass than we are." Pierson swiveled back and forth in his desk chair that was old when Eisenhower was president. "We've handled worse than this. Remember that cartel down on the border? They didn't know what hit 'em."

"We were on those guys before they knew who they were dealing with." Sanz licked his lips. "We mowed 'em down on the street and the cleanup crew loaded them up while we got the hell out of there. Nobody's looking for those bodies out in the desert, and for sure there weren't as many people close by to hear the shots. Nobody cares if a bunch of gangsters got shot, except their bosses."

"That's why I chose this guy Crawford's place and told them I was him. See, this is the kind of stuff Cross doesn't think about, double-checking. If he'd done that at the outset, I doubt we'd be having these problems with Snow."

"So are we gonna meet her at the Love's like you said?" Sanz asked.

"Nah. There's no need. I just wanted to make sure I had the right place. And I do. The Crawfords have a big ranch with the house way off the highway." He spun the laptop so they could see the satellite image of the ranch. He was right, the nearest house was well over a mile away, perched on a bluff over the river bottoms. "Made up that story off an arrest I read about on the internet. Shooting out in the country is common. No one will notice, if we're all careful with that first shot, and that's the way to do it. Aim careful. Shoot. Game over."

"What do we do with the people who live there?"

"Mr. Cross wants them gone just like the Ramseys. Once we've dealt with them and the Snow brothers, the cleanup crew comes in to take out the few pieces of hot hardware and we're gone."

Barnes studied the vinyl floor at his feet. "Cross is pissed because that dumbass driver sold a load of hot drill rods and pipe to a welder instead of delivering them to Stem Recyclers. All this because his nose is out of joint."

The company had already been advised that a different kind of radiated load was coming in, and when it didn't show, they started making noise about contacting the feds. Mr. Cross was also working on that issue, and ChemShale was doing its best to bury the report.

"I still don't get it," Truitt spoke up. He was the newest member of the team with the least bit of experience. "From what I read, it's not unusual that drilling through some of these formations brings a little radioactivity to the surface, but it's not that dangerous."

"It's not TENORM we're worried about." Pierson sounded like a pompous college professor. "Rocks in and around certain formations may contain radioactivity when waste materials are brought to the surface. People have been buying and selling those pipes and rods for years without a problem, unless they try and sell them to a scrap recycler."

"Why?" Truitt was like a kid brother wanting to fit in, but full of questions he should ask one-on-one in private.

"They run a Geiger counter over them before they'll weigh the material. If it clicks, they refuse it. But TENORM's exacerbated by DrySoil, and cap that off with real radioactive material one rig drilled through after some dumbass buried it out there decades ago, and the rods are hotter'n hell."

Truitt shook his head, still not understanding. "I don't understand the lingo. TENORM?"

"The term stands for Technologically Enhanced Naturally Occurring Radioactive Material." Sanz picked up the thread and cut off Pierson's lecture. "We had the bad luck to drill through some of that stuff, *and* low-level nuclear waste. Combine all that with DrySoil, and it's pretty nasty.

"Ten years ago out in West Texas, Halliburton lost a seven-inch metal fracking rod contaminated with americium-241 and beryllium. That means it was classed as a category three radiation source. They're used in horizontal drilling—that'd be fracking—and lowered into wells to find the best places for ChemShale to drill for oil and gas.

"If someone found it and picked it up, exposure to that little bitty rod could be fatal, and at the very least, it could cause permanent injury to someone, but to make matters worse, if that material made it into the scrap metal chain, it could contaminate everything it touches. Think about it, if one little piece of metal seven inches long could do that, imagine what damage an entire eighteen-wheeler load could do. And then think about how many people could die as that stuff makes its way around the state."

Pierson stopped listening when two more black Suburbans pulled up out front. "The other team is here. Looks like we're a go."

Barnes and Sanz exchanged looks that spoke volumes.

Chapter 29

My GPS took us to the Crawford place all the way up to the Red River. It was a sprawling ranch for that part of the state, nearly three thousand acres tucked up against the serpentine river thick with sand and silt. Unlike most people, the Crawfords built their house well away from the two-lane highway running east and west through Red River County, providing themselves plenty of privacy.

The two eight-foot pipe gates painted white were wide-open, so we drove under a tall arch bearing the ranch's brand, the Rocking T, symbolized by the letter *T* standing upright in a wide rocker.

"Fancy." Harley turned to look over his shoulder. "At least that one makes sense from both sides."

We rattled over two cattle guards, and finally made our way to the house. I pulled to a stop in front of the house and tapped the horn twice, an age-old country way to tell the owners we were there, and to alert any dogs in the area.

I was surprised there was no barking to greet us. Ranches of that size usually had at least one blue heeler to help with the cattle, and two or three hands at a minimum. The barn to our right had a bunkhouse attached. Despite the heat, the door was wide-open. No one appeared either there, or at the house.

We waited in the air-conditioning for a minute and still no one appeared. I left the engine running. "Guess I'll have to knock on the door."

I knew someone had to be close by since they were expecting me. There were two trucks parked in view near the barn and bunkhouse on our right, and a sedan that likely belonged to Mrs. Crawford.

"The hands may be out, and these folks are like Mom and Dad when they got old. The TV's probably turned up so loud they can't hear it thunder."

Harley laughed. "Good goddlemighty. With the TV so loud and them being cold all the time and keeping the house hot, I took to talking to them on the porch." He plucked the phone from his pocket. "I have a signal. I'm gonna call Tammy while you're in there to make sure everything's all right."

Just for to hear him holler, I left the door open so hot air could get in. He was too busy with his phone, but he'd start squawking pretty soon.

Crawford did it right. The two-story house with cedarwood exterior was built on a pier and beam foundation. A wide wrap-around front porch with comfortable-looking lounge furniture was a cool, shady place to get out of the hot sun.

Thankful for the relief, I tilted my hat back and rang the doorbell at the same time the blue heeler I'd been expecting raced around the corner. Whining instead of barking, I saw he was running on three legs, favoring his right front.

"You get a sticker, buddy?"

"Dammit, Tuck!"

Pleased that I'd aggravated my little brother once again, I noticed blood on the dog's coat when he came up to me and rolled over on his back.

I knelt to check the dog for wounds, and my hat went spinning off my head at the same time the report of a gunshot slapped off the house.

"Look out!"

Harley's voice reached my ears at the same time I threw myself to the right, half rolling off the porch and into the soft dirt of a flower bed. Brittle stems snapped as I landed. Enveloped in the thick aroma of rosemary, I snatched the .45 from my holster. Tail tucked between his legs, the little blue heeler vanished around behind the house as the staccato burst of a fully automatic weapon came from the direction of my truck.

Good ol' Harley.

Other automatics chattered from more than one direction as others joined in. It sounded as if a small army was attacking from all directions. I've never been in the military, but I've been under fire before, and this one was way too close and intense.

A bullet smacked into the wooden foundation skirting beside me. Another splintered the porch post just over my head and went whirring away toward the river with a nasty buzz. Staying low, I saw the shot came from a big John Deere with a bucket on the front and threw two shots in that direction. Half a second later, Harley was beside me with his warbag in one hand and firing with the other.

There was no way he could connect with the shooters crop dusting like that, but spraying lead in the air to throw off our assailants' aim was the idea. He pitched the heavy bag toward the front door, where it slid against the frame, grabbed me by the collar, and yanked me onto the porch.

"Inside!"

A flash from my left gave away another man's position behind a wide water oak between the house and the river. I fired twice in his direction, and he fell back around the tree, heels drumming against the ground. I grabbed the doorknob and gave it a twist while Harley dropped to one knee beside the wall and emptied his magazine into the open bunkhouse door until it ran dry.

Lucky for us, the house's front door was unlocked and we spilled inside.

On the opposite side of the coin, there was a man with a pistol standing in a doorway twenty feet away. Harley dropped to his right and landed on his shoulder to roll toward the questionable cover of a couch facing a fireplace. I juked to the left as the guy fired three times, uncertain who to aim at.

It was the classic response when dove hunters are suddenly presented with a large flock of birds. Instead of choosing one, many are overwhelmed at the number of targets and give in to the instinct of firing into the mass of birds and hoping to hit something. That technique usually fails in the field, and it did then, too.

He squeezed one off at me and two at Harley's rolling form, missing us with every shot.

Hearing my old man's advice from when we were kids, I took careful aim that seemed to take hours. Aligning the sights on center mass, I methodically pulled the trigger three times and he fell.

There was no time to consider the impact of those few microseconds. Still on the ground and with rounds punching through windows and walls, Harley kicked the door shut with one foot and dropped his empty magazine.

"Loading!" He slammed a fresh mag into the well of his M4

and released the charging handle. Using his feet to push himself away from the window and behind the cloth sofa, he wormed around to cover the door in case someone decided to come charging in. "Loaded!"

Hearing he was ready, I dropped the magazine on my .45, stuffed in a fresh one from my belt, and pushed the slide release to chamber a fresh round. "Loaded."

I stuffed the Colt in its holster, belly-crawled to the warbag, and pulled out my own AR. Bullets walked across the front of the house. Powdered dust and razor-sharp glass filled the air as I stayed low and dragged the now much lighter bag away from the window.

Like Harley, I pushed around behind the couch and paused to catch my breath. Both of us were panting as if we'd run ten miles. The shooting stopped. For the first time I took stock of our surroundings and the room's layout.

"Dammit!" Realizing our backs were to the second-floor staircase, Harley flipped around and swept the room with the muzzle.

I twisted myself nearly in two trying to cover the hallway containing the dead man, and the door. "Where'd they come from?"

"All directions." He wriggled back to see more of the room. "I was leaning over to the door you left open to give you a good cussing when I saw somebody beside that big water oak with a rifle. He was already drawing a bead on you. I saw you go down and thought you'd been shot."

"He put one through my hat when I bent to check on the dog."

"What dog?"

"The one I was leaning over to check on when that guy started shooting."

"Well, you're lucky. After that, everything went on

autopilot when somebody opened up from the bunkhouse. I grabbed the warbag and rolled out your door to keep the truck between us.

"As soon as I hit the ground and got straight. Shot under the truck and shut those guys up in the bunkhouse, but there was one behind the tractor and at least one other behind those two pickups. Seemed like there were twenty of 'em shootin' at us, though."

It was impossible to cover every opening in the living room, but I slithered around to keep an eye on the door and the hallway containing the man's still body. "I don't know how they screwed up and missed us that first time."

Harley raised up on one elbow to peek outside. The windows were fairly good cover with the sunlight reflecting off the glass. Unless someone was right up on the porch to look in, they couldn't see us inside.

"The guy behind the tree had you dead to rights. He just didn't account for you bending down."

"I'm calling for backup." I reached for the phone in my shirt pocket and realized I'd left it in the console. "Dammit! Phone's in the truck. You'll need to call."

His mouth twisted in disgust. "Can't. I plugged it into the charger and it's on the dash."

Two rounds punched through the front door and we ducked.

Harley scanned the room. "You have a plan?"

"Not one I'd like to follow. You?"

"Yeah, let's creepy-crawl out the back door and take this fight to them. They'll come in and kill us if we stay on the defensive."

He's always been one to attack, even when we were kids. It didn't matter if there was eight of 'em against one on the schoolyard, he'd plow in and take out the biggest guy first.

"I have a better idea. Let's crawl out the back door and run like hell."

He held up a hand. "Listen?"

The sound of gravel under tires reached us. I raised up enough to see over the couch. A black SUV flashed past the shattered windows and sped away in a cloud of dust. I took a deep breath to calm down. "They're leaving."

"I would too if my ambush didn't work. New plan. Let's give 'em a minute to get away and slip out the back and check around."

I laid my head on the hardwood floor and waited for my nerves to quit jangling.

Chapter 30

In Shelly's kitchen, Chloe and Jimma backed up to the pantry door with the boys close in behind them. Breathing hard and fast, Chloe held a sharp boning knife in one hand and a hammer in the other. She'd seen hundreds of movies where terrified heroines grabbed one of the big wide-blade chef's knives from the block for defense.

Uncle Harley always snorted at the sight when they were watching movies. "Hollywood. If you're ever in that situation, get the boning knife or the utility knife. It's easier to slash and stab with it, and remember to keep the sharp side up."

The smooth handle in her hand didn't instill much confidence, especially if the man at the door had a gun, but her dad and Uncle Harley showed her and Jimma how to attack and slash fast, as a last-ditch effort.

Her dad had repeated over and over. "I'd rather go up against a man with a gun than a knife."

On the other hand, Jimma was conditioned by movies and had the chef's knife. It was sharp, though, and the two of them could do some damage if that man tried to get past them. Their job was to protect the kids, and she wouldn't let anyone down.

At least Aunt Tammy with her pistol was between them and the stranger. She was a good shot and it was quiet in there for a few moments. Obeying her aunt's orders, Chloe tried not to hyperventilate as they unplugged the TV and turned off anything with a speaker.

Jimma cleared her throat to speak, but terror robbed her of the ability. Licking her lips, she tried again, but the words were dry and sticky. "What do you think they're doing in there?"

"Talking, I guess."

"You don't think he stabbed her and she's laying there dying while we're in here?"

The revelation jolted Chloe's stomach. "No. Kevin's not barking. She'd warn us before she went down." She paused, thinking. "And she'd be shooting if he attacked her."

"Why's this happening again?" The reedy question almost came out as a whine.

This was new for both of them, but Chloe knew what Jimma meant. "I don't think this guy is here to kidnap anyone. There are too many of us to round up."

"Well, why then?"

Chloe's face reddened in anger. "I don't know! Dammit, I'm just as scared as you are and I don't know what to do! Why's this always happening to us...?"

"What are you talking about out there?" Danny's young voice was way too loud for the situation, and if anyone came into the kitchen, they'd hear him and know where the boys were hiding.

Chloe whirled, her voice low and full of threat at kids who wouldn't listen. They were always questioning their mother, when they should be glad they had one and should listen when she talked. "Will you shut up in there?"

"Hey, don't yell at my brother." Matt was like his dad and was prone to attack first and ask questions later. "You're not the boss of us."

Chloe wanted to slap the door and scream for them to be quiet. It would be so easy to lose it and shriek until her voice was hoarse, and that was exactly the wrong thing to do.

She also wanted to hear what was going on in the hallway. It was better to get away from the boys for a moment and regain her self-control, which was fast slipping away. "You stay here outside of the door. I'm going over there to see if I can hear what's going on."

Jimma's chin quivered. "That's not a good idea."

"I'm out of good ideas."

Chapter 31

The guy in the hall not far from where we were barricaded was dead as nickel coffee and it should have made me feel bad, but I was more relieved than anything else. "I think they're gone, but we need to clear the house before I can breathe normal again."

Rising slow and careful with his rifle at high ready, Harley swept the living room while I made sure the adjoining dining room was empty. We came together on the way to the back door.

Harley glanced down at the man's sprawled body, which lay still in death. "Two in the engine room. Good shootin', Tex."

He'd always been glib at what some would say was the wrong time, but that's the way my little brother dealt with mayhem and death. After that, he'd have a steak and a beer and sleep like a baby.

I'd lie in bed that night, reliving the past hour and swallowing down nausea and guilt.

"Not that good." I shook my head, knowing what some money-grubbing lawyer would say in a court of law. "I'll be on desk duty for this whole thing, and the hole in the guy's back where he spun around while I was still shooting."

My first round caught the man in the right side of his chest, spinning him around. The second entered his left side and continued out the right. In the heat of the fight, his momentum was such that the third round caught him in the left side of the back before he dropped.

It was exactly the kind of shooting scenario that lawyers love. Technically, I'd shot the attacker in the back, and there was a good chance someone would say that I shot him while he was fleeing. I'd have to rely on an understanding grand jury on this one.

The house was empty, save for the cooling body, and as far as we could tell, no one was waiting for us outside. An old-fashioned wind-up clock ticked our lives away from another room. Nerves jangling and tense as a bowstring, we slipped out the back to find nothing but birds and the little blue heeler watching us from underneath a defunct old Poppin' Johnny tractor.

Walking, twisting, and watching over our shoulders to cover the area all around and behind us, we made our cautious way across the dry yard to the bunkhouse. If there was anyone still around, they'd have opened up on us when we were far from cover, but we still practiced safe procedures and bracketed the open door.

Standing off to the side, Harley nodded at me. "I'm the alpha."

"Good. I don't want to go in there anyway."

Taking a deep breath, he ducked inside and to the left. I immediately followed and went the opposite direction, taking care not to trip over the corpse sprawled just inside.

"I see brain matter." Keeping his rifle on the still body, Harley kicked a wicked-looking rifle away.

I kept the muzzle of my rifle on a second body lying farther inside, as if the man was wounded and tried to flee through the back door. The room reeked of the coppery scent of blood and the sharp stench of perforated bowel. "Lots of blood. He's dead."

While Harley secured their weapons, I checked their pockets to find nothing but one piece of wrapped peppermint. "Pros."

"Even pros make mistakes. They didn't expect us to respond so fast." Still holding his rifle at high ready, he studied the yard, our truck, and the oak tree beyond. "We might have bought the farm if you hadn't taken that guy behind the tree out. They had us in a cross fire until he went down."

I came back from checking the rear of the bunkhouse, which had everything from six bunks to a full kitchen and two full bathrooms. Only three of the bunks were in use, and there was a bra across the foot of the one that was made.

The nearest bunk to that one had a small table full of pill bottles beside it. Only one of the containers was turned so I read the name on the label.

Bill Sloan.

I passed through and found the back door was cracked. I peeked inside to find a barn full of equipment. "You see the body?"

"Nope. The tree might be hiding him if he fell straight back."

"I saw his heels drumming."

He pointed with his chin. "Let's clear the barn."

"I don't want to."

"Neither do I. This time you're the alpha."

I nodded, and we repeated the procedure. There were lots of places for people to hide, but the only living thing we saw was a rat that disappeared behind several square bales of hay. He was lucky; I was already squeezing the trigger when I realized the movement in the dim light was a rodent.

A blue tarp covered a sedan. I pointed and Harley nodded.

There could be a shooter underneath or inside the car. Readying myself, I got a handful of the stiff material and yanked the tarp onto the floor to reveal a black Charger. Harley swept the car and dropped to one knee to make sure no one was lying underneath.

Together we approached the sedan, prepared to open up through the windows, but the lights on our rifles lit the interior and it was empty.

I took a deep breath and relaxed for the moment.

There was nothing between me and the open back door except for an empty stall. With the bright sunshine outside threatening to take my vision from the dim barn, I turned to wave Harley out.

Carrying our weapons more at ease, we returned to the bunkhouse door that opened onto the yard. I stopped there, watching for any sense of movement other than what was provided by nature. I finally decided all was clear. "Let's get to the truck so we can call this in. We should be able to see that last guy from there."

"I'll lead." With Harley providing cover, I hurried across to the truck and grabbed my phone from the dash, but it wouldn't work. It was hot to the touch, and I remembered hearing that they'll often quit working if left in the sun.

Harley's phone had fallen onto the floorboard and was fully charged. The tension drained out of us while I called the local sheriff's office. Dispatch was shocked, but the young man on the other end of the line was a professional. He listened without interruption, other than to confirm my name and our location. When I finished, he wanted me to stay on the line, but I had other things to do. Dispatch assured me help was on the way, and I hung up.

Harley went over to the tree. "Hey, hoss. There's a lot of blood here, but he's gone."

"What?" A puddle of already-drying blood and a number of brass shell casings were all we saw. "Maybe he drug himself out there."

A tangle of berry vines, briars, wild muscadines, and an assortment of small bushes acted as a natural windbreak. Beyond them was a steep slope down to the river.

"I don't think so." Harley made a 360-degree turn. "No drag marks, but there're several sets of tracks."

There was little undergrowth beneath the wide tree, and the bare patches in the sand showed more than one pair of shoe prints. "They could have discussed it here in the shade before we showed up."

Harley studied the area. "Maybe. Or your dead guy in the house and another might have walked around to the back. We're lucky both of them weren't inside."

The back of my neck prickled, and I glanced up at the second floor. "We didn't clear the upstairs."

His eyes snapped to the second floor at the same time the low roar of an accelerating engine reached us. Harley paused. "Listen!"

The still air reverberated, coming from behind the house, and I strained to see what was there. Half a second later a black SUV exactly like the first roared into view and shot toward the gate. Both of us raised our rifles, tracking the vehicle, but neither of us fired at the fleeing Suburban.

When it disappeared down the long drive, Harley turned to me. "They'd parked it way around back."

"Those first guys hauled ass quick." I knew what they'd done. "While we were inside, this second bunch hauled this guy away."

I felt deflated. "I'll bet you the farm my guy's not in the house anymore."

We rushed to the front door, and sure enough, the body in the hallway was gone.

Harley finished my thought. "They got him in here, and a dollar says when we left the barn, they came through the other side and picked up those other two bodies." For the first time in years, he shivered. "They could have wasted us at any time."

I drew a deep breath, thinking. "We'd already outshot them, and they were rattled. They knew we'd call for help, so they needed to get out of here."

"Like you said. They're pros."

"They took everything except the bullets they shot at us, and the casings."

"What are we up against?" He thumbed his phone alive. "I'm calling Tammy. I don't think they're safe at Shelly's house anymore."

"Tell her to get her friend and get gone, too. These guys have a far reach."

Taking a knee to gather myself, I forced my hands to quit shaking.

Chapter 32

The sun came through the windshield with fury, baking the dash and lower parts of Barnes's legs. The slender ChemShale employee barely felt the heat from the steering wheel as they shot down the barren two-lane.

He was furious, and terrified. Their ambush and training had failed.

Training? They hadn't truly trained in more than two years, relying mostly on their memories of past successes and the occasional day at the range. They thought they were too good, dealing with sheep most of the time, and hadn't truly anticipated the responses of two men who were obviously wolves.

The second team that had just arrived from Houston certainly hadn't been ready. They got out of the cars looking confident and fit. Three hours later three of them were dead, and Warren, who'd been wounded, was chalk-white in the back.

Beside Barnes, Sanz looked over his shoulder at the rear cargo area that contained men once known as Brandenburg, Coyle, and Handley. Only Warren was still breathing, and from the sounds back there, he wouldn't be for much longer. Eyes wide and sucking air through his mouth, Barnes forced himself to concentrate and drive the speed limit.

In the seat behind him, Truitt was on his phone, talking urgently to a cleanup crew waiting half an hour away. "That's right. The job went sideways. There's no cleanup on-site, but we're bringing you the leftover materials for disposal."

He listened for a moment. "No casings, though. That's all."

Sanz turned back around. "We barely got out of there. Just who'd we tangle with?"

"Men better than us." Barnes checked his speedometer as they came up behind a farm truck driving almost ten miles below the speed limit. He and the boys had seen men as tough down in Central America, but they didn't expect anything like that here. Delta, yes, but these guys weren't military. It was all he could do not to pass the man, but instead dropped back and followed at a safe distance.

"We can't go back to the motel right now, looking like this." Both men were covered in blood from retrieving the bodies of their team members.

Sanz glanced over his shoulder to get an answer from Truitt, who frowned and shook his head.

Barnes forced his hands to release their white-knuckled grip on the steering wheel. "No. We'll meet the cleanup crew so they can pick these guys up."

"Everything's covered in blood. It's an ocean back there where they're leaking all over everything, and Warren's pumping blood like a fire hose."

"That's their job. To clean up."

"But how…?"

"Shut up, will you!"

Sanz clamped his jaw shut, but there was so much adrenaline

pumping through his system it was hard to calm down. "I can't believe those guys didn't check the top floor. They'd have cornered us."

"We were all lucky on that one. Any or all of us might have died if they did."

Waiting at the top of the stairs, Barnes and Sanz had the perfect kill zone if the two they were after had decided to clear that part of the house also. But when their targets worked their way outside, they came down and waited in one of the rooms the men had already checked, emerging only when the Snow brothers made their way to the bunkhouse and barn.

Rattled to the point that they were terrified of the brothers who reacted to the ambush like war machines, Barnes and Sanz resorted to self-preservation and their fears of Cross. They'd failed, and in doing so, endangered the entire team and ChemShale as a whole. There was no way they were going to continue the firefight with responders likely already on the way.

That's when Barnes saw an opportunity. They dragged the bodies outside, and while Barnes carried them one by one down a two-track lane to the Suburban hidden several yards away, Sanz crept to the tree to retrieve Warren. He was surprised to find he could still walk, but barely.

It was so absurdly easy; they came up behind the barn and listened in until the Snow brothers finished checking on the bodies of Coyle and Handley, two more of the newcomers. Sanz wanted to engage them again, but when the stock agent turned to where they were hidden in an empty stall and seemingly looked directly into his eyes, Barnes panicked and almost gave away their position.

Somehow the cow cop didn't see them peering through horse-chewed slats. Sanz looked down at his shaking hands, wondering if he and Barnes had somehow become invisible for a moment.

Knowing they had only a few minutes before first responders arrived, they threw the corpses in the back and took a chance to speed past the house, hoping the brothers wouldn't shoot.

And they didn't.

In the second row of seats, Truitt hung up the phone and leaned forward between Barnes and Sanz. "We have a meeting place, but Mr. Cross already knows what's happened."

A death rattle came from the back seat as Warren expired. They continued in silence down the road, following the farm truck, and lost in their own thoughts of what might happen to them.

Sanz broke the quiet. "We tell the truth. Pierson told us it was Mr. Cross's decision and we followed orders, since Strap wasn't there."

Truitt twisted the top off a bottle of water and drained half of it in one gulp. "He's gonna have Pierson eliminated." He used the remainder to wash the sticky blood off his hands, the pink water splashing onto the carpet at his feet. Finished, he pitched the empty onto the floor and dried his hands on his shirt.

They came to a gravel turnoff and Barnes glanced at the in-dash navigation system. It showed the road wound around for several miles until intersecting with the highway that would lead them to the rendezvous point. Taking the back roads would be better than following the two-lane, where their black vehicle would stick out like a sore thumb. It beat the possibility of running into a local constable or highway patrol.

He slowed and angled off toward the west. Lowering the visor to block the sun, he held up his right hand. "Pass one of those water bottles up here."

Truitt cut two free from a plastic-covered cardboard tray on the floorboard beside his feet and passed them forward.

Barnes twisted the cap off and pitched it over his shoulder and took a long swallow.

"You're wrong about one thing, Truitt."

"What's that?"

"Mr. Cross isn't going to eliminate Pierson. I'm gonna kill him first."

Chapter 33

"Now what?" Fred Belk cracked another beer and took a long swallow as the last real bodark fenceposts in the county flashed past on their way back to the Crawford place.

Sloan cut his eyes across the pickup's cab. The whites that were once bright were tinged with yellow. "We keep on keeping on."

"What are those guys into?"

"You mean the Snow brothers?"

"That's who we were just talking to."

"Well, we were also listening to those other people talking to them, but yeah, Tuck and Harley."

A hawk hung low over an overgrown fencerow as they passed down the highway, watching its next meal in the dry grass as Sloan's truck passed underneath. "Something I'm afraid we created."

Fred watched the little drama in the side mirror as they passed. "It's not about the stock we've stolen."

"No. It's about those drill rods we bought."

Unsure of where Sloan was going, Fred took a swallow of beer. "Do tell."

"How long did it take me and Mitch to weld those pens and arbors?"

"Better part of two weeks." Fred nodded to himself in thought. "Would have been faster if I hadn't been down with that virus. The three of us could have done it in four or five days."

"Yep, and then Mitch and Strawn sell out overnight, and the next thing you know, those pens and everything are gone and no one knows where they've gone. That gets me to wondering."

"There's a lot to wonder about, that's for sure."

Sloan hung a hand over the top of the steering wheel. "It beats me why those guys are on Snow, and why the metal is gone. They didn't take the old fence, just what we built with the material me and Toby bought from that guy."

"I knew something was fishy about that whole deal. It was like that time when me and you were at that gas station when those two guys pulled up with a case of jewelry to sell for cheap."

Sloan chuckled. "He must have thought we were a couple of rubes, telling us about a tornado in some town we'd never heard of and they just scooped up big handfuls of jewelry from the street in front of a store and hauled ass."

"I wonder how many people fell for that story."

"We for sure didn't. Fifty dollars for a ring that I bet came out of a claw machine from some arcade." Sloan shook his head. "That wasn't as good as those two who waved us down at a light, trying to sell us oil-filled stereo speakers because their company loaded too many on their delivery van and they didn't want to take them back to the warehouse."

Fred threw back his head and laughed before draining his beer. "Those old boys were shocked when we said we'd look at them, and then pulled into the chamber of commerce parking lot right next to the sheriff's car."

The two old boys who grew up together howled at the recollection.

Sloan turned onto the country road leading to the Crawford ranch. "None of them knew they were dealing with a couple of old pros."

"Who started back in high school."

They bumped knuckles.

"So my thought is we bought from the wrong guy for once, and he took *us* instead." Fred opened the little YETI cooler and fished around in the ice and water for another beer.

"That really wasn't Toby's fault, though."

"Never said it was. It would have been the same if we'd run into that guy before her. Now they want all that drill and tool steel back for some reason, and it's getting on innocent people."

"We don't know that for sure."

"We don't, but look at the facts. Mitch is gone. Strawn, too, and I helped him build pens with some of those rods. Then I heard Mr. Crawford on the phone the other day, talking about using the last of them to build a fence on the road. Said Mrs. Crawford was tired of having nothing between the house and the road other than a bobwire fence. If I'm right, those people who're after the Snow brothers are out gathering up all that metal and the Crawfords are next in line."

"So what do we do?"

"Keep an eye on the old folks for one thing, and have Toby call that guy who sold us the rods and find out why these people are so hot to get them back. You talk to her today?"

"Yep, she's there right now, visiting Mrs. Crawford, who's teaching her how to make teacakes. So what do we say, 'Hey, call that old boy who sold us those drill stems for cheap and ask him why in the world a drilling company would want to collect them all back'?"

"They're not just collecting them like picking up litter."

"Nope, they're serious about getting those rods. Maybe they're numbered somehow and the company is somehow responsible to the EPA or something to keep them and maintain records."

Sloan was tapping his fingers on the console and quit when a thought hit him. "Fred."

"That's me."

"No, I'm serious. When did I start getting sick?"

"A week or two after you finished Mitch's pens and arbor."

"When did he get cancer?"

"About that same time. Why?"

"And when did we build Strawn's fences?"

"Right after. What is this, some kind of deposition?"

"Then he had medical issues. They both worked with me and you didn't because you were sick when we were at Mitch's, and then you got called in by the National Guard for that month I was at Strawn's place. You're fine."

"A little buzzed."

"Something's wrong with those rods. I handled them a lot, and breathed the vapors from welding them. It was the rods that made all three of us sick. Those company people are trying to collect all the evidence so it can't be traced back to them."

Fred was quiet as they approached the ranch gates, studying on Sloan's theory. As was his way, he compartmentalized the information and switched topics so he could mull it over later. "We moving cows tonight?"

"Naw." Sloan shook his head. "I'm not feeling real good right now. Toby has her eye on some stock we can pick up in a day or two. We both need some spending cash."

"Yeah, 'cause we need to get you well."

"Ain't that the truth."

Chapter 34

Strap owned more than one house, and one was a two-story Craftsman on Swiss Avenue. One of two hundred historic homes in the shadow of the Dallas skyline, the neighborhood consisted of Mediterranean, Spanish, Tudor, and several other styles representative of the turn of the twenty-first century. The house was a gem among diamonds.

Owned by a shell corporation with no clear ties to Strap, the house was one of his getaways between jobs. He'd done most of the interior renovations himself over the years, hiring out the exterior work in order to avoid being seen too much by the neighbors and to avoid conflict with the strong homeowner's association that preferred outside projects be completed without delay.

There was very little activity outside in the oppressive heat. Two yard crews finished in the late evening sunshine, and there were no pedestrians or cars on the sidewalks and street. That would change toward dusk, when those more tolerant of the Texas summers came outside to walk and jog.

He pulled the black SUV into the paved drive, through a

side portico that was so narrow the fenders almost scraped, and around back to a garage that once housed Model T cars. The Suburban couldn't fit inside, but it was hidden from the street.

Tammy and the kids got out, and Chloe and Jimma paused beside the car. Kevin jumped out last, sniffed the air, and trotted to a bush to lift his leg.

Jimma's eyes were wide with wonder. "This is, like, the greatest house I've ever seen."

"It's an amazing neighborhood, too," Chloe added. "But I still don't like being here. Where are we?"

"Old East Dallas." Strap reached into his pocket and dug around, pleased that the girls had finally spoken. They sat in the back like silent statues all the way from Gainesville. "This is my place, and you'll be safe here."

They obviously still didn't trust the big stranger, but he heard Chloe whisper to Jimma as they were loading up for the trip that he reminded her of The Rock. He noticed she kept one eye on him as he scanned the area.

"Does Dad know where we are?"

"I hope not." Strap led them to the back door and unlocked it. Knowing they were all still nervous, he handed Tammy the key. "You can leave when you want. You're not prisoners here. This is a safe house."

"Cool." Danny studied the exterior and grounds. "A safe house like in the movies."

Strap shook his head. "No, it's not a safe house in the sense of CIA agents and stuff. It's a safe place for you to be right now. No one knows I own it. No one knows you're here."

Danny pondered the implications. "Then if you wanted to, you could just kill us and drive away, and no one would ever find us."

Jimma rolled her eyes at the youngster, who would someday

be her little brother after the adoption processes was finished. "*I'm* gonna kill you if you don't stop asking dumb questions."

Tammy paused at the door. "Is there a phone inside?"

"There is. An old-school landline."

"Security?"

"Nope. Nothing modern. No cameras. Not even a television. Nothing that can be electronically accessed."

The boys moaned, and Danny slapped his head. "What're we gonna do all the time we're here? Mom, can I use your iPad?"

Strap answered for her. "She didn't bring it." Since they still hadn't made a move to go inside, he pushed past and flicked on the warm yellow lights to brighten the vintage kitchen full of shiny new appliances with an old-school look. Kevin squeezed between his legs and trotted inside to investigate the new digs.

"Honestly, guys, the only thing I can suggest is for you to read." Strap waved to the inside. "There are a few board games, and some cards and dominos are in a drawer somewhere. Look around and find them. You have the run of the house, but you don't need to go outside, not until I give you the all clear."

Tammy put her purse on a vintage quartersawed oak table and looked around. "You know I'm going to call my husband, to let him and Tuck know where we are."

"Of course, but only on that phone you said he gave you." Uneasy that one of them still had a cell phone, he led them into the hallway where a black rotary phone sat in a tiny alcove in the wall. "Or you can use this."

Matt and Danny leaned close and squinted at the antique communication device. Danny put his finger into the dial and pulled. "How do you use this thing?"

Tammy put one hand on his shoulder. "I'll show you later when we order some pizza."

Strap watched the boys disappear down the hallway with a cheer. "Don't use a credit card."

"Dang it. Everything's trackable these days." She shook her head. "I don't have much cash."

Strap took a roll of bills from his pocket, suddenly concerned with how long he'd been gone from the motel. He peeled off four hundreds.

She shook her head. "This is way too much."

"I don't know how soon I can be back. This will help until your husband and Snow get here. Then y'all can come up with a plan."

"You know they'll be here soon?"

"That's what I'd do."

Time was crunching in on him. Two hours to Gainesville, and he used up most of an hour to convince Tammy to leave with the kids while her friend Shelly went on an unplanned vacation to Cancun with a friend.

Being recently single, there were benefits to not being tied down.

Two more hours down I-35 to the house on Swiss, and now another two hours back to the lodge might raise some eyebrows. He was already working on an alibi for the guys, but *their* timeline wasn't impacted. He planned to get a cleanup crew out to the Crawford farm and eliminate all the damning drill rods and contaminated pipes.

Mr. Cross wanted Snow permanently out of the picture, but that wouldn't be happening. He'd oversee the clearance of the radioactive material, but vowed there'd be no more killing. Strap realized on the way out to meet Tammy in Gainesville that despite "national security," he was finished with eliminating such problems with wet work.

He paused, looking out the window at the line of fine stately historic homes up and down the famous street. With these five in hiding, Strap could tell the team that he'd eliminated the human issue himself, and they could go back to Houston.

The boys stomped up the stairs, reminding Strap of when he was a kid. He and Tammy returned to the kitchen to find Chloe and Jimma sitting at the table. Strap paused where he could see the back door and down the hall to the front entrance. "Guys, I'm going to get you out of this, but don't ask me how right now. I have to leave for a few hours, but you'll be fine here until I get back."

"I'm worried about Dad." Chloe's chin quivered and dimpled as she tried not to cry.

"There's nothing to worry about—"

He was interrupted by Danny's excited voice.

"Wow!" He and Matt rushed down from the second floor, sounding like a herd of elk on the wooden stairs. Danny was holding a brightly colored cardboard box. "Look what we found! Lawn darts! What're these?"

With the typical blank look of a tired mom, Tammy simply shook her head from side to side.

Chapter 35

Standing in the front yard surrounded by an army of first responders, Harley looked at the burner phone in his hand as if it were alive. "You're where? With who?"

Tammy's voice came through, sounding tired and more than a little worried. "We're in a historic house on Swiss Avenue." She didn't have to tell him where the street was located, because she and Harley once drove through the historic area when they were in Dallas on one of their date nights.

For once I wasn't sure what to do, other than to pour a bottle of water on Harley's head to cool down his rising fury. Instead, I tilted my hat with the bullet hole to shade my eyes from the setting sun. "Tammy, what's the address?"

She told me and I wrote it down on a scrap piece of paper from my truck's dash. Harley was getting another mad on. He hadn't yet told her about the shootout, and his fuse was dangerously short. "You just let some *stranger* come waltzing in and let him talk you into getting into a car with him and going to *Dallas*?"

I was as shocked as he was, but yelling at her wasn't going

to help. The guy must've been a helluva talker. "Tell us what happened."

Harley's eyes grew flint hard as she described the man named Strap, who came to Shelly's house and convinced them to leave. Harley kept interrupting her with questions, and I finally had to put one hand on his arm.

It didn't help much, though. "Have you lost your damned mind?"

Those kinds of questions weren't helping, in my opinion. "Is he still there?"

"No, he left. Said he had to go back, but he gave me four hundred dollars for food, so take it easy, guys. He also gave us the keys to the house, but said there was a whole corporation of killers out there who know all about us."

"We're coming to get y'all."

"Hold on," I said to Harley. "Let's think this through."

"Tuck's right." Tammy's voice sounded tired. "He told us a lot on the way out here, and even though this might be a bad guy with some folks, I think he's telling us the truth. We're fine, and boys are playing games and we just ordered pizza."

Harley mouthed, "Pizza," at me. We'd been in a gunfight, the bodies we needed for evidence were gone, more bad people were likely after us and our families, I was about to fly a desk for the next ten years if I wasn't flying a bunk down in Huntsville, and they were ordering pizza in a stranger's house in Dallas.

I forced myself to relax. "What phone is this? We didn't recognize the number."

"A landline." For the first time since she called, her voice had some energy to it. "He has an old-school landline here and the boys wanted me to use it when we called Pizza Hut. It's just me and the girls in here right now."

Harley chewed his bottom lip. "So you're telling me this guy is supposed to hit us, and y'all too, and he got a sudden case of religion?"

"I didn't say religion, but he told us that he's from the country, and this corporation's had him do some bad things in the past. It's his raising that made him come to us, because they already knew where we were, get it? Those bad guys that threatened you and Chloe knew where we *were*."

I made eye contact with Harley. "They're tracking us every minute."

Harley took the lead with Tammy. "All right. Stay there right now. You have your pistol?"

"Sure do, and both girls have one of their own. I got them out of your safe."

We'd trained Chloe and Jimma on their shooting skills, and both went through Harley's class. They were as well trained as we could make them.

"I need to tell you something else. Strap says there are a couple of dirty FBI agents on his company's payroll."

"What company?"

"He wouldn't say, but he says the first thing those people do when they begin what they call an operation in a particular area is to pay off some crooked officers. They get dirt on them somehow, and trade their silence for information. Once those guys are on the payroll, then they're squeezed even more and can't get out of it. He says don't trust anybody investigating whatever it is you guys get into."

She paused. "Are you into something?"

I answered. "We sure are."

"Then listen to what I said."

"Fine then." Harley adjusted the drape of his shirt. It would have been a tell that he had a firearm. It was a familiar mannerism we'd learned not to ignore when a criminal was unconsciously concerned that the pistol they were carrying either printed against the material, or they were afraid the handle or butt was sticking out.

I was wearing my badge, and Harley had his retirement shield hanging from his shirt pocket. We'd convinced the sheriff and his deputies not to take our guns when they arrived, and they wanted them pretty badly, but since Harley was no longer officially on duty, he wanted to keep his firearm off their minds. I also reminded him that a black bag full of all kinds of weapons was in the bed of my truck, but right then wasn't the time.

Some of the tension went out of Harley's face. He squinted into the distance as if Tammy was looking right at him. "One little inkling that something's wrong, one dog that barks and then immediately quits, one little feeling of uneasiness, and y'all get in a safe place and shoot anything that comes through a door without sliding a badge under first. You hear me? We're gonna take care of this here, and then we'll come get you."

"What are you guys taking care of there? Are you all right?"

Harley raised an eyebrow and I shook my head. Tammy was operating on a woman's intuition that something was wrong, likely from the tone of our voices, but she didn't need to know what we'd just been through.

I was wondering how my daughter was taking all this, and Jimma, too. "Is Chloe listening in?"

"Hard to do on an old rotary phone, why?"

"I'd forgotten. Listen, this is big. Bigger than anything we've ever run into, so be careful."

She gave out a long sigh. "You're not going to tell me anything right now, are you?"

"Nope. Not over this phone."

"It's a burner, isn't it?"

"It is, but that doesn't mean someone hasn't already triangulated it and is listening in. You shouldn't have even said where you were."

"I had to tell you something." Her voice rose in fear, anger, and frustration.

I put a little water on the coals. "You did what you thought was right, and I feel better knowing where y'all are, now that you left Shelly's house. Just hang in there for a little while longer until you see us."

"We will. I don't like being alone in this, but we'll do what we have to."

I turned away so Harley could say goodbye to his wife. There wasn't any long emotional *I love you*. Those weren't in him. "Be careful."

He hung up and looked over the bed of my truck and at the crowd of men either working the crime scene, or standing around in groups, occasionally turning an eye toward us since we were probably part of the conversation.

"I'm headed to Dallas the minute we get out of here."

"I'm with you, little brother."

"You have a plan?"

"Yeah, get to the girls and then decide what to do."

One of the last people to still wear a watch, Harley checked the time. "We have a couple of hours of daylight since it don't get dark until damn near nine."

"Then let's get there early."

He nodded at the sheriff, who'd taken over the scene. "Think he's gonna let us go?"

"He's gonna have to." I dialed my supervisor. "Jimmy, I have a long story to tell you, but first I'm gonna give this phone to the local sheriff and let you explain why he has to let me go right now, without questions."

A long sigh came through the speaker.

"What happened? I need to know that first."

I walked toward the river to relay the events of the past two hours. "And we have an informant who tells us there's a distinct possibility that at least one of the FBI agents here, and possibly a local officer on the scene, may be dirty. We have to trust this guy to protect our families."

"The whole world isn't on the take, Tuck."

"But the one or two who are make me suspicious. I can't take that chance with my daughter, and Harley feels the same way. Hang on."

I caught Harley's attention and we watched a member of the local volunteer fire department come running up the two-track leading down to the bottoms. He was out of breath when he reached the sheriff and his deputies. As highway patrol officers and two constables gathered around the group, I knew something else had happened.

"Jimmy, I hate to ask you this, but I'm gonna need you here to run block for me." I went back to explaining the situation to my supervisor.

When I finished, I could tell he was already moving. "It won't be fast."

"Where are you?"

"Just finished a meeting here in North Dallas. Be there in an hour and a half."

"Run your lights and make it faster."

Constable Rich Lawrence stepped up to me and Harley. I'd known him for years. "They followed their little heeler down that way to a pretty deep draw. The Crawfords' bodies are back there."

Harley licked his lips. "I figured they were somewhere around here."

Constable Lawrence swallowed. "Yeah, and the Texas Rangers are on their way. Said to hold you boys, but I heard what y'all told the sheriff over there. You two need to get shed of this place before the big boys get here."

"They'll come a-huntin' us if we do." Harley had that dangerous twinkle in his eye, and I saw that we were leaving in a matter of minutes. "They're not gonna stop me from going to protect my wife."

I had to say it out loud, for my own peace of mind. "You'll go to jail."

"And you're gonna get fired, I 'magine."

"Only if I leave."

"I have an idea, then."

"What's that?"

Harley turned, watching the reaction of the other officers grouped around us. "I go on ahead, and you stay here to straighten this out. Maybe you can talk to the rangers, and without telling them where Tammy and the kids are, you can get them to understand what kind of mess we're in. With Jimmy doing the same when he gets here, you might have some luck."

I'd forgotten Jimmy was still on the phone in my hand. "Are you hearing any of this?"

His voice came through. "Might work. I'm gonna call a friendly judge I know and run something by him. Maybe with the three of us working together, we can get you out of there pretty quick."

"I believe it's our only shot. It's like when we were working narcotics. They knew *what* we were doing, but not *how*. Maybe that's the way you play it. We broke no laws here, and clearly it was self-defense."

"No bodies, though." The constable toed the ground. "None but that couple over there. I'm not saying anybody here's gonna think you killed the Crawfords, but I'm afraid you boys are gonna need a good defense lawyer in any case."

Harley took a step away and looked around. "Well, all these bullet holes in everything, and the four blood puddles will tell them what happened."

"They should. They'll at least take your gun and badge, even if you're not in cuffs."

It felt like Harley and I were backed into a corner. "We have plenty more pistols at home in the safes."

Harley's eyes flicked to the sheriff, then the drive. "Okay. I'm gone. If they don't cuff and stuff you, how're you gonna get home?"

"I'll take Tuck," Constable Lawrence said. "But first I believe I'm gonna go over there and stand so's the sheriff's back is to the drive, and maybe he won't notice your truck pulling out."

Chapter 36

In the soft light of early dusk, Strap left his charges behind, turned right out of the Craftsman's driveway, and steered toward the Dallas skyline. It was still hot but not as oppressive as under the blazing Texas sun.

Though heat radiated from the concrete sidewalks and the western sides of brick houses, the softer light also had a psychological effect, making people think the temperature had dropped. Already, walkers and joggers were making an appearance as the neighborhood's residents got their exercise in before it became full dark. The Swiss Avenue oasis wasn't a fort or protected area, and some of Dallas's meanest neighborhoods were only blocks away.

After a mile, Strap turned south near Baylor Hospital's towers, past dangerous-looking apartments and rundown houses, and headed for I-45, which intersected I-30, a fairly straight shot to the town of Mt. Vernon, and then northeast to the Red River Lodge.

The eight-lane interstate wound through the Trinity River bottoms due south of the city, a thick, still almost impenetrable tangle of woods that periodically flooded in heavy rains. The great forest was full of mosquitoes, wild hogs, deer, and any number of buried or discarded human bodies.

Using his indicator, he merged into the building traffic and onto the highway that was almost picturesque in the late evening light. He crossed one of the many bridges above the river where a single kayaker paddled downstream and away from civilization.

Uncomfortably late and anxious to get back to the motel, Strap resisted the urge to call Pierson and check in. He'd never liked the man, and lately he'd been puffing up, acting as if he was more than a technician for the team.

Pierson wanted to be tough, a bad man to deal with, and considered himself smarter than anyone else. That's why his cowboy charade failed. It was the one charge given to him by Mr. Cross to make his bones, and he couldn't do it.

Strap was barely four miles east when a silver Range Rover drifted over into his lane without signaling. Dallas traffic being what it was, failure to change lanes without a signal was a weak violation, and he wouldn't have paid much attention had the Toyota pickup in the lane to his left not matched his speed and hung there, just over his shoulder.

Raised in the country, Strap hated city traffic, and it was all he could do to endure Houston traffic on a daily basis when they were near headquarters. Dallas was no different. This guy on the left frosted his flakes, though. He always hated for someone to stick to his flanks on either side but especially in the hammer lane. That one was for passing, and it irked him to no end that the man neither accelerated to pass, nor slowed to get behind him.

"Get out of there, you idiot."

To take his mind off the irritation, Strap punched the radio alive and glanced in his rearview mirror. The traffic wasn't bad, but it was starting to clot up as people went out for dinner, or traveled that stretch of interstate to avoid the usual tangle of traffic and accidents on I-30 that ran right along the southern edge of Dallas proper, parallel to the highway he was following.

A Honda Odyssey with one weak headlight followed. He checked his left flank. Yep. The moron was still there. The only lane that was open was on his right, and seeing few cars in front of him, Strap turned on his indicator and changed lanes.

He stiffened when all three cars around him did the same thing in unison.

He was bracketed, and the only thing on his right was the shoulder, then the darkening woods beyond. It was a classic maneuver designed to separate a vehicle from traffic before launching some kind of action.

Eyes to the rearview mirror. The Odyssey closed the distance.

Back to the lefthand mirror. The Toyota truck was in exactly the same place as before.

Up ahead. The Range Rover slowed, and the distance was closing.

Behind their cluster of cars, traffic was starting to back up as impatient drivers who typically exceeded the speed limit found themselves trapped against the rolling roadblock.

In the movies or on television, the hero always produces a pistol and checks to see if it's loaded by pulling the slide back. There was no need for all that showy and useless nonsense. Strap kept his Sig P320 loaded, with a round in the chamber at all times. That single second it took to go through such a ridiculous task might be the difference between getting out of a situation alive, or not.

Heart pounding and not understanding what was happening, Strap adjusted the seat belt so it wouldn't interfere with drawing his weapon. He took a deep breath and jerked the wheel hard to the right. The Suburban responded, though the vehicle's weight made it feel as if he were about to lose control. The moment he was on the shoulder, he slammed on the brakes and all three cars shot ahead.

Horns blew in fear or anger. Innocent drivers hit their brakes, uncertain about what was happening. Without hesitation, he stomped the accelerator and whipped back into the right lane before the traffic could close up around him. Pressing even harder on the accelerator, he muscled his way into the next lane, eliciting an even longer barrage of horns from those already driving too close for comfort.

Another hard maneuver to the left as brake lights up ahead flickered like fireflies when the drivers of the rolling roadblock struggled to respond as the lanes closed up behind them. The sound of crumpling hoods and front and rear fenders came from different directions as drivers overreacted. Puffs of dust knocked loose from the impacts looked like smoke in the dim light.

Using innocent and unsuspecting drivers as a shield, Strap hit his brakes. Those in line behind him stacked up one after another with soft impacts. He hit the gas again, while cars in the other two lanes zigzagged left and right to avoid being involved in dozens of little and large wrecks happening around him.

And there it was, exactly what he'd been looking for. An opening in the line as someone behind slammed on their brakes and slid sideways, blocking two lanes and creating even more chaos. He threaded the needle through a maze of maneuvering vehicles, and up ahead freedom availed itself as an off-ramp appeared.

The three vehicles that blocked him in were well beyond taking the ramp as he stood on the accelerator and rocketed up to the intersection. Breathing hard and exhilarated, he turned right and headed due south. Evasive maneuver. He turned right again, and then back around to regain I-20 going in the opposite direction.

"What just happened?" he spoke aloud.

His new spur-of-the-moment plan was to return to I-45, head north, and pick up I-30, which would lead east, eventually intersecting his intended route where he could drive though the country as fast as possible to rejoin his team.

Traffic was light in this side of the tangle he'd created and he leaned back in the seat, letting out a long-held breath. Half a minute later, the Toyota pickup passed on the left and he glanced over out of habit. Two men rose up in the back and shouldered rifles with a distinctively familiar shape. They opened up on full automatic with AK-47s, spraying his car with lead.

Strap stomped his brakes, leaving behind a cloud of white smoke as he cut the wheel. The heavy Suburban slewed right, down the steep embankment toward the line of dark woods. He managed to maintain control to the bottom and slid to a stop only feet from trees that would have barely registered the impact. Two more vehicles left the road, and bounced toward his SUV to join the Toyota.

Strap was out in an instant. He ducked around the front of his vehicle as the Range Rover angled in too fast on the steep incline and crashed into the Toyota, tearing off fenders, chrome, and plastic trim. Two men flew from the truck's bed, landing like tossed dolls.

The light was almost gone, and all he could see were figures stumbling out of open doors. Those thrown over the Toyota's side rose slowly, taking stock of themselves. Uncertain what to do, others stood beside the Odyssey that had barely missed being a part of the collision. Two with clear heads took cover, and those were the lucky ones.

Using his hood as a shooting bench, Strap took advantage of their disorientation and opened up with his Sig, taking his time and picking out targets. Screams filled the air and shouts of terror erupted and bounced off the trees.

Only a couple fired back, but their shots went wild, ricocheting off into the trees. Shaken men rolled from the SUVs and scrambled to cover on the back side of the cars.

Strap fired until the slide locked back. At least two of his bullets found flesh. He dropped the empty mag and stuffed a fresh one into the well. He hosed the wrecked vehicles, shattering windshields, punching holes in their radiators, and forcing his attackers to duck.

The last of the 9-mm rounds chattered through. He dropped the mag, slapped in another fresh one, and making sure they were still in hiding behind whatever cover they could find, Strap disappeared into the blackness of the great Trinity Forest.

Chapter 37

Chloe and Jimma sat on the edge of the queen-size bed in the upstairs bedroom they had selected as theirs. Instead of taking separate rooms, the teenagers were more comfortable sleeping together. Though the hundred-year-old house had updated wiring, plumbing, and a state-of-the-art HVAC system, it was still almost uncomfortably warm on the second level.

Each of the girls had a revolver lying on the nightstands bracketing the bed. In the months since their kidnapping, Harley had put them through extensive urban defense training and both were more than proficient in firearms and hand-to-hand combat.

Even so, they weren't yet fully trained to defend themselves against a grown man who might get hold of the diminutive pair. All of this was fairly new to Jimma, while Chloe was raised around it and slightly more confident.

Kevin lay curled up on the floor at the foot of the bed. He usually stuck close to the boys, who shared a room with Tammy, but for some reason known only to the dog, he wouldn't let the girls out of his sight in the old house.

Every door on that floor was closed, just in case an intruder managed to make entrance. Uncertainty about which room they were in would hopefully slow down a bad guy, or guys, if there were more than one. Maybe the opening and closing process would squeak a hinge, or click the old hardware.

The antique doorknob had an old-fashioned keyhole Jimma had been eyeing for some time. She rose and padded on bare feet across the polished hardwood floor into the bathroom. Both girls kicked off their flip-flops as soon as they walked into the room.

"At least you could close the door." Chloe looked around the room and felt her back pocket, a motion she'd already repeated fifty times since they entered the house.

Nope. Her phone still wasn't there and for a teenager who constantly had one in her hand or pocket, it felt as if a part of her was missing.

"I wasn't using the bathroom." Jimma held up a piece of toilet paper. She crossed to the door and stuffed it into the keyhole. "We don't want anyone peeking through when we do, though."

That done, she closed the Venetian blinds over both windows, ensuring that no one could look in from the street.

As soon as she was done, Chloe came behind and angled the slats so she could look outside without being seen. "You know I can't stand it when all the blinds are closed. It's like a cave in here. The only people who keep their curtains drawn all the time are probably doing something they're not supposed to."

She needed her mom, not Tammy and Jimma, though they were family. A rising irritation threatened to take over, and when it did, she was afraid she wouldn't be able to stop the words forming on the edge of her tongue.

"Truth. The blinds were always down in Atchley's trailer."

"I thought it was your mom's."

"It was, until that creep showed up. He had a fit when the curtains were open, even in *my* room if I was in there alone." She suddenly looked drawn. "I guess you're right about why they were always closed. He didn't want anyone to see when he came in at night."

The feeling of irritation Chloe was biting down faded in an instant with the thought of what Jimma had endured at the hands of her stepdad. They all had trauma in their lives, and everyone had to deal with it in their own way.

Jimma's fingers danced over her bare legs, down to the handmade quilt, and back again to the hem of her shorts. She always showed the same nervous mannerisms when they talked about her abuse by her mom's common-law husband who was now rotting in a Huntsville prison cell.

"You know, I'd enjoy this place any other time." Jimma looked around the room as if seeing it for the first time. "Do you think Harley and your dad'll get here tonight?" It was too soon to bring herself to call Harley *Dad,* or anything else.

"Knowing them, they're probably on the way right now." Chloe drew back from the window as a white Lincoln Navigator passed. She *harrumphed* to herself, knowing there was no way a driver could see inside.

Jimma swung her legs on the bed and leaned back against a drift of pillows. "I can't take much more of this."

She looked small and frail to Chloe, who sometimes felt that she was a chubby giant next to her friend. It was all perception, because the slender, well-proportioned teenager was the envy of most girls in their high school.

From Chloe's angle, half of Jimma's face was hidden by a

pink pillow. Chloe grinned at the one eye she could see. "You're tougher than anybody I know."

"How's that?"

"We both know what you went through, and then us together up in Oklahoma."

"Well, you're tough too. I never knew a girl that could be hit with a man's fist as hard as he could swing and still wake up."

"It took over an hour." Chloe touched her cheekbone with the tips of her fingers. It was weeks before the soreness went away from Atchley's violent attack.

"I wish there was a TV in here, at least. He could've put one of those old tube styles in there. We had one in the trailer. No one could listen in through that."

Chloe joined her on the bed and they lay side by side. "Yep. He could have set one on the dresser there. They have those new antennas you can use to watch local TV. At least that'd give us something to do."

"Are you scared?"

Chloe reached out and took Jimma's hand in her own. "I sure am, but Tammy knows what to do."

A joyous shriek came through the closed window and Chloe was on the floor in an instant, cracking the blinds so she could see out into the front yard. Awakened by the boys, Kevin put both feet on the windowsill and pushed the blinds out of the way with his nose.

The light was almost gone, but there was enough for Chloe to see Matt and Danny on opposite ends of the yard, surrounded by hundreds of flickering fireflies. Danny threw an object in the air that arced up and came down to bury half its length only feet from Matt who raced forward to pick up a gigantic dart.

"That was close! My turn!"

He threw one in Danny's direction. It arced high and Danny had to dodge out of the way when the huge dart barely missed him. "Hey, watch it!"

Kevin gave a soft woof as Chloe shot out of the room and yanked the door open. "Tammy!"

Chapter 38

Harley drove like a bat out of hell toward Dallas, accelerating Tucker's truck to over ninety on the straightaways when there were no lights ahead. There was always the possibility that a deer or hog could dart out in front of him, but he needed to get to Tammy and the kids.

He came over a hill and encountered the one thing he hoped to avoid. A highway patrol car running radar. The state trooper hit his lights as Harley passed.

"Dammit!"

He immediately let off the accelerator and was already pulling off to the side when the trooper shot off the shoulder and in behind him. They both came to a stop with plenty of distance between the vehicles and the highway. Harley turned on the inside lights and plucked his badge from the back pocket of his jeans.

Knowing the procedure, he remained still, watching the trooper step out, approach the truck, and place the palm of one hand on the truck's left bed side. Cautious, he glanced into the back, advanced, and checked the back seat.

He reached the open driver's window. "Evening, sir. I clocked you at eighty-five here in a seventy zone. Can I see your license?"

Harley held up his retirement badge. "You're gonna want to hear this."

The trooper sighed. "I probably don't."

The man's face changed from impassive concern to disbelief, to outright fury as Harley explained the who, what, when, where, and why he was racing to Dallas. "I just got a call about you. Fled a crime scene."

"I wouldn't call it *fled*."

"Snow. I heard of you and your brother."

Not wanting to engage in pleasantries, Harley waited, knowing the man was weighing his options. "I've already called this in."

"I know."

"Not even a warning ticket will fix this."

"I know."

The trooper stepped back. "I'm gonna radio ahead, tell 'em you're coming through. That'll get you to Collin County, but then you're on your own."

"I owe you one."

"You bet your ass you do."

Chapter 39

Strap was lucky. Had it been a wet year, he would have bogged down in the bottoms made up of sloughs, swampy areas, huge mudholes, and meandering streams and cuts leading to the river. With the drought firmly in place, the Trinity wasn't much more than frightening sludge moving at a trickle.

Few of Dallas's residents living in apartments and houses only a mile away knew there was an entire ecological habitat of creatures that sang all night long to the steady drone of cars on the elevated highway bridge. Tree frogs, crickets, owls, and other night birds filled the dry air with clicks and calls and songs designed to attract a mate.

The darkness was Strap's friend and provided much-needed cover as he worked his way north. His days of hunting with the kids he grew up with in Nacogdoches returned as soon as he set foot on the dirt trail. Never completely out of earshot from highway traffic, he used the roars and hisses of tires on pavement to maintain direction. There was enough moonlight to allow him to avoid thorny thickets and tripping hazards.

He was familiar with the woods and moved through rough

terrain with ease. The game trail he followed was wide and flat in most places, packed by thousands of hooves belonging mostly to hogs, but some whitetail deer as well. Gritting his teeth against the mosquitoes swarming around his sweaty face, he pushed on.

More than once he heard large animals crashing away at his approach. He almost ran into a sounder of hogs rooting up the forest floor. They scattered in all directions, piglets squealing and adults grunting in annoyance and fear.

The trees occasionally thinned out enough to see streetlights off to his left, illuminating the miles-long bridge over the bottoms. The glow from downtown Dallas was constant through the leaves. Torn between wishing he could get up there on smooth pavement and glad for the cover, Strap jogged as much as he could when the trail was clear.

He finally came upon a railroad track and made better time jogging between the rails. Covered in sweat and dirt, he followed the tracks to a four-lane bridge crossing overhead. Using both hands and feet on the riprap leading upward, he scrambled up and paused, evaluating his position.

A late-model sedan passed on one of the last rural roads that close to Dallas, its headlights bright in his eyes, which had become accustomed to darkness. He faded back into the shadows of the bushes and trees to watch it pass. The next one that came by caused him to squint, but seeing was easier once his eyes adjusted to artificial light.

He knew better than to try and wave anyone down. No one was going to pick up a stranger on that road. It was too dangerous and a quick call to 911 by a suspicious driver would have ended badly. He'd have to come up with a way to get into a car.

The road was bracketed by shallow ditches bordered by trees

and thick undergrowth. Walking west toward an industrial glow, he stuck to the highway's shoulder, and each time a pair of headlights approached, Strap stepped into the trees.

The glow became distinct as he realized dozens of sodium lights lit a salvage yard. He hoped to find someone working late. Strap wasn't a carjacker, but he wasn't against stealing a car at gunpoint. Like the urban wilderness he'd just left, it was survival of the fittest at that point.

Those two words, *urban wilderness,* almost made him smile. Cities and towns were a different kind of wilderness, full of humans doing their best to survive. In his world, the world of ChemShale and people like Mr. Cross, they were the alpha predators, and he didn't like being prey one damned bit.

Luck was against him when he saw the scrapyard's dark office and empty parking lot. Needing a breather, he stopped near a cluster of cedar trees that grew thick and full. Inside the growth, little sunlight reached the ground during the day and the trees formed a crude shelter hidden from the road. A kid's hideout anywhere else.

Wiping sweat out of his eyes, he ducked into the natural sanctuary and took a knee on soft dead needles. For the first time since the attack on the highway, he relaxed and rested. Sleep almost washed over him and he shook himself awake. He doubted daylight would reveal his shape in the enclosure, but staying there all day would have been miserable, thirsty, and would have put the people at his house in danger. He had to get back to Swiss Avenue and get them out.

Shaking himself alert, he saw another set of headlights approaching.

Planting his feet and gripping the rifle, one way or another, that was going to be his ride out.

Chapter 40

"He's already given you a statement, and it's late." Jimmy Meeks was sitting on the tailgate of his truck. Two Honda generators hummed quietly, providing electricity for four freestanding lights that flooded the scene enough to make it look like a movie location.

A pair of Texas Rangers stood between us and the gaggle of lawmen who'd arrived on the scene before them. I'd watched the hierarchy of investigations change through the years whenever outside agencies arrive at a crime scene. It was the same there. Local law enforcement was in charge until the rangers arrived, and I had to go through the same questions again.

They went over our part in the shooting with glacial speed, and I'd repeated my story so many times I was about ready to clam up.

Jimmy had my back as usual and he finally slid off the tailgate. "Guys, you have his statement and I have it in writing. He's concerned about the safety of his family, and I want to let him go be with them."

We hadn't told the rangers that Harley and I sent Tammy and

the kids away, or that an unknown individual had moved them to another location. Following protocol, they would have gotten on the radio or their phones and informed their superiors. If that had happened, the chances of the bad guys intercepting the conversations would have multiplied tenfold.

The rangers exchanged glances. The older man who had taken the lead on questioning shrugged. "I can't see a reason why not."

The other addressed Meeks. "Agent Meeks, you'll put him on desk duty…"

"…pending the outcome of the investigation," Jimmy Meeks finished for him.

"That's right."

Relieved that we could leave, I started for Jimmy's truck when two more unmarked cars pulled up the drive. Doors opened and men wearing FBI jackets emerged. Jimmy slapped me on the shoulder. "We're getting out of here. Don't make eye contact."

I knew what he was doing, hiding in plain sight. There were a lot of people, and the feds had no idea what I looked like. It was time to go. With their arrival, the hierarchy of investigators elevated, and I wouldn't have been surprised if the CIA didn't show up.

Something similar had happened years earlier. Harley and I were working a case when we got a report that a high school was evacuated because of a terrorist attack.

We were deep undercover, doing our best to get enough evidence to put away a team that was selling drugs to schoolkids. A new player arrived, undercutting the first group, and it became a fight for territory and we were determined to bust them all.

A call had gone out from the school that someone had released some kind of gas into a classroom, causing students and staff to become sick and pass out from the fumes. By the time we arrived, both fire and the local PD were there. Harley checked in with the police chief and brought him up to speed on what we were doing while I drifted over with another undercover officer I recognized to watch.

Campus administrators transported over thirty kids and two staff members to area hospitals. Everything seemed to be in hand and the school dismissed the remainder of the kids. Three hours after the incident was reported, the FBI showed up and took control of the scene.

Officers, paramedics, and firefighters tromped in and out of the building from the outset, but the stone-faced feds ordered everyone away and donned hazmat suits. They went inside with suitcases full of test equipment.

The cops rolled their eyes, the firemen left, and Harley waved me over. "We're done here. It's nothing."

"What's nothing?"

"This wasn't the dealers we were after. A student in one of the upstairs classes started choking on a sandwich they'd snuck out of their locker and someone sent for the school nurse. She's pregnant and tried to run. Her blood pressure spiked and she passed out, and the rest of what happened was made up by kids who wanted to leave, and maybe even a little mass hysteria."

Shaking my head, I thumbed in the direction of the police gathered around a spokesperson. "I heard they found something in the trash that was supposed to have released the gas."

"It was an empty plastic bottle, and their instruments picked up on the chemicals in the fake fruit drink."

We left, and this new incident was on the verge of repeating itself when the feebs showed up once again, hours late and after everyone was finished and tired.

Jimmy Meeks and I split up and climbed into the cab as some of the agents took stock of the scene. Others spoke with the rangers, who turned their backs on us in professional courtesy. We knew they were giving us an out, and we took advantage of it.

I looked over at my supervisor as I closed the door. "If we stay here, it'll be morning before we can leave."

"We're not staying." He started the engine.

"You're gonna get in as much trouble as me and Harley."

"I don't answer to the feds and neither do you."

He pulled out onto the highway, vanishing into the dark. I glanced back to be sure the new arrivals weren't following. All that those guys knew was that two cowboys left at the same time they arrived.

Jimmy dropped me off at my dark house forty-five minutes later. The single pole light beside the barn threw harsh light over the cattle pens, the side yard, and the barn.

I unpinned my badge and held it out, along with my service weapon. He glanced at it and a slight grin curled one corner of his mouth. "You better keep those."

"I'm on desk duty."

"They said that. Not me." He stuck out his hand and we shook. "Stay out of the news."

"I'll do my best." I slapped his hood, and my supervisor circled the drive and left.

Disabling the alarm, I gathered up my warbag in the silent house and loaded it into the Suburban.

It was time to get away from all the investigative parties in the area and get after those who'd killed people and threatened my family.

Chapter 41

More relaxed than he should have been only moments before carjacking a ride, Strap watched a pickup slow on the highway, come to a stop on the shoulder, then accelerate past where he hid in the cedars and whip into the scrapyard's parking lot.

Strap whirled toward the place where the Toyota stopped, pistol in hand. There was an open gap in the trees, wide enough for him to see three armed men coming down the side of the road. Lit from the glow of the security lights, they made perfect targets.

"Dammit!"

He'd allowed himself to get trapped inside the thick cedars growing beside a chain-link fence topped with concertina wire, and an open four-lane road. It was the perfect kill zone for those after him.

Without hesitation, for they'd brought the fight to him, Strap fired twice, dropping two of them before the third ducked for cover. An empty water bottle crackled under his foot and two men behind the Toyota opened up at the sound. A hail of bullets cut through the green cedars and he dropped flat.

His only option was the one thing they didn't expect. Most of today's predators and opportunistic criminals expect their victims to give up, cower, or run. None of the three options appealed to him, and Strap burst through the trees. Providing his own cover fire, the big guy exploded into view.

What they didn't know was that his shots were directed *over* the Toyota. A pickup full of bullet holes wouldn't do him any good. He needed a vehicle that wouldn't attract attention. Racing around the front of the truck, he caught the driver and one terror-stricken employee of the company waiting for the shooting to stop so they could finish killing them.

Their rifles came up, but it was too late.

Strap slid to a stop and neutralized them both. He snatched up one of the dead men's AKs and threw lead at the one man left on the opposite side of the cedars. He kicked the other rifle away and patted the nearest corpse's pockets, looking for the key fob. It wasn't there. Rising just enough to look through the cab, he checked for the fifth man, who was still out of sight.

He checked the other man's pockets for the key fob, but again came up empty. Anxiety rising in his throat, Strap yanked the door open and leaned inside to find the fob in the console's cup holder.

Throwing the hot rifle muzzle down on the passenger floorboard, he squeezed behind the steering wheel and had to waste valuable seconds adjusting the seat far enough back that he could fit into the space. The engine was still running. The last man still hadn't appeared.

Strap grabbed the shift knob in the center console and slammed it into gear, throwing pebbles into the air as the tires squalled on the pavement.

Once away from the scrapyard, he wondered how they'd found him so fast.

Chapter 42

Watching the navigation system in the dash of Tuck's pickup, Harley turned onto Swiss Avenue and drove well under the speed limit until he reached the address Tammy gave him. Any other time he would have enjoyed the well-lit stately old homes in what some called the Grand Experiment, but right then the only thing on his mind was to gather up her and the kids and leave.

Antique streetlights provided enough illumination to chase most of the shadows back under trees and into manicured shrubs hiding the houses' pier-and-beam foundations.

Instead of stopping in front of the house, he continued past, giving the classic two-story Craftsman a good look. Both floors were lit as if every light in the house was on, though the blinds were all closed. The porch looked inviting, and he realized how tired he was. It would be great to sit there in the swing and have a drink, with Tammy snuggled up close and the boys playing in the yard.

And Jimma curled up in a chair with her phone.

He reached the end of the block and turned around at the closed post office. Retracing his route, he drew close to the address, and pulled to the curb one house down to watch the street.

Nothing moved in the warm darkness as he shifted into park to keep the air conditioner going at full speed. A tabby cat crossed the street and ran under a car. In the distance, sirens wailed and a plane circled high above, its lights flashing.

Harley opened his phone and dialed up his brother. Instead of hearing through the tiny speaker, the rings came through the Ram's sound system. Harley dropped the phone and reached for the volume knob when Tuck answered.

Tucker's voice was so loud Harley jumped. "Where are you? Everything all right?"

"I was gonna ask you the same thing." He cranked down the volume. "I'm here at the house where that guy brought Tammy, but haven't gone in yet."

"Does it all look quiet?"

"Like a TV neighborhood. Glad to see you're not in jail."

"Got out just in time, about five seconds after the FBI showed up."

Harley checked all three mirrors. A man on his side of the street approached, walking a little dust mop of a dog. "They always screw things up. You on the way?"

"Just leaving the house. Be there as soon as I can."

"We need to get away from here." Harley scanned the silent street. Realizing his headlights were the brightest thing in the neighborhood, he flicked them off. "I'm not waiting."

"Didn't expect you to. Load 'em up and get gone. I can meet you anywhere."

"That's the problem; right now I'm not sure where to take 'em."

It was silent for a moment while Tucker considered their options. "You remember where we used to fish with Uncle Bill?"

"That cabin..." Harley paused. "Where you caught those fish the otters stole from you."

When they were teenagers, Harley and Tuck fished the Mountain Fork River in southeastern Oklahoma with their favorite uncle, who had a cabin set back in the woods. Pushing eighty, he still lived there alone, spending most of his time with a fly rod in one hand and a beer in the other.

"Yeah." Harley watched the man and his dog pass the truck. The dash lights, nav system, and radio were bright enough to read by.

Curious, the man in shorts and a Hawaiian shirt slowed and peered in the window while the dog sniffed the grass. Not feeling especially friendly, Harley threw up a quick wave and checked the driver's side mirror to see an empty street.

"Meet me there."

"I guess that's as good a place as any, but it's a long way for you."

"It's a long way from everything. That's just what we need."

Their conversation was interrupted when the guy stepped off the sidewalk and rapped his knuckles on the passenger window. "Hey, buddy."

"Hang on a minute, Tuck. Some neighborhood guy's at the window." When Harley flicked the switch to roll the glass down, a wave of hot air filled the cab. "Help you?"

"You can't park here."

Tucker's slow sigh came through the speakers.

"I'm not parked," Harley explained. "I'm stopped. Hear it? The engine's still running."

"And polluting the air with unnecessary exhaust."

"It's safer than driving and talking on the phone at the same time. The emissions are still the same."

"Our neighborhood watch prefers that people don't sit in their cars in front of houses that aren't theirs, especially at night."

"How do you know this isn't my house?"

The guy straightened and jerked a thumb across the sidewalk behind him. "Because I live there."

"You know, if I was a bad guy, I don't believe it would be safe for you to come up here after dark, knocking on windows and announcing where you live to an irritable stranger."

The man's eyes widened. "I suggest you leave."

The front porch lights went on behind him and a woman in workout clothes stepped out. "Harry? What's going on?"

Harley went back to his conversation with Tuck. "Can you believe this?"

"I hear."

The man pointed a finger at Harley. "Leave now before I call the police."

The situation amplified when the woman came off the steps. She held a phone in one hand. "You want me to call 911, baby?"

Flabbergasted, Harley did his best to remain calm. "Y'all, I just pulled over to talk to my brother."

Hawaiian Shirt turned to his wife. "He won't leave. He's arguing with me."

The woman, whose name had to be Karen, rushed up to her husband, held out the phone. "That's fine. I'm recording this! I see you as clear as day."

"Lucky for you. Get my good side."

Her voice rose when she rounded the front of the truck. "I'm filming your license tag so the police will know who you are! This is private property! You have no business here."

In response, Harley flicked on his bright lights, startling her.

She squeaked and jumped back onto the well-manicured and watered parkway.

Her husband also produced a phone. "I'm taking pictures of you."

Sensing that the couple was upset, the little dust mop began yapping.

With the situation spinning out of control, Harley considered badging them, but that would open another can of worms.

"Fine then. I'm going."

The woman rejoined her husband on the sidewalk. "What are you doing out here, casing our house! This is private property."

"You've already told me that. I wasn't casing anything. Just looking for an address."

The dog kept yapping as the guy used the flashlight on his phone to illuminate the back seat of the truck. "Don't tell me you're delivering boxes this time of night."

Harley'd had enough. "Look, Karen, I said I'm going."

"Hey, buddy, don't call my wife Karen."

"I was talking to *you*."

She punched at the phone in her hand as exterior lights across the street came on. "Hey, smart mouth. I'm calling the police right now. You need to stay there."

"Dad!" the Dodge rocked as Danny jumped up onto the truck's running board and shouted through the closed window. "We've been waiting for you!"

Harley turned to the now silent couple. "Thanks for letting everyone in the neighborhood know I was here. You can go back into your house now."

Chapter 43

Despite the hour, traffic was still heavy when Strap pulled back onto the interstate heading north into downtown Dallas. Lights flickered on the screen of a cell phone and reflected in the cracked windshield. He plucked it off the dash to clear his field of vision and pitched the useless device out the window.

One less thing they could use to find him.

There was no doubt about it. That three-vehicle maneuver back there on I-20 was a coordinated company effort. How did they know he was at the scrapyard? He could have come out of the bottoms anywhere.

It couldn't have been dumb luck. There were too many streets and roads for it to be a coincidence. The company didn't operate that way, and they wouldn't waste time driving around in the hopes of running across one man on foot in the southern part of Dallas.

For sure it wasn't anyone who knew his personality and training who figured out where he was. He didn't recognize either of the men he'd killed beside the Toyota. The others were too far away in the darkness to be more than shapes.

Tucking in behind a white Taurus, he drove north, back toward his house on Swiss Avenue. There he'd have a fresh change of clothes and ammo.

Keeping an eye out for lights of suspicious cars, he flicked on KRLD radio, a local twenty-four-hour news station. They regularly provided a traffic report, and he wanted to know what was going on behind and ahead.

Dallas traffic is never predictable, and half a mile farther, he came to another clot of cars that slowed and stopped. Resisting the urge to hammer the steering wheel, Strap again adjusted the pistol under the seatbelt and watched a DPD car come up behind him. They were at a complete standstill and the officer's headlights reflected off the rearview mirror into Strap's eyes.

Tense as a coiled water moccasin, he did his best to remain calm. Blue lights came on behind him, and his breath caught. They must have already been looking for the Toyota. There was nowhere to run in the traffic jam. He'd just have to take his chances with an arrest and a good lawyer, one he'd have to pay for, because it was the company that set him up.

He was almost ready to pull over when the cruiser cut right and accelerated past on the shoulder.

Relief washed over Strap, and he settled back. Struggling to breathe normally, he finally relaxed in a herd of stalled cars. There was no way the company could find him, unless it was with a drone attack, and not even they would do that in the middle of Dallas traffic.

His thoughts returned to why and how they were keeping up with him. There was no doubt that Pierson had ratted him out with Mr. Cross, telling him that he'd gone rogue. Using whatever means they had available, they must have tracked him to the house in Gainesville, and then on to his safe house on Swiss.

He could see how they'd do it in one way. Supposedly none of Mr. Cross's SUVs operated without computerized tracking devices. The company's technicians used all their skills to override those devices that come on all new cars, so unless for some unknown suspicion he'd ordered a bug to be placed on the Suburban that Strap drove, it wasn't that.

Up to this point, Strap was a model company man, someone who might have even achieved Mr. Cross's position if and when he moved up or out.

It wasn't his burner phone, and he'd left everything but his rifle with the SUV.

Then how?

He glanced down. The only explanation was something hidden in his clothes. Maybe his belt or shoes, but that could have only been done when he was in the shower. There was no other time anyone would have access to his personal possessions.

In that instance, more than one of his team members might be involved. He wouldn't put it past that smug Pierson.

Strap leaned back in the seat as more cars joined the tangle idling on the bridge. A commercial came on the radio urging listeners to get a Covid booster shot.

That was it.

Nothing was hidden *on* his person. He was carrying it around *inside* his body.

A sick feeling washed over him at the realization of how they were following him so easily. Two years earlier they'd all been ordered to accept Covid vaccinations from a lab retained by the company. To a man they'd all complained that the injection sites hurt more than anyone expected, and they took almost two weeks for the soreness to subside.

Had they all been chipped?

Microbots?

Nanotechnology?

No matter how they did it, they'd be coming again, and his breath caught.

They'd know his destination, because he'd already been there once that day, when he should have been up in Red River County.

The house on Swiss Avenue.

Chapter 44

Bill Sloan and Fred Belk saw flashing lights in the night long before they reached the Crawford Ranch. Half a dozen news vans were parked in the shallow ditches, towers raised to broadcast. Locals were also on the shoulders, talking in small groups.

A deputy sheriff's car was parked across the entrance gate. An officer standing beside the cruiser waved the pickup on. Sloan turned off the highway and rolled down his window. Fred set his open beer into a holder inside the door.

The trooper's face showed irritation when they didn't follow his directions. He held out a hand to stop them. "Can I help you gentlemen?"

Fred answered from the passenger side of the pickup. "What's going on?"

This was way too close to the law, but Sloan didn't show any signs of nervousness. "We work for Mr. Crawford. What happened?"

The officer's demeanor changed. "Names, please."

They told him and he nodded. He took a step back and spoke into the microphone clipped onto the epaulet on his shoulder. A male voice came through, clearing them to advance.

The officer waved them on. "They'll tell you when you get down there. Give me a second to move my car."

Fred took in the well-lit scene as the trooper pulled his car a few feet forward. "This is bad."

"Take it easy. They're not here for us. This is a helluva lot for a few stolen cattle that we may or may not know anything about."

Sloan squeezed behind the deputy's Chevy Tahoe and crept down the long two-track drive. Attendants were loading two bodies into an ambulance when they reached the house. Fred drained his beer and dropped the empty onto the floorboard. They quit talking when another officer directed them to park on the grass near a cluster of other sedans and trucks.

He waved for them to get out. "You boys work for Mr. Crawford?"

"We do."

He pointed at a cluster of Texas Rangers and men wearing FBI windbreakers. "Talk to them."

"Which one?"

He chuckled. "Any other time, I'd say the man with the biggest hat, but right now you'll have to figure that out for yourselves."

Confused and more than a little nervous, Sloan heard a bark and his blue heeler, Maggie, shot out of the barn and made a beeline for the two ranch hands. He knelt and rubbed her ears, then roughed her up on the sides the way she liked it. Her hair was tacky and stiff. He examined his hand and held it out to Fred.

Seeing them with the dog, one of the Rangers separated from the group and waved them over. "Which one of you is Sloan?"

"I am."

"You're Belk."

Fred nodded. "What happened?"

"I hate to tell you boys, but the Crawfords have been murdered."

Shocked, Sloan absently rubbed his sticky hand on the legs of his jeans. "Why? How come somebody killed 'em?"

"Can't say." The ranger watched their reactions. "Y'all live here on the property, or somewhere else?"

Sloan took the lead. "It depends. Most of the time we're at our houses, but we stay here at the bunkhouse when we're working cows."

The ranger wrote on a pad in his hand. "Where were you this afternoon?"

"Nowhere in particular, except I had a doctor's appointment. We brought in a load of feed, then went back out and bought some beer. Just been riding around…"

"Drinking cold beer." The ranger emphasized *cold* in a time-honored tradition of farm and ranch hands and rodeo cowboys.

"Yessir. We went to town, came back, and stopped to visit with Agent Tucker Snow and his brother…" He stopped when the ranger's eyes snapped up from his notepad.

"When and where was that?"

"This afternoon. He was at Mitch Ramsey's place."

Sloan and Fred shared a look, warning each other not to say anything right then about Agent Snow's phone call and their concerns. It was an age-old country alliance against anyone wearing a badge, even though Snow had a badge of his own. It seemed as if he were one of them.

"I assume Agent Snow will corroborate your statement."

Fred spoke up. "Don't see why he wouldn't."

Sloan looked around the yard at dozens of small orange cones and flags. "Looks like a lot of shooting went on here."

"Can't say for sure." The ranger's eyes flicked up and around before returning to his notes. "We're gonna need for you guys to provide any other witnesses as to your whereabouts today. Do either of you own AR-style rifles?"

Fred nodded for the both of them. "Of course we do. This is Texas."

"Where are they and when was the last time y'all fired them?"

Sloan took the lead. "Been a week or so...those rifles at least."

"So if we test your hands for nitrates, they'll come back negative."

"I doubt it. You're in the country, son, and we shoot all the time. Shot a couple of pigs last night with a .357 'cause that was the closest pistol handy when they came into the yard."

Another nod. The ranger pointed to the federal agents working the scene. "These guys'll want to talk to you, and I expect they're gonna want those rifles and tests anyway."

"I don't understand this."

"There was a murder here, sir. They'll want to talk with you tonight and probably tomorrow, too."

"That's not possible. I have an appointment in the morning to see my doctor."

"What time?"

"Ten."

"Where? What doctor?"

Sloan told him.

"Are those rifles of yours in the bunkhouse?"

"They're in the truck."

Unfazed, the ranger made another note. "That'll make things easier. We're gonna take 'em and compare them with the shell casings we've found here. Also, is that Charger in there yours?"

A student of the *NCIS* television series, Sloan suspected

they'd already run the car's plates and were asking to see if he'd lie about it. "Yessir."

"You don't keep it at your house?"

"Inside the barn's better; Mr. Crawford doesn't care. Are we under arrest?" Sloan saw the ranger's eyes soften and knew he'd passed the test.

"Naw, but you're being detained for a while."

Fred waved a hand toward the truck. "So can I have a beer?"

"I wish we all could."

Chapter 45

"How could you guys have let this happen?" Pierson stalked back and forth beside an SUV owned by ChemShale and the truck he used as cover. They stopped bumper to bumper in an unlit rural roadside park.

Barnes shoved his arrogant colleague with both hands. "*Let* it happen!? This whole stupid plan was your idea, and when it got out of hand, you ran out on us!"

Pierson rubbed his forehead with a shaky hand. "I thought you were all dead when I left."

"I was talking to you through comms. You never answered."

"Mine quit working." Pierson struggled to remove Barnes's hands from his shirt. "Probably because the shots were too loud and fried some circuits or something."

Truitt and Sanz stepped in and separated them as an old two-tone farm truck slowed to get a good look at the scene in the shadows from only yards away. Once past, the truck sped up.

Barnes whirled as if to walk away, then spun back. "I told you we should have waited for Strap to get back."

"He ran out on us." Pierson wouldn't admit that he'd panicked when their ambush failed. Orchestrating such an operation wasn't as easy as he thought it'd be, and the whole thing went to pieces in a way he never could have anticipated.

"He didn't run out on anything." Barnes backed away, breathing hard. "He was out doing his job, and you tried to take over."

"I have everything under control! I called Mr. Cross a few minutes ago. When he found out Strap bugged out and our assignment went wrong, he sent people to deal with him and has a car on the way out here to help us out."

"There you go again! Making decisions without talking to us." Barnes doubled a fist. "This is all on you!"

Pierson pushed Barnes away. "You guys were quick to join in."

Barnes walked away for a moment to get control of himself. "Strap wouldn't have let this happen."

Sanz drew a Glock from under his oversize shirt. "I'm gonna kill this son of a bitch!"

"I want to do it, too." Barnes grabbed his hand. "But you can't shoot him here."

Pierson blanched and raised his own shirttail, reaching for a gun. "You're not shooting anybody."

Sanz held up both hands and spoke as if Pierson wasn't standing only a few feet away. "Easy, men. We'll tell Cross how Pierson lied to us, saying he'd told us that Cross okayed the mission."

"It won't do any good." Truitt took a deep breath and addressed them as if they'd stopped at the pullout just to get out and stretch their legs. He turned his attention to Sanz and Barnes. "This guy's covering his own ass. He's already turned Cross against us. Let's just calm down!"

Sanz backed up. "Cross is gonna kill us all for this."

"I'm just as worried about Strap." Barnes kept his hand on

Pierson's chest, maintaining pressure on him and backing the frightened man up two, then three steps. "There'll be hell to pay when he gets back."

"We have to get off this road." Truitt walked around, rubbing his head. "Let's go back to the lodge and decide what to do."

"No." Pierson squared his shoulders. "We still have our original orders from Mr. Cross."

"Our orders were to work as a team and take out that nosy cow cop and then let a cleanup crew deal with the Crawfords and pull the dangerous rods and clear out." Sanz looked up and down the dark, deserted highway.

Barnes shook his head in disgust. "Don't you see that we're all dead men? Explanations and asking for forgiveness won't work with this company. The best we can do is..."

A gunshot lit the park in a brief strobe of light. Pierson took one step to the side and fell. Sanz and Truitt jumped and grabbed for their weapons, but Barnes had already flipped his Glock to hold it by the hot barrel and not seem to be a threat. "Now, let's get out of here."

Shaken, Barnes licked his suddenly dry lips. "Fine then."

"We can't leave him lying here." Truitt wiped his sweaty forehead. "And we still have to do something with these bodies in the back."

"That's why we're here, and there they are. Right on time." Barnes took over as a white panel van pulled in behind them. He stepped into the open as doors opened and men in dark coveralls emerged.

One carried folded body bags, and Barnes waved him over. "This one and the others in the back of the Suburban." Kneeling beside Pierson's body, Barnes ran his hands over the dead man's clothes, finding a burner phone and the keys to the pickup.

Their passwords on all the operation's phones were the first five letters of the op name. He woke it up and read the screen. "This is the one he used to call Mr. Cross. I'll call him and explain the whole situation and clean up Pierson's lies."

The men they'd never met moved with practiced efficiency. In less than five minutes they had the bodies in the van. One of the men slipped behind the Suburban's steering wheel and pulled onto the highway, followed by the van.

Barnes, Truitt, and Sanz stood beside the truck and watched them leave. Truitt lit a cigarette and drew smoke deep into his lungs. "What about Strap?"

"I'll tell him the truth about that, too." Barnes opened the driver's-side door. "Then it'll be up to Mr. Cross. Get in and let's go clear out of the motel. It's time to move."

"The truth's always best," Sanz said.

Chapter 46

It was all I could do not to drive toward Dallas and meet Harley, just to lay eyes on Chloe and the rest of the kids. Instead, I trusted he had hold of the situation, and I headed toward Uncle Bill's cabin in Oklahoma to secure the area before they arrived.

So far away from any city or town, I drove my old-technology Dodge under a bright, clear, star-swept sky. An armadillo scurried across the road, reflected in my headlights, and I let off the accelerator to let him get across.

I was completely out of my element against Cross and his guys, who weren't-run-of-the-mill criminals. They had unlimited funds behind them, and technology I couldn't understand.

Speeding through the night, I tried putting all the pieces together, still not understanding what was happening. Cross was keeping tabs on us, and I had to assume his people knew everything about us, where we were, and even where we were going. A car passed, its headlights almost blinding me. Using the dimmer on my steering column, I flashed the driver to let him know his lights were on bright. He passed and I watched his taillights recede.

This had all started when Mitch Ramsey called about a mama cow and her calf. I adjusted myself in the seat, leaning one elbow on the console.

What was the connection?

I was warned away from the start. Did it have something to do with one old cow? Why would a corporation care about her? Was she stolen? Naw, no business cared about her and a calf. That was ridiculous.

So what was it?

He and I talked that day. He smoked.

I thought back. Mitch was at ease while I was there, and made no mention that he intended to move. And it wasn't just a move. In a matter of weeks since my visit, he died and his wife vanished, along with everything they owned.

The math wouldn't work out. Ranchers and surviving spouses selling out generates interest. There are auctions for equipment and cattle, and the property is put up for sale. Nothing made sense.

The silence was too much and the whine of tires on pavement was bothering me.

I flicked on the radio and an old spoken-word song came on. Tex Williams rattled about smoking, playing cards, Saint Peter at the golden gates, and making the old white-haired man wait until he finished his last cigarette.

That was old Mitch in a nutshell. I wondered if it was the smoking that killed him, but then again, I knew a lot of old folks who smoked until they died of something else. Like Mitch, it wasn't cigarettes that caused him to lose his leg, or at least he made it clear the disease started in his shin.

The first time I saw him after he learned to walk on his new prosthesis, he emphasized that it wasn't the cigs he was always inhaling. "Hell, they keep me sane." He lit a fresh one that day. "If I didn't smoke, I'd be as nervous as a mouse. I even asked ol' Doc if it was somehow connected to these Marlboros, and he said he didn't think so."

We didn't dig any deeper into his cancer that day. It wasn't any of my business, and those old ranchers were tough and didn't show much interest in talking about their own trials or infirmities.

As my truck punched a hole in the night, I kept feeling there was a connection, though. The last time we talked kept replaying like a loop. There he stood propped on his corral, his metal leg resting on the rail...

No, not a rail in the typical sense, but one made from a drill rod.

The corral that he or someone else sold for scrap, maybe.

I jerked upright and pulled off to the side. No one sells corrals and arbors set in the ground. Leaving the corrals where they were would bring more money to the table during the sale. New owners might dig them up and remove them, but not a guy's wife getting out of the business.

The pipe and cable fence was still out there, along the road in front of Mitch's house.

What was the connection?

I plucked my phone from the dash and looked to see if I had a strong signal. Nope, not so far out there in the country. I'd have to wait until the next town to call Harley and check on their progress. I doubted there'd be much signal at Uncle Bill's house, so I had to find out before I got there.

A pair of headlights appeared behind me. I had the cruise set on sixty-five, and the lights were coming up fast. The road was fairly straight and level, with wide, easy curves that wound around left to right. Each time I reached a straight stretch, he was closer.

Running fast and wide-open out in the country wasn't especially safe, but it was a common occurrence in our part of the world. I wouldn't have paid much attention before, but after what I'd been through, it was smart to pay attention.

My AR was lying muzzle-down, resting beside me on the passenger seat. I pulled it closer and made sure it wasn't caught on anything. Shifting my weight, I adjusted the .45 on my hip.

The headlights caught up on the next straightaway and rode close, filling the interior of my truck with light. Had the rear window not been tinted, the headlights would have been way too bright. The driver followed for a moment, then seeing there was no yellow line in our lane, a dark sedan pulled around me, accelerated, and was back in my lane for only a few seconds and was gone.

The guy was in a hurry, and disappeared over a low rise. I relaxed and settled back.

Caution was my watchword that night. I cancelled the cruise control and the Dodge slowed down to sixty miles an hour to let the car ahead increase his lead. When I crested the incline, the sedan was on the shoulder.

Without any forethought, I slowed, made a U-turn, and punched the accelerator back the way I came, meeting a dark SUV going the other way. It might have been an innocent situation, but it changed my mind.

I hoped they wouldn't follow. If they did, none of us would like what happened next. I turned at the next country road, punched the accelerator, and turned again at the next. Cedars obscured a gravel road, and I saw a sagging abandoned house. I pulled up the overgrown drive and around back.

Time crept by as I zigzagged to throw off anyone tailing the truck and it hit me then. That's all I'd been doing since Sara Beth and Peyton were killed, zigzagging through life with little awareness of where I was going.

Those two vehicles might have belonged to Cross's men, or they were nothing more than late-night travelers the same as me. I waited as long as I could and then retraced my route, driving to Bonham.

Tears welled, and I wiped them away just outside of town, the result of so much time alone and thinking after what had just happened. I hadn't had time to grieve, moving from one trauma to the next. Were those tears leftover from the shootout back at Crawford's, or for my lost family?

My chest hitched and I choked back a sob that rose. Now wasn't the time. I wiped my cheeks again. When this was over, I vowed to take Chloe with me and talk with a police chaplin who'd been friends with me and Harley for years.

Reaching Bonham, I found the Walmart and went inside. A couple of shoppers stared at my badge and gun, and they nodded. Used to it, I built a stiff smile as I hurried to the back of the store and snatched a cheap prepaid cell phone off the rack, along with a card to load more minutes.

Sitting in my truck under a light near the door, I followed the instructions and activated the phone. I pulled back on the highway and dialed Harley's number.

He answered almost immediately. "What?" It was his standard answer when he didn't recognize a phone number.

"It's me. Picked up a new phone. Where are you?"

His answer sent ice water down my back. "Running like hell out of Dallas."

"What happened?"

"That big guy, Strap, showed up looking like he'd been drug

behind a truck. He told us they were tracking him by an implant they put in his shoulder."

"He's not with you now, is he?"

"No. Sent us out before those people showed up at his house. We're good. Said he's going somewhere to get it cut out."

"So I guess he's gone, then."

"Nope. That guy's an encyclopedia of information we need. We have a place to meet up at daylight."

"How's he gonna get that done this time of night?"

"Has an old buddy from the military who was a medic and he's now a doctor here in Dallas. Said it'll be done in no time."

"Fine. Change of plans. I think I was followed toward Oklahoma, so we're not going there anymore."

"Dammit. Where to now?"

"Percy's house."

He hesitated and I could tell he didn't understand the name. I repeated it, this time with a lilt. "Oh! Percy!"

It was a nickname we gave a college friend one night while everyone was loafing around in our living room. He played the bass guitar in a little band, and Harley, who was ten beers into a twenty-beer night, announced only guys named Percy played bass. The nickname was a joke between the three of us and no one else.

Harley grunted. "I can't think of a better idea right now."

"I'll meet you there, and then we're going to work."

"About time."

Chapter 47

Light filtering through heavy gray clouds found me over two hours south of Dallas on I-45, halfway to Houston, and not far from the little town of Centerville. Caught in time just before it died, like a prehistoric insect in amber, the community was one step above being on life support. It was a reminder of what small towns used to be before urban sprawl became the norm.

There was no traffic on the rural roads leading off the interstate, and it was too early for any of the handful of struggling businesses to be open. I saw only a couple of trucks parked on the street and a single cruiser in front of the sheriff's office.

For the first time in months, enough of a light shower fell to wet the road. Even heavier clouds built up in the northwest, and quickly overcame the dawn. I drove on through town and back out into the country, anxious to reach Russell's house, the real name of the guy we called Percy.

No one paid one bit of attention to my old Dodge truck that had over four hundred thousand miles on it. Despite its age and use, the body was sound and the engine ran like a clock. Folks out in the country aren't prone to disposing of vehicles when they still have life in them, so mine wasn't the only old truck on the back roads. I passed a couple of 1960s vintage pickups, and nearly every yard in that rural area had at least one old cranker that still served the owners.

After several miles, a narrow and crumbling potholed blacktop split off the road to weave through the pines. I followed it past pastures full of sleek, fat cattle and the occasional farmhouse partially hidden in the trees.

Years had passed since I'd been there, but little had changed in East Texas, including the weather. I wasn't surprised to see much-needed moisture falling. That part of the state can be heavy with water from the sky, creeks, rivers, and lakes. It looked as if the drought was finally breaking, but that could bring another set of problems.

I remembered an old weatherman on Channel 5 in Dallas who always said a drought ends in a flood. Based on my experience and observations, he was always right, and I wondered if this was the weather system that would drive off the heat.

Trees grew almost to the edge of the road, and I slowed down to look for a blue mailbox on a cedar post. Even though I was watching for it, the turnoff hidden by a new growth of brush came up suddenly. I had to brake and back up to make the turn, but once I was off the blacktop, the still-familiar two-track trace through the piney woods was easy to follow.

I slowed to examine a clear set of fresh tire tracks that were sharp and defined in the sand that wasn't covered by pine needles. It had showered sometime in the night and they stood out against the dimples in the sand. It was a relief to see there was only one set. I figured they belonged to my SUV driven by Harley. It looked as if he hadn't been pursued, and I breathed out a long sigh.

From there, the narrow lane leading to Russell's cabin was heavily wooded. Massive pines mixed with a variety of hardwoods overgrew the dirt track, dripping water and blocking out nearly all light in a leafy tunnel made darker by the heavy sky.

The winding lane was barely wide enough for my side mirrors. It lifted my spirits for the first time in days. The road meant comfort and safety. At the end was a childhood friend and my family.

While Harley and I had embarked on careers in law enforcement dealing with the dregs of civilization, Russell concentrated on directing his own career down an entirely different path. As the old folks I grew up with would put it, he made a psychologist.

The years passed and he also invested a large percentage of his rather substantial income into land acquisition, expanding his Leon County holdings in small increments until he was surrounded by acres of trees. He eventually insulated himself from outside influences with a safe cushion of undeveloped land on all sides.

Russell's backcountry retreat rose from a secluded hill, nestled securely in the pines, and miles from any major highway. Success as one of the nation's leading clinical psychologists allowed him to eventually move into a highly paid speaking circuit, lecturing with a "down-home" flavor and delivery.

The years passed and he withdrew from public speaking, tired of the travel, and communicated with most of his clients and publishers from the isolated cabin through emails and Zoom calls while his wife, Jenny, established her own successful career writing children's books.

Some outsiders who didn't understand their way of thinking suggested they were survivalists, but their lives were a long way from that definition. They simply preferred to be left alone, and invested time and resources in withdrawing from society only because they didn't like the direction it was going.

At the end of the lane, I rounded a particularly large tangle of trees, yaupon hollies, and wild shrubs, the kind of vegetation that costs an arm and a leg in city nurseries, but grows in profusion like weeds in undeveloped areas.

Their log cabin, large as cabins go at around twenty-five hundred square feet, was perched high on a pier-and-beam foundation overlooking a wide spring-fed pond at the bottom of the hill, and the heavily wooded Trinity river bottoms a mile farther below. The house seemed as if it were part of the landscape under tall pines, pecan, oak, and hickory trees.

Russell heard me coming and rose from where he'd been sitting with his feet propped on the porch's waist-high rail. An old WWII-era .30-caliber carbine leaned within reach against the wall, a thirty-round magazine curling upward.

Two mixed-breed mutts loped around the house to meet me, barking all the way. My stomach clenched when Harley's dog, Kevin, followed them and sat down when someone shouted at the dogs.

They were there and safe.

The front door opened on the substantial porch stretching around the front and both sides of the house, and the boys boiled out, making more noise than the barking dogs. I pulled up close to the steps and killed the engine.

"Uncle Tuck!" They raced to my side of the truck, shouting over each other to be the first to tell me everything that had happened in the past twenty-four hours. Danny jumped on the running board and, apparently thinking I'd lost my hearing since the last time I'd seen them, shouted through my open window. "We're all here!"

"I can see that." I stepped out as the boys tugged my hands and belt.

Danny pulled me toward the house. "You gotta see this place!"

"We've been on the *run*!" Matt waved his arms and almost tripped over Kevin, who wrung his tail and twisted himself into knots of joy. "Look where we are!"

Chloe came out, followed by Jimma. They raced off the porch and almost knocked me down with their hugs. Eyes burning, I had to blink several times to clear my vision. Tammy and Jenny were next.

Jenny hugged my neck, though it seemed forced. We were never close and shared different political ideas. After they married, she made sure Harley and I knew Russell was hers now, and one night she emphasized to us his name wasn't Percy and she didn't like it much.

I figured her fresh stiffness was because we'd brought trouble to their door without asking. She pulled away. "Good to see you made it safe." A light shower rattled on the leaves and collected on the pine needles above to fall in great fat drops "Y'all get in out of this weather."

The porch was wide enough to live on, giving the structure a solid feel. I always thought the house belonged on the side of a mountain, above a clear chuckling trout stream somewhere in Colorado. They'd equipped it with enough rocking chairs to make a veteran merchant marine seasick if everyone rocked at the same time.

Chloe wrapped her arms around my waist, and I reached out to draw Jimma in as well. Crow's-feet at the corners of Russell's eyes deepened. "You're a sight for sore eyes, Tuck."

Harley came around from the east side, carrying his M4 rifle.

I felt suddenly drained, as if I'd run a marathon. The clouds lowered and it was darker under the trees. Light from the single floor lamp in the huge living room shone through the large picture window, giving the interior a warm yellow glow as if from the stone fireplace.

Although the exterior logs were rough and rounded, they were planed flat on the inside. Finished smooth and the color of warm honey, they created an environment both comforting and inviting.

Jenny softened the harsh edges of the interior with well-chosen leather furniture, bookcases, curtains, and just enough of a feminine touch to make the interior attractive to everyone who entered. Spacious rooms, an oversized kitchen, vaulted ceilings, and large windows gave the house an open, airy feeling.

Once on the porch and out of the falling weather, I hugged the girls up until the boys forced themselves in between us. Chloe whacked Danny on the head. "Don't be a brat."

Jimma used one hand on top of Matt's head to turn him toward the door. "They can't help it. Let's go inside so the adults can talk."

Unfazed, Danny grinned and rushed back into the house. Matt followed and it was quiet again.

Harley nodded and joined us with the rifle carried muzzle-down by a strap over his shoulder. "Good to see you made it."

"You too."

"Are the laws looking for us?"

"There's a possibility that everybody in the state is, but I don't know for sure. I haven't talked to you or anyone else since I called you about coming here."

"I almost didn't answer when I didn't recognize the number."

"That's the idea."

I desperately needed to sit on the big porch and let my mind and stomach uncoil, but there was a lot to do. I finally shook Russell's hand. "Percy."

Russell hadn't changed since college, except his once shoulder-length brown hair was now cropped short and salted with gray. He was six feet tall and carried very little extra weight. He had a pleasantly worn face, not too much sun, but not the pallid fish belly white common to people who stayed inside most of the time.

He turned loose and hugged me. "The last time I saw you was at Sara Beth's funeral."

I recalled that day with a sharp pain in my chest. "Thanks for coming."

He wouldn't let the mood become somber, despite the reason we were there. He laughed. "It takes something like this to get y'all back out here."

"That's the hard truth."

He was the same man who had acted as a spark to our tinder. Russell was our unofficially adopted brother and we had held him close since childhood.

More than once, either Harley or I had to seek his advice to save our mental health after months of working undercover, on the heels of a shooting, or to clear our minds of the horrors we'd seen on the streets. Humans are the cruelest animals on the planet, and our dealings with abused children, meth-addled parents, and murder played over and over in our heads.

Russell wore hiking boots and a nylon fishing shirt to offset now-moist heat. "I thought you'd never get here."

Russell, Harley, and I settled into wooden rocking chairs near the small table holding the bourbon. I raised an eyebrow. "It's morning."

"It's for medicinal purposes, if you need it."

"Not now, but keep it handy for when we come back through."

Waving pine trees creaked and rustled their needles in the breeze high above us. The sky continued to weep moisture from the clouds. A rumble of thunder in the distance promised a real rain.

Confused by the dim light and thinking night was approaching, a whippoorwill out in the woods whistled a lonesome call. I leaned back in one of the rockers, calm for the first time since it all began.

Russell went inside and I could hear him talking to Tammy and Jenny. He flicked on another light in the living room and returned to the porch with three cups of steaming coffee.

The long spring on the door *creened*, then the wooden screen slapped shut with the *pop pop popping* sound of our youth.

I took a sip of black coffee and sighed. "I'll need to eat something soon."

"Bacon's frying on the stove right now."

"Thanks for taking us in, brother. This is the safest place I could think of. I guess Harley told you why we're here."

"He did." Russell inclined his head toward the M1 carbine leaning nearby. "They'll be fine here. I have security cameras at the entrance and all around the house."

"I didn't see 'em."

"That's the idea. Whenever someone breaks the beam, I get an alert on the security system. I knew when you turned off the road." He pointed past my Dodge. "There's a camera in that bluebird box, and half a dozen others in different places." He pointed down the lane. "See that one with the blue top?"

"Yep."

"That's exactly fifty yards."

He'd marked shooting distances around the house. "Anywhere you see a blue top, it's fifty yards. Red is one hundred yards." He grinned and shrugged. "Just in case."

Harley blew across the surface of his cup. "These guys are pros, though. They hacked Tuck's security system at his house."

"Nothing is absolutely safe, but no one knows you're here."

"Harley fill you in on *everything*?"

"Mostly. Up to the point where you changed your mind last night and he came here."

"At least now we have time to think." Swallowing a sip of coffee, Harley glanced down the lane. "We can't tell what we're going to do next."

"You don't know, do you?"

I raised an eyebrow at Russell's observation. "Not completely, but we're through reacting. Now I'm going to find out who these people are and what they're up to."

"I can answer a lot of that," Harley said.

We finished our coffee while he related everything Strap told them back in the house on Swiss Avenue.

Chapter 48

The sky was clouding up when Toby pulled her pickup to the curb in front of MedCom Drug Store on the old square. She saw a couple of young men who slowed their stroll down the street to watch her step up on the high walk and push through the glass door. Any other time she might have flirted with them some, but the Crawfords' deaths were too fresh on her mind.

Life had to go on, and so she needed to pick up Bill's meds at one of the last old-school independent drugstores in that part of the state. The vintage soda fountain along the right-hand side was still functioning, though it was too early for customers. Dusty shelves still contained older compounds popular for decades. Resinol Salve, Bactine, and Baby Percy Medicine shared space with more modern ointments and treatments.

The pharmacist heard her bootheels on the old linoleum floor. He glanced up, saw her coming down the aisle, and plucked a brown paper bag off the shelf beside him. "Good morning, gal."

"How're you doing, Arnold?"

"Fair." He rubbed his large nose with a finger. "Woke up with a bad old summer cold."

"That's funny, the pharmacist being sick and all."

"You'd probably be the same with all these sick people coming through here day after day." He laughed and put the bag on the counter. "I suppose you're here to pick up Bill's meds."

"I am."

He poked the bag with a finger. "It's hard to believe that boy's still blowing and going, as sick as he is."

She plucked a slim credit card holder from the back pocket of her skintight Wranglers and slipped one out. "He won't quit, that's for sure. What have you got for him today?"

"The usual, I figured it'd be him coming in to pick this up."

"Him and Fred are working cows this morning."

"See, that's what I'm talking about. That boy's tough as nails, but the other day after he got that CV line, he came in and picked up an antibiotic. He was telling me about being sick for so long and mentioned that he'd thrown up for nearly a month when all this started."

"He couldn't keep anything down, all right. I kidded him about being pregnant."

"That's what he said. Told me he had a sensitive stomach." Arnold chuckled and looked past her when the bell over the door rang as another customer came in. His thick eyebrows met in the middle. "Bill's symptoms reminded me of what I've read about radiation poisoning. You sure can't get that here, though, I don't believe, or at least I hope not."

A chill went up Toby's back. "What makes you think of that?"

Arnold shrugged. "I went and looked it up when he took a round of iodine a few months ago, and now his cancer. None of it makes sense, though."

Toby's breath caught. It all fell into place. She didn't know about the iodine, though he had no obligation to tell her about it since they weren't married. The tense phone call about something so innocuous as drill rods, Bill's cancer, and the disappearances of Mitch Ramsey and Luke Strawn, who'd both used those same rods, all made sense now.

She made up her mind right then and there that she wasn't having anything to do with those damned rods again. She'd talk with the boys and they'd come up with a plan. She shivered.

Arnold noticed. "Possum walk over your grave?"

She shook her head at the old saying. "Just thought of something."

"You all right, kiddo? Thinking about the Crawfords? It was a terrible thing. I know y'all were close."

"I'm fine." It took an effort to shake it off and she felt her eyes burn. "It was a shock."

"Y'all hear anything new? Have they caught whoever it was killed 'em?"

She knew better than to tell all she knew. "No, just what y'all heard, I 'magine. They're still investigating. Once the FBI showed up, they shut everything down. I thought they were gonna arrest the boys, but they told 'em to stay close and not leave town."

The pharmacist spoke to the customer walking in their direction. "Be right with you, Miss Emerson."

Toby glanced over her shoulder at the elderly woman with a giant purse over one arm. She gave the lady a wan smile then turned back to Arnold and handed him her credit card. He rang up the sale and handed her the receipt. "Hey, I meant to ask Bill when he came in, but I 'magine you'll know. Do y'all have any steers I can buy for the freezer? I'm getting low on meat, and I'd rather buy from you than the grocery store."

She nodded and tried to shake off the blues that threatened to settle on her shoulders like a heavy yoke. "I bet we can come up with one for you. I'm pretty sure the family'll sell off all the Crawfords' stock." Her breath caught, and she took a moment to get control of herself. "The hard part's getting a kill slot, though. Everybody's doing the same thing and the processors are backed up. I'll have to check for you."

"No hurry." He handed her the bag. "Tell Bill I hope he gets to feeling better."

Chapter 49

Mr. Cross sat at an empty polished board table in one of ChemShale's Dallas offices. He showed no emotion as the men seated around him one by one recounted their versions of what happened at the Red River Lodge, and later at the Crawford ranch. Familiar with the routine, each man included everything they thought, saw, or experienced. It was their typical debriefing after an assignment.

A master at hiding his emotions, Cross listened impassively until everyone finished.

There was no other furniture in the room but that table and eight chairs. The soundproofed walls were devoid of paintings or prints. The spartan room was swept twice a day for listening devices and microcameras, and one final time only minutes before they arrived.

The last person to finish speaking was Barnes, who'd assumed command in the field. Sitting on the edge of his seat, he outlined the events of the previous day in great detail, leaving nothing out. When he was through, he rested both hands flat on the table, fingers spread as if offering the digits for compensation.

The silence was broken only when Mr. Cross neatened his tie and drew a deep breath.

"Mr. Barnes, in your estimation, what triggered the failure of this operation? Boil it down into two words if you can."

He considered his answer. "Pierson. Strap."

"Exactly. Pierson was an arrogant, narcissistic fool. However, Strap has been my right hand for years. What do you think happened?"

"I don't know, sir."

"Anyone. Thoughts?"

With no random objects to hold their attention, Barnes and Sanz stared down at their hands and laps.

"Gentlemen, I once watched a prosecuting attorney spar with a witness. He showed that man a color photograph of a cow and asked him what color it was. The witness responded by saying that he didn't know what the opposite side of the animal looked like, but the side he could see was brown. It was the precise answer."

Not knowing how to respond, they waited.

"When an attorney asks a question, a good attorney that is, he or she always knows the answer beforehand. So would anyone venture an observation on what led up to your failure?"

Truitt swallowed. Sanz laced his fingers, and Barnes finally drew his hands into his lap.

"I do." Cross's voice was soft, calm. "I know exactly what happened, because that's my job. No matter what you've heard in the past, or what I've told you, all company phones and vehicles have tracking devices. You're under surveillance at all times. The weapons provided to you have the same. That's why you've never been permitted to bring your own.

"And most importantly, I know where each of you are at

any given moment of the day. Each of you has a tiny device implanted in your left bicep that shows me your whereabouts." He studied the expressions on their faces. All three started to reach for their upper arms and stopped. "Oh, I don't watch you every moment of every day. I don't have the time or inclination, but I *can* look back at a later date and see where you've been.

"It's called insurance." He straightened a file on the table. "I've been over your movements, and we've accessed your phones and laptops, which recorded your conversations over the past few days. I only asked for your verbal reports to see how loyal you are. You see, like that well-prepared attorney I mentioned, I know the answers. I simply wanted to hear them from you, and your reluctance is annoying, to say the least.

"Mr. Barnes, though you exhibited poor judgment in allowing Pierson to lie and convince you to operate outside the parameters of my plan, you showed me you could be trusted, but events conspired to work against you. Good work and thank you for removing Pierson from our payroll. You have the potential to be a leader in some other organization.

"Strap, on the other hand, has gone rogue, something I least expected of him. This has put our country at risk, and that can't be allowed."

Cross paused to collect his thoughts.

"Truitt and Sanz. You two aren't the best operators in the company, which is why I'm removing all of you from anything that happens at this level here at ChemShale."

Barnes straightened to speak, but Mr. Cross raised a finger from the table, indicating that he wait. "We need to finish up out there and get out of the area. There's way too much going on, and I suspect people are starting to talk. There's a fresh team waiting for the authorities to finish their investigations at the Crawford ranch."

There was no need to tell them that when the authorities were finished, one of their program technicians was instructed to upload the proper legal forms to a fictional attorney who in turn would contact a shell company that would purchase the property and distribute funds to anyone in the Crawfords' recently "updated" will, another fictional document. In a matter of days, the property would sell to still another shell company that would soon divide the property and sell it once again, muddling the ownership of the land and further hiding any information about the radioactive pipes and drill rods that had been there.

At least Crawford hadn't built anything other than one little pen with it, adding to the distribution of the deadly material's impact on others.

He smiled. "For your peace of mind, you'll be glad to know that I have men who will deal with the Snow brothers, who have been way too much trouble. Truitt, would you have believed that one man could cause so much havoc?"

The man started to respond. Cross held up his hand and cut him off. "It was a rhetorical question. He simply showed up at the wrong place and time. One damned wandering cow and calf interfered with this entire process, which should have gone like clockwork. Not your fault was it, Sanz?"

Instead of answering another rhetorical question, Sanz made eye contact and then looked back down at his laced fingers.

"So, gentlemen, Strap will be dealt with and we will close the books on this entire fiasco. Barnes, a direct question for you. Did Strap make any effort to deposit those medical appliances out in Well 3233 like he was supposed to? Did he arrange for someone else to do it for him?"

"I don't know sir."

Mr. Cross chewed his bottom lip. "Very well. We don't know, but I assume those appliances are still in the hands of those who dealt with the Ramsey and Strawn bodies. Anyone?"

The three men remained silent.

Mr. Cross rose and scooped up the file from the board table. "Fine then. There are people waiting in the hall. They will escort you from this building. You will leave with nothing except the clothes on your backs. Place the contents of your pockets on the table, please. That includes money, wallets, phones, and anything else you may have in your possession."

They emptied their pockets, and he held a hand toward the door. "You'll be contacted about severance pay that will go directly into your accounts, and gentlemen, let me remind you of the contracts you signed. One word about this company or your parts in any operation, and your families will bear the cost."

Truitt opened the door to find six men who looked just like them, waiting in the hallway. Sanz followed him out, and Barnes paused in the doorway, looking back like a dog going to be put down. "I expected more after all these years."

The answer was chilling. "Me too."

Chapter 50

A soft beep came to us from the inside of the house. Russell rose as if he was expecting it and hurried inside. Knowing the sound for what it was, Harley and I stood and waited, ready to see what the security cameras revealed. Kevin sensed our concern and rose from where he'd been lying against the wall to stand between us.

Russell came back in a few seconds. "Car coming. Camry. One occupant, and he pretty much fills it up."

"That'd be Strap." Harley relaxed. "No other cars behind him?"

"Not on *my* property. Could be someone hiding in the back seat or the trunk, or maybe coming in on foot."

"I was thinking the same thing." I stepped off the porch and crossed the open space where my truck was parked. Grabbing up my AR, I slipped into the dripping trees and found a position where I could get a clear look at the oncoming car and a clear shot if necessary. I waited for the Camry to appear.

Though the engine was quiet, I still heard the hum as the driver steered down the lane. The white car finally appeared, and I brought the rifle up to high ready. Harley'd described Strap perfectly. The big guy probably didn't get *in* the car, he had to put it *on*.

He passed slowly, watching both the lane and woods around him, but it was impossible to examine every tree. I'd taken up a position behind the thick trunk of an old pine. Bushy yaupons grew around the base and crowded the open lane in search of light. There was a lot of stuff for him to see before he could find me peeking out from cover.

He was probably relying on movement, which attracts the eye when you're in the outdoors. Our dad taught us to hunt when we were big enough to drag around behind him in the woods, so I held perfectly still.

He crept on past and the undergrowth obscured my vision. Instead of following, I waited where I was, just in case another vehicle came roaring up, or if men followed on foot. He tapped the horn to announce his presence.

The woods were silent, except for the sound of dripping water, a crow passing overhead, and the thunder getting closer. Doing my best not to move, I waited.

A car door slammed. I relaxed after a few seconds and took a deep breath. The quiet told me there was no confrontation. I remained rooted to the spot. If men were moving in on us through the woods, they'd be much slower, and careful. I became part of the landscape where I watched and listened.

A flicker of movement caught my attention, and all my senses vibrated to life. It was just a flash and I waited, looking for others that would be scattered through the trees as they advanced on the house. Moving only my eyes, I focused on where I'd seen motion. It could have been a squirrel, a bird… or the little doe that stepped into the open and looked around.

I relaxed. She wasn't concerned, so unless a squad of bad guys was moving with glacial speed, we were alone.

I lowered the rifle, and she vanished.

I didn't like how easy it was for him to drive down the road, just as we'd done when we got there. Not far from where I was hunkered down, a substantial limb had split off one of the pines from high above and lay only yards from the road.

Leaning the rifle against a tree, I grabbed the big limb with both hands and walked backward, dragging it across the drive. Now anyone coming in would have to stop and move the blow-down out of the way before they could continue.

Walking back to pick up my rifle, I saw one of Russell's cameras and gave it a wave. Feeling a little better about the situation at hand, I headed back to the house.

Rain fell, the first edge of the approaching storm. The trees blocked most of it, but my shoulders and cap were wet by the time I reached the house. Harley and Russell were on the porch with someone who looked like a mountain. The man was in tan 5.11 fatigue pants. His gray nylon short-sleeve fishing shirt stretched across his shoulders.

A fresh white bandage on his left bicep almost glowed in the dim light.

Harley waved when I came out into the open. "All clear?"

"All clear."

"Come over here and meet Strap. You're not gonna like what he has to say."

The big guy turned, and I remembered him from that day in my front yard that seemed to be years in the past. He was the man in the dark suit who waited by the black Suburban as Cross intruded on my porch and tried to bribe me.

Seeing me appear, Strap twisted his lips in a "sorry 'bout that" expression and waited while Kevin thumped his tail on the boards where he lay.

Chapter 51

From behind his desk, Cross glowered at his new technician, who was tapping a laptop resting on his thighs. "Completely gone?"

The man from Mumbai used his fingers as a comb to get a lock of black hair out of his eyes. "Yes, sir. We have no signals from Strap's implant. His last position was in Bren-hum, Texas, before it went offline."

"You had the same problems pronouncing Mexia and Nacogdoches, Patel, so don't hurt yourself trying to say it right. The town's pronounced Brenum."

"Got it."

"Vehicle? Phone?"

"Those devices are also silent." Fingers on the laptop's home keys, he cleared his throat and gazed up at his boss without moving his head from its original position. "He's gone dark."

"That shouldn't happen." Cross thought for a moment. "Run a list of associates, both in and out of the company. Get a list of men who served with him in Afghanistan and cross-reference their last known whereabouts."

"That will take some time."

"The phone in your pocket is nearly thirty-three thousand times faster and stronger than the Apollo computers. It performs instructions one hundred and twenty million times faster, and even the charger for that laptop you're using has more raw processing power than the Apollo guidance system that landed astronauts on the Moon, so Mr. Patel, I suggest you find them."

Expressionless, Patel once again addressed his computer while Cross studied a stack of papers on the table in front of him. Ten minutes later, Patel straightened.

"I have six men he served with in Afghanistan that he frequently calls. One is in Bren-ham." That time he pronounced it properly.

"Outstanding. Now, I want background on Tucker and Harley Snow. I want to know who their friends are, and people who they frequently call. I want to know everything about Snow down to his childhood vaccination record. Better yet, I want everything down to their permanent record."

"What's that?"

Cross flashed a rare smile. "It was something teachers held over our heads when I was in school."

"Something they held over your head in class?"

"No matter. Just like Strap's background, get me a list of people and addresses. No one can go completely dark these days. Now, email me those names and locations for Strap while you do it."

The technician tapped on the keyboard and punctuated his work with a hard punch on the enter button. The phone in Cross's hand vibrated, and he read the list of names on the screen. Recognizing none of them, he made a call to his new team leader, Denver.

"I have a location for you to check out. You and Heller

make a little visit to a former combat medic specialist named Rodriguez who works as a doc in the box at a little clinic there. I believe he's removed a tracking device from an individual who has been under surveillance."

He listened for a moment. "Yes, it's Strap. We need to confirm that it happened and if Strap said where he might be going next."

Cross hung up and stared at the wall, thinking. "Patel, while you're at it, see if Strap shows up on any flight lists heading out of this country."

He picked up a traditional fountain pen and unscrewed the cap. Instead of writing, he tapped the nib with one finger for a moment and replaced the cap. "And where is that research on the Snows? We've underestimated them, and I need that information as quickly as possible."

Patel raised an eyebrow in a "we?" expression, nodded once, and went to work.

Chapter 52

Some folks might have called it a gray, dreary old day, but I've always been a fan of what my dad called falling weather. I used that term once with Chloe and she looked at me as if I'd just grown an extra head. I had to explain that it meant anything falling from the clouds.

It wasn't the first time I'd used an old-time phrase she didn't understand. Once when Chloe was around thirteen, we were trying to pull onto a busy road and couldn't find a gap in traffic. I told Sara Beth that it looked like someone let the gate down, and Chloe asked what that meant.

Sara Beth and I laughed together at the thought that she didn't understand what it was like when a gate was left open and cattle poured through the opening.

Now I listened to a steady rain rapping a staccato beat on the cabin's tin roof as water ran in rivulets off the porch overhang. There was a crowd of us outside, and had it been under different circumstances, it would have reminded me of the old days when Sara Beth and I used to visit Russell and Jenny to spend the evenings sitting by a campfire.

Strap had center stage, sitting in a rocker that put his back to the woods, allowing me, Harley, and Russell to position ourselves against the cabin's wall to keep a lookout for any upcoming trouble. Tammy, Jenny, Chloe, and Jimma all gathered around to listen, while the boys stayed inside with Kevin and built Lego models from kits Russell kept on hand for young visitors.

He rolled his left shoulder. "My old army buddy cut it out last night. ChemShale required several shots over the years, especially when we left the country. Called 'em vaccinations, but they weren't. Half the shots we get these days are called vaccinations, but they're nothing more than a shotgun approach to keep us from getting sick.

"Anyway, they required a Covid shot a couple of years ago, but me and the guys had an idea it was more than that. They hurt like hell and ached for two weeks, but none of us ever figured they'd implanted these in our arms. My friend who took it out said it was something he'd never seen before, and had actually allowed the tissue to bond with the contraptions."

Russell picked up on the word that was common to many Texans. "Contraptions. Where are you from?"

"Here in East Texas."

"Figured. So why are you doing all these things so close to home?"

Strap's gaze slipped off his face. "Money, like everything else."

Harley was impatient. He wanted to get back to the problem at hand. "So your buddy cut it out and now you're on our side."

"I'm on your side," Strap repeated. "and I'm out of the business, 'cause I don't like the way these people operate anymore, Harley."

"But you didn't mind it last month." My voice came sharper than I expected, and the kids registered the tone. Chloe caught my eye and held one hand flat, Sara Beth's subtle signal for *maintain*. They were just alike.

"Look, I know how y'all feel, and I'd like to apologize, but that's all hollow in the wake of what's happened. I did what I did, because they told me it was national security, and I bought into it, just like when I was in the military, but now I'm thinking for myself."

Blue-jeaned knees together and a cup of coffee in both hands, Jenny leaned forward. "Since I'm new to this discussion, give me the nutshell version of what you…used to do, so I can get a handle on what's going on in my home."

I felt a little embarrassed at what we'd brought after going so long without coming by to see them.

"Fair enough." Strap adjusted his seat. "I worked for a shadow company called ChemShale. It's an umbrella oil company with several legs, like an octopus, but I only have knowledge of two. Here's the CliffsNotes version. They developed a new way to extract oil, without getting it approved by the EPA, or anyone else. It worked for a while, but then they found out there were problems.

"This process required deeper drilling, and doing so went through layers way down that have more radiation in them than others. That means the drill rods were more dangerous than typical drill metal. Because of that, they disposed of them at a facility specializing in such things. It went on for a while and everyone got lazy. Then one day a year or so ago, ChemShale drilled into a well containing nuclear waste."

We all leaned forward. Russell pulled at one earlobe, a sure sign he was thinking. "I know there's a deep backstory here."

"There is, but I don't have all the details, or time. It was something they had to keep away from the media. It would've been the story of the century, sending a lot of people to prison for a variety of things. They had to keep it away from the public, in the interest of national security."

He looked even more uncomfortable than before. "ChemShale's in bed with the government on this, and their funding comes not from the oil they drill, but from a shadow governmental agency. They have unlimited funds and resources, as well as the autonomy to do what they want.

"The drill rods were seriously hot, so ChemShale decided to shut the well down and keep everything quiet. People were paid off. People disappeared, either of their own accord, or ChemShale did it for them, because if the story got out, people would start investigating the company, and the other legs of that octopus would be exposed. No one wanted that. These guys make the CIA look like boy scouts.

"Anyway, they shut the well down and sent the last few loads of hot drill stems to the disposal company that was supposed to bury them. Instead of disposing of the drill rods in the right way, they sold them off to a shell company."

"That's what got all this started, then." Harley's mouth twisted in disgust.

"Yessir. People throw that term *transparency* around all the time, but no one really wants it. ChemShale decided to do the same thing those people did with the nuclear waste. The truck-loads should have gone to an old lignite pit in East Texas before they covered it over, but one of the truck drivers got greedy. That's how this kind of thing gets started. One guy needs money and then things snowball."

"Everything comes down to money." Harley and I said it a lot, just as Strap had admitted earlier.

"You're right about that. The guy's name was Jack, and he

knew someone who knew someone who was looking for drill rods to use in welding. He delivered them to a man named Carl Cunningham who then resold them. One extremely hot load went to Mitch Ramsey." He nodded at me.

I felt sick. That's why Mitch lost his leg and was fighting cancer. Because of money.

"Other rods went to Mr. Strawn, but our company tracked them down and we bought them from him, except for some he didn't tell us about. He sold those to Mr. Crawford. That's why we had to go back. Our job was to…" Strap swallowed. "Eliminate the evidence."

"So you were supposed to find the drill rods and collect them." Jenny took a sip of coffee, as if to punctuate the sentence.

"No, ma'am. We were to eliminate the people so they couldn't talk and lead back to where the rods came from. Then, our job was to recover the rods."

Her eyes went flat. "You're an assassin." Her head snapped toward me. "You brought a murderer into our house, and he's sitting there pretty as you please, telling us everything he does!"

Strap shrugged and winced when it pulled the fresh incision in his shoulder. "Was an assassin."

"You don't just quit and walk away to wipe your hands of murder. You still are!" She rose, and I thought she might take a swing at him.

"No, ma'am."

"Tuck!" Jenny's face was red as a beet. "You represent the law here, and this falls under your domain. Arrest these people!"

"Under normal circumstances, I would." I had to choose my words carefully. I was glad she had addressed me instead of Harley because it always torqued him off when anyone told him what his job was. Those kinds of things rolled off me, for the most part.

"But right now there's a greater issue, and that's the safety of all y'all. After that, I need to track down this Cross guy, but Strap is our go-to guy right now. When Harley and I worked undercover, we could have arrested any number of people we had dead to rights, but they were more useful on the streets than in jail. You see what I'm saying?"

"No!" Jenny refused to listen. I'd seen it before. Sometimes people get fixated on one subject and won't allow themselves to be pulled off, whether by common sense or facts. They become emotional, and that's something you simply can't argue against. "He just admitted to killing people!"

Harley stepped in to cool our old friend down as Strap stared at his feet instead of Jenny, who was throwing daggers at him with her eyes. "Right now, Strap's more valuable as an ally. We'll deal with his crimes later."

Tammy agreed with her husband, speaking quietly. "Strap's out. The boys' job isn't to prosecute him."

"Look, I'm sitting right here." Strap obviously didn't like for people to refer to him in the third person. "I want to put an end to this, and that includes my boss, whose last name is Cross, as well as ChemShale. It's the only way I know to make amends while I can."

Chloe had a suggestion that rang true in her limited experience. "Go to the media."

"That might have worked decades ago, or hell, ten years ago, but not now." Strap shook his head as if hearing of a close friend's death. "I wouldn't trust the media today to tell me the sun is shining and the sky's blue. They're fed by corporations that pick and choose which issues they want to concentrate on. They'll only do it for a short while, as long as it serves their purpose of gaining viewers, and then they'll glom onto the next big thing and leave everyone behind."

Jenny's concerns were valid, but she was about ten steps behind where we'd already been. "Let's get the police involved. Call and tell them."

Strap shook his head. "We can tell them, but there's little evidence I can point to, and the truth is that some people are paid off. Mr. Cross has more people than you can believe in his pocket."

"We'll tell them about your company."

"No way to prove it. ChemShale lies for a living, and every question brings up more questions that can't be answered."

"So how do we shut them down?" Russell was looking for a definitive answer. "If they've followed y'all so close and are there at every turn, how do you defeat such a system?"

"By cutting the head off the snake." Harley's statement made me look hard at him. "And I think Strap knows how."

"I do, but it's gonna be hard. They're everywhere, and right this minute Cross is looking into your backgrounds. We need to stop him first."

"How do we do that?"

"I. Don't. Know. But we'll figure it out."

Chapter 53

Laptop in hand, Patel knocked on Mr. Cross's door in the Houston office. No one in their right mind would simply walk in without announcing themselves in some way. "Sir?"

"Come in." Cross looked up from the papers on his desk with a look akin to a college professor entertaining a grad student. The desk was positioned to overlook the Katy Freeway, the widest highway in Texas. Twelve main lanes, eight feeder lanes, and six managed lanes that carry mass transit vehicles during peak hours, it was a massive north-south artery that clotted several times a week, despite the engineers' best efforts.

"What do you have for me?" No one ever came to Cross's office to visit.

"Some news. Misters Truitt, Barnes, and Sanz were found murdered last night in a crack house in the East Terrell Hills neighborhood of San Antonio. Of course the local police of San Antonio don't know their identities, but from the descriptions I read this morning on the internet, it was them."

Cross put down his fountain pen. "That is news, but they were no longer employees of this company."

Having informed his boss, Patel dismissed the comment and held the laptop up like a visual aid. "I did as you asked and have been searching for obscure information on Tucker and Harley. I created a spreadsheet of friends and relatives stretching back to when they were in elementary school. Then I cross-referenced that one with a list of frequent telephone calls and even ran a program of keywords that appear in phone logs that might lead us to their whereabouts, or if nothing else, the way they think and approach problems."

Cross laced his fingers and waited. Tech people always wanted to tell him how a watch was made, when all he truly wanted was the time.

"After I cross-referenced those names, I had an idea about friends outside of their immediate circle of family and colleagues. That came when a childhood friend of mine in Mumbai reached out to ask the best places were to live in this state."

He tapped at the keyboard with one hand. "When people from my country move here, they prefer to be with others of our own culture and religion. You can see that by researching school district data to find where the neighborhoods are predominately Indian..."

"And you found?"

"Ah. Yes. Get to it, as you say. Talking with my childhood friend sparked an inspiration that Snow might have an acquaintance with whom he touches base now and then. His wife was killed in an automobile accident, and when I brought up her obituary, I found that one of his associates who attended her funeral was also listed as a pall bearer, the only person who performed that duty and wasn't a law enforcement officer."

He waited for Cross to respond, but the silence stretched until he could no longer stand it. "Then I researched that individual named Russell Monroe, who was a well-known psychologist and public speaker who essentially went off the grid not long after the funeral. I went back into the phone records and saw they'd spoken often until Snow's wife was killed, and then nothing."

"So why are you bringing me this?"

"Because he was apparently a close chum for most of their lives, and now I can't find anything."

"Chum." Cross mused the antiquated word. "Where does Monroe live?"

"Not far from the community of Centerville, Texas, halfway between Dallas and here, as a matter of fact. Using a mapping app, I located the house situated in the woods off a farm-to-market road. Once I had the coordinates, I used ChemShale's satellite system and downloaded the most recent images of that area. Out of one hundred photos within the dates of the death of Snow's wife, there was little activity around the house, and only two vehicles were ever in evidence. One was a blue sedan, and the other a maroon utility vehicle.

"Then I referenced the past few days and saw nothing until yesterday when a large SUV arrived. However, when the satellite passed this morning, there were too many clouds for an image. The rains have obscured the location, but I feel that it's imperative that we investigate. I think Russell Monroe's property is where at least one of the Snows is now."

Cross plucked the phone from his pocket. "Denver, Patel here thinks he knows where Snow has gone, and if I know Strap, he'll be there, also." He issued instructions and ended the call by saying, "Handle it."

Patel remained standing in the same spot, waiting.

"Anything else, Mr. Patel?"

"I'm glad to say we were successful, but I am also sorry to say I failed in one research venue. Though I've tried, I can find no mention of a permanent record, nor anything called a permanent record for anyone. Is that a misnomer I am unfamiliar with, or is there a local definition leading me to misunderstand you?"

For the first time in months, Mr. Cross laughed big, not his usual forced chuckle.

Chapter 54

Lunch was sandwiches, and we all gathered around a large pine farm table just off Jenny and Russell's kitchen. The heavy, gray clouds seemed to rest on the pine tops and the rain was tropical. Once it started, there was no letup.

After he ate, Harley paced the rooms and hallways like a caged lion, grumbling about having to eat sandwiches. I almost laughed, because he despised them, saying we'd eaten nothing but deli meats and fast food for years, and he no longer had the stomach for slimy processed foods.

But then again, this was the guy who loved Cheetos and corn chips, because they crunched and were therefore not slimy.

I waved him into Russell's study. "Come with me. We need to get legal before we can do anything else."

"What do you have in mind?"

"Judge Elliott Hiragana."

"You think we should tap him again?"

"He's exactly what we need. Remember what our old buddy Curtis Mack said when he got his fifth divorce?"

Harley laughed. "Don't hire a just lawyer. Hire a bulldog lawyer."

"Yep, and that's Judge Hiragana." I opened an old address and telephone notebook I've had for decades and flipped to his last name. Long ago I realized people no longer memorized phone numbers, relying on the phones themselves to keep up with such information, but if the phone wasn't nearby, or malfunctioned, as they often do, they were of little use.

We'd worked with Judge Hiragana back in the old days when we needed judges on speed dial for a variety of late-night warrants. Some were by the book and wouldn't respond until they were officially on duty in court. Back in our undercover days, we had a couple of judges who worked on the right side of the law. We could call them at work or at home at any time of day or night.

Judge Elliott Hiragana was our main guy, and we drove to his house more than once when we had enough evidence or probable cause to wake him up and get a warrant for some bad guy we intended to take down. We'd called him only months earlier for another warrant and though our reasons were thin, they were valid.

I flipped open the drop phone and punched in the numbers. He picked up on the third ring. "If this is a spam call, this is Judge Hiragana and I'll do everything in my power to reach out and touch you, no matter where you are. Now, what do you want?"

"A warrant."

He was silent for a moment, until his voice lifted with recognition. "Tuck?"

"Yessir. How're you doing, Judge?"

"Well enough to be upright and taking nourishment." I heard ice tinkle in a glass and knew it was sweet tea, something the judge drank by the gallon. "What're you two into now? I assume Harley's close by."

He leaned in. "Right here, Judge."

"You two could call just to catch up from time to time, you know. There's a place not far from me that makes the best chicken fried steak you ever ate. Their sweet tea is just like Mama used to make, too."

I had an image of his little Asian mother mixing up iced Southern sweet tea and had to laugh. "We'll take you up on that pretty soon, but right now we're in a tight spot."

Hiragana's voice went flat and businesslike. "Shoot."

I told him the entire story while he listened without interrupting. I had to prompt him a couple of times when the silence on the other end made me think the call dropped. When I was finished, there was a long spell of nothing while he considered what had happened.

"I've never heard of ChemShale."

"Neither had we, nor radioactive drill rods."

"Forgive the pun, but this goes deep. It's one of those scenarios where you pull a string and before long, the entire sweater unravels."

"That's a good way to put it."

"So without EPA approval, they changed drilling processes, and common radiation contamination increased dramatically, and because they were drilling deeper and using an unapproved process, they inadvertently drilled into nuclear waste deposited by shadow individuals who maybe utilized an outlaw well that should have continued to produce, and now the cover-up for illegally sold drill rods is worse than the originating incident and involves murder, more cover-ups, and the exposure of a company that has power and resources provided by the U.S. government."

"Sounds worse when you say it." Harley rolled his eyes.

"You're asking for warrants for a Mr. Cross, though we don't know if that's his real name or an operational nomenclature."

"Yessir. He's our initial target, but like you said, once we start to pull at this string, I expect to uncover a lot of players."

"But you can't arrest these players that aren't listed."

We knew that. He was working through the process like he'd done in the past. In Texas, an arrest warrant is issued by a judge and gives law enforcement the legal right to arrest the individual whose name is listed. These warrants are generally only granted if there is probable cause the offense in question was actually committed.

He took so long that Harley got worried. "You know, Judge, issuing a summons won't work in this case. You can bet this guy won't appear, because that isn't his real name, and like we said, he has resources. I wouldn't put it past him to have a lot of politicians on his payroll, or probably the other way around."

"I wasn't thinking of a summons. I'm just trying to get a handle on how to word this warrant."

"A John Doe warrant makes sense to me." Beside me, Harley nodded in confirmation.

In Texas, John Doe warrants are issued for individuals whose name is not known by law enforcement, but can be identified and known by sight. They're usually issued for cold cases, but have found favor in cases like the one we faced.

"Here's the deal with a John Doe, boys." The judge sounded like he was addressing a couple of law students. "The federal government does not allow nor recognize this type of warrant. That could be a problem down the road when the nuclear waste comes up and this thing goes to the feds, or we pull in other agencies. Then we're talking about the EPA and a dozen other alphabet organizations."

I needed to nudge him a little. "It still provides enough of a suspect's description, though."

He mulled it over. "You're right. There's reasonable certainty that this description can later identify the person in question. But let me tell you boys, all your ducks need to be lined up for this to work."

"We're lining them up right now, sir."

"Don't 'sir' me. The only time you do that is when you want something."

"You're right, but we need to get rolling on this, because I'm afraid these guys are coming after us right this minute. The informant I told you about says that's how they operate."

"This man, Strap."

"Yes, and that's an op name. He's turned and working with us like a hundred other informants in the past, and we need him."

"Do you want a John Doe for him, too?"

Harley shook his head, and I agreed with him. "Nossir. I'm pretty sure this guy's gonna disappear at some point, and even though I woulda shot him a couple of days ago, he got my daughter and Harley's family out of harm's way. In my book, that cleans most of his record."

"All right. I'll issue the warrant. When are you coming to get it?"

"Uh, can you email it to us?"

There was silence on the other end. "I can, but you'll need an official document within a damn few hours of when you pick him up. I'll need an affidavit of fact. Once you make the arrest, you sign it and return it back to me. I must be crazy, 'cause any other judge down there'll raise hell for such deviation from normal procedure."

He grew silent for a moment. "You need a search warrant, also?"

I could have used one, but that might have gotten sticky down the road. A search warrant specifies a place, vehicle, storage facility, boat, or any other location. Usually the place is identified by an address, including a detailed description of the structure, down to the exterior of a building or the color of a roof, or in the case of a vehicle, it would be the make, model, or color.

All of that needed another affidavit before the warrant was issued. Then we'd have to attach an inventory of items seized, if and when that was necessary, and return it to the judge also.

I raised an eyebrow at Harley. "You think we need a search warrant?"

"Strap tells me we might be going to Cross's location, but that'd be like trying to get into the White House. I say we…you pick him up somewhere else. We don't want this to turn into some kind of Waco event."

He was talking about the FUBAR created by the ATF when they attempted to arrest David Koresh at the Waco compound instead of waiting for him at a grocery store or somewhere in town. He had to correct himself because Harley wasn't an official law enforcement officer. He played it fast and loose when it came to working with me, though.

"Do you still like Buffalo Trace?" That was Harley's way of ending the conversation, since his attention span had been strained to the limit.

"I do, when I can find it, and you better not be offering me any kind of bribe."

"I wouldn't think of it. I just wanted to make sure you had some for me to drink the next time I see you." Harley paused. "Hey, I have an idea. You swore me in a few months ago when we had to go into Oklahoma and pick up that Atchley guy. How about you do it now, and keep me on the tab indefinitely as an undercover agent? It'll be like old times."

"You were an officer back then. You're retired now."

"I still think it's a great idea."

"Ummm humm." For a second I thought Judge Hiragana was going along with Harley's idea. Instead, he cleared his throat as if to punctuate a thought. "What's the email address you want to use?"

My stomach sank. We couldn't use mine, or Harley's. "Hang on a minute."

I went into the living room that was loud and alive with noise from four kids and three adults. "Russ, can I have a judge send me a document through your email?"

"Sure." He gave me the address and I repeated it to Judge Hiragana.

"I'll have this to you within the hour."

Harley was grateful. "We owe you more for this."

"You better remember the other times, too."

Chapter 55

Patel closed his laptop and rushed back down the hall to Cross's office. He rapped and pushed through before Cross finished saying for him to come in. "I have them."

"You have what?"

"I was right. They're at Russell Monroe's residence. I've been monitoring all electronic traffic going in and out of that house, even though he has a sophisticated system, and when I...."

"Get to the point, Patel."

"Right." He nodded three quick times. "Monroe just got an email from a Judge Hiragana in Dallas."

"So?"

"It's an arrest warrant for John Doe. I looked it up and..."

"I know full well what a John Doe warrant is. Why is this important?"

Patel blinked a couple of times. "Well, sir, no other legal documents have come through Monroe's email, other than some paperwork for land..."

"Because you checked and cross-referenced certain keywords."

"Exactly. And above all else, the name Agent Tucker Snow is listed as the arresting officer."

"That means they're getting ready to move on someone."

Patel waited while Mr. Cross flicked dust off the lapel of his suit coat. "Do you think he's coming after me, or you?"

He grinned at the horrified look on Patel's face. "Don't panic. I was just kidding."

"Sir, do you need anything else from me right now?"

"A complete file on Monroe, from birth to this moment, and that includes immediate family and grandparents, if they're still alive. Also updated satellite images of the area, and that will include those I just mentioned."

Patel looked past Cross and out onto the Katy Freeway, which was a chaotic glut of traffic in the rain. Emergency lights clustered around two far left lanes that blocked the wide artery. He shivered at the thought of what Cross had in mind. He could stall on the bios for a while, and maybe somehow warn the others of the danger they were in. "Of course there won't be current images due to the weather."

"Of course not." Cross flicked his fingers in dismissal and picked up a desk phone. Punching in numbers, he issued a series of instructions intended to eliminate all their problems.

"And at the same time, send someone back out to where all this started. Go to this man Crawford's ranch and load up some cattle, then collect those two cowboys we've been monitoring. Right, the ones who've been stealing cattle. I knew they would come in handy when they were gathered with Snow at the Mitch Ramsey site. Set it up so that it looks as if they stole the cows, crossed with another outfit, and were shot. That will give the local sheriff something to hang his stupid hat on and will go a long way toward cleaning this up."

He hung up and spoke to the empty room. "And then I hope we never have to go back to that godforsaken county again." He opened a drawer and took out a bottle of sixteen-year-old Lagavulin Scotch. Pouring a small amount into a glass, he breathed deep of the smoky barley-malt flavors.

Instead of sipping the whiskey, he carefully poured it back into the bottle and replaced the cork. It was a ritual he had performed a number of times in the past when events threatened to overwhelm his position, which he'd fought too hard to create and maintain.

He addressed the bottle as if it were a living thing. "When we are finished with this foolishness."

Chapter 56

Still inside because of the rain drumming on the house's tin roof, we gathered beneath wide beams and the steep A-frame cathedral ceiling in the open-concept living room. I had to speak to Harley in bits and pieces because he continually moved from window to window, disappearing into other rooms and returning. It reminded me of a pacing lion at the zoo.

The TV was on in the guest bedroom, where the boys had holed up. Tammy and Jenny shared the brown leather love seat. Chloe and Jimma were curled up on the matching L-shaped sectional. The teenagers seemed as if they didn't know what to do without having a cell phone in hand, and it reminded me that we needed to talk with them about their constant reliance on the devices.

They were like winos weaning themselves off the bottle, and bore the same expressions.

"We can't just go charging in there without a solid plan," I told Harley, who was gung-ho about running Cross to the ground.

Strap agreed with me. "This guy's good, and he has an army behind him. You made an enemy of this man who's had few people stand up to him. He's the most vindictive person I've ever known, and his pride won't allow it. To top it all off, he's convinced you know more than you do from Mr. Ramsey."

"All I know..." I paused. "What I know for sure is that Ramsey's cancer came from those hot drill rods. Good God. He either gave others away, or sold 'em. There could be contaminated rods all over that county, and the people who have them are getting cancer and dying from radiation poisoning. That's why he's determined to clean it all up."

"Yessir. I didn't want to tell you, but Mr. Ramsey and Mr. Strawn were...removed on Mr. Cross's say-so." He gave us all a look and slight shrug that said, "In for a penny, in for a pound." For the first time, I saw real regret in his eyes. "They will never be found, and I'd bet a dollar to a donut that he's working on some way right now to make the same thing happen to all three of us."

I pointed to my family, who was soaking it all in. "And them too?"

"I'm afraid so. I told him I wouldn't do anything, but there are men who will, and he'll be sending them along. This is a harsh thing to say, but now that you've told them, Mr. Cross will figure they'll tell someone else." He rested his gaze on Russell. "And I hope he never finds out about you."

Without an immediate answer, Russell tapped his computer to life and checked the cameras. Frowning, he turned from the screen and grinned at me. "Good idea, dragging that limb across the drive."

"I'm always trying to think."

Satisfied we were safe, at least for the moment, he turned back to our conversation.

Strap had positioned himself to see out one of the great

windows that provided tons of light in the airy home. "I've been with him for years and know how he thinks and operates."

Tammy pulled a strand of dark hair behind one ear. "How long?"

"Since I got out of the army. I worked as a roughneck for a while until I made driller, and Lago Energy hired me on and I punched holes in the ground from Texas to North Dakota. We had some trouble with a bunch of environmentalists up there who didn't like the drilling and the pipeline, and I helped handle the situation. Mr. Cross saw something in me he liked and needed..."

"The ability to murder, for example?" Jenny's caustic tone did nothing to improve the conversation. Kevin sensed her anger from where he was lying under the kitchen table and raised his head to watch.

Strap nodded as if she'd said he was good at drilling for oil. "There was none of that up in North Dakota, but you're right, he saw someone who would be faithful to the job and take orders. I've been with him ever since."

"It's all about blood money."

"Miss Jenny." His soft method of address caught her off guard. "Everything is about money, in my world *and* yours, and yes, blood is involved more than anyone will admit. ChemShale's employees in my area of expertise are paid a lot of money for what we do, and believe me when I say there are a lot of us. The man has an army at his disposal, if that's what you want to call it. We get paid a base salary, plus a tiny royalty on the oil that's pumped, but it adds up quick."

"Blood money." It was as if Jenny couldn't help herself. Of course, we'd invaded her home, with Russell's blessing, and her free-spirit self couldn't handle it. I didn't blame her a bit, but right that moment wasn't the time for debate.

"You can't hang all that on the oil companies." Strap wasn't bad at debate. "If you want to discuss these things, let's do it at another time and start with the pharmaceutical industry. Blood money's appropriate if you want to call it that, but the whole world operates on the love of the dollar, everything from the workingman to politicians."

"Workingman and -woman, you mean?"

"That's enough." Harley'd had enough of her, and his voice was sharp. "This isn't about our beliefs and political correctness. It's about ending this threat here and now."

Not liking their tones, Kevin woofed softly and rose to pad around like Harley had been doing earlier.

"We can't do that sitting here. If we arrest this Mr. Cross, I suspect our troubles will be over." I needed to pour a little water on the coals that were fast flaming up. "So now we have a John Doe warrant for your boss, Cross, and you know where his office is."

"Yessir, but like you said, I think we stay away from the ChemShale offices and pick him up on the street somewhere."

"There's a good chance, and I'd say a hundred percent chance, that somebody's gonna start pulling triggers." My mind spun with possibilities. "Innocent people might get hurt on the street."

"That's why we stop by his house or pick him up somewhere he's least expecting."

Harley tilted his head. "You know where he lives?"

"Yessir. Like I said, I learned a lot from him, and one of those things was to gather as much information as possible about who I worked for. I have a friend named Patel who is on staff, and if I know him and Cross both, they're doing their best to track us down."

We all glanced out the windows at the world drowning in a steamy downpour.

"Patel is going to find us, but you can bet your bottom dollar he'll do a little misdirecting, too, as well as finding a way to let us know if and when they're coming."

"How's he going to let you know? We've dumped all the electronics that can lead to us."

Furious, Jenny rose and stalked out of the room.

Strap pretended not to notice. "He'll find a way. But I say we beat them to the punch."

"How and where?"

"Well, Mr. Cross is a creature of habit. He likes nice things, and each evening when he's in or around Houston, he dines out." Strap grinned. "That's his only weakness, good food on a specific schedule. Tonight is the night he goes to Sazerac's to eat prime rib, or maybe we set up outside his house and wait for him there. This is your call."

I'd never heard of the restaurant, but Russell had. "That's the one out in the woods not far from Pinehurst."

"It is. The place sits pretty much alone out in the trees and that should make things easy for a couple of old country boys like yourselves."

A buzz came from Russell's computer. He rose, white around his mouth, and rushed to check the screen. "Car coming, and it's moving fast. Just turned off the road."

"Just one?" Harley crossed the room and picked up his M4.

"That I can see."

Harley pushed out the front door and disappeared into the rain.

Chapter 57

Rain produces a special sound in the woods, making me think of what it must be like in a South American jungle. The thick air was gray with mist and fog. Each breath filled my lungs with steamy air and water poured off the brim of my hat. My shirt was instantly wet, and stuck to my skin. Had it been a different situation, I'd have enjoyed the scent of wet pines and loam.

Harley was nowhere to be seen, but I knew my brother well enough to guess that he'd run down the two-track drive where it was easy to make time, and then ducked right into the woods.

How'd I know he went right? Because that's what I would have done if I'd left first.

That put me on the left side, and I did the same as Harley, running fast in the open before plunging into the woods several yards short of the limb I'd used to block the drive. Harley saw me and waved at the same time lights flickered through the trees down the long drive.

A white sedan lurched and bounced over the uneven ground, headlights dancing on the rough road, reflecting the falling raindrops that looked like ice as they fell through the beams. Those inside must have been bouncing their heads off the roof at a speed that was way too fast for the conditions.

The growl of the engine reached me at the same time the driver saw the limb I'd dragged across the two-track lane. There was no way to go around it, and the main part of the branch was too thick for the low-slung sedan to drive over. The driver hit his brakes and the car I recognized as a Nissan Maxima slid on the wet sand covered with pine needles. The front bumper rammed into the roadblock with a crackle of snapping limbs and splintering fiberglass.

The driver slammed the car into reverse and, seeing there was no way through the woods, shifted hard back into drive. He hit the gas and the tires spun in the same skid marks, causing the rear end to slide to the right, digging into the soft ground before they gained traction. I gave the guy props for trying. He shifted his angle and hit the thinner end of the limb full of dead needles again trying to muscle his way over the obstacle and into the clear.

Anyone driving like that told me they were either terrified, chased, or damned mad. Another option was that it was a suicide bomber and he was determined to get to the house. These days, I wouldn't put such a thing past anyone.

Partially shielded by the trunks of mature pines, Harley and I stepped out at the same time. The headlights were unnaturally bright in the gloom, and almost blinded me.

Left knee bent and leaning into his stance, Harley was ready to fire if necessary. "Driver! Out! Out of the car! Let me see your hands!"

Rifle against my shoulder and the stock tucked against my cheek, I sidestepped into the open so whoever was inside could get a good look at me and realize they were about to absorb about two pounds of lead from both sides of the trail. "Get out of the car!"

The driver's door popped open and a frightened man wearing a mop of thick black hair bailed out with both hands high and empty. "Don't shoot! Strap, Russell, Tucker Snow, uh, Harley Snow! It's me, Patel! People are on the way to do you harm!"

Chapter 58

Strap could have joined them, but he remained in the living room, watching out the back side of the house. The response by Tammy and the kids impressed him as they armed themselves and rushed up the stairs to join the boys. Chloe and Jimma had handguns, and carried them with care. They'd been trained well.

"I do love Texans." Drawing the Sig from under his shirt, he moved back into the living area to find Russell in front of the computer, checking his surveillance cameras. There was no movement in the woods.

Jenny came from their bedroom holding a Mossberg Maverick 88 pump twelve-gauge. She was tall enough that the shotgun's barrel looked shorter than its actual size. She paused when she saw Strap holding his pistol low by his leg. "I didn't say I wouldn't protect my home."

His grin was tight. "I figured as much."

Russell had his M1 carbine leaning close to hand. "Still only one person in a white car. Looks Indian. The boys have him out."

"That'd be Patel." Strap tucked the pistol into the small of his back and pushed through the front door and down the porch and into the rain, which still showed no signs of letting up. He trotted down the drive to get there before the Snow brothers took his old friend to the ground.

It wouldn't have mattered if he'd waited. They had Patel over the hood and Harley was patting him down. Strap kept his voice low and steady when he arrived. "Easy, boys. He's with us."

"That's what he says." Grabbing Patel's upper arm, I stood him up. "Tell Strap what you were telling us."

Patel gave Strap a white-toothed smile. "I knew you would be here."

"And I figured you'd show up sooner than later. What do you have?"

Patel's forehead wrinkled. "Cross is looking for you, of course. He also has people coming here." He turned to me. "You are Tucker Snow, correct?"

"I am."

"I am sorry to say I intercepted a warrant intended for you to serve."

Harley frowned, and his face reddened. "And now you're here to tell us? Why didn't you hide it, or not tell your boss?"

"Because there is another person in this organization who monitors my work. There are many overlapping layers of security to ensure loyalty and commitment. I had to tell the truth."

Harley's eyes were diamond hard. "So you ratted us out and then just jumped in your car and drove out here."

"It was the only way I could reach Strap. I often work from a variety of locations, so it isn't unusual for me to be somewhere else."

"What makes you think you aren't being tracked?" I'd positioned myself so I could see down the drive.

"I am. Like Strap, I have been planning to leave the company for some time. Today is the day."

All the while we were talking, the steady rain funneled off my hat and the one Harley wore. Strap wore a ball cap that did little to protect anything other than his eyes. Patel looked as if someone had stuck his head in a swimming pool, and we were all that wet.

We didn't need to be there any longer and now that Patel said Cross's men were on the way, I wanted to clear out. "We have to go, and here comes Russell. Probably to tell us that exact thing."

Instead of walking the distance to where we were, Russell drove an old maroon Bronco. He pulled up close and got out, leaving the engine running. "Guys, I'm getting a bad feeling."

"Us too, and there's a good reason." Strap walked a few yards toward the highway. "There's no reason for any of us to stay here right now."

"Let's take it to them." Harley looked ready to bite somebody's head off. "We have the warrant."

My mind was racing and something was bothering me that I couldn't put my finger on. Something I recalled from when Russell and Jenny first bought the property. "Russell, is this drive the only way in and out to your house? I seem to remember a trail…"

"No. There's a dirt county road hunters and fishermen use that runs not far from here. It's one folks never reach and goes down to the Trinity. And if you know where to look, it parallels the river and winds around and eventually comes out on Highway 7. It's pretty overgrown."

That's what I remembered. We'd been down it a time or two, and I recalled that it more closely resembled a trail winding through the woods than anything else. "Any houses or anything down there?"

"No. Nothing but woods and a few pastures." He grinned. "The road's hard to see on a satellite image, too."

Harley turned his attention back toward the house. "That's not good news. These people could come from that way." He turned to Russell. "Do you have cameras covering anything in that direction?"

"No. Never occurred to me. We weren't expecting to be raided from that direction."

"Fine then." I remembered Russell's Bronco was so old that the only electronics were the radio and tape player. "I say we load everyone in your Bronco and head for the hills. Even with all their technology, they can't track something that doesn't have electronics on it."

Harley adjusted the M4's three-point strap hanging over his shoulders. "Where do you think we ought to take 'em?"

"The sheriff's department in Centerville, Russell. Tell 'em everything." I finally had a plan. "Tell them to call on my burner and I'll tell 'em what I know. Then I'm calling a U.S. marshal I know and tell him we're about to pick up this Cross guy here in his region and he might want to be in on it."

"But he needs to keep it quiet when he finds out." Harley ducked his head and water funneled off onto his soaked boots. "And at the same time we can see who *he* trusts down here."

"You got it." I turned to Patel, who was wiping rain out of his eyes. "Do you know if any of the lawmen here are on Cross's payroll?"

"I have no idea, but there are many people who get paid for a variety of jobs. Do not trust anyone."

"I don't. You have any idea how long we have before they get here?"

He shrugged. "It won't be long, but Cross is planning something else. He isn't finished at the Crawford ranch. He still wants the last of the rods, because they are now the only evidence out of his hands, but the shooting there has attracted a lot of unwanted attention. He plans to put all the blame on two people there, Bill Sloan and Fred Belk."

"You guys realize we're standing here in the rain like we ain't got good sense." Harley jerked a thumb back toward the road. "If we're gonna keep talking, how about we do it inside?"

"Nope." I shook my head. "We're done here, except Patel. Would you warn Bill and Fred? Then make yourself scarce."

"I can do that, but since they don't know who I am, they probably won't believe me."

He was right. "Tell them to call my drop phone." I rattled off the number and he quickly thumbed it into his cell phone. "This is how much I trust you, Patel, because of Strap."

Strap slapped Patel on the shoulder. "Thanks, buddy. Go. I'll see you on a beach somewhere."

His friend nodded and got back in his Nissan and backed down the drive. He disappeared from view, still backing up because the trees were too close to turn around.

I headed for the Bronco. "Russell, drive us back." The three of us piled into the big rig at the same time two shots reached our ears, muffled by the rain.

Chapter 59

The man named Pratt followed what he thought of as a deer trail angling uphill from the Trinity River bottoms toward the Monroe house. The men with him, Aguilar, Hudson, Jennings and Stav spread out through the trees. They'd been hired by ChemShale two years earlier after doing contract work for the corporation in Colombia, where they'd planted dozens of common thieves bent on stealing oil and gasoline from the *Aceite de Pueblo* pipeline.

Such thefts exploded in popularity after the Covid-19 panic revealed weaknesses in governmental control. Lawlessness exploded in a number of Latin American countries and crime increased dramatically as oil theft from pipelines cutting through remote terrain increased a hundredfold.

The process was simple and provided ChemShale with any number of targets in the jungle. Well-funded gangs and leftist guerillas turned their attention from cocaine to tapping the pipelines with nearly a thousand illegal valves, hauling away up to twenty-five hundred barrels of oil each day. That equated to an annual loss of around forty million dollars each year.

ChemShale and the Colombian government fought back with a vengeance, sending in teams led by people like Pratt, who dealt with the vicious People's Liberation Army guerillas with swift gunpowder-propelled vengeance.

Now his team was moving against another enemy of ChemShale with the same instructions they followed when dealing with the PLA. End the issue.

Confident in their abilities based on months of killing well-armed thieves either through ambushes or sniping, the four-man squad almost swaggered through the piney woods. These people were sheep compared to the hardened guerillas who killed and stole for a living. Taking out an academic sheltering a cattle agent and retired police officer wouldn't be much trouble.

They'd be having drinks in one of Houston's many strip joints by dark.

Armed with M4 rifles and body armor, they approached the back of the house after following a long, overgrown trace through a mix of pines and hardwoods that reminded Pratt of the jungle trails they traversed in Colombia.

The team leader held up a fist when he finally saw the log house on the hill above. He didn't like having to advance uphill, but there was little to worry about. This wasn't a fortified position. Still, he had Jennings and his M24 sniper rifle. He could sit somewhere comfortable and reach out and touch someone at such a short distance without straining his eyes.

"Spread out and cover the outside." Pratt pointed at Aguilar. "You and Hudson there. Jennings and Stav there. Set up and find a good field of fire that'll let you do your thing. I'll go in alone."

As one they advanced in the rain, which would help obscure their approach.

Chapter 60

Tammy had the boys hemmed up in a well-appointed media room on the second floor. They were watching a movie while Chloe and Jimma found themselves in another strange bedroom with nothing to do.

The rain falling on the tin roof only a few feet above their heads made Chloe think they were in a drum. She watched Jimma walk back and forth between the bed and one of the two windows looking out on the back and side of the house.

Jimma looked miserable. "Normal families don't have things happen like this."

Chloe barked a laugh. "We're far from normal. How many people do you know have been kidnapped, or had their houses almost burned down by lunatics, or had to run away from bad guys who hate them because their dad is an officer?"

"That's what I mean. Nothing is normal about us."

Chloe smiled at Jimma saying *us*.

"We're snakebit for sure." She frowned when she realized she sounded like her dad. He always had sayings that drove her nuts.

If she complained about how much homework she had, he'd ask her if she knew how to eat an elephant.

"Just one bite at a time," he'd say and she almost felt like pulling her hair out when she heard it.

Now she was channeling him, and didn't even realize it.

Jimma must have read her mind. "You sound like Tuck. How about, 'Less is more'?"

"Right?" Chloe wasn't surprised they were on the same wavelength. They'd grown close in the last several months and had bonded through their own sisterhood. "What does that mean, anyway?"

"It means he's old and we're not."

"It wouldn't be as bad if we could go outside." Jimma fell back on the bed. "Even sitting on the porch would be better than this." She sat up. "I'd love a cigarette, too!"

Shocked to hear such a thought spoken out loud where her aunt Tammy could hear, Chloe stepped over to the open door to peer into the hall. The door to the media room was open and Tammy was sitting where she could see out, but with the TV on, she didn't appear to have heard.

Chloe knew Jimma smoked sometimes, because she'd seen her do it when the dark-haired girl lived with her mom and Atchley, and she'd snuck one now and again at school, but it wasn't something they should *talk* about.

She closed the door, leaving only an inch between the edge and the frame. "You can do that some other time. You don't have any with you right now, do you?"

Jimma gave her a wink. "Maybe. Maybe not." She stood and walked to the window looking out behind the house. "I'm just wondering if they've gotten themselves all worked up over nothing. You know, after what happened to us, your dad and Harley might be seeing boogers behind every bush."

"They know what they're doing. I don't think we should second-guess them."

The conversation stalled as Jimma watched the rain, but Chloe saw something different in her stance. Jimma turned, her face white. "There's a man out there with a rifle."

"Hunting?"

"Wrong time of the year."

Chloe spun and yanked the door open. "Aunt Tammy!"

Her aunt shot out of the media room as if she'd been expecting such a panicked call. Kevin followed close on her heels. He split off and ran downstairs as Tammy stopped in the hallway. "What's wrong?"

"Jimma says there's a guy with a gun out there."

"What kind?"

"Like Dad's."

She responded as if the whole thing was rehearsed, like a fire drill. "You and Jimma get in here with the boys. Do you have your guns?"

"Yes."

Jimma came into the hall with one in each hand. She passed a small revolver to Chloe, taking care to be sure it was pointed away from everyone. "That guy is almost to the house."

"Close the door and y'all stay in there until one of us comes to get you out."

Jimma hurried into the dark media room and Chloe followed.

—

Tammy hurried to the bedroom and peeked outside. She didn't see the man anywhere, but knew he was probably so close to the house that her perspective hid him from view. She had her own

.38 revolver in the turquoise fanny pack she wore when walking through their neighborhood for exercise. She unzipped the pouch and drew the Lady Smith.

She whirled and hurried back out into the hall to warn Jenny. Knowing better than to shout, she started down the stairs and saw Jenny flash past, shotgun in hand.

"Someone's out back." The woman's face was blank. Her mouth a thin, straight line. "I saw a gun."

Tammy's heart was in her throat as she reached the first floor where Jenny was watching out the window over the kitchen sink.

The moment was surreal. Looking like a movie set, the kitchen was neat and clean. A bowl of fruit brought color to the white quartz island. On the cabinet between the sink and stainless refrigerator, two wineglasses and an unopened bottle waited for just the right moment. A red toaster and vintage canister set were the only other items on the spartan countertop.

Tammy paused as Jenny raised the shotgun and backed away from the window. She stopped with the island between her and the back door. Mouth open in fear, she raised the shotgun, positioning herself like a shooter at a skeet station.

Movement in Tammy's peripheral vision was the only warning she had as an intruder dressed in khaki fatigues and tactical vest leaped onto the covered porch and kicked in the back door. The frame splintered and the door slammed against the counter, glass exploding from the impact.

Kevin raced across the kitchen, ears laid back and teeth exposed in a snarl. Instead of following through and targeting Tammy, the intruder's attention immediately went to the threat of a charging dog. The muzzle of his weapon swung in that direction, giving Tammy plenty of time to raise her revolver.

Squaring her stance, Tammy's pistol rose. She couldn't

see the intruder, but one step inside and she'd have the angle. Instead, the man never entered the kitchen, and Kevin didn't have time to complete his attack, because the man was blown back outside by Jenny's Mossberg. The shotgun's blast in the enclosed space sounded like a hand grenade.

His vest took most of the charge, but one of the twelve-gauge pellets punched through his left trapezius, another through the arm on that same side. The assailant stumbled back on weak knees and he landed hard on his back, eyes wide in shock. As he fell onto the wraparound porch, the man's finger tightened on the trigger and a single round punched through the glass and through the kitchen ceiling, barely missing Kevin, who grabbed the gun hand in his teeth and jerked back and forth, using the weight of his body to sling the man around.

Blood pouring from his wounds and disoriented from being shot, the attacker struggled to raise the rifle. Jenny shucked another round into the chamber and the empty hull rattled off the counter and then danced on the hardwood floor.

"Kevin! Release!"

Hearing Tammy's voice, the lab turned the man loose and trotted back into the house.

This time Jenny aimed. "Don't raise that rifle."

The muzzle came up and with tears in her eyes, she pulled the trigger again. This time the charge took him in the neck. "This is my damned house."

Chapter 61

Those two shots were all that cut through the rain, but from the Bronco's back seat, I saw a man in khaki fatigues and tactical vest rounding the side of the house as it came into view. He had what looked like an M4 tucked up and ready to fire, but we surprised him.

Russell slammed on the Bronco's brakes, and Harley and I rolled out of the back seat, each of us through a different door. Drawing a handgun, Strap popped out of the front seat and crossed the front of the house to intercept anyone coming around from the other side.

The guy beside the house reversed direction and vanished like smoke. We split up while Russell charged straight up the porch and into the living room. "Jenny! It's me!"

Separated by several yards, Harley and I veered off into the woods to better get an angle on the back of the house, creeping from tree to tree. I was wishing I'd put on my vest, but it hadn't seemed necessary only an hour earlier. Who would have thought that a private residence in rural Leon County would come under attack by armed individuals? This was something I'd expect in a third world country, but not in my home state.

But then again, parts of our world were quickly becoming unrecognizable, and we were in a war that was bearing down on us like a freight train.

Harley extended his left arm and waved me farther away. I guess he felt we were too close together. When I swung out, I realized my little brother might have had another plan. He shouldered his rifle and took a knee at the edge of the house and waited for me to reach the edge of the trees bordering the back of the house.

I'd let him use me as bait.

Thankfully, there was a large hickory tree that looked as big around as a Volkswagen bug. I ducked behind it and studied the area that could have been hiding an entire army. Russell's "backyard" extended out probably forty feet from the house and ended abruptly at the edge of thick woods leading down to a steep gully.

I didn't see anyone, but that meant nothing. "Special agent! Put down your weapons and step out into the open or you will be shot!"

There were any number of hiding places there and my heart was in my throat. The one thing I wanted was to go charging into the house to make sure everyone was safe, but I couldn't because I didn't know if there were any others out there. After what we'd seen of ChemShale, there was a damned good chance the woods were full of armed men.

Common sense told me there were only three or four men out there, but fear is a strange mind killer and thief of reasoning. I kept expecting hundreds of armed men to emerge from the trees, so much so that my knees were almost shaking.

I knew one thing for sure: anyone shooting at me was going to watch grass grow from the wrong side.

Russell's voice came through the driving rain. "One man down here!"

Had he said one down, both Harley and I would have lost it, thinking that one of the girls or the boys was injured, but the addition of "man" made it clear that someone in the house had defended themselves.

As I leaned against the back side of the hickory on that gray day, I wondered what had happened to our world. Harley and I were walking an equally gray line in both defending Russell's house and our families, and in our actions that would come into question in a court of law.

I decided right then to worry about it later, but for the love of Pete, I was a *brand* inspector in Northeast Texas, and this was about as far from my duties as I could get.

Not seeing any movement, I again wondered how many people were out there. I backed up a little, thinking that there might be a guy with a scoped rifle. All a good sniper would need would be a sliver of face, a shoulder, or an elbow.

During training with a SWAT team several years earlier, Harley and I played the bad guys in a scenario where we took over an abandoned school building and let the team of well-trained professionals root us out. We were there all day, shooting at each other with Simunition, nonlethal training ammunition that comes in 9-mm, .38, and 5.56 calibers. They fire a reduced charge paint projectile that breaks upon impact to mark where the round hits.

At the end of that day, my right elbow looked like an abstract painting, and was so sore I could barely bend it, despite the low velocity of the bullets. When I asked the SWAT leader why they'd continually shot me there, because we're all trained to fire at center mass, he laughed and told me that's what they could see when I was hiding around corners and raised the Glock they'd supplied me.

Because of that training, I kept my right elbow tucked against my body, and that's all that saved me when someone sent a burst of three rounds toward my tree. Two chunks of lead knocked great long splinters off the trunk, while the third whistled past so close I could almost smell it.

In response, Harley squeezed off two quick bursts, and I saw the impacts against the small limbs on a yaupon. Without moving, he squeezed off another three-round burst and stepped back into the protection of the house as even more twigs and leaves fell.

Shots came from the other side of the property in ragged pops like a string of Black Cat firecrackers. It wasn't repeated. Harley rose from his crouch and charged in my direction. I fired half a dozen rounds at the trees, just to make sure no one would shoot at him.

He whirled around my tree and continued in a sweep that took him parallel to the back of the house. It was quiet for a moment before I heard him. "Move!"

He wanted me to alternate with him and work our way through the timber.

"Moving!" I followed a similar path, passed behind him, and several yards into the woods where I found another tree for cover. Yaupons growing thick and lush slapped my hat, nearly knocking it from my head. A thorny vine caught my boot with a ripping sound against the leather, almost causing me to fall. I stumbled and caught myself with one hand against a tree where I took a knee.

I'd barely stopped when an arm came out of nowhere and wrapped around my throat from behind. The guy was a pro, and in half a second I felt the arm tighten, cutting off the blood supply to my brain.

Lucky for me I didn't have the rifle's strap over my shoulder. I let it go and almost gave in to the instinct to grab the arm to reduce the pressure, but instead I bent, ducked my left shoulder in and under his right side. Twisting hard, I planted my left leg behind his and threw my weight against his fall. With the change in leverage, I was able to throw him off-balance and backward.

Physics took over and his grip was gone, stripping my hat and what seemed like all the skin and hair from my temples in a hot path of friction. His shoulders and the back of his head hit the ground with a wet thump.

Had it been an arrest situation, things would have proceeded differently, but this was a murder attack. The next thing I knew, my .45 was in my hand and I stuck it into his stomach and pulled the trigger several times. The guy twitched, groaned, and grew still.

Breathing hard, I holstered the 1911, slapped my hat back on my head, picked up my rifle, and let Harley know I was set. "Move!"

"Moving!"

My heart was pounding out of my chest as he rushed toward the position where we'd taken fire and stopped, easing forward with his rifle at high ready. I saw him jerk to a stop and aim downward. It was a moment before he relaxed. "I see brain matter!"

Whether he did or not, it was a signal that the shooter was down and out of commission. "Moving!"

I answered, "Move!"

He took two steps and someone opened up on him, the shots coming hard and fast, sounding flat and muffled. Harley dropped to the ground at the same time I saw a muzzle flash through the rain. Already geared up to fire, I was on the shooter in a second and pumped round after round at the bursts of light, saturating the area.

A high-pitched yelp told me I'd connected.

Seconds later, we heard heavy receding footsteps as another assassin showed good sense and ran away. I had to make sure the guy I'd hit was really out of commission. "Moving!"

"Move!"

Running in a low crouch and anticipating the impact of a bullet, I reached the body that lay still in death. The guy was dressed like the first man we'd seen behind the house, and I shook my head in wonder that his vest hadn't turned every bullet I'd fired.

It looked to me that at least one or more hit him hard enough that he twisted in pain, allowing a single round to penetrate his chest through the armhole. It was a lucky shot on my part, but not so much for him, and proved the fallibility of body armor.

"Dead man!"

"Moving!"

I heard the adrenaline in his voice when Harley broke from cover. I was moving slower than when we first began, and wobbled to a stop to catch my breath. Harley must have felt the same way because the next time I saw him going through the woods, his movements weren't as fluid.

We swept through the trees, looking for more targets and hopefully clearing the area. By the time we came to a thin trail leading to the east, we'd covered most of what Russell might have considered his back woods without finding another shooter.

Crouching beside a thicket of yaupon hollies, we squinted through the rain and let our ears do the work for us while our lungs caught up with what we'd asked of them. It was quiet if you didn't count the constant slap of drops on hardwood leaves.

Strap stepped out into the open. I don't know if he knew exactly where we were, but he waved a hand to call us in. "Clear!"

Not taking any chances, we again separated and, hoping the rain would cover us from any long-distance snipers, emerged from the woods. Strap was already on the way toward the back door and we followed, alternately twisting and sweeping around and behind us until we were inside.

Chapter 62

As I climbed the steps, Strap grabbed a body by the collar with his free hand and drug it off the porch. Nothing is as limp as a dead mammal, and this guy was no exception. His head lolled as Strap pulled, and his heels thumped down the steps. Strap dropped him without ceremony, and the body folded in two before gravity took hold.

His other hand held an M4 rifle that he took off one of the bodies.

Harley barely gave the corpse a glance as he went inside, taking care to step around a wide puddle of blood. "That one's DRT." The old slang used by cops, paramedics, or other first responders, was short for "dead right there."

It was a beehive of activity inside the house. Russell and Tammy were gathering kids and preparing to hustle them out to the Bronco. Russell picked up Matt and Danny's little backpacks with one hand and held the M1 carbine with the other. "They came up through that county road we talked about. We can't go that direction."

Chloe held the boys by their hands. Harley gave her a pat on the shoulder as he went straight through the kitchen and out to my truck. She took a deep breath to steady her voice. "There were more than two, Dad. Me and Jimma counted three, and there may have been four or five." She told me what they'd seen through the upstairs window.

Strap passed. "They're all neutralized."

Tammy and Jenny took turns bringing us up to speed on what happened in the kitchen. Jenny's eyes were glassy. I'd seen that look before when someone was under duress, or had been attacked. It was a look that couldn't be faked, and came from the adrenaline that flooded her system.

Tammy's eyes looked sleepy, the opposite reaction some folks experience. It meant shock could be setting in and I'd have to watch her.

My mouth was dry from fear and effort. I opened the fridge to find it stocked with water bottles. I took one out and sat it on the island, then passed others around. "Drink. Everyone needs water right now."

I twisted the top off mine and drained half the contents.

Harley came back inside with our tactical vests. We'd loaded them with magazines, first aid kits, knives, and fire before we left. We slipped our arms through the holes and shrugged into them, smoothing the Velcro straps that held them tight against our bodies.

He gave me a wry look. "These things didn't help those guys much, but they've saved our bacon more than once."

He wasn't kidding. The first time I'd gotten into a fight as a young cop, a couple attacked me in a house when my partner and I'd been called out on a domestic disturbance. Half a minute after I arrived, I was in a wrestling match with the man who'd been fighting with his wife. Seeing me on top and trying to cuff him, she switched sides and came in from the kitchen with a butcher knife, raking it down my back several times.

The officers who arrived drug her off, and after they cuffed her too, insisted that I lie down and wait for an ambulance. Feeling just fine, I asked what was wrong and one of the older officers told me to take off the vest.

The back of the vest was shredded from the sharp butcher knife, and the only thing that saved me that night was the fact that she'd slashed me instead of stabbing me in the back.

Kevlar won't turn a knife thrust.

Adjusting the vest on my shoulders, I took up a position giving me a clear view of the woods out back. "The thing that saved us was that they didn't expect us to be outside in the rain. We surprised them, and they didn't have time to adjust to our defense."

Rain washed the blood off the body Strap dragged out of the way.

I thought back to how this had all started, and even further, dealing with Jess Atchley only a few months earlier. "It's hard to believe something like this is happening. I've had enough of this."

Harley's grin reminded me of a lion. "I'm just getting started."

"There's something wrong with you." I turned to see Strap thumbing fresh shells into a pistol. "Thanks."

"Just trying to make amends." He tucked it into the back of his belt. "Cross doesn't send two-man teams for anything other than knock and talks, so your daughter is right. These guys aren't amateurs, they just didn't expect this kind of response. And Russell's right. We can't go that way, because they're fading back to the vehicle that brought them, and have probably called Cross already."

"Will they go?"

"Hard to know. I recognize that one on the porch. Name's Pratt, and he was one bad dude. I was surprised to see him here. He's been working down in Colombia, putting down oil thieves out there."

Tammy stood with her back to the refrigerator. "What does that mean?"

"It means they deal with thieves a different way in South America. Gangs are stealing oil, and people like Pratt are killing all of 'em they can find."

Running one shaky hand across her forehead, Jenny finally leaned forward and braced herself against the island. "Look what I did. How can people be like that? How can they make other people do what I did?"

"People have always been killing each other." Strap set his jaw. "Some to defend themselves, others trying take something, or their lives from them. It's nothing new."

Her voice was sharp. "And *you* did these things."

"Yes, ma'am. I'm ashamed to say I did, but now I'm trying to make amends."

"It's too late."

"You're probably right, but my old grandmother said we can all be forgiven."

It was hard to believe, but the intensity of the rain increased, overwhelming the gutters and running over the metal sides in sheets.

Russell put one hand on his wife's shoulder and drew a deep breath.

"It probably wouldn't have been smart to go down by the river anyway. This much rain is running off pretty fast. Some parts of that road are sugar sand, and sometimes it doesn't know how to act when it gets wet. It can pack, or it can just bog down a car even with four-wheel-drive like the Bronco has. If any were left to get away, they'll probably have trouble getting out."

"I'm not worried about them if they go that way," I said. "I hope they wash off into the Trinity and drown. All right, me and Harley'll use my truck to lead y'all out in the Bronco, Russell. Once we get on the highway, you stay on our bumper until we get to Centerville proper, then peel off at the sheriff's office."

He nodded.

So much had been going on that I hadn't paid much attention to Chloe and Jimma until that moment. They were so close they could have been attached at the shoulder. It was the revolvers lying on the island in front of them that made my heart hurt.

What had happened to our world?

Strap checked the safety on the M4 he'd picked up, dropped the mag to make sure it was fully loaded, and then pulled the bolt back to see the brass of a chambered round. He shrugged. "I don't have a stamp."

He was referring to the NFA tax stamp required to own a fully automatic weapon.

Satisfied with his newly acquired weapon, he flicked the selector switch to full auto. "This. Will. Do."

I took Chloe's arm. "We have to go now."

Chapter 63

Jennings's rifle and scope wasn't much use in the rain and thick trees, but he wasn't inclined to shoot anymore, anyway, with a hole in his stomach. Wondering how everything could have gone sideways so quick and holding his left hand over the wound in his side, he left the carnage behind and made his way back to their company-issued Jeep.

Pratt had parked it nose-in in a thick grove of cedars that served to break some of the rain and prevent the vehicle from being seen from above and most sides, except for the way they'd come in from the river. They'd been crowded inside with three big men in the back, but the empty interior seemed enormous when he opened the back hatch and pitched in the rifle beside a MOLLE pack.

Panting, he half sat in the shelter of the raised door and dragged the pack close and opened the first aid kit attached to the exterior. They usually each wore a pack full of ammo, food, water, and emergency supplies, but this was supposed to have been an easy mission. Taking out unsuspecting civilians didn't require such supplies.

Pratt was wrong. It was like they'd run into a buzz saw and it was completely unexpected. They were lazy and unprepared, and the result was a dead or dying team and a hole in his stomach.

Water dripped off the brim of his khaki cap as he ripped out a packet of quick-clot gauze and stuffed it over the hole not much bigger than a pencil in his abdomen. Hissing with pain, he applied pressure and covered the area with a self-sticking battle dressing. Pulling a crackling plastic bottle from half a case of water, he drained most of it in a series of loud swallows.

He pitched the empty over into the back seat and tugged a phone from the cargo pocket on his right leg. "Damn it!"

The words, No Signal, were the most frustrating things he'd ever seen.

"I told them we needed SAT phones!"

Jennings jammed the useless block of plastic and circuitry back into the pocket and grunted to his feet. He closed the hatch and peered around the Jeep to make sure no one was following. The trace was empty. Using his hand to maintain pressure against his side, he rounded the vehicle and dropped in behind the wheel.

At least Pratt left the key fob inside, in case they had to evac quickly. Jennings grunted. It wasn't much of an evac, if you asked him. The word *rout* came to mind. The Jeep started with a quiet hum, and using the rearview and side mirrors, he backed into the ribbon of space they'd followed in.

A soft crunch and abrupt stop caused him to jerk, sending a jolt of pain through his side. A crash of water on the roof made him think the pine tree he'd backed into had split up high and dropped on the Jeep.

"Dammit!"

Despite the bandage, his lap was filling with blood. He had to get out and find help soon. That little .223 or 5.56 round must have rattled around inside, putting holes in lots of important parts.

Gritting his teeth at the pain, he shifted into Drive and pulled away from the tree. It was almost too much to take, but he twisted around to look out the back glass and see if there was a wide enough opening to back up.

The underbrush was too thick, so the only option was to drive forward for a few yards, looking for an opening. Luck was finally with him when he came upon a wide enough gap to nose in, then make a three-point turnaround to get back on the cut. Resisting the urge to drive fast, he found a speed that wouldn't beat him up too badly and followed the serpentine trail down to the bottoms.

The wiper blades barely kept up with the volume of falling water, and steering became squirrelly at one point, but he kept his cool and shifted into four-wheel-drive at the last minute to get out of trouble on the softening ground. Whenever it was wide enough, and that wasn't often, he found that driving with the wheels on grass, sticks, and decaying vegetation gave him better traction.

Branches squealed and scraped along the passenger side, but it was of little consequence to the ChemShale employee. He needed to get back onto the highway, find a signal for his phone, then a hospital.

There he'd play dumb until someone from ChemShale came to pick him up. Of course, that might take a while, because the first thing the emergency room doctors would do was notify the local police or sheriff's department and report the shooting.

A little cash under the table would take care of all that.

Jennings breathed a sigh of relief when the trail began to

ascend from the Trinity River bottoms. Still, the heavy rain caused problems as the tires sometimes slipped and got bogged down. After what seemed like hours, he reached a blacktop road.

He turned onto the hard surface and stopped to check the signal on his phone. Three bars was enough. He leaned back in the seat and punched in the emergency number as rain sluiced down the glass and the wipers swept sheets of rain from the windshield.

A gruff voice answered. "This is Murphy."

"Jennings. Our mission was compromised. People were waiting. I'm the only survivor."

"This Pratt's team?"

"Was."

"Did you complete your objective?"

"Not hardly."

"Are you damaged?"

"Worse than you can imagine."

"Do you need extraction?"

"Yes."

There was a moment while the man on the other end of the line played a keyboard. "I see you. Can you drive?"

"Some."

"Follow that road to a highway intersection. Turn left. There's an abandoned farmhouse about five miles further. People will be there."

"What about the others?"

"Did you leave them behind?"

"It would have been hard to carry four dead men at once. Of course I left them."

The was silence on the other end.

"Just get to the pickup point."

The line went dead and Jennings drove to the end of the blacktop. Once he reached the highway, there were no more trees to break the rain and it was a deluge. Water flowed down ditches on both sides of the road, looking like natural streams.

His vision blurred after a mile and his forehead felt heavy and full of cement. His eyes drooped and the Jeep strayed off onto the shoulder. Jennings's heart ran out of blood and ceased to pump his empty arteries. The Jeep nosed off and into the bank-full ditch, sending up a splash and wave of water that covered the hood.

Five minutes later, a Dodge pickup followed closely by a Ford Bronco passed without slowing.

Chapter 64

"Oops." Harley watched a Jeep that was nosed into the ditch recede in our mirrors.

I kept one eye on the road and the other on the Bronco behind us. They weren't following as closely as I would prefer, but my truck was throwing up a pretty good fan of water and they had to back off. "We'd stop any other time, but I can't risk those behind us."

"I didn't see anybody behind the wheel." In the back seat, Strap turned to look through the glass over his shoulder. "Maybe somebody already picked them up."

"Could have."

We went over a hill and met a dark SUV coming our way. I tensed, wondering if it was another ChemShale vehicle. It was difficult to see inside as we passed, as the dark clouds reflected off the glass. I breathed a sigh of relief when the only glimpse I got of the driver told me it was a woman.

It disappeared over the hill behind us, and the road dipped. I slowed, expecting water to be collected at the bottom of the drop, but the engineers were good and the road's slope carried runoff away. It was up and down after the next couple of miles, typical of land draining toward river bottoms.

There was no more traffic other than a white panel van going the opposite direction until we pulled into town. The few streetlights and storefront signs reminded me of dusk. Lights on the inside and two cars in the parking lot were all that told us the local grocery store was open. We slowed when we reached what amounted to the town square. The parking lot in front of the sheriff's office was almost empty. I turned into the drive and slowed down between the parking slots on either side.

Behind us, Russell pulled the Bronco into an angled parking space right in front of the door. I waited, engine idling, as he popped out the door and checked the surroundings.

"Good boy." Harley nodded, his hand on the grip of the M4 riding muzzle down on the floorboard between his legs.

Russell leaned into the Bronco and said something, probably telling those inside that it was clear. The other three doors opened and the group rushed through the rain, just like we'd ordered. Kevin made a single loop around the Bronco as if checking to see that no one was left behind before he trotted into the station.

The moment they were inside, I drove through the lot and onto Highway 7. I turned right and we drove through what was left of the town to the entrance ramp of I-45. Harley's phone rang.

"You guys all right?" He punched the speaker icon so we could hear.

It was Tammy. "We're good. We just told the deputy working dispatch. Everyone else is out working wrecks because of the rain, but Russell knows the deputy here, who believed us, and we're locked inside now."

"Better put the boys in a cell."

"Believe me, I wish they would." She sighed. "You two be careful."

I leaned a little toward the phone. "Did they want to know about us?"

"Sure did. I told them you were a stock agent and were serving a warrant. They want to talk to you."

"Can't hear you." Harley made crackling noises with his mouth. "You're breaking up. Prob..e..ther. . .rain."

He punched the phone off and Strap chuckled. "You guys are Cross's nightmare."

I met his eyes in the rearview mirror. "Why's that?"

"Because he can't plan for you two. He truly realized you were different when you turned down the money. I thought his head was going to explode over that one. He's a chess player, you know, and he likes to plan. You guys are damned random."

"Which is why we're going to meet him at Sazerac's. He won't be expecting us to show up there."

An eighteen-wheeler passed us, throwing up sheets of water that the wipers could barely keep up with. I was driving almost ten miles under the speed limit, but big truckers on the interstate considered time as money, and had no intentions of driving so slow.

Despite the rain, the interstate was busy, and by the time we reached Huntsville, the traffic had increased. As we passed the prison, I glanced into the rearview mirror to see Strap studying the walls, wire, and gun towers on the far side of a wide pasture full of horses.

"I won't be going there, guys."

Neither of us turned our heads. Harley stared straight ahead. "You do right with these guys, and I probably won't see you disappear like the Lone Ranger at the end of an episode."

"You too, Tuck?"

A sedan passed, the driver holding the wheel tight with both hands. Despite the rain, I saw the elderly woman driver's big knuckles and driving glasses.

"A beach sounds pretty good right now."

—

We reached the Woodlands, a twenty-eight-thousand-home master-planned wooded community north of Houston. The interstate had widened to six lanes of traffic and slowed down to less than thirty miles an hour. I took the first exit west and we found ourselves stuck in bumper-to-bumper traffic negotiating lights that held us up at every intersection for over twenty miles.

Harley was like a caged lion on a short leash. He twisted, turned, crossed and uncrossed his legs so much that Strap leaned forward to watch. "You didn't take your meds today, did you?"

"I don't take anything except aspirin." Harley adjusted the rifle and tried to loosen his seat belt.

A police car passed us. "Little brother, this guy over there sees the butt of that rifle, and we're gonna have some 'splainin to do."

"It's perfectly legal for me to have it here."

"You and I know that, but I'm pretty sure our names are out there and more than one person is looking for us."

"Some kid tries to mess with me today, and I'm gonna bring the world down on his shoulders."

"You're preaching to the choir." I checked the rearview mirror at the next light holding us up. "Black SUV behind us." I was now paranoid of any dark SUV.

In the back, Strap shifted to lean his back against the seat and the passenger-side door, stretching his legs out behind me. "Cross won't do anything with this many people around. There's no way to clean up the mess when it happens. He's probably busy with crews dealing with what y'all left at Russell's house."

"I wish I knew that for sure."

"I do."

"So what does that entail?"

"Depends who he has close. Guys come in and pick up bodies when they need to. That's the first order of business, and they'll even get the brass when they can. Vehicles have to disappear, and while all that's going on, a couple of guys are working the scene to make it look like an accident occurred there, or a suicide."

"What'd they do at the Ramsey place?"

"That was easy. A big crew came in and pulled up all the hot rods. Once they were gone, it was nothing but a hired landscape crew to clean up behind them."

"But you had experts in hazmat gear, and truckers, and heavy equipment out there at first."

"Sure did. Those guys are paid well, and they understand how dangerous it is to talk about their jobs. They're fast, though."

"This is conspiracy territory."

"It's not conspiracy. It's reality." He pointed with a big hand. "Turn up there. I know a back way we can use to get to the restaurant."

I followed the route but wasn't through with our conversation. "What about the people like Ramsey and his wife?"

"ChemShale deals with a lot of dark issues. We sometimes had to move people out of their homes for a variety of reasons. Most of the time they're persuaded to take a huge amount of cash in addition to what they get for their property. Money deposited into a bank can account for the house and property, and a couple of suitcases of cash under the bed makes everybody happy."

Harley crossed his arms and leaned back against the seat rest. "You're gonna run out of cash when the government forces companies to quit pumping oil."

Strap barked a laugh. "That'll never happen. This green movement is bogus. Sure, they can make electric cars and everyone'll be happy to say and think they saved the environment, but no one looks past the sound bites and surface reporting.

"We'll *always* need oil. It takes petroleum to make everything on an electric car from fiberglass to metal, nylon, plastic, and safety glass. But no one thinks about the oil it takes to make damn near everything in your house. Good Lord, everything you touch is manufactured in some way with petroleum or energy from oil.

"Look around. Oil is used to make ballpoint pens, faucet washers, dyes, soap, TVs, and the cabinets they sit on. The sealant on the logs in your house, upholstery, the water pipes bringing water into the house. The credit cards in your wallet, and most likely everything else in there, the trash bags under your sink, most of the bottles under there, the glasses sitting on your nose, and I hate to break it to you, even the blades on the wind turbines so many people love come from oil. The whole *world* is made from petroleum products.

"Even all the way back to the cargo ships themselves that bring everything over from China and the other countries we trade with. Politicians are like magicians. 'Look at this hand doing all this work. Watch this hand, watch these fingers wiggle, and watch this hand some more. It's the liar.

"The other hand we can't see is doing all the work. Get this, guys. Today's modern cars contain from one thousand to three thousand microcircuit chips. You don't think those plants are powered by electricity, do you? And where do the materials come from? They all trail back to a manufacturing process that's fueled by oil.

"And then they have to get it here. Transports, loading equipment, and all the parts that make them up. Look at all the cars around us and think of the parts that make up cars and think about getting them from overseas. *One* container ship from other countries emits pollutants equivalent to fifty *million* cars. That's *one* ship."

"How's that?" I used my indicator to change lanes and get around someone driving with a phone to their ear.

"Because the low-grade fuel that cargo ships use contains up to two thousand times the amount of sulfur compared to the diesel used in cars and eighteen-wheelers. And now there's a new breed of super-size container ships that use fuel not by the gallons, but by tons per *hour*! To top it off, shipping across oceans now accounts for ninety percent of global trade."

Harley drew a deep breath. "Oil is here to stay."

"And drilling, too, and companies like ChemShale. Guys, there's no getting away from this." He paused. "And don't even get me started on what it takes to put up a wind turbine. Petroleum builds the world, and that's a fact."

The rain slacked off enough that I could turn the wipers down one notch, and a few minutes later, we were out of most of the traffic and headed for Sazerac's restaurant in the little town of Pinehurst.

Chapter 65

Bill Sloan and Fred Belk watched it rain through the open door of the Crawford bunkhouse, along with Toby James, who'd arrived only minutes earlier. Also known as the Smythes, Toby and Bill were talking about the murders of the rancher and his wife.

Checking to make sure no one was close, she pulled Bill to her side. "This is my fault."

"How can you say that?"

She told him about the phone call from the truck driver and his offer. "I wasn't going to go, but then I got to thinking we needed money, and I decided that I'd meet them, but they never called back."

She drew a long, shuddering breath. "It had to have been those guys who killed the Crawfords. I didn't lead them here, but I might just as well have."

Sloan held her arm. "What makes you say that?"

"I slipped while I was talking to the guy. Said their name. It isn't hard to run it and find this ranch." She wiped a tear. "Stealing cows is one thing, but outright murder is another. We need to get out of here and find another line of work, or at least relocate."

She looked past Bill at a shelf beside the door that displayed her little owl Mr. Crawford made for her, and his first two attempts to create little artistic critters. Those people wanted the drill rods back and the irony was that even the little figure had been part of that load.

Fred leaned on the doorframe, looking out. Lying on one of the unused bunks, Maggie the blue heeler watched the three of them. "I hate what happened to the Crawfords, but there's a lot of stock out there that needs to be rounded up and sold. We can't just leave. Somebody needs to take care of this ranch for a while."

"You don't think you're gonna sell 'em for cash, do you?" Toby was shocked. "That'll have Tucker Snow on us like a tick, and I don't want to go back to jail. Not with my record. If Snow sees me with hot stock, he'll make sure I wind up in the Goree unit down in Huntsville."

"We don't sell 'em here." Sloan couldn't help touching the new CV line his doctor had inserted into his chest. The new central venous catheter would remain in place until they called to tell him he had a new kidney waiting and the surgery was way in the past.

Fred tucked a dip of Skoal into his bottom lip. "We load them up and head for Oklahoma or Arkansas. Maybe across the river in Louisiana. There are some small sale barns down there that aren't as particular about keeping good records. We sell them using Mr. Crawford's name and clear out."

Toby gently touched Sloan's CV under his shirt. "Can you work with that thing in your chest?"

"Sure can. They wanted to put it into my groin, but I told

'em that was your territory and nobody was shaving anything around there but you."

She gave him a punch in the shoulder. "Behave."

"Look, those rods they wanted to buy are hotter than the hinges of hell. That's what killed Mitch and Strawn, and ultimately the Crawfords, and it's killing me too. Those guys are something we don't need to mess with." Sloan turned toward Fred, who walked back to his go-bag resting on one of the bunks. "We're little pawns in some big game, and even though we started this mess, we need to warn the Snows and get the hell out of here."

Fred agreed with him. "Well, I say we do this fast and don't come back. It gives me the creeps to be around here with the Crawfords gone. Too many feds around here anyway."

"So we sell the stock down there in the lower pasture and find another way to make a living?"

"This one doesn't seem healthy anymore." Bill Sloan chuckled. "But one sure thing, we'll be gone and the laws will be looking for some other rustlers who took advantage of the situation here." He looked at the others. "When it comes to money and survival, friendships tend to take a back seat."

Chapter 66

It rained on us all the way to Pinehurst. That happens in Texas a lot, especially when the southwest winds come up from Mexico and intersect cooler weather. Of course the steady rain would eventually come to an end, but I hoped it kept up at least into the night. We needed the cover.

I'd gone over the plan with the guys on the way out there. We'd wait until Cross arrived at the restaurant, then simply catch him in the parking lot between his car and the building. That would keep us away from as many innocent citizens as possible, in case he did something stupid.

The John Doe warrant would give us the authority to cuff and stuff him in one county, and then hightail it out of there back to Judge Hiragana and friendly territory, where I could defang the man who threatened me and my family.

Tucked off Stagecoach Road in a clearing cut into thick woods and designed to look like a rustic lodge, Sazerac's Restaurant wasn't much on the outside. The exterior was fake logs, a far cry from Russell's real log home. A large throwback neon sign on the two-lane highway out front flickered red and blue through the low clouds and rain fifty feet above the ground.

The muted colors reminded me of traveling carnivals on cool, foggy fall evenings. Except the air was thick and juicy. I pulled up in the busy gravel parking lot and backed in against the trees between two other pickups.

Despite the rain, mosquitoes were bad, and we had to leave the engine running and the windows up. I turned the headlights off and hoped no one would pay too much attention to three men sitting inside the cab.

The woods behind us were thick and dark with an occasional lightning bug flickering three or four feet above the ground. No one would be walking past back there, which allowed us to concentrate on the parking lot quickly filling with customers.

Harley watched a young couple walk along a cedar porch rail, past half a dozen people waiting outside for a table or others to join them before they went inside. The porch was wide enough to stay out of the weather if patrons sat in a line of rocking chairs against the front wall.

Harley studied the exterior. "Those people are tougher than I am. I couldn't sit still and let skeeters eat me up."

I cut my eyes at him, knowing what was coming next.

"But I can't sit here without knowing what it looks like around this place." He opened the door and stepped out. "Need to do it before it gets too dark. This dome light's like a million-candlepower flood."

We'd taken off our vests for the drive out, and he adjusted his untucked shirt covering the M9 pistol on his belt. "I'll be back in a second."

He closed the door and took a look around. No one was paying any attention to him, so he adjusted his ball cap to protect his eyes from the rain and walked straightaway from the tailgate and into the woods.

I watched a sedan turn off the highway and into the parking lot. "Your old boss must really like the food here to drive so far."

Strap slid to the middle of the back seat. "He loves this place because it reminds him of when he was a kid in Louisiana."

"He doesn't have an accent."

"He does when he's upset or mad. Cross works hard to keep it under wraps."

It felt like when Harley and I were on stakeouts back in the old days. "Does he come early, late?"

"You never know. He'll be here before nine, though."

I checked my watch. Most people have given up on wearing them, but Harley and I depended on wristwatches when movement was critical. There was no digging a phone out and punching it awake. Using a phone to check the time in the dark would be like shining a flashlight into our faces.

"We might be here awhile."

I kept looking for Harley, but he was far enough back in the trees that he remained hidden. I reached under my seat and pulled out an old shop towel. Pitching it into his seat, I waited as rain beat on the roof.

It was past eight when the gloom gave way to darkness. One minute there was nothing behind us, and the next Harley appeared between the trucks and opened the door. Soaking wet, he slipped into the seat and grabbed up the ragged towel.

"Thanks."

"Well?"

"Skeeters are bad, like I thought."

"And?"

"Two men sitting in a truck right on the opposite edge of

the parking lot. Nothing else, but I think they're not supposed to be there. The woods go back a ways all around." He pointed. "That's the only way in and out. I think we need to go cuff and stuff 'em. How do you want to do this?"

"They could be guys waiting for someone to go in and eat."

"They could be guys waiting to shoot us when we get out. Let's bag 'em."

Strap grunted from the back seat. "Does he always talk like this?"

"He's doing it for you." I dreaded getting out in the rain. "All right. Let's go see. I'll walk up to the driver. You cover the other side."

"Just like the old days."

"It usually wasn't raining. Strap, you hang here."

"Gladly."

We slipped out of the truck and again I cursed the dome light that lit us up like aircraft landing lights. There was enough of a glow coming from lights around the restaurant to let us see our way on the periphery of the woods, walking right against the edge of the darkness.

We came up behind the pickup Harley saw, and there were two in it all right. The driver's window was down and cigarette smoke filled the air. There wasn't much room between their truck and a sedan parked beside it. Drawing my .45, I came up on the driver's door, surprised he didn't check his side mirror, where he would have seen me the moment I stepped between the vehicles.

I came up fast and shoved the Colt behind his ear. "Police! Hands on the wheel and don't move." Being a special agent is different from the police, but most civilians are geared toward that title, so I wanted them to be sure they understood what was going on.

Harley jerked the back door open on the crew cab and jumped into the back seat. He grabbed the man's left shoulder and squeezed. "You move and I'll shoot you through this seat. Tuck, lots of guns back here."

"Driver. Open the door and stick your left hand out." He did and I snapped a cuff on his wrist. "Slide out and back. Hands behind you. Passenger, do what he says back there."

We had them out and cuffed before they could get a good read on what was happening. The rain covered our movements on the dim side of the parking lot, and we pulled them deeper into the woods.

"Don't kill us." The driver was terrified, and I would have been too if a couple of guys had snatched me and Harley out of our truck.

"You'll be fine if you do what I say." I turned him to see Harley. "He'll shoot if you so much as sneeze."

Harley gave him his crazy grin. He'd used it a hundred times when we were working together, because it was so creepy and unnerving to antsy criminals. "How about we cut their throats and leave them to bleed out? I don't want them yelling."

The passenger almost yelped. "Don't! We won't make a sound."

"I don't believe you." Harley unbuckled the man's belt. "I hope you're in good shape."

"Why?"

"You'll see."

He had them on their sides trussed with the belts looped around their ankles and up their spines and around their necks. "Y'all stay in that position, and you'll be fine. If you try to wriggle around or yell, those belts will tighten and you'll strangle yourselves."

"This is inhuman." The driver's voice squeaked off when the belt tightened on his Adam's apple.

"See? Now, y'all be still."

We left them and worked our way back around to the truck. Strap looked relieved that we were back. "What happened?"

I took off my hat and put it on the dash. The only thing that wasn't wet was the top of my head. "Put a couple of old boys out of commission."

"You kill 'em?"

"No, tied them up, but they'll be all right."

"They're gonna yell."

Harley grinned. "No they won't."

I checked the parking lot. "Nothing?"

"Not yet," Strap answered.

Harley used the already wet shop towel to dry his face. "How many cars does Cross show up with?"

"I only expect him and a driver."

"Well, it should be pretty easy to pick him up, then."

"We'll see."

—

It was dark when a black Suburban turned off the highway, across the oncoming lane of traffic, and into the parking lot.

Strap sat upright. "That's him."

We'd already put our tactical vests back on. We watched as the Suburban circled the parking lot, then pulled into an unmarked space at the outer edge, the hood facing the highway.

"Let's go." I opened the door and slid out, leaving my AR in the seat. Harley and Strap followed and let me lead the way, carrying their weapons low against their legs.

Cross's driver went around and opened the door for his boss. Cross stepped out, looked around, and spoke to the driver, who nodded and went back to slip behind the steering wheel. Cross moved fast in the rain and was halfway across the parking lot when I intercepted him.

My Colt came up, and he froze. "Cross! Hands where I can see 'em. You're under arrest!"

He stopped with a shocked look on his face, and when he saw Strap, the devil flashed alive in his face.

Harley and Strap spread out, and Cross grinned.

Chapter 67

What we didn't expect was the number of cars that discharged armed men who were all throwing guns on us. His men had beaten us to the restaurant and had been waiting for that moment.

Harley and Strap instantly swung on the men nearest to them. Strap didn't say a word, but Harley was vocal. "Put the gun down! Police officers! Guns down! We're the po-lice!"

His voice was lost in the shouted orders coming from half a dozen different directions, demanding we drop our own weapons. More than one was also shouting the word *police.*

I know my brother, and the man who was looking down the muzzle of his M9 pistol was the closet person to death in that parking lot. I put the sights of my .45 directly on Cross's chest. "Cross, we're all half a second from dying."

He held both hands out, palms down. "My people! Calm down and be quiet."

Knowing better than to take my eyes off Cross's face, I waited half a second and spoke to Harley. "Little Brother, take a breath. Strap."

"Yo!"

"You do the same. Cross, we have situation here that's likely being recorded by everyone in the parking lot with a cell phone."

"It's your fault, you know."

"I have a warrant here for your arrest."

"I don't doubt that, but I'm not going in."

"You will. In about five minutes, there'll be a dozen police cars here, and we'll all go in."

"No, we won't. You'd an admirable opponent, but I'm walking away. You can't shoot me in the back, and if you pull those triggers, my men will cut you down. I will be talking with you soon."

He turned and walked back to his car. It was the second time we'd been involved with a Mexican standoff with those guys and Harley couldn't stand it. "Hey! Get back here."

The men holding guns around us tightened their weapons against their shoulders, and I knew Harley was moving. "Don't!"

"He's leaving!"

"So are we."

Instead of aiming my .45 at Cross, who couldn't see it, I shifted my attention to the next man to my left. It was the first time I'd seen how many were around us. "Back out of here, boys."

Growling like a mad dog, Harley did what I said. We backed out of the ring of ChemShale men who remained rooted where they stood, watching us like hawks. Cross's car pulled out of the parking lot and sped away.

We continued to back up. It was the first time in my life I've ever retreated, and I knew for a fact that it was Harley's first time, too. It was hard to stomach, but we were so outgunned that the only thing that saved us was the professionalism of those we'd stood down.

By the time we were back in the truck, half a dozen cars were leaving the lot, splitting off into two different directions.

"I hate this!" Harley slammed his door in fury.

I was already moving before Strap closed his own door. We were close to the restaurant's parking lot entrance and were gone in seconds. Half a mile down the road, the first responder running code was a sheriff's car. His brake lights flashed as he whipped into Sazerac's parking lot.

A county road came up a hundred yards later, and I immediately took a right off the highway. Beside me, Harley let loose with a string of cuss words that would make a merchant seaman take notes.

I used my burner phone to call the emergency number. The calm voice came through loud and clear. "Nine one one, what's your emergency?"

"There are two guys tied up in the woods out there at the Sazerac restaurant."

The was silence for a beat. "Did you do it?"

"I did, and y'all better hurry, because the way we did it, they'll be in trouble in the next few minutes."

"Why…?"

I hung up and dropped the phone into the console's cup holder. A big hand rested on my shoulder for a moment before Strap leaned back. "You're a good man."

"He is, but I'da let them sonsabitches strangle." Harley went back to looking out his window.

The next half hour was a series of turns down back roads that finally brought us back to I-45. We drove south toward Houston and once again I turned off the interstate and back into the country.

Harley'd finally calmed down by then. "Do you know where you're going?"

"I do. I have a friend who owns a camper set up in Independence. He's always said I could use it, and told me where the key is. It's the safest place I can think of."

"Then what?"

"We go to plan B or C."

Five minutes later I turned into the Live Oak RV park and drove down one of the big resort's eight loops to a massive forty-foot camper with four slides. The key was where my buddy said it was, in an empty Tic Tac case taped to the underside of the bottom step.

We went inside and turned on the rig's AC unit. There were two recliners facing a huge flat-screen television, and Strap settled in. "I have an idea."

"What's that?"

"A page out of Cross's playbook."

Harley opened cabinets until he found a bottle of Wild Turkey. There was a 7Up in the refrigerator, and he mixed two drinks. "Before you start, you want some of this, Strap?"

"I do. Neat."

I settled into the other recliner, thinking I should take off my damp shirt. Harley brought the drinks and leaned against the big rig's island that separated the kitchen from a dining nook. "All right. What's your idea?"

"A couple of years ago I saw a handwritten return address in Louisiana on an envelope on Cross's desk. He was pretty casual about it and raked it off in a folder."

"Where you say Cross is from."

"That's right. I may not know his real name, but that address was in Thibodaux."

Chapter 68

Chloe answered on the first ring. "Daddy!"

"How're you doing, kiddo?"

"It'd be better if you were here."

"Don't tell me where here is."

"All right. It isn't over?"

"Not by a long shot, but I have something I need for you to do, if you can." I still didn't trust anyone but family, and she'd always been good on a computer. Kids are natives to this electronic world, while us older folks are immigrants.

"What's that?"

"Is there a computer where you are?"

"There is."

"All right." I gave her all the info I had and spelled Thibodaux.

"What a weird word."

"Not really. You've heard it when I play 'Jambalaya.'"

"What's that?"

"A Hank Williams song."

"I never listen to that stuff when you have it on."

"Looks like I failed again." I sighed. "Anyway, I need to know who lives there, pays taxes, all that stuff. Find out everything you can about this guy and his family. Do you know how to get around paywalls on these search sites?"

"Is it okay if I say I do?"

I laughed. "It is this time. See if you can get me names."

"I'll have to download a paywall evasion app. Somebody might have to pay for it. How's that for ironic?"

"Have Russell do that for you."

"Okay. How fast you want it?"

"As fast as possible. How're your aunt Tammy and the rest?"

"The boys are driving us nuts, but we're good. Uncle Russell and Jenny have been a big help."

"Jimma all right?"

"She's good. Says she's ready to go home."

"Aren't we all? Okay, sweetheart, call when you get that info for me."

"I'd ask where you are, but you won't tell me."

"You're right about that. I'm probably taking a chance calling you, but we should be all right."

"Fine. I'll let you know quick as I find something out."

Chapter 69

Cross had barely closed his office door the next morning when his cell rang. Glancing at the screen, he gave a slight smile and answered. *"Sa ou fe, ma-mawn."*

His Creole great grandmother's voice came back soft and low. "Good morning, *mon petit douce*. Have you forgotten me?"

"Of course not. I've just been busy."

"How's it going?"

"Nothing to complain about."

"Well, I just wanted you to know that I'll probably die before you come see me again."

Her passive-aggressive way of shaming him wasn't new. He grinned and rubbed at the short hair on his temples, an unconscious habit from when he was young and she greeted him this way. "You're not old enough to die yet."

"But I am. Miz Guineaux gave me a birthday present yesterday. It was a house dress that had *shudders* on it. I put it on for her, but it made me look like an old *maman*. I'll put it in the top of the closet where it will stay, but don't you bury me in it."

He laughed. *Shudders* was Cajun for *flowers,* and *maman*

translated into *old woman*. The fact that his grandmother was in her early nineties wasn't lost on either of them.

"I know it's been too long since I been down home." His accent thickened every time he talked to her, and it always embarrassed him to think that he sounded like the Cajun country musician, Doug Kershaw. "How about *je venir see vous prochain* weekend?"

How about I come see you this weekend? He'd switched to Creole mix without thinking about it.

"Hurry before *ils* have to *mettre moi dans* the ground, and *il 's* too hot *pour moi to pondre* out *pour joliment* long."

He translated it to *Hurry before they have to put me in the ground, and it's too hot for me to lay out for very long,* and laughed again. It was always a delight to speak with the old woman who'd raised him.

"I will see you Saturday."

"*Samedi il is, my douce. Faire* attention." *Saturday it is, my sweet. Be careful.*

"You too." Cross hung up and turned his attention to the Snow brothers.

Chapter 70

Harley, Strap, and I were looking out the RV's "mountain view" window at the rear of the rig. Instead of a sweeping majestic landscape the big rig's designers advertised to new clients, they only saw a cow pasture that was ankle-deep in water. The rain had stopped, but it would be a long while before all that water soaked in.

Right then, it was turning to steam in the bright sunshine, promising hot and humid temperatures for the next several days.

My phone rang and it was Chloe. "Got it."

I drew the ever-present notepad I'd carried since getting the job as brand inspector. "Whadda ya have?"

"It wasn't hard to find. The address is an old house southwest of New Orleans. Looks like it's in the swamp from the satellite picture I pulled up."

"You get names?"

"Sure did. You're gonna love this. Leo and Lavonia Babineaux." She was excited to tell me what she'd found, so I just listened. "I dug around some more and found out that Leo died thirty years ago, but Lavonia is still alive. Then I wondered if they had kids, so I looked some more and found a boy named Louis. It seems they liked names that begin with the letter L. Anyways, he got killed in an offshore drilling accident."

My ears perked up at the mention of oil.

"So I found the obit for him, and he was married to Hestia..."

"Is that a Cajun name?"

"I wondered myself. I found out it's an African American name. Creole."

The puzzle pieces started to click, because my daughter is a native in the world of technology. Since I'm an immigrant into that world, I'd have never found that information in ten years of digging.

Chloe was on a roll. "So she had a son who had a son. I found it in the obituary. There's a lot of information in obituaries. It's kinda scary. Anyway, his name is Traver. Traver Babineaux, and the only thing on him was when he graduated from Tulane and went to work for Humble Oil right before it became Exxon. Is it pronounced 'umble' or 'humble'?"

"'Humble,' and in the way I feel right now about your computer skills."

"Funny. Another dad joke. Anyway, I can't find anything else about him, or Hestia."

"That's everything I need. You did great, sweetheart."

"Be careful."

"I will."

I looked at the boys and grinned. "We have a name for your Mr. Cross, Strap."

"Do tell."

"Traver Babineaux."

"How do you know for sure?"

"I don't, but this is what Chloe found for us. We're going to pay him a visit."

"At that address in Louisiana?"

"Nope." I jerked a thumb southwest. "Strap, take us to Cross's office."

"You think that's wise? Y'all said you didn't want another Waco, and you'd rather pick him up at his house."

"His house won't have any papers we can use. We need to hit him where it hurts, and we're taking half a dozen deputies and U.S. marshals with us to serve this warrant."

Harley looked up from his phone. "You know what *Traver* means when it's translated into English?"

"No, what?"

"Roughly translates to *Cross*. We got him!"

My phone vibrated again, and it was Bill Sloan. I had to sit down as he laid out a sinister story of cancer, highly radioactive drill rods, and the murder of the Crawford family.

Chapter 71

It didn't take but one phone call to Judge Elliott Hiragana and a brief explanation about what we'd found to get the ball rolling. The three of us met a squad of Harris County deputies and U.S. marshals in a hot, steamy grocery store parking lot only a few blocks from the ChemShale offices.

Strap and Harley had disarmed themselves before the officers arrived, to alleviate any potential problems. I wore my wrinkled shirt and jeans, holster, badge, and hat. This time my clothes were wet from sweat and not rain. Folks not knowing any different might have assumed I was a rancher, or someone who'd just come in from a night of dancing and beer.

The rest of them looked as if they planned to assault a fort and were sweating buckets. I understood how they felt. "I know you're hot, boys, but these guys are stone killers. Keep that armor on."

Several sets of eyebrows went up.

Marshal Mark Cameron pulled the neck of his vest down to get some air. "Then do we need SWAT?"

"No. I don't think they'll do anything stupid in an office

building, but keep those rifles close, please. I just want to walk in and pick up this guy."

To a man, they looked uncomfortable, but they did as I asked. I didn't have to explain to those professionals that since I was the affiant, I had the point and was making the assignments.

Strap could have been one of them and they gave him a questioning look, probably wondering what department he was with, and why he wasn't wearing protective gear. They all noticed the thin nylon face mask in his hand, but no one asked about it. This wasn't the first time they'd worked with undercover officers, and I figured they assumed that's what he was, which was fine by me.

Never quiet, Harley introduced himself. "Boys, I'm the good-looking brother that works with the cowboy there." They'd already seen the badge on his belt, but I doubted they cared that it said "Retired." That withstanding, he stood tall and lean before them as if it were his operation, the same way he addressed the men under him when he and I worked undercover.

His comment was funny, because he looked like a U.S. marshal standing there in a hat and jeans. "Me and Tuck here were on the job when y'all were dragging on your mama's dress tail, so he'll take the lead."

"I've never served a warrant with a cattle cop," one guy built like a weightlifter said. "Or with a tagalong civilian." He gave Strap the eye.

Harley crossed his arms, looking small next to the mountain that was Strap. "You have now."

Satisfied that my little brother wasn't going to back down, the weightlifter grinned. "Good enough for government work."

I looked at each of them in turn. "Y'all ready?"

Nods all around.

—

The three of us rode with Marshal Cameron. Blond hair and built like a cowboy with a brush-pile mustache, he looked the part. His Chevy Blazer led, and we slid to a stop in front of ChemShale's glass doors. The line of cars discharged the boys who moved like a well-trained unit under the portico.

The blessed air-conditioning inside felt like we'd stepped into a freezer and I remembered Sara Beth always said indoors in Texas was the coldest place in the world in the summertime. A uniformed security guard in a horseshoe-shaped booth rose when we hit the lobby with me in the lead. "Can I help you boys?"

I held up the paper that carried all the weight we needed. "I have a warrant for a Mr. Cross."

His eyes snapped to the men around me, as if speaking to them all would help his case. They were all stone-faced. "There's no one here by that name."

With the face mask pulled down, Strap was unrecognizable in a black T-shirt and ballistic vest that read SHERIFF on it. I'd already wondered where he got it, and gave up on the puzzle.

He pushed past the startled guard. "We don't need you, Clem. Sit down right there and go back to playing solitaire."

Eyes wide in surprise, the man reached for the phone on his desk, and I pointed. "Don't you move!"

One of the deputies circled the end of the horseshoe and grabbed his arm. "Sit down in that chair right there and visit with me for a while. I'll tell your supervisor you did your job before we leave."

I pushed on past. "Cameron, stick with me and Harley."

We hurried through the lobby and on to the bank of elevators.

It was a busy building housing several businesses, and more than a few people stopped what they were doing to watch us pass.

Strap punched the elevator buttons and pointed past the bank of metal sliding doors. "There's a staircase there."

Without me issuing orders, another deputy with a rifle at low ready peeled off and took up a position where he could see both the elevator doors and the stairwell. "I have it. African American, gray temples."

Professional.

"Right." I was proud of those boys who, despite having not worked together, acted like a well-oiled machine. The deputy would pick him up if someone warned Cross before we reached the top floor of the high-rise.

The doors opened and we crowded in. Vests, guns, and big guys built like linemen were sardined tight with little room to move. I had the brief thought that if the door opened on another floor and someone was waiting with a weapon, automatic or not, we'd be in a kill slot.

The ride to the top seemed slow, especially because of a symphonic version of George Strait's "Amarillo by Morning."

The doors opened and we boiled into ChemShale's chrome-and-wood lobby. A huge logo filled the wall across from us, and dozens of old black-and-white photos of oil derricks and drillers completed the art ensemble.

Security was tighter here, and two guys behind a console drew pistols and rose quickly at the sight of my armed crew. They found themselves looking down the barrels of fully automatic weapons in the hands of men who knew how to use them.

The boys around me spread out as best they could in the wide hallway and advanced. "U.S. marshals!"

"Sheriff's office!"

"Sit down!" I hadn't yet drawn my Colt. "You two put those guns on the ground now!"

The situation was tense for a long moment until the guards realized they were dealing with something way above their pay grades. Eyes on my team, they knelt, placed the weapons on the ground, and backed away.

A receptionist blinked her fake eyelashes at us. Her mouth was a small lipsticked *oh*. She swallowed. "Can I help you?"

"Looking for a Mr. Cross or Traver Babineaux."

"There's no one here with those names."

She wasn't a good liar. There were doors behind her on either side of the wide curving reception desk that looked like a giant amoeba. Strap gave her a wave and led us past the desk and to the left. "Go home, Nikki."

She frowned at the masked man who knew her name. We pushed through the open-air business complex. Men and women in casual clothes rose as we passed their workstation cubicles. Marshal Cameron, following right behind me, waved them back to their seats. "Sit down, folks, and don't get involved!"

I liked his style.

We came to a set of wide double mahogany doors, and Strap hit them like a locomotive, leading us into a plush corner office. "This is Mr. Cross."

He peeled off to the side and positioned himself beside the only other door coming into the room.

Cross was behind his desk and jerked upright. He stood. "What is this!?"

He deflated when he recognized me and saw the assortment of law enforcement officers fanned out through his office. Finally seeing red over what that man had put us all through, I crossed the room and went around behind his desk.

Sara Beth's soft voice inside my head warned me to cool down. *He's not worth it, Tuck. Chill, pill.*

"Cross or Babineaux"—I took a deep breath—"I have a warrant for your arrest."

He jerked open the top drawer beside his hand, and I slammed it shut with my hip, barely missing his fingers. The man took a swing at me, but I didn't mind. I stepped into it and hit him square in the nose with everything I had. Blood spurted, and he went over backward.

Sara Beth shrugged in my mind. *Fine then. He started it.*

Harley stopped in the middle of the room. "That's the kind of guy who'll provoke you."

The adjoining door burst open and a man rushed in with a pistol in his hand. Strap grabbed his arm and swung him in and around, bending his elbow backwards. The guy gasped, lost the pistol, and landed hard on the carpeted floor. His feet hit hard enough that he lost a shoe. The guy was determined to protect his boss, though, and came up in a fighting stance that showed some practice, but he made the mistake of charging Marshal Cameron.

I've never seen anyone hit so hard, so fast, and so many times in such a short space. The man had no chance. A soft pop and his wail told me Cameron had dislocated the employee's shoulder.

Cross rose, holding his bloody nose. "You people don't know what you're dealing with!" He pushed up in my face. "Your family is dead, Snow!"

"Traver Babineaux, I'd think your old granny Lavonia Babineaux would hate to hear something like that from her boy."

The shocked look on his face told me we'd hit the nail on his head. He understood my meaning and deflated like a blowup clown. "You can't do anything like that. You're a *law*man."

"Your man Strap isn't. I think we found *your* Achilles' heel."

I'm not like that and would never hurt an innocent person, but Cross didn't know that. The man spent his entire career eliminating people, no matter who they were. In his world, killing someone for the good of the country was just fine, even within our borders. Collateral damage.

Terrified, Cross stiffened as Strap stepped out through the office door and was gone. "Where is that man going?"

"Who?"

"The one who just left. Was that Strap?"

Me and Harley knew Strap well enough by then. He'd play the part, but he didn't have it in him to harm someone's old grandmother. He'd done his job and was headed for a Pacific island somewhere, and I didn't blame him for that. His disappearance would muddy the waters some, but it would also serve to keep Cross looking over his shoulder at his granny's house for the rest of her life.

"One of the guys must have needed to use the restroom." Harley stepped around the desk and hit Babineaux hard enough that Miss Lavonia's eyes watered over in Louisiana. "That's for scaring and threatening my family."

Marshal Cameron came around and helped Cross/Babineaux to his feet. "You have to watch your step there, sir. I don't want you to fall again."

I read him his rights as Cameron cuffed him. Blood dripped off the man's nose, splashing onto his tie and white shirt. As if he wasn't wearing a suit, Cross wiped his nose on his coat's shoulder. "You found my nanna through Strap."

His thin upper lip lifted in a sneer. "Well, do your worst because you've won, this time. I have lawyers who'll have me out in the morning. But tell me what it was that Mitch Ramsey told you to get all this started? How much?"

"Mitch didn't tell me anything."

A flicker passed behind those eyes. "He said nothing about… nothing?"

"No. He and I talked about his cows and his cancer once. Then when I went back, it was all about a stray mama cow and her calf."

"You didn't know." He wiped his bloody nose again on that same shoulder. "You don't know?"

"Not until the last few hours. Mister, whatever it is that put a bug up your butt about me is all in your head. But now we have all the goods on you, and we know all about well number 3223, Achilles' Heel, and the people you've killed and endangered."

"You're not a real lawman!"

"I'm a brand inspector, and that's all, until you pissed me off."

"You're more."

"And that is?"

Cross's shoulders slumped and for a moment, I saw sadness flash across his face. "Something I used to be, but not anymore."

We were talking in mysterious circles, and I was finished with the man. "Marshal Cameron, would you secure this office until we get a search warrant?"

"Yessir."

"Deputy Ball."

The Harris County deputy gave me his attention. "Would two of you corral all those folks in the cubicles out there and get their names before they leave? Then we're going to secure this entire floor. I think this place will be crawling with feds pretty soon, and I want things done right here."

"You bet."

Cameron led Cross out the door. I walked over to the window to take a breath. The parking lot below was rapidly filling with law enforcement vehicles converging from several directions. Lights flashing, one city cruiser had to slam on its brakes when a dark-colored Charger almost failed to yield the right of way.

A dark Charger in the way. A black Charger under a tarp in Jim Crawford's barn. Then I remembered something that had been in the back of my mind. The Dodge and the mention of Mitch Ramsey's mama cow reminded me.

I plucked the phone from my pocket and called Ganther Bluff's Sheriff's Department. Chief Deputy Frank Gibson answered, and I brought him up to speed on the arrest of Cross, and soon others he was involved with. "Now, one last thing."

"What's that?"

"Go out and find Bill Sloan and Fred Belk."

"I have them already."

"Why?"

"Loading up some of Crawford's stock, like them cows belong to them. Funny, a sheriff's deputy came out to make sure the crime scene was still secure and saw them with a catch pen full of steers."

"Good for you. I have a hunch they're the ones stealing cattle with a little gal, Toby James. I have a hunch that if you mention Loren and Tracey Smythe and online sales of cattle and mules, they'll fold.

"The Charger they used to run block between me and the stolen cows that night my truck was shot up is in the Crawford barn, or I expect it to be. Just mention it and tell 'em I'll be talking with them soon. I'll call Captain Meeks to send someone out to do the paperwork.

"And they also have a stack of radioactive drill rods that have given Sloan radiation poison and are killing his kidneys."

"How'd you know that?"

"I have a witness who told me about contaminated materials. Sloan helped Mitch Ramsey weld those rods to make the corral and other things. I think when Mitch was in the hospital, Sloan and Toby and whoever else was working with them hid some cows in their back pastures for a while until they could get 'em sold. That's where that cow and calf came from, the ones that started all this for me.

"I figure they got away while they were loading 'em up and came to the house because they were looking for the others, and because that old mama cow was pissed about the whole thing and couldn't get over it.

"Get Toby off in a corner and bring up Sloan's failing kidneys. That should give you everything you need to know. They're hurting for money, and it always comes down to that."

The chief deputy grunted. "Well, they're gonna need it, because all three of them are sick and in the hospital."

My stomach clenched. "From what?"

"Well, you already know about Sloan's kidneys, but Fred Belk has been throwing up, and the ER doctor says him and Toby're showing signs of what he thinks might be radiation poisoning."

"I'll check in when we get back later today or tomorrow. I know they're sick, but you crossed your *t*'s and dotted all the *i*'s, right?"

"I did. Don't worry about it and I'll see you when you get here."

Harley frowned when I hung up. "That's harsh. They seem like good guys."

"They are, in a way, but they're thieves, and I can't abide a thief, even if they're sick and I like 'em."

I sat down behind Cross's desk and spun around to look out his window at the traffic snarled up on the Katy Freeway way down below.

Harley crossed his arms. "How do we keep getting caught in messes like this?"

"Because we'll stand up to wrong when we see it, and to hell with all the chains that try and hold us back." I paused. "And because we're there when it happens."

"So you're saying we're snakebit."

"You could look at it like that."

He waved a hand toward the freeway and the apartment buildings and housetops as far as we could see. "Who could live in all this mess?"

"Not us. You ready to go home?"

"I'd be tickled to death."

Chapter 72

Six weeks later I sold that crazy mama cow and calf, that were fat and healthy despite being in the radioactive pens, and the money went to a local charity. Chloe and I were cleaning up the dishes after supper and I'd just gotten off the phone with Russell and Jenny.

All was well between me and Jenny, though she'd reverted to her old hippie ways. It's just the way she was, and I could no more change her way of thinking than I could change Harley.

My cell rang. I didn't know the number, but answered anyway. "If this is a spam call, you may as well hang up."

"Special Agent Snow, this is Strap."

"Well Mr. Strap, you shouldn't be calling me. You're a fugitive from justice."

"I just wanted you to know that I'm sipping tropical drinks on a beach, but I just got off the phone with Miss Lavonia Babineaux down in Thibodaux, Louisiana. She's a nice old lady, and she's glad I call every now and then to check on her, now that her grandson's heading for prison.

"She says Mr. Cross doesn't like it that I touch base with her and have people come by to take care of the yard and the house. He says he doesn't know me and would prefer that I stay away."

"But you're going to keep taking care of that little old lady, and making amends through her at the same time. It's kinda mean, in a way."

"Yessir. It kills two birds with one stone. I'm not a nice guy, but I'm trying, and I've gotten to like the old gal. Reminds me of my own grandmother. Are you folks all right?"

"We're fine."

"Good. I'll keep a watch on your family, too."

"I really wish you wouldn't do that."

"I know, but it's something I have to do. Hey, I have good news for you. If you'll check your bank account, you'll see that all your money is back."

At first I was ecstatic, but then I paused. "Uh, I hope it's the exact same amount I already had. You know, if there's even a dollar more, I can get in trouble."

He chuckled. "Down to the penny, though I know a guy who can set you up with an offshore account..."

"No!"

He laughed big. "Well, fine then. I'm gonna keep an eye on y'all, just to make sure none of this ever comes back on you. I'll know if you ever need help."

"Wait. What? How?"

"It's been good talking to you again, Agent Snow. Take care."

He hung up, and I made a note to have a company come out to sweep the house and area for cameras or microphones. It just never ends.

THE END

READING GROUP GUIDE

1. Tucker Snow is a special agent, also called a "cattle cop," in Northeast Texas, whose job is to catch cattle thieves. How surprised were you to learn that cattle-rustling is not just a thing of the old Wild West but continues in modern times?

2. Tucker says his deceased wife, Sara Beth, was his best friend and therapist. As he confronts dangerous situations after her death, he often hears her cautionary advice in his head. Do you think he's actually hearing what she'd say, or is his own conscience counseling him? Why do you think it seems to be easier for him to assign these thoughts to her rather than to his own internal warning system?

3. In their pursuit of money and avoiding arrest, Sloan's girlfriend, Toby, and his accomplice, Fred, break laws and take chances that seem to make them uncomfortable. Do you think they feel justified in doing so

because of Sloan's illness? Does his health situation motivate them to cross lines?

4. After shooting at Special Agent Tucker Snow's truck, Fred Belk says, "Us old boys ought not be shooting at one another when we're all on the same side." He explains that he's referring to the "right" side and "country folks." Throughout the book, the author shows us the distrust country folks have for city dwellers. Even as a lawman, is Tucker perceived as one of them? Do you think the contrast drawn between city slickers and rural ranchers is accurate today?

5. Tucker and his younger brother, Harley, seem to think alike in dangerous combat—and in life. How does their relationship evolve during the course of this case?

6. As a retired officer, Harley has special skills and experience, but does his status as a civilian entitle him to join Tucker in taking on criminals, opening fire, and not "playing by the rules"?

7. How does Cross's relationship with his Creole great-grandmother inform your opinion of him?

8. What do you think motivated Strap to change sides and decide to help Tucker and Harley protect themselves and their family? Do you think the earlier mentions of Strap's veteran status—and his relating to the cattle agent's role to pursue justice and protect

property—foreshadowed his change of heart? Did you pick up on those hints?

9. What did Cross mean when he said Tucker was something he, too, used to be but not anymore?

10. Russell and Jenny put themselves in danger when they allowed Harley and Tucker's family to hide out at their remote property. Would you have done the same? Was it too much to ask of their friendship?

A CONVERSATION WITH THE AUTHOR

Do you base your richly drawn characters on real people you know?

To be specific, Tucker and Harley Snow are *loosely* based on two real retired undercover agents for the Texas Department of Public Safety. They're the only brothers to ever work undercover here in the state and did so only through special dispensation from Governor Mark White. These guys have stories! We've become good friends, and I took their own characteristics and amplified them for *Hard Country* and now *The Broken Truth*.

I don't know about other authors, but the rest of my characters come unbidden and usually fully developed as I write. They tend to walk onstage without conscious intent on my part, coming in when needed and all with something to say.

Depending on the manuscript, some might be framed on people I've known or have run into through the years, but they will be a collection of personalities, traits, and qualities as a whole. Certain mannerisms might come from someone I saw at an airport or at a store or from an individual I heard or read about. The rest comes from life and experience, where I take those little foundation pieces and infuse them with those many parts to fully develop a fictitious persona.

How has living in Texas informed your writing about the contrasts between city folk and country folk?

I grew up both in the country and the city. My parents came from a rural background. Dad picked cotton when he was six, served in the Japanese theater in WWII, then moved to Dallas when he and Mom married. Technically, I was both a city boy and one who lived his best life in the country, a kid who spent all my weekends, holidays, and most summers with my maternal grandparents on their farm in Lamar County. They lived half a mile from my dad's folks, who also raised cows and crops. They were all country folks and touched me in myriad ways.

When I wasn't running in the woods and fields around their little frame farmhouses, I lived in Old East Dallas and attended school in Urbandale and Pleasant Grove, eventually graduating from W. W. Samuell High School. During those years, I observed the adults who shared many characteristics rooted both in rural and urban locations, and they all imprinted on my psyche.

Those two viewpoints made their way into my novels and allowed me to examine both their differences and similarities.

How far ahead do you plan a plot? For example, did you know before you started writing the novel that Strap would have a change of heart and decide to help the brothers and their families escape and assist in the arrest of Mr. Cross?

Both readers and authors alike are surprised when I tell them I don't plot, outline, or consider what my characters will do at any given point in time. I simply sit down each morning and put my fingers on the keyboard and start typing. I'm as surprised as my readers at what reaches the page.

Strap began as an enforcer, someone to do Cross's bidding. When he first stepped onstage, I thought he'd wind up being one of the Snow brothers' antagonists. He was big, bad, and experienced, but he evolved into a complex character who developed a conscience. I was just as surprised as everyone else when Strap saw that Cross and ChemShale were evil and wanted out. I didn't expect him to switch sides, and when he did, I investigated that branch of his evolution.

This isn't the first time I've been surprised. When I reached the climax of my first novel, *The Rock Hole,* I threw up my hands when the serial killer's identity was revealed.

"I can't believe it!"

My wife came running into the office, thinking I'd lost the entire manuscript for the second time, due to another technological burp. It had already happened.

"What's wrong?"

"I know who the *killer* is!"

She stared at me for several long moments, probably wondering exactly when I'd lost my mind. "You knothead. It's *your* novel. Of *course* you know who the killer is."

"Yeah, well, I thought it was someone else."

She sighed and turned away.

You must have thoroughly researched radiation poisoning to write this novel. Do you find doing research an enjoyable part of your writing process?

I love research, but it comes at a cost. As I said above, I don't plot or outline, so I have no idea where the story is going. When I reach a point in the manuscript that requires specific research, I stop, dig around, and often wind up going down a rabbit hole.

While burrowing down one particular Bugs Bunny hole, I found references that led to other branches and wound up reading a lot about drill rods and radiation. My dad was a roughneck in the 1940s and told me about drilling wells out in West Texas, then immediately capping them for later.

When I asked why, his answer was succinct. "Because we knew that at some time in the distant future, oil would become a precious commodity, so the people I worked with said we'd buy and use foreign oil until it was gone. Then we'd have those wells to fall back on."

I also know someone who knows a lot about hot drill rods, and he directed me to further information.

I do love research and discovering fresh, new, fascinating information. It's an excellent reward for the time I spend digging around. I file much of this information away if it doesn't relate to that particular manuscript, but it rests there in a mental folder until a twist triggers a memory and I find a way to make those details part of the work in progress.

Who was your favorite character to write?

I'm not sure I have a favorite. Each fictional entity is fun, and I enjoy looking at the world through each character's viewpoint. Tucker is fun, because he has a strong moral code but will veer just a little when it comes to protecting his family. Harley is a hoot, because he represents the kid in all of us, yet he's the most dangerous of the two when circumstances force him to react. Mr. Cross was evil yet had strong roots he'd forgotten, and I enjoyed exploring that aspect of his life. Of course, Strap was fun, and the evolution of his character was fascinating. I like looking into Chloe's world, because we raised two daughters, and she has some of their characteristics.

As you wrap up writing a mystery, are you already developing the characters' next set of challenges?

If I am, it's purely subconscious. Since I don't plot, they're always a surprise. I'm always looking around for ideas. Something will come, and when it does, I'll draw a tight rein and ride it out.

What are you reading now?

I always have more than one book going at the same time:
White Smoke by John Gilstrap
River, Sing Out by Nick Wade
The Grapes of Wrath by John Steinbeck
The House at the End of the World by Dean Koontz
Hunting Time by Jeffery Deaver

ABOUT THE AUTHOR

© Shana Wortham

Two-time Spur Award–winning author Reavis Z. Wortham also pens the Texas Red River historical mystery series and the high-octane Sonny Hawke contemporary Western thrillers. The Texas Red River novels are set in rural Northeast Texas in the 1960s. In a Starred Review, *Kirkus Reviews* listed his first novel, *The Rock Hole,* as one of the "Top 12 Mysteries of 2011." *The Rock Hole* was reissued in 2020 by Poisoned Pen Press with new material added, including an introduction by Joe R. Lansdale.

"*Burrows,* Wortham's outstanding sequel to *The Rock Hole,* combines the gonzo sensibility of Joe R. Lansdale and the elegiac mood of *To Kill a Mockingbird* to strike just the right balance between childhood innocence and adult horror."

—*Publishers Weekly,* Starred Review

"The cinematic characters have substance and a pulse. They walk off the page and talk Texas."

—*Dallas Morning News*

His series from Kensington Publishing features Texas Ranger Sonny Hawke and debuted in 2018. *Hawke's War,* the second in the Sonny Hawke series, won the Spur Award from the Western Writers Association of America as the Best Mass Market Paperback of 2019. In 2020, the third book in the series, *Hawke's Target,* won a Spur Award in the same category.

Wortham has been a newspaper columnist and magazine writer since 1988, penning nearly two thousand columns and articles, and has been the humor editor for *Texas Fish & Game Magazine* for twenty-four years. He and his wife, Shana, live in Northeast Texas.

All his works are available at your favorite bookstore or online, in all formats.

Check out his website at reaviszwortham.com.